THE LOST ARCANUM

A SECRET LOST FOR TWO THOUSAND YEARS...
A SINISTER PLOT TO UNCOVER IT...

NAVIN REUBEN DAWSON

Invincible Publishers

First published in India in 2018

ISBN: 978-93-87328-28-0

Invincible Publishers
G-120, Sushant Lok III, Sector 57, Gurgaon-122002

Registered Address: Opposite Kasturba Ashram, Radaur, Haryana - 135133

This book is a work of fiction. The characters, incidents and dialogues are the product of the author's imagination. Resemblances to any person, living or dead, are entirely coincidental.

Truth may be hard to fathom sometimes, but fiction must always be based upon truth. That being said, the artwork, catacombs, historical sites, locations and organizations described in the novel are real. The science and technology at the core of the novel is based on current research and discoveries.

DEDICATION

I take immense pleasure in dedicating this piece of work to my late father, Mr. Samson George Dawson, Granny and Grandpa, Manoramma and Danayya Prakash and to my dear uncle, Sadanand Prakash.

Thanks for endowing me with your abundant wisdom that is the cornerstone of my book. Your words fascinated me throughout my childhood and while penning this work and will continue to influence many more future ventures...

ACKNOWLEDGEMENTS

First of all, I am grateful to the Almighty God for making this book possible and to my sweet mother, whose unceasing love and support throughout this project is immensely appreciated though it can be ever indemnified.

I would like to express my deepest gratitude to my friends Varun P Jajee and Siddharth Valkeri for providing me with everything I needed while on my journey of writing this book.

My heartfelt thanks to Miss Pavithra Venkataraman, Mr. Mallinath Algundi and Zuveria Sultana, my first critics and my greatest supporters, who lived, nurtured and supervised this dream project, turning it into a reality. I'm really indebted to you all, thanks for being there for me. Thank you for continually and convincingly conveying a spirit of enthusiasm in regard to my work. I am extremely grateful to you all for never leaving my side.

Special thanks to two of my greatest role models. Shailesh Dinkar and Arun Kumar Karodi. Thanks for your wonderful support, by inspiring me with your amazing vision in all the aspects of life. You both are exemplary individuals, whose endeavors will be greatly cherished and followed.

I also take special privilege to thank a very special person, Mr. Venkataraman, who is a great mentor and a father figure. Thanks for being on my side on the journey of publishing this book.

Special thanks to my Publisher Mr. Ajay Sethi, for having deep faith in my work, who has been a great person, taking care of all the aspects, from marketing to distribution, in publishing my book.

I place on record my special thanks to Raghuvendra Joshi (*Guruji*) for those countless late night sermons, providing me with deep insights into *sadhus* and their wonderfully mysterious world.

I appreciate and thank Rahul Narsikar, an architect and great artist who endeavored many nights rendering design and shape to ciphers that evolved in my mind.

I also express my deepest regards to Mr. Vincent Narayanan, a mentor and a great friend whose knowledge and wisdom I always admire and absorb.

I thank Kanakraj and Ravi Talikoti, two of my best friends. Thanks to Harshvardhan, Kanni, Jeswin and Prabhuling Talwar, my other friends.

Finally, I take this opportunity to thank my entire family, to each and every one who directly or indirectly lent a helping hand to this venture.

PROLOGUE

Bajarat,

Thar Desert,

23 BC.

The secret must be buried…

Since the inception of the secret brotherhood, this desperate cry to protect something of momentous worth from peril, had been burnt into each initiate's consciousness.

A man bundled in a crimson hooded-cloak recalled the line, tightening his arms around a metal chest and guardedly hastened across the twilight-kissed desert, towards a monastery. Even from a distance, its gigantic rock-cut dome rose imposingly against the dimming sky.

I'm almost there, he reassured himself for umpteenth time, eyeing the monastery. *Now there's nothing I should fear.*

As he hurried, his cloak billowed behind him, swelled up by the turbulent desert winds that made his haste laborious. He discounted it, but a more serious concern weighed heavily upon his mind: blood dripping from a bone-deep cut across his back.

He reached across to the wound with one hand and tugged the freshly ripped skin, as if in doing so the stinging pain could be momentarily eased. Yet, his efforts were in vain. He felt a hammering throb in his head.

Ignoring the pain, he peered over his shoulder to ensure that no eyes tracked his progress. More valuable than his own life was the safety of something precious that he had vowed to protect: a metal chest, now tucked safely in his embrace.

A while ago, in the orange flicker of a blazing sconce high up the wall in a cavernous chamber, he had knelt before a circular stone altar in a perfect circle with his crimson-cloaked brothers—brothers who were tied to each other not by blood but by a greater cause, one that would dictate the future of the world.

Their attention was focused on the Grand Master of the brotherhood, an old man whose long salt-white hair framing his leathery wrinkled skin did little to obscure the intense concern burning in his shallow eyes.

Foreseeing the danger upon the secret his brotherhood had guarded for centuries, Old Grand Master had summoned them to this urgent congregation to remind them of the agenda of their secret association and the purpose to protect and safeguard what had been held precious all along that had been passed down to them by their forebearers.

Their brotherhood was nearly as old as human civilization. Its inception dated back to when mankind, following in the footsteps of the first man and woman who fell from grace in the Garden of Eden, revolted against its very Creator, the Almighty. The brotherhood was created to guard access to the knowledge that the Creator had denied mankind. The knowledge—secret and precious, dangerous and beneficial—had been forbidden to mankind and taken away and hidden, lest it might sever human ties from the very purpose of their existence and extricate them from the one who had forged them into flesh and bone.

Enraged at what they considered their birthright being withheld from them, men began the great hunt for the lost secret knowledge. In the wake of this search that the brotherhood secretly came into existence to protect and safeguard the arcane knowledge that in the wrong hands would be devastating. Taking a solemn vow to guard and keep the knowledge alive, the brotherhood began the clandestine task of disseminating the knowledge only to those considered worthy, those who understood its immense mystical powers and would use it for their spiritual growth and to access an ancient truth—that the Creator would have allowed free access to the knowledge if his first creation had not betrayed Him and brought upon themselves a holy wrath by violating His divine instructions.

With the passage of time, owing to the brotherhood's inconspicuous summons and discreet manner of conduct, its cause was misinterpreted. It came to be considered as a clandestine society with macabre and sinister intentions. The brotherhood was accused of heresy and deemed evil. Its associates were burnt at the stake, branded as a Satanic cult that safeguarded the knowledge they believed was entrusted to them by Lucifer--the fallen angel and the cause of the fall of humanity from heavenly grace. On the run from those hunting them, the survivors of the brotherhood had wandered like nomads. Changing location from time to time, they crossed from one part of the world to another, carrying with them the precious trove of knowledge, finally finding a safe haven in a secluded Buddhist monastery in the Indian desert of Thar, where they took refuge among the pious monks, preserving and sharing the knowledge among those deemed worthy.

It was only after word had reached his ear that a band of assailants from a religious sect had been dispatched from the Far West to hunt them down that the old Grand Master felt the need to replicate the knowledge in multiple languages and have it shipped to various parts of the world, where it could be well preserved and guarded by the worthy. Men with a strong conscience and sharp linguistic skills, who had proved their worth, were chosen from the nearest regions and entrusted the translation of the arcane knowledge.

Now, as the Grand Master looked at each one of them with his fear-riddled eyes, they nodded somberly to indicate that the work entrusted to them—of replicating the arcane knowledge into different tongues— had been accomplished.

Relived, the Grand Master looked down at what lay before them on the altar, glowing magnificently under the amber flicker of the torchlight.

Placed before each one of them were chests forged out of cast iron, one square foot in length and breadth, secured with keys. Their corners elegantly fashioned with intricate lacework of mysterious symbols with one familiar symbol carved at the center: a hexagram star inscribed within another symbol: a snake feeding on its own tail.

Even in the dim glow of the torchlight, it had the sheen of mystery to it. In the deafening silence of the chamber, the Grand Master gazed at the symbol carved at the center. It was the insignia of the brotherhood that had earned a notorious title: **The Brotherhood of the Serpent.**

Despite, history had misinterpreted this symbol as a Satanic seal--symbolic of Lucifer, he knew it was on the contrary. He had a comprehensive understanding of its true meaning that only a wise man could grasp.

"They're coming to get this knowledge," he said anxiously, his voice laden with concern and fear, "the lost knowledge of Gods."

He lowered his hands upon the chest and opened the lid on its hinges like a book.

A look of deep veneration crossed their face as their eyes fell upon the opened metal chest, filled with birch bark scrolls. Inscribed within the scrolls was the arcane knowledge that in the wrong hands was dangerous. It was meant only for those learned enough to understand its true essence and put it to appropriate use.

"They intend to confiscate this knowledge in the name of heresy," the Grand Master said gravely. "They want to destroy it. But we should protect it from slipping into their hands. This knowledge should survive for future generations. This is the only living testimony to the truth that God had a divine plan for mankind, how his creations could have evolved into spiritual beings should they have not disobeyed His commands, letting temptations get the better of them."

During the last minutes of the discourse, they had heard a faint stomping of hoofs which soon turned into a loud galloping of horses, winding through the cavern where the brotherhood had gathered.

Terrified, the Grand Master handed over the keys to the chests and said in urgency, "Now take these and leave the place. Go along the four directions and keep the knowledge alive. And don't forget," he reminded them again, for the umpteenth time, "in the face of peril…the secret must be buried."

No sooner had the four members of the brotherhood departed with the metal chests and keys than a band of horse-mounted assailants burst into the chamber and had the old Grand Master assaulted. All the men, a cavalry of some religious sect, wore knee-length creamy white tunics over dark chausses and pointed boots which gave them an air of medieval European knights.

Three of the four associate entrusted with the metal chests had long gone, but a sense of acute curiosity had kept the fourth one waiting in a corner, from where he saw his old Grand Master taking several butts of swords on his body before finally dropping to his knees.

An assailant from the band urged his horse onward till it gingerly came to a halt beside the Grand Master. The man had shallow eyes and shoulder-length auburn hair, fair and tall and wore a mantle that represented the authority of a leader.

Without dismounting from the horse, he freed his sword from its scabbard and brought it closer to the Grand Master's face, parting the ruffled hair that formed a cascade down the Grand Master's face, obscuring his features.

Deep, fiery eyes of Grand Master climbed the length of his body before they rose to meet his. And in them, the leader saw an acute resolution and a fierce determination to protect what he sought.

"The forbidden knowledge," the leader rasped, coming straight to the point, "where is it?"

The Grand Master knew what the leader was referring to: the sacred knowledge forbidden to the human race from the beginning of time, now locked safely in the metal chests and shipped out away from harms distance.

"It's safe and in a place beyond your reach," the Grand Master replied, cursing under his breath, "I wager you'll never find it."

"That's quite an impolite statement," the leader said scornfully, lifting the Grand Master's chin on the tip of his sword, "but what you don't realize is that your resistance to compliance can cost you your dear life."

"That which is dear to me is already secured," the Grand Master said proudly, recalling the metal chests with scrolls. "Now, there's nothing I fear."

The leader smirked. "You're doomed for carrying Lucifer's legacy, by preserving and sharing the forbidden knowledge that cast humanity out of the divine grace."

"I see you don't understand what you seek," the Grand Master said, "do you?"

The leader glared at him with scorn. "You pursue something that eludes your comprehension. Something that is perceptible only to those who are worthy."

"You know not what you are guarding." The leader nudged the tip of the sword into his skin. The Grand Master struggled under the grips as the leader spoke. "You're fostering a monster that will unleash an evil force of immense magnitude, enough to strip the human race of their values. It will corrupt their ethics, drawing them away from God."

"If only unworthy men like you," the Grand Master said, writhing under the sword, "those from the past and from generations to come, could grasp its true potential..."

"Unworthy? Me?" the leader let a loud devilish laugh. His throaty voice echoed in the cavern. "And you assume you are worthy enough to receive knowledge that is blasphemous?"

"The knowledge you call blasphemous," the Grand Master said, struggling in agony, "is the divine wisdom that will liberate mankind from the bondage of ignorance and set him free from the slavery called religion." Gasping, he whispered aloud, "In the name of God and religion, you wage war on innocents, control the weak and enslave the downtrodden. Religion is but a tool to control the masses."

"God will despise you for what you say."

"If only you knew the true meaning of God!" the old Grand Master replied, proclaiming, "Knowledge is the only God through which man himself can become God."

Realizing the old man was too tenacious to yield, the leader made one last attempt. "You tell me where the scrolls are or you're doomed."

"The scrolls are long gone. Indeed, as we speak, they are crossing the borders. They will migrate into far-off lands and make known the truth. And they will spread the message that the time is near when every man on earth will break free from the shackles of religion and will have access to the arcane knowledge that will elevate him to physical and spiritual perfection and allow him to live infinitely."

Enraged by his obstinacy, the leader thrust his sword under the old man's jaws, lifting him off his knees. With that single thrust, the old man's body fell flat on the stone floor, his hands over his bleeding neck, his body writhing like an injured snake and gradually, his endless crusade of protecting the arcane knowledge came to an abrupt with his body going rigid than silent for eternity.

Horrified at the sight of his old Grand Master with slit throat, blood spurting like a fountain from the slice, the fourth associate let a loud gasp. It was loud enough to draw the eye of an assailant. Panicked at having his cover blown, he hastened through the winding passage and slipped out of the cavern.

The assailant reacted instantly and urged his horse in the direction the hidden man had escaped. Not far from the cavern, the assailant cornered him and engaged him in a fierce fight when he'd received a nasty sword gash across his back. As he disarmed the assailant, injuring him beyond recovery and prepared to escape with the metal chest, he had a glimpse of the leader and his band in hot pursuit.

Putting a safe distance between him and the assailants, he climbed the stairs to the monastery. He regretted his choice of staying back too long within the cavern, which now brought to mind the danger his Grand Master had always feared and warned him of. With his back bleeding profusely, he was sure he would not survive long enough to fulfill his duty of conveying the scrolls safely out of harm's reach. Lest he would succumb to his injuries, he made a decision. One that was a last instruction from his Grand Master.

In the face of perils…the secret must be buried.

With that thought resonating in his mind, he entered the deserted monastery carved deep into a series of small hills, its entrance so well concealed that it was very easy to miss unless one was looking for it.

Anticipating a siege from the west, the occupants of the monastery had long since abandoned the place. It was colossal and cavernous. The ceiling was a stunning one hundred feet high, supported by monolithic black granite columns. When the torches were lit, they washed the interiors in a golden blaze and more amazing features of the monastery became apparent: The grotesquely engraved floral and animal motifs with narrative panels on all the walls, an expansive oculus cut into the ceiling that let in a bright shaft of sunlight to illuminate the monastery's prominent feature—the thirty-foot tall sculpture of a seated Buddha, dominating the eastern wall in the sanctum.

It was here in the sanctity of this cavernous space, in a divine congregation of monks and in the solemn presence of the Grand Master that he had proved his worthiness to learn the arcane knowledge. And it was also here under the serenity of this lofty structure, he reminisced, that the Grand Master, impressed by his mastery of various arts and great prowess in various languages, had assigned him the task of translating the arcane knowledge into multiple languages, including his native language– Pali.

Now, holding a torch, he hastened across to the rear wall of the hall and slipped through a door into a small chamber behind.

The chamber was spacious. At the center sat a large altar, hewn from a single block of black marble.

He crossed over to it and fell to its foot, letting out a deep moan of respite.

I'm only seconds away from fulfilling my duty…

With a final glance at his surroundings, ensuring his solitude, he placed the metal chest on the altar and opened it. He lowered his hands inside the chest and delicately lifted the scrolls with his fingers, spreading it open on the altar until his eyes basked in the pleasure of the strokes of his own handwriting. Caressing his script in the glum silence of the chamber, he reflected on those sleepless nights he'd spent under the golden glow of the lamp, stressing, sweating and endeavoring to recreate every word in the statement by God—the divine wisdom in its most quintessential flavor—with intense care and utmost precision. His brows had pinched in deep contemplation and risen in excitement when struck by both, the amazing potential of the hidden knowledge and the dangerous powers it would entrust into the hands of anyone who beheld it.

Shaking off his rumination, he took a deep breath and shifted his fingers across the face of the altar, adjusting his fingers into two depressions separated by an arm's length. With a slight jerk, he pulled the front panel which creaked open like a drawer, exposing a large cavity.

The cavity was three hands wide and two hands deep. He let the key free from his waist to lock the chest, but a sudden slash of a sword sent the chest skittering off the altar, spilling the scrolls.

Afraid, the man turned to find an assailant brandishing a sword from a yard's distance. He drew back a step, preparing for a fight.

The pain from the laceration on his back was bothering him to the point of passing out, but he conjured his strength and channeled his focus on the assailant.

Initiation into the brotherhood had required novices to master the arts of self-defense, to tackle the threat of deadly ambushes from religious sects, bandits and pirates on their voyage to distant lands. Now like a skilled ninja, the man drew a long breath and lunged at the assailant with great agility.

The assailant leaped forward too, in an attempt to slice the sword across his torso. Parrying the attack, the injured man thrust the bottom of his palm into the assailant's chin, sending an electrifying shock through his skull and into his eyes and brain, disorienting him momentarily. Seizing the moment, he pinned the assailant under the weight of his hand and elbowed him squarely in his face, before snaffling the sword from his hand and slicing it across his abdomen, thrusting him backwards. The assailant dropped to the floor with the sword in his gut, blood spurting from the wound.

By now, five more assailants had appeared behind him, dropping from their horses. Noting their silhouettes from the corner of his eye, he already had the sword in position. He swung it outward as they unleashed an assault on him. He took the first assailant by blocking a strike with one hand and driving the sword into the man's intestines before thrusting his heel into his chest, sending him hurtling backwards. The assailant bumped into the wall behind and slid to the floor lifelessly.

He regained his position just in time as two assailants lunged at him with fierce force. Nimbly angling his sword, the associate sliced it across the head of one of the assailants while blocking the second one with his other hand, throwing him back into the bloodied body of the second. The two assailants crash-landed on the floor. One of them bled heavily, but the other recovered only to take another fierce strike of a fist in his face and the sharp edge of the sword down his throat, before being yanked out of the way.

The guardian of the metal chest took a moment, gasping heavily. His agile mind and sharp eyes caught two more assailants circling him like sharks. With brandished swords, they pinned him under their sharp focus. Hidden behind his earthy attire, they sensed were the self-defense techniques of a skilled warrior who'd leave his opponents lifeless in a matter of seconds.

With calm and steady gaze, he gathered his bearings and studied his assailants. His trained eyes caught the first assailant signaling the attack. As they pounced on him, one from the front and the other from the back, he dropped onto his right knee, swinging his arms like a windmill, striking the front assailant's groin with his open palm with great force. The impact lifted the assailant off the ground. Manipulating with sufficient leverage, he sent the assailant flying over his head to hit the stone wall at the back. The assailant bounced back from the stone wall and dropped to the floor, his hands around his bleeding groin.

He rolled over his shoulder and gained his foot just in time as the other assailant attacked from the back, bringing down his sword in force upon him. Parrying off the slice, he grabbed the assailant by his elbow and then wrapping his powerful arms around his torso, hoisting him up over, yanked him down to the floor.

The fall sent a crushing force up the assailant's body, squashing his lungs and stifling his breath momentarily. The assailant writhed on the ground. Snaffling the dagger from the assailant's waistband, the associate of the brotherhood stabbed the assailant to death.

Ere he could take a long breath of relief, to his misfortune, a chilling pain speared his body. Startled, his eyes crept down toward the source of pain and discovered the sharp point of a dagger, protruding from his torso. Grief-stricken, he realized there was another assailant behind him who'd harpooned him with a dagger.

He couldn't stomach the idea of being killed. Not until he had accomplished his obligation of hiding the chest of scrolls. He and his brotherhood had sworn to protect it forever, to guard the secret knowledge from the ones who wanted to destroy it and wipe its traces from the face of the earth. With every breath at his disposal, he was ready to resist death. Regardless of his end, the secret as far as he knew would survive, must survive.

He remembered that he owed it to his brotherhood to keep the knowledge alive, for the chosen few, those who were enlightened. But he could not let the knowledge fall into the hands of the maniacs who desired control over the human race in the name of religion. With that fierce determination racing through his veins, he reached out to the sword on the floor, swung it outward and thrust it right across the assailant's torso just as he came in close.

Only after the sturdy frame of the assailant had collapsed lifeless to the floor, did he identify him as the first in command: the leader who'd hacked his old Grand Master to death back in the secret chamber. He sighed, having avenged his old Grand Master's death.

Saving the world always comes at a price, the price he realized was the life of his Old Grand Master and now his own.

Through his death-burdened eyes, he saw the tumbled metal chest and the scattered scrolls on the altar. *I do not have much time. Before my soul detaches from my body, the secret must be buried…*

Hoarding grateful gulps of air for his craving lungs, letting his drained body regain what little energy he had left, he dragged his battered body with his palms towards the altar. With every inch he moved, he felt his consciousness diminishing and his chances of fulfilling the task. Despite this, he pushed courageously until he crept the distance to the altar.

Reaching the altar, he felt relieved when his outstretched hands came to rest upon the metal chest on the altar, while three-fourth of his body lay senseless, immovable on the floor. With trembling hands, he set the metal chest straight, gathered the scattered scrolls back into it and pushed it into the cavity, sealing off the panel.

I'm done. His soul squalled from deep within. *The secret is buried.*

He sunk to the floor, falling flat. He knew he was only seconds away from his death, but he also remembered that there was one last thing need to be accomplished—another objective of their secret brotherhood.

The secret must be buried but with a key to its location concealed in a cryptic gesture that only someone worthy could uncover.

Summoning the cryptic clue to his memory, he coiled the middle, ring and little fingers of his right hand, while stretching his index and thumb outward. Gasping loudly, he breathed for one last time, freeing his soul from the confines of mundane flesh, satisfied at the accomplishment of his vow, unaware that some scrolls and the key to the chest had slipped from his hand while the rest was being secreted. But it was too late now. He lay dead. Woefully, his work was only half- done. The valuable key and some of the scrolls lay vulnerable, insecure and unguarded on the altar.

So much was doomed to happen, so much he could not have anticipated and for all the wrong reasons. This served as a harbinger of a devastating event that would unfold in the future. One whose repercussions he never knew would push the world to the brink of mayhem.

Thar Desert,

27^0N 71^0E,

November 1991,

3 PM.

This is mysterious…

George Stevens, senior head of the department of Archaeological Survey of India (ASI), whispered to himself. He leaned closer to the ground and suspiciously analyzed the right hand of a skeleton, splayed face up on the sand-covered floor.

Amongst the score of skeleton uncovered, this one, half buried in the sand with only skull and rib cage visible, was distinguished by the unusual pattern of the bony fingers of its right hand, arranged in a strange fashion.

It had intrigued him.

Middle, ring and the little fingers were coiled while the index and thumb were outstretched. This unusual hand gesture weighed upon his mind, triggering a suspicion and a sense of dejavu as if he'd seen this icon somewhere before. But definitely not on any of the excavations he had conducted earlier.

After giving at it a close scrutiny, he rose from the ground. He stood there with his hands resting on his waist, his tall and lanky frame draped in a white linen half-sleeve shirt and denim trousers. As he strained to make sense of the shape of the skeleton's hand, lines creased his temple, indicating signs of aging and his eyes furrowed in deep thought.

He gradually turned full circle on his heels, taking stock of the place just to ensure that he had missed nothing that would substantiate his suspicion that things here were as they were made to appear.

The scorching heat of the desert drew him from his reverie, making him take off his hat. His tousled hair spilled thin grey strands over his broad forehead that he neatly groomed back in place with a stroke of his hand.

The previous day, this place was almost nonexistent. Buried beneath layers of sun scorched sand, this monastery, now covered in centuries of dust and cobweb, was an accidental discovery stemming from a terrorist search operation in which a cross-border terrorist being hunted down by the Indian army, by the twist of fate, had slipped and fallen to his death through the hole that once formed the oculus in the ceiling of the structure.

George Stevens was still in the process of understanding its significance when he heard a voice calling out to him, "Sir."

When he turned, a soldier from the Indian army was escorting a sturdy man in Military uniform towards him.

George had heard about this man just yesterday. Being the director of the Mechanized Forces in the Indian army, the man was dressed in a razor- sharp military suit. Noticing turban atop his head, George confirmed yet once again a well established fact that Indian Army preferred to recruit a large chunk of its battalion from Punjab territory than any other region in Indian country.

This man was a little over six feet tall and was distinguished by a stocky nose. It was him who had informed Archaeology department about the discovery last evening and had even assisted the archaeological team in setting up the excavation. From setting up makeshift tents to dispelling the cavernous darkness with a series of flashlights using a battalion of soldiers, this man had ensured that the initial plan of action was launched in full sprint.

"This is Mr. Balbeer Singh," the soldier introduced, once they arrived. "And this," turning to George Stevens, he said, "is the senior archaeologist."

Director Balbeer Singh shook George's hand with a somber smile. "Nice to meet you, Mr. George."

"It's my pleasure," George reciprocated with an affable smile. "And thanks for this generosity," he said, gesturing to his left.

The director swept his eyes in the direction with a proud grin. He was glad to find his soldiers lending a helping hand to the archaeological team in setting up a makeshift table as they prepared for a preliminary investigation of the recovered skeletons. Archaeological equipment like shovels, trowels, dustpans, tape measure, plumb bobs and other basic tools came in handy as they prepared for the analysis.

Neither the previous day's terrorist search operation nor its outcome had kindled his interest in touring this find. Instead, it was his inclination towards ancient discoveries and ruins that formed the core of his interest, compelling the director to fly down here across hundreds of miles.

Bright flashes from cameras drew his attention off to the side, towards a few individuals from the archaeological team who were capturing the walls from all angles. On each wall, he observed, were engraved the songs of architectural brilliance of the past. The intricate floral designs, the iconic blend of animal themes, the Hindu-deities and the grotesque God-like figures adorning the wall evinced the remarkable impressions of great artistic compositions of a bygone era, left intact and covered by the dusts of time. It seemed to him he was strolling along the galleries of a museum of ancient world and its wonders.

Few minutes when he had abseiled down the makeshift ladder into this chamber through the oculus in the ceiling, he was taken aback by the sheer beauty of a masterpiece on the eastern wall of the monastery hall—a magnificent sculpture of Buddha, chiseled from a single block of jet black granite, whose shimmering attributes had withstood the destructive forces of time.

It had mesmerized him.

As the solider hurried off, the director looked straight at George. "Well, Mr. George, what do you have to say about this place?"

"Ah!" George ventured in an excited tone. "This is an absolutely thrilling discovery. Something akin to the caves of Ajanta and Ellora that expounds the significance of Buddhism and the artistic brilliance prevalent during their times."

The director cast his eyes upon the skeleton on the floor. "How old could this place be?"

George shrugged. "We've have taken samples for radiocarbon dating. The reports are due in a week. But my rough estimation place the age of this monastery somewhere between the first and seventh century AD, making this place at least close to two thousand years old."

From what George had been told, Director Balbeer Singh had a penchant for ancient discoveries. It was the only reason, George suspected, that had motivated him to set up the excavation in such a short time.

Finding the director on the same wavelength, sharing a common ground of passion for the remains of the past, George realized he definitely had something worth this man's interest.

"There's something more I think you might want to see."

The director was intrigued. George motioned him toward the table near the rear wall of the chamber that had a reading lamp, a laptop, infrared spectrometers, portable petrographic microscope, GPS, notes and a magnifying lens.

As they reached, the director glanced over all the items, but his gaze settled upon something very interestingly crude that was laid out under the white glow of the reading lamp.

Scrolls?

He immediately recognized that it was some ancient manuscript. More scrolls were neatly transferred into a wooden casing beside on the table.

"Those are scrolls," the director said in awe.

"Birch bark scrolls," George corrected him, his face replete with excitement. "Ancient scholars used the barks of the birch tree for writing documents. This is one of the materials they used for propagating their knowledge, culture and history down the ages."

The scrolls were deep yellow to olive brown in color, laced by copper wire through holes on the left hand corners. The edges were weathered and chipped, making them so frayed that they would crumble to pieces if handled roughly.

With the touch of his finger, the director had confirmed this.

He looked closely at the scrolls. His brows pinched at the writing, etched in dark brown ink, bearing inscriptions of some language he couldn't identify.

"The manuscript is in ancient Pali," George elucidated, almost reading his expression.

"You know the language?"

George nodded. "It's a form of Sanskrit highly laden with Prakrit vocabulary and its inflexions."

Noting the director's interest in the texts, George offered him his tweezers with a nod to pry open the scrolls and explore them.

Feeling honored, the director accepted the tweezers and with little effort, turned the first scroll delicately to see what was on the underside and what was on the ones under it. He continued to turn the scrolls, from one to the next and the next, until something very disturbing caught him off guard.

The director's brows furrowed and his face contorted. Then his eyes gaped wide as soon his eyes drank in the numerical calculations of some sort of mysterious diagrams and geometry that made him stare up at George in surprise. "This is impossible!"

George smiled proudly. "Isn't it an amazing piece of evidence to the lost wisdom of the ancients?"

The director riffled through scroll after scroll.

"This could be it," George continued, "a testament to a high level of skill and proficiency in every aspect of social and life science. Or simply put, a clue to more such treasure troves of knowledge that might be hidden in here...somewhere," George concluded suspiciously glancing back at the skeleton's right hand.

In disbelief, the director flicked through the scrolls. Although he couldn't read the script, he knew what he was looking at under the soft yellow glow of the lamp. With rapt interest, he went on to spot uncanny pictures, schematics and illustrations that were far beyond the understanding of humans. Too mysterious for ordinary eyes to recognize, too advanced for modern-day scholars to comprehend.

Examining the manuscript in silence, the director was locked in deep contemplation. His face was rattled with anxiety. Then he looked up at George. "Has anyone other than us..." pausing for a beat, he glanced in the direction of the archaeological team near the skeletons and insisted, "I mean other than the two of us, has anyone seen these scrolls?"

The statement was confusing, but George after a long unsure pause, replied, "No."

The director sighed. His expression turned from fear to one that was of relief. "Now, I have a new home for these scrolls."

George was puzzled.

"The National Defense Research Centre," the director furnished, putting back the scrolls inside the wooden casing and lifting it into his hands. "From its face value alone, it seems that these scrolls contain some kind of ancient knowledge on warfare that requires meticulous examination. These scrolls need to be analyzed and subjected to serious experimentation." He paused. "I'm confiscating these scrolls in the interest of national defense."

George hesitated, trying to make sense of what the director was saying. "I'm sorry, I cannot approve this. These valuable ancient records belong to the ASI." George moved closer to take hold of the scrolls from the director's hand. "And I cannot have you take them..."

The director stopped George in his tracks, pinning his index finger into his chest.

George felt his chest tighten as he gazed straight into the director's steel-cold eyes; it seemed as if the weight of the director's rugged military frame had been concentrated at a single point on his chest through the man's index finger alone.

The director glanced around, relieved that no one from the archaeological team had witnessed this tussle. Turning to George, he kept his voice low as he spoke, "I appreciate your allegiance to your profession. Now, be wise enough to stay out of the affairs of national interest."

George made a face, clueless.

The director gave him a grave stare and then turned and walked out of the chamber, emerging into the main colonnaded hall, clutching the wooden casing in his hand. As he headed to the makeshift ladder running up the oculus in the ceiling, out into the desert, he had George close on his heels.

All around them, soldiers bustled around aiding the archaeological team in whatever manner they could.

"What is this all about?" George pressed clamorously, following the director, "can you be clear on what you're up to?"

The director stopped and spun around, his gaze unwavering and serious. "I don't see any necessity to make myself clear on this. But seeing it was you who had discovered this treasure, I owe you an explanation. That these scrolls have great future in our hi-tech military research facilities than lying worthlessly caged in the display panels at the museum." he paused. "Before I leave, I want you to remember one thing about the scrolls. This will remain between us." He paused again letting the statement to linger little longer. "Just you and me."

"You have no authority to confiscate anything you desire," George sounded flustered. "Not here. Not at a dig run by the ASI."

The director looked at him sternly. "If you want to talk about authority…yes, I do. I have the authority to do what I feel is right in the interest of national defense. And my profession grants me that leeway." He inched closer, meeting George's eyes. "If you remember, it was I who informed your department about this discovery. If I had wished I could have surveyed this ruin first and confiscated the scrolls, leaving you nothing but one option," he said in a deep grating tone, "that of pouring over the piles of skeletal remains that are not even worth a dime."

His fierce response left George speechless.

Giving him a sharp look of disgust, the director turned and walked over to the ladder. He climbed the ladder with the scrolls and disappeared overhead.

Helplessly, George stood at the foot of the ladder, realizing that the director was right. It was the director who'd first informed their department about this accidental discovery and had even arranged for their travel to the site by military chopper. But George also knew that the director had no authority over the ancient find. Whatever was found at an ancient site entirely belonged to his department. No one could lay their claim over the remains of ancients, save for the ASI. Still, for a man with this caliber, of his rank, confiscating anything from anyone from anywhere with or without permission was a left-handed game.

Weighing on his mind, however, were a bunch of questions awaiting answers. Like what had the director uncovered within the layers of those scrolls? What disturbing thing had he grasped that his own trained eyes had missed? Had the contents of the scrolls, as the director had insisted, really depicted any relevant connection to warfare that needed further research in the interest of defense of the country? Or had it contained some reference to mysterious weapons or some advanced technology that he found too dangerous to reveal?

The deeper he dived, the heavier was his desperation. Letting go off the worries temporarily, he went back to the chamber and found himself staring again at the skeleton that lay near the altar.

George moved away from the archaeology team, focusing his full attention on its right hand. He believed that this strange arrangement of fingers had some story to tell. Like a guiding hand, it must have been pointing at something which he was missing.

Then, it struck him. *Good Lord!* George moved closer to the skeleton and observed the finger arrangement again in a new light of recognition. *It is the same hand,* he whispered in surprise, now fully understanding the pattern and its symbolism.

This hand gesture was an ancient symbol---a classical icon that served as a map to discover the location where the greatest secret of mankind awaited—the secret that was kept from man for a reason, accessible only to those who understood its true meaning.

CHAPTER 1

Sunday, August 5, 2017.

10.30 AM.

The pattern is strikingly unusual...

CBI officer Jake Stevens thought as he stood by the poolside and observed the hands of a dead body sprawled in a puddle of blood.

The fingers of the left hand were outstretched but did not seem unusual. The fingers on the right hand, however, were coiled except for the thumb and the index finger, which were arranged like a hand gesture from a signboard, directing or pointing at something nearby.

His eyes trailed the direction of the index finger only to land on the bare wall in the verandah. After a moment of introspection, he abandoned the theory that the fingers were pointing at something, finding the idea absurd.

A bright flash yanked him from daze and he turned to see photographers from the forensic team capturing the dead body from all the angles. A fleet of men with sniffer dogs rummaged the place for evidence against the murderer.

Two hours ago, in broad daylight, when the whole of New Delhi was teeming with life, a man named Ramanujan was brutally murdered at his bungalow in one of the city's busiest localities, Connaught. The dead man was around sixty and had been found draped in a towel, lying lifeless by the poolside.

According to the forensic preliminary examination of the crime scene, the man was suspected to be shot dead immediately after he had emerged from the pool.

"Zoom and capture his hands," Jake told the photographer, pointing to the fingers of the dead man. "This could be important."

Clad in denim trousers and a navy blue blazer over a pale blue shirt, Jake stood full six feet tall. He was in his early thirties, fair, with a sophisticated charm that many in his field lacked.

From the time he had been absorbed into the Central Bureau of Investigation (CBI) as chief officer in the Special Crimes Division some three years ago, he had never looked back. Resolving offences related to internal security, espionage, antiquities and international rackets to suspicious deaths and crimes of national importance from early on in his career, he had risen through the ranks faster than any senior official in the agency.

None of the earlier cases had challenged his ingenuity in a manner quite like this one though; this and the murder that had occurred the previous day, both of which had involved victims with right hands frozen in the same position and pattern.

Realizing it was too early to make connections between two different murders, Jake brought his mind back to his surroundings. He strolled around the green lawn, past the pool, observing the bungalow that was fortified with a huge iron gate and a tall compound wall. After a brief inspection of the crime scene, he arrived back at the spot where the body had been found and gazed down, trying to picture the scene from various perspectives.

The head of the forensic team, the chief medical examiner, rose from his examination of the body, removing his gloves. "Single shot to forehead at point blank range." he informed, adding, "death was instantaneous."

"Any marks on his body?" asked Jake, "of physical assault?"

"None that I can see," the forensic doctor replied curtly.

"I think I do," a voice interrupted.

Jake turned to find his associate walking towards him. "Marks of forced assault, yes, but on his belongings," Riya Sonal said.

Riya Sonal was tasked with assisting Jake. Draped in elegant dark blue suit, even in her late thirties, she appeared as stunning as ever, endowed with a well-toned figure that belied her age. A high pony-tail--her signature hair style, swayed as she brisked gracefully through the lobbies of the CBI building, swaying along hearts from her profession. Be it her mannerism or her attire, both typified professionalism.

"His room is ransacked. His closets, stripped." Riya paused, glancing at the dead body. "The killer came looking for something he thought the victim possessed."

Jake saw that her gaze had gone distant. Behind those pretty eyes of her, he sensed, her mind was churning various possibilities. It hadn't taken him long to realize that it was her acute sense of reasoning that had earned her his assistant's post soon after her recruitment into the CBI.

Jake turned to the chief medical officer beside him. "When can I expect the complete forensic report?"

"Forty-eight hours," the forensic officer replied.

As soon as the forensic officer had left the scene, Riya started briefing Jake on the profile of the victim, noting that he was survived by his wife who was presently out of town. Halfway through, Jake stopped her.

"Wait. What did you say about his qualification? A PhD?"

"Yes, he holds a PhD in fluid mechanics," repeated Riya, adding, "a branch of science that deals with the mechanics of fluids."

"His branch is not my concern," Jake said. "His degree is all that matters."

He turned and moved closer to the dead body. "You should see this," he pointed to the pattern the fingers of the dead man made. "Ring a bell?"

Riya rounded up the dead body from the other side, squatting, analyzing it as Jake spoke.

"Isn't it too much of a coincidence to have two victims, murdered on consecutive days, both retired professors with doctorates, whose circumstances of death bear a striking resemblance?" Jake informed studying the fingers meticulously. "The fingers on their right hands are fashioned in a similar pattern."

Riya realized Jake was linking both the cases. However, there were minor irregularities that cannot be overlooked: both of them had retired from different universities and the pattern formed by the fingers on the left hands was entirely different.

"The left hand pattern does not match. They are entirely different." Jake refrained from commenting.

"Sir, I think you should see this," one of the members of the forensic team called out to Jake.

Jake and Riya hurried to the spot where the forensic specialist had crouched on the ground. His focus was riveted on something on the paving around the pool. They saw what he was looking at: footprints cast of wet soil, now caked.

Jake let his eyes trail the footprints and found that they had emerged from the lawn.

"Capture it," Jake directed the specialist.

"Jake," Riya continued, "we have someone from the neighborhood who claims to have seen a stranger prowling around this bungalow thrice yesterday."

"Put him through to the artist and get a sketch ready," said Jake.

Shortly thereafter, Jake heard his cell phone chiming in his pocket.

He answered the call, spoke for a brief moment, hung up and turned to Riya.

"AD wants to see us. We have to leave right away."

Riya was already on the move.

"Unearth more information about his background," Jake was telling her as they moved towards the gate. "His bank accounts, a background check and anything else that might be crucial. I want nothing to be missed."

"Sure," Riya nodded.

As they walked, Jake glanced over his shoulder, casting one last look at the dead man's right hand, thinking it definitely held a crucial tale to be told.

CHAPTER 2

Three blocks away from the crime scene, a man on the seventh floor of a hotel building, finished typing a message on his cell phone.

OPERATION: THE LOST ARCANUM.
TARGET: RAMANUJAN.
TASK: INCOMPLETE.
TARGET STATUS: TERMINATED.

He ensured the images of the crime scene was tagged along with the message and then hit the send button, tossing the cell on the bed. He reached for a pair of binoculars and parted the blinds, looking down the window through the binoculars at the dog squad spread all over the lawn beside the pool.

"Sniffers," he mumbled under his breath, finding the investigation team combing for clues at the crime scene. He then turned, adjusting the diopter ring on the binoculars, fine-tuning it until a dead body lying by the pool came into sharp focus. "That's quite an end you've made for yourself," he grunted under his breath. "Wouldn't be lying dead, if you'd given me what I wanted."

An hour and a half ago, waking up to the first hint of sunlight, Ramanujan, a middle-aged home alone professor had dived into the pool waters, letting his drained muscles gain some semblance of life, giving a quick energetic soak to his body lethargic from the previous night's comatose sleep. He floated in the water for a short while before emerging from the pool and befuddle at the sight of a stranger trespassing on his territory, barging into the lawn and walking straight in his direction.

The stranger on the prowl was tall, lean and clad in a long, black coat. His eyes obscured behind sunglasses and under the shade of his hat, his face was almost unrecognizable.

"Who the hell are you?" Ramanujan had barked in panic, collecting a towel from a nearby chair and draping it around his waist. "Who let you in?"

A terrible smile crinkled the stranger's lips

"Security!" Ramanujan's eyes searched for the guard on duty. His desperate cry went unheard. Before he spat out another call for help, the stranger was in front of him and had retrieved something from jacket pocket, waving it at him.

Chills ran down his spine. His eyes reflecting sheer terror as sunlight glinted off the hard steel shaft pointed in his direction.

"What do you want?" Ramanujan hesitated, seeing a 9mm Beretta in the stranger's hand.

"The Lost Arcanum."

"What?" Ramanujan went numb on hearing that.

The stranger stepped closer, threateningly, lifting the gun to Ramanujan's temple.

"What in the world does that mean?" Ramanujan stammered. "I don't know what you're talking about."

"I hate repeating myself," the stranger rasped.

"Security!" Ramanujan screamed again, his voice barely audible.

The stranger grabbed Ramanujan's jaw with one hand, holding the gun's muzzle to his temple with the other. "Don't make this any harder for you."

His eyes were as hard as cold steel. He leaned menacingly over Ramanujan. His cigarette breath washed over the professor as he hissed, "You scream one more time and I bet…" He paused. "You'll take the secret with you to your grave."

The stranger smirked at the fear of death reflected in Ramanujan's eyes.

Ramanujan realized that this menacing stranger had come here to acquire a precious trove that had been kept for thousands of years, tucked away in a safe location, far from this place and way beyond his imagination. For the first time since the stranger had walked into the villa, Ramanujan registered that the man was broad shouldered and dark skinned with stubble and small eyes obscured behind the glasses.

"Where's the Lost Arcanum?"

With the gun fairly close to his forehead, Ramanujan ascertained that death was at his doorstep. *My death is inevitable. Whether or not, the Lost Arcanum is compromised, I'm sure to die.* Expecting his death at any second, Ramanujan inhaled a long courageous breath and broke his silence. "It's safe, intact and in a place far from your reach." The stranger gritted his teeth. "Then you die, bastard!" Thud…

A single bullet burst out of the muzzle, drilling into Ramanujan's temple, throwing him to the ground, limp and lifeless, with blood gushing out of the hole at the back of his head.

A low hum from his side drew the stranger back from the flashback. He turned from the window and found his cell vibrating on the bed. He walked to the bed, picked it up and saw an unknown number flashing on the screen.

The previous day, too, he had received a call from the same number minutes after he texted the update about the execution of Anurag Chopra along with the images as a proof, following which, his hirer had guided him to his fortune waiting with a street boy.

He pushed the talk button.

"What about the situation at the crime scene?" a mysterious hollow voice inquired.

"CBI is up with the smelling thing," the stranger replied. "I suppose you've covered your tracks."

"Not a question about it."

"Good," the caller replied after a second, "and that's why you've been hired." Following another pause, the caller noted, "Your fortune awaits at the second left from the main road, with a fruit vendor."

A greedy smile curled the corner of the gunman's lips.

"I will update you on your next move shortly," the caller concluded and hung up.

Reaching the basement of the hotel, the shooter climbed into his black Honda SUV and drove away to claim his prize.

As a child, he'd often fantasized about a short route to fame and riches. His fate has been excessively favorable for the past few days. Yet his past continued to haunt him, specifically his identity as an orphan.

What makes one stone-hearted? This grieving question had stayed with him since he'd learnt from his caretakers that his family had forsaken him at the doorstep of an orphanage when he was only three days old. There he grew up as Soori, 'the wise man', named by the caretaker from orphanage, before he was adopted by a rich man at the age of ten. Beside assuring best education to Soori, he had promised equal rights at home and a well defined status in society as those from the rest of his wealthy family.

That was end of his life as an orphan. Or at least that's what Soori had thought. If only he had known that happiness was ephemeral.

Within a year of his adoption, the man had turned into a dictator of sorts, putting an end to his studies and forcing him to assume the role of a domestic help. One ill-fated day, provoked by resentment and driven by a juvenile impulse, Soori had stabbed the rich man to death.

Thereafter, like a nomad he moved from place to place, growing up in the narrow streets of Kolkata between haphazardly parked vehicles and pushcarts teetering with food, and substandard clothing. His adolescent years were spent like a paranoiac, fretting about his fate. He would hang out in the same busy streets and loiter in old cafes and antique bazaars, subsisting on junk food from the street vendors and passing the nights curled against a crypt in the nearby cemetery. Eventually, he was handpicked by a notorious gang leader who honed his aggressive side. From extortion to killing for money, he took on every notorious project that came his way.

Now, the money he'd been chasing laboriously was within his reach and the time was not far when his dreams would transform into reality.

From street thug to the highest-paid contract killer. He smiled wickedly. *I'm the most desired professional killer.*

The killer stopped his SUV on spotting the fruit vendor. *There's my prize!*

He got down from the vehicle and approached the fruit vendor, attentive to his surroundings.

The fruit vendor produced a black briefcase and placed it on the cart.

Soori looked at it and then looked up at the vendor. "Who gave this to you?"

"A man," the vendor replied.

"What did he look like?"

"I'm not sure," the fruit vendor responded bluntly. "I saw only his silhouette in the backseat. The windows were tinted."

Who could that be? The killer Soori was intrigued at the man who demanded such high secrecy over his identity. Whoever he was, Soori realized, he wished to stay anonymous. He was deft at picking his moves carefully and with precision, ensuring not even the slightest of hint of his identity escaped.

"How did you recognize me?" The killer fished for more.

"They have your picture. The car driver showed it to me."

That astounded Soori.

These were not ordinary people.

With that thought circling in his mind, he walked away with his prize.

CHAPTER 3

Central Bureau of Investigation,

Headquarters,

New Delhi.

The magnificent edifice of the CBI headquarters at the CGO Complex on Lodhi Road flaunts an exceptionally dazzling corporate look. Spread on five acres of prime land and said to be modeled after the Interpol Headquarters at Lyons, France, this eleven-storied structure is a contemporary building paneled with deep green tinted solar reflective glass, standing out from other conventional-looking government offices around.

As if competing with the extravagant exterior, the interior of the nation's premiere investigation agency building leaves no stone unturned in trying to match the external design as well. An exquisite combination of yellow and green tiles is laid out on each floor, the pillars are painted in vibrant strokes of dark grey and open offices fitted with modular cubicles are marked in shades of pink and grey. The elegant furniture adds a touch of vibrant glitz to the interiors.

Each branch is allocated a separate floor with interrogation rooms, lock-up rooms, dormitories, media rooms and conference halls. The topmost floors—the tenth and the eleventh—are reserved for top officials, including the CBI directors, the additional directors and special directors. The sixth floor accommodates the gallery that showcases the history and accomplishments of the CBI.

Post World War-II, inglorious and anti-social activities of bribery and corruption soared, pushing up the expenses of the Government of India. The police and other state law-enforcement agencies seemed futile. To tackle the crisis, a Special Police Establishment (SPE) was launched in 1941. With time, more powers were awarded to this division, diversifying its operations across all union territories and into different states with the consent of concerned governments. It wasn't long before another enforcement wing took over, loaded with extra privileges to curb offences relating to import and export.

Soon, the central government felt the need for a central police agency that could, in addition to cases of bribery and corruption, manage cases regarding violation of central fiscal laws, economic fraud, crimes on the high seas, crimes on airlines and serious crimes committed by organized gangs and professional criminals. This led to the setting up of the CBI in April 1963, categorizing different divisions under its wings.

In one of the chambers on the top floor of the CBI headquarters, nestled in a leather crafter chair was Rajat Singh, additional director, Special Crimes Division.

He peered through the glass wall into the office corridor, eagerly awaiting the arrival of his junior officer, Jake.

Rajat Singh, also known as AD, had a great admiration for Jake. His compassion for Jake came more from a paternal instinct than the ingenuity that Jake was usually known for. In a short span, Jake had scaled heights, cracking crime cases within days of its occurrence, accomplishing what none of his fellow officers had been able to do despite years of service and experience in the CBI.

Now, expecting the same level of efficiency once again, Rajat Singh had summoned Jake for an immediate debriefing on the progress in the investigation of the murder of another home alone scientist Anurag Chopra, killed the previous afternoon.

The sound of footsteps in the corridor interrupted his thoughts. When he glanced up, the door to his chamber swung open and Jake walked in, frustrated.

"Ugh! Traffic sucks!"

AD threw him a serious look. "Then I suggest you get yourself a bicycle. That's sleeker, more compact and sexier than your limo."

Jake pulled out a chair in front of AD's desk and sat down, making a face. He was well acquainted with AD's dark sense of humor hidden beneath his stern countenance.

Offering no response, Jake silently set the case file on the table.

AD chuckled. He picked up the file and leafed through it. Sitting quietly opposite, Jake admired AD as he went through the case file. Regardless of the two decades he had spent in the Indian army, prior to his posting here, AD's dedication and commitment towards his profession had endured countless challenges in his tenure and continued to be ceaseless. Even in his early sixties. That was quite apparent from his rigidity. AD's once dark hair had turned silver. Even so, a cleft on his left cheek, his unwavering voice, his matchless gait, all spoke of a stern, dignified bearing that had remained unmarred over the years.

"A threat?" AD's face clouded over as he read from the file.

"There's only one we've gotten hold of," Jake added. "It talks about some shadowy organization threatening him to keep silent about whatever he knew."

AD looked up at him from the file. "What organization?"

"Not clear on that." Jake's gaze was distant. "I suspect it's the same organization that might've wired adequate funds in his account to encourage him to maintain his silence over that secret."

AD appeared intrigued. "And the account?"

"As expected," Jake said flatly, "it's fictitious."

AD reclined in his chair and thought for a moment. "What's your take on this angle?"

Jake was silent for a few seconds, before he replied, "As per my analysis, this scientist was working for that organization. Probably doing some research on something on their instructions. At which point, he might've discovered something this unknown organization hadn't wanted him to and got rid of him."

AD realized Jake was probably right, but there was another possibility. Giving it a thought, he rose from the chair and walked to the side table and reached for his coffee maker. "I seriously doubt that this organization has a hand in his murder. If they had to kill him, they would've done that much earlier instead of bothering to bribe him to keep mum."

"It might also be," Jake countered, "that he was doing research on some mysterious technology on instructions from that organization. At some point, they realized he was a liability, a probable threat in the near future, which got him eliminated."

That made sense to AD.

He turned from his machine and asked, "Any other clues?"

"We are still working on it," Jake said, looking at the photographs of the previous day's victim, Anurag Chopra, specifically at the pattern the fingers on his right hand made. Jake recalled that the pattern matched the ones he had seen an hour ago. He was sure that if this puzzle could be solved, many secrets would spill out into the open.

"Would you like some coffee?" AD asked Jake, glancing over his shoulder, aware of Jake's profound lust for coffee.

"Sure," Jake shot instantly.

AD returned to his seat with two mugs of coffee and held one out to Jake, before he imbibed his own fresh, piping hot beverage.

Jake took a sip and gaped at him. AD chuckled. *I knew you'd love it.* "It's one of the finest brands of coffee, from Coorg." He took a long sip as he spoke. "You can pick it up if you're stopping by home for dinner tonight."

Jake gave him a look that seemed to ask for an explanation. The invitation hadn't surprised him at all. AD often asked him home for dinners and lunches and Jake received them devoutly, without hesitation. But this time, it was quite surprising, since two nights ago, he had been there hogging his favorite cuisine.

Understanding his confusion, AD clarified. "Riya and her daughter are invited for dinner. My better-half will be glad if you can join the party."

Jake smiled, thinking of Mrs. Singh, who was like his own mother, loving, affectionate and very caring.

Flipping through notes, Jake continued. "Sir, I think you should know this."

AD gave him his attention.

"The victim had opted for voluntary retirement, some good five years before his official tenure came to an end."

AD stretched back in his chair, contemplating another confusing piece of information that only rendered the case more intricate, like a mass of snarled wool, rather than fleshing out any positive outcomes.

"It suggests," AD said, "that his professional history might tell us something about this unknown organization."

Jake agreed with a nod and glanced at his right hand. He stretched his index finger and thumb, while letting the rest coil, imitating the pattern found on the victim's hand.

AD watched him. "What is that?"

"Nothing," Jake replied, thoughtfully.

CHAPTER 4

Exiting AD's chamber, Jake strode into the long corridor outside, stopping by a reception desk, where a young girl, wearing a graceful smile, received him.

Ishita, receptionist-cum-personal secretary to Jake, was just twenty-four, blessed with gracious curves that drew considerable attention from her fellow men.

"How are you doing?" Jake asked on reaching her desk.

"Fine, sir."

He saw her shuffling through some papers. "You look stressed!"

"Do I?" She glared at him worriedly and then snapped the papers on the desk, opened the drawer in her desk, picked up a mirror and looked into it.

"Good lord! You've got dark circles too," he said, playfully motioning to her eyes. "Is something really bothering you?"

"Nope," she replied after a long pause.

She's crazy. Jake smiled to himself. He knew she was obsessed with her looks, a situation he suspected had bloomed out of her keen interest in him. Attention from females of all age groups was something Jake had got accustomed to from his teenage days. He grew up with a magnetic charm that many admired, while some secretly desired him in their beds. However, raised in an orthodox family, he grew up to be someone who knew how to draw boundaries in the matter of carnal appetites.

"Anyway, anything important that needs my attention?" Jake asked and waited for a few moments, but she was still watching herself in the mirror.

"Hello, I'm speaking to you." Jake's voice rose.

"Oh! I'm sorry, sir." She looked up at him apologetically. "Anything of my concern?" Jake pressed again.

"No. I'll let you know if something crops up."

"Ok. Now, relax." Jake finished and left her desk, striding toward his chamber. Midway, he heard her calling him again.

"Sir, you have an appointment with Mr. Ravi Raj today."

Jake turned back. "Now, this confirms that something is really bothering you."

Jake then headed straight to his chamber, picturing her big round eyes that spoke more than her lips.

A frivolous young woman obsessed with her looks.

Inside his chamber, Jake crossed over to his table, pulled off his jacket and hung it on the chair. Computer, intercom, fax machine and heaps of official files and papers were neatly arranged on the desk. Cozy beams of sunlight filtering through the tinted glass window illuminated the interior.

First things first. Brewing some fresh coffee topped the list of his daily chores, especially on the days like as today, when he'd had to sacrifice the first cup of the day on account of duty call. Although AD had offered him a cup a while ago, he was still habituated to brewing coffee in his own coffee maker and relishing it in the comfort of his chamber.

Once his coffee was ready, he returned to his seat and sipped from the cup as he checked his emails. As usual, except for a couple of official mails, the inbox only contained notes from his college buddies. One mail, however, came from Eileen.

She was someone whom he thoroughly disliked. He had never met her. Nor had he ever spoken to her, but he knew that she was accountable for the agony he'd endured in his past. For that, he'd never forgiven her nor he would ever. Regardless of the effort she invested in trying to reach him, he stonewalled her, even warning her against ever calling him. She had since begun to shoot him emails, with the same subject line: THE TRUTH LIES WITH ME.

Whatever the truth she had, he was clearly not interested.

The clock on the wall chimed: 12.30 PM.

Time to meet Mr. Ravi Raj. Jake placed his computer in hibernation mode, picked up his car keys, jacket and left the chamber.

Down in the basement, Jake started the car and sped out.

La Piazza was where Jake was now heading to. He glanced at the buildings passing in a blur by the roadside. They rose and fell, some even spiked high, representing themselves as a testimony to Delhi being the fastest developing city in the world. It was on the same bustling streets, he recalled, that he had spent some happier times with his parents in his boyhood. His mind travelled down the tunnel of time and soaked in the warmth of those memorable instances.

Things have changed far more than anticipated.

Small shops where his parents had bought him Christmas gifts were now history, replaced by huge malls. Fast food sold from carts was long gone, supplanted by lounges and cafeterias, complete with glass paneling. One old structure, however, had remained unbelievably intact: Katherine's Orphanage.

It wasn't because it was an odd structure that he couldn't forget it. Coincidentally, it bore the name of someone he had loved the most in his life: Katherine, his sweet mother.

Things have changed since then, Jake thought, *and so have the people.*

Nothing is perpetual, his mother had whispered to him while on her deathbed, in an effort to console her sobbing son. He was only fourteen when hypertension had led to a stroke, paralyzing her body. After a year of suffering, she finally passed away, leaving behind an indelible scar of pain and grief.

Jake could still feel himself sitting next to her bed, holding her hand, staring into her sorrowful eyes when she had breathed her last. It was a heart-wrenching moment that kept recurring in his mind. But he always blocked it with an understanding: *Life was a long journey of sufferings, although some momentary carnivals of joy came along in installments.*

CHAPTER 5

Jake glanced over his shoulder at the tempting lamb *kofta* skewers being served to patrons on the adjacent table.

A smile escaped his lips as memories of his childhood returned. The aroma of food from the next table would tease his taste buds, his mother would frown but his father would wink his approval and order the same delicacies. That was a tender phase of his childhood marked by innocence and naiveté when such actions were impulse-driven rather than the result of rational inference. Although that time had elapsed, this was a trait he couldn't rid himself of, even after decades.

With hunger making his stomach growl, Jake pointed to the adjacent table and told the waiter. "Get me that one," The waiter smiled and hurried off.

Jake glanced at his wrist watch and wondered what was keeping Mr. Ravi Raj.

Some two decades ago, his father George Stevens had introduced this man to their family. As a family attorney, he had taken care of all legal matters, professional and personal. His pockmarked face, bushy brows over deep-set eyes and plum nose suggested a typical villain straight out of the movies. His monstrous looks had once caused the younger Jake nightmares, sometimes to the point of bedwetting. But in truth, the man was quite harmless and on the contrary to his first impression. Virtuous, loyal and trustworthy, he had carved a niche for himself in their family. His villainous image transformed into one of the most likable when conscience had struck Jake at the age of thirteen.

The waiter arrived at his table and served him lemonade. Jake hadn't even taken a sip when he saw the attorney walking into the restaurant with an attaché case.

The attorney appeared fit even in his late fifties. Clad in off-white, narrow-bottomed trousers and a black coat over a grey striped shirt with long cuffs, he was among a handful who preferred a fashion reminiscent of the past.

"Long time," Jake said, smiling widely as the attorney arrived at the table and took a seat in front of him.

"Not as long as it required you to make up your mind on trivial decision," the attorney gave him a half smile.

Jake knew what Ravi Raj meant. It had taken him years to decide on the legal affairs concerning his family. In fact, he was still unsure if he was really ready. The thought had made him uneasy. Jake tried to hide it, taking a moment to register their order for lunch with the waiter.

As soon as the waiter left, Jake looked back at the attorney. "Hey, you seem to have put on weight. That seriously scares me."

The attorney gave a plain smile. "And I'm scared of your ignorance, Jake."

Jake hesitated.

"Jake," the attorney said, finally voicing his concern, "you need to learn to take things in life as they come. Hardships are part of everyone's life and things that are gone will never come back. At least not in this life." The attorney implied God's will in his mother's untimely death. "You cannot continue to bury your head in the sand. You must learn to face the facts."

Ravi Raj examined Jake over a moment of pause.

Jake regarded his suggestion like a kid, quietly sipping from the glass. Ravi Raj was like a father figure to him. Any suggestions or advice from this man were heartily welcomed. On the other hand, the attorney was well informed about Jake's affairs. He remembered Jake was only fourteen when his father had abandoned them. At fifteen, his mother had passed away. Growing up in a boarding school was the most difficult part of his life. Deprived of love, only the bitter truths of the past had seemed to be his companions in loneliness.

A matter the attorney had never wanted to bring up and Jake ever wanted to recall.

The ambiance had gone dead silent. The food reached their table just in time, sparing Jake any further awkwardness.

"Ah! Here's the food," Jake said aloud. "I'm insanely hungry." The attorney reacted with a restrained smile.

Over a long conversation, both devoured their meals, with the attorney briefing him on his workload, while Jake discussed the investigation he headed presently. At the end of their lunch, the attorney had pulled out some papers from his attaché case and had tossed them on the table.

"If this is about the same will of goddamn assets worth millions my father has bequeathed to me, then I'm sorry," Jake said. "My hard- earned money, though little, is just enough." A thoughtful second later, Jake declared. "Let me know if there's something else that might interest me."

The attorney watched him silently. He was also familiar with Jake's rude attitude towards his late father, whom he'd despised and blamed for all the pain he and his mother had endured, even to the point of holding his father responsible for his mother's untimely passing. Hatred and contempt was all that Jake had nurtured for his father over the years.

The attorney mutely flipped through the papers and slid it across to Jake, tapping on it. "This is your mother's will."

"What?" That surprised Jake. He instantly snapped up the papers. "She has bequeathed something to me?"

The attorney noticed Jake's face glowing as it did whenever anything related to his mother was brought up.

"In a way, yes," the attorney clarified. "Your father had gifted this property to your mother. That now, after her death, you inherit it."

The hatred emotions he felt for his father reappeared as he listened to the attorney with anger soaked mind.

"And if you refuse to accept this inheritance, the property will be transferred to a trust."

Jake wondered. "What trust?"

"An orphanage," the attorney replied, stating, "called Katherine's Orphanage."

That knocked Jake over. "You mean the one next to that mall?"

"Yes," the attorney said, nodding. "Your mother was oblivious to it. Only your father and I knew about it. He demanded secrecy."

Jake was taken aback. It was unbelievable that the orphanage that stood in the middle of the posh street that he always admired had belonged to his mother. He mulled over it for a few seconds.

"He maintained secrecy for what?"

Ravi Raj leaned over the table. "He loved you and your mother more than anything. He placed you both before all his needs and the wealth he'd hoarded. His assets worth millions were you two. He was involved in works of charity, catering to the needy so that the rewards of those deeds would be bestowed on you two. He was a God-fearing man and magnanimous at heart."

Jake flared up. "You knew my father for more than fifteen years. Tell me, was what he did to us fair? Leaving us out there all alone to die?"

That question silenced the attorney.

"Do God-fearing people ever forsake their dear ones?"

The attorney said tiredly, "Jake, your father might have had his own reasons which I cannot comment on. Besides, I want to leave before this official meeting turns into an argument. So, have a look at this will and decide how best it suits your needs. Meanwhile, I'll take a leave."

Jake suppressed his anger. Picking up the file, he flipped through the pages and put it back on the table. "Too many pages to read. I'll take it home if you're okay with it?"

"That's fine," the attorney said. "Take your time. And do let me know how best we can go about it."

The attorney stood up and held out his hand.

Jake accepted the gesture and before the attorney turned to leave, he held him back with his words. "I see my father in you. You remind me of my father, who was caring and lovable before he abandoned my mother and me."

"Thanks for that honor, Jake. I'm immensely moved. But trust me, your father was a gentleman. He never betrayed you. Nor your mother. Like you assume."

With a warm smile, the attorney picked up his attaché case and walked away.

Jake watched him striding out of the restaurant, acknowledging the man's fatherly concern for him. That made Jake trust him to the core, really meaning what he had said. He was like a father figure.

In fact, very much like my father, his heart whispered silently.

CHAPTER 6

Jake had picked a silk, dark mauve shirt and pearly chinos for the evening. He cast a cursory glance at his facial features in the rear-view mirror as he drove. He remembered how much he had always admired his straight nose and sharp jaw line setting off his long neck and curvy brows over almond-shaped eyes.

Sliding his fingers over his face, he felt the texture of his skin. Supple and conditioned, not too different from what it had been a decade ago. 'Debonair', that's what his friends would often call him when they spotted him in attire that seemed to make a fashion statement of its own, admired by many and envied by more.

Squeezing his mind from the thought, through the windshield of his car, Jake's eyes caught sight of AD's beautiful white mansion, rising against the vivid backdrop of Rajauri Garden, a posh locality in Delhi chiefly inhabited by Punjabi families.

Since Jake's absorption in the CBI, AD had taken Jake under his wing in many ways, filling the void left by his mother's untimely passing. Jake had found that in addition to the steely reserve and rigorous methods he was known for, AD had affection and warmth in his soft ageing eyes. Filling his barren wife's desire for a child, AD had seemed to have adopted Jake to make a small loving family bonded with love, if not by blood ties.

Giving a welcome bow, the security guard opened the heavy metal gates and Jake brought his car to a stop under the porch. He climbed down and reached for the mansion's main door crafted of solid teakwood. He buzzed the door bell and waited until a pleasing face emerged on the other side. *Mrs. Singh*—Jake smiled—the other person he loved the most.

AD's better half was dressed in a satin gown and smiled widely at Jake. Although in her early fifties, Mrs. Singh used yoga and constant workouts at the gym to maintain her health and her vigor and high spirits were enough to mask her age quite gracefully.

"Good to see you, Jake." She expressed her joy, kissing him on his forehead.

Jake accepted her warm gesture and followed her to the living room where Riya had already settled on a plush sofa with her eight-year-old daughter alongside.

Jake had to admit that each time he visited this mansion, he couldn't resist an instinctive glance at its interiors. He was aware that AD nurtured a great taste for extravagance and had his house ornamented with the finest pieces of furniture shipped from various parts of the world: a hand-carved rosewood table from France, a Persian carpet, a Kashmiri tapestry, an ornate crystal chandelier and artifacts from different eras were all immaculately displayed. AD joined them shortly.

It was a small family get-together, a rendezvous that allowed them to catch up on each other's personal and professional lives. As usual, AD, his wife and Riya insisted that Jake to get married soon, they all showed their affection for Riya's physically challenged eight-year-old, Shikha, and their appreciation for Riya, a divorcee, for striking a perfect balance between her personal and professional life, giving her little daughter every possible care and share of love, both of a father and a mother.

Talk came to a halt when Mrs. Singh rose to set up dinner. Riya and Shikha joined her in the kitchen. While AD and Jake threaded their way up the stairs to the balcony, settling on the cushioned swing. Lighting a cigar and taking a long puff on it, AD asked, "Any leads on Ramanujan's case?"

"No," Jake replied, "His wife returned this evening and seems to be in deep shock. We won't be able to get any details until tomorrow morning."

AD allowed this information to settle.

"But we're looking for one clue in specific," Jake added.

AD threw a curious glance at Jake.

"The artist's impression of the prime suspect," Jake continued, "who was spotted thrice yesterday closer to the victim's bungalow. The witness is on a business trip until tomorrow. Once he's back, we'll put him with the artist and get the sketch done."

AD nodded and walked up to the parapet. Jake followed him and stood by his side. From the balcony, Jake admired the incredibly beautiful and scintillating skyline of New Delhi.

AD dragged a last puff and stubbed out the cigar in an ashtray. "Find out what his wife has got to say. I'm sure she knows something about this murder."

They heard Mrs. Singh's calling to them downstairs.

At the dining table, Jake's taste buds salivated as his favorite delicacies were spread lavishly across the length of the table. Soft wheat *rotis* were piled up in a basket and roasted chicken was arranged on a platter. Steamed rice was in another dish, while dal garnished with coriander leaves and a fresh vegetable salad soaked in mayonnaise helped fuel his gustatory desires. Amid the entire set-up, a bottle of exotic wine leaning in a basket came as a big surprise.

"Ah!" Jake excitedly reached for the bottle of wine in the basket and picked it up. He read the label: "Dom Perignon."

"Famous French wine," Jake told Riya. "AD really has a great taste for vintage wines."

AD acknowledged the compliment with a wink.

Halfway through dinner, AD remembered. "Jake, you didn't tell me about your appointment with your attorney."

"Oh!" Jake said, recalling it. He recounted the conversation with the attorney.

"I think he is right," AD commented, sipping from his glass of wine. "Wind up the pending legal formalities and have the bank accounts closed."

On several occasions, knowing Jake's hatred against his father, George Stevens, AD had given his assessment that his father was a gentleman. Although he hadn't known the man personally, his opinions were drawn from what he had heard from others, Mr. Stevens' colleagues and friends. These very opinions, at times, placed Jake at crossroads, compelling him to wonder if he had misunderstood his father.

CHAPTER 7

In the comfort of his loving home, lazing on the couch, Jake was enjoying his favorite cartoon, *'He-Man'*, when his mother in a beautiful floral-print dress, blocked his view and gazed down at him angrily.

Oops! Jake realized that it was time for homework. But he tried convincing her, "Mom, please…just ten more minutes."

"Nope." She took away the remote and switched off the television. "It's time for homework, sweetie." She forced him off the sofa to get his books from upstairs.

Jake was a little disappointed but he knew his mum wasn't hardheaded, strict and rigorous like the parents who burdened their children with studies all the time. On the contrary, she was soft and tender-hearted but could be strict to get him to adhere to the schedule chalked out for his academics.

It was while treading down the stairs that he had seen his mother hang up the phone. The charming smile on her face revealed that she'd talked to his father, George Stevens.

"Sweetie, your dad will be late. He's in a meeting."

"Okay," he replied, settling onto the sofa with his books.

As Katherine went on to clean the dusty shelves next to the television, she couldn't help pondering over how she considered herself very fortunate to have a wonderful husband, George, who loved her deeply, fulfilling all her desires, her dreams besides also being an ideal father to their son.

Some minutes later, the buzz of the phone sounded once again. "In your place," she ordered Jake when he was about to jump for the receiver.

Jake dissolved back into his seat, angry. But in the next moment, he saw his mother's face turning pale, enshrouded in distress. She placed the receiver back in its cradle and collapsed on the chair next to it, submerged deeply in some thoughts.

What had happened to her? Jake worried, finding her lost as if she had heard something unanticipated that had brought her world crashing down. Whoever had called and whatever she'd been told, it was definitely something of great concern as deep creases etched across her otherwise lovely face.

"What's the matter, mom?" Jake asked.

She shook her head sluggishly, pushing up from the chair. She crossed over to him. He noticed tiny droplets of sweat on her temple, which further added to his worry. "Mom, are you alright? Who was on the line?"

"It was a blank call, dear," she told him in a hesitant voice.

Silence reigned before she added, "Jake, I've got to pick up groceries from the supermarket. You keep studying while I'm away." She picked up the car keys. "I'll be back soon."

Soon after she left, heavy rain lashed the city. She returned a full hour later, drenched. Her hair was dripping and her puffy eyes and flushed cheeks suggested that something serious had come to pass.

Jake wanted to run and embrace her. But something held him back, pinned him down to where he was. He tried again and sprung upright in bed, breathing heavily. He realized he'd recessed into a dream… actually, a memory from his yesteryears, seared into his psyche which was the cause of frequent nightmares.

Shaking its sting away, Jake checked the timepiece set on the table next to his bed: **August 6, 2017. 7.45 AM.**

I'm late.

Getting out of bed, he walked to the shower. The steamy hot water poured on his bare body, sending chills down his spine, stimulating his inactive muscles. Its steamy warmth cushioned his agitated mind which often traveled back to that horrific night that had turned their world upside down.

Casting away its acrid bite, he emerged from the shower before the mirror and observed his bare chest. His muscular frame that had once resembled a chiseled sculpture was now out of shape. His predominant collarbone had been flattened into the surrounding muscles. Biceps and triceps had sunk and what was once a well-developed chest had smudged into the flesh around his rib cage. His light, unmarred complexion and almond shaped eyes snuggled under curvy dark brows were his saving grace. And his straight nose with the tiny pair of lips underneath was the gift of his father's genes.

I still look great at 33.

His answering machine chimed.

Normally, his day would have started out like any other. Out of bed at seven, a shave and shower, treating his taste buds to some steamy coffee while glancing at the newspaper, followed by a light breakfast before he was off to work. But for the past two days, urgent affairs had had him flying out of home and it seemed today would no less than that..

The voice on the answering machine belonged to his assistant Riya, who promised to reveal some significant leads on the recent murder cases if he could pick her up and took her to a certain place.

Jake glanced down at his attire in the mirror. Off-white striped shirt, blue denim trousers and a navy-blue jacket with a bold CBI logo imprinted on the back.

It's perfect.

He rushed downstairs after a parting look at his two-bedroom space, filled with cozy furniture, from the comfort of which he relished his daily routine if emergencies like today's did not occur. However, one thing still awaited him in the basement of his apartment that promised an indulgence. His limo: a Honda Civic-CVR, a hybrid version.

Jake climbed into the limo, cranked up the engine and sped away. On the way, he picked up Riya.

Turning his attention from the road, he asked Riya, "Where are we going?"

"Ramanujan's home."

"His wife okay now? Is she ready to give her statement?" asked Jake.

"I already have her statement," Riya said, smiling.

Jake appeared slightly surprised. "She was supposed to give her statement today. Then, how did you…"

"She called me last night," said Riya. "She thinks she knows who might've killed her husband."

Jake grew curious. "And who is it?"

"Someone she believes had insisted her husband to opt for voluntary retirement."

That made Jake curious. Like Anurag Chopra, Ramanujan was a scientist. He too had been forced to opt for voluntary retirement. Except that…

As if sensing his thoughts, Riya handed him a document. "This confirms your suspicion."

Jake took the paper. He alternated between steering and glancing through the statement and finally looked up with a victorious smile.

"So, this man as well had a huge amount of money wired into his bank accountant from a fictitious account."

"Appears so," Riya replied, visibly excited. "But one thing doesn't add up."

Jake looked at her.

"If this organization was funding them to keep their silence over whatever it was that they knew, then why ransack their houses?"

As their car crawled through a traffic-heavy area, they both pondered the case from their own perspectives.

"What else did she say?" Jake asked, fishing for more.

"Nothing significant."

"However," Jake smiled, swerving the car skillfully through thick traffic, "it seems we might be closer to cracking the murder mystery than we think."

A shrill sound cut through their conversation. Riya's cell was ringing. The call was from AD. She listened for a few seconds and then hung up.

Jake turned to her.

"Its AD." Her voice was laden with concern. "We should head back to headquarters."

"What is it regarding?"

"Don't know. He wants us to abandon what we are doing and report to him immediately.

CHAPTER 8

"Well, ho far has the investigation has progressed?" AD broke his silence, turning his attention from the computer screen, a long minute after Jake and Riya had arrived and settled into the chairs opposite his desk.

Jake and Riya exchanged an uncertain glance at each other, wondering if this was the urgent matter that they were asked to abandon their pursuit for.

Riya answered, "To an extent, we've found links between the two cases."

AD asked, "Can I have the reports?"

Riya handed him the files. As AD scanned through the report, as Jake briefed him.

"It's this fictitious account that's the link between these murders. That shadowy organization had been using this account to funnel funds to these two victims. Ramanujan and Anurag Chopra."

Jake realized AD's reaction seemed surprisingly calm considering that they were on the verge of a breakthrough.

AD mulled over the data and closed the file. He rose from the chair and stood looking out the window at the busy street below with his back to them. Then, following a minute of silence, he turned back to face them.

"It's undoubtedly a case of a serial killer on the loose, who seems to be working for this organization to acquire whatever they possessed or hid." He paused, returning back to his seat. "So what'snext?"

Jake took over. "Whoever is behind these murders has a motivation. Something do to with their past. We have to peek into the victims' past

lives and see what's waiting for us. We might even have to visit their previous place of work..."

"That's not required anymore," AD cut him short curtly, gazing seriously at Jake and then over at Riya.

A look of utter mystification washed over their faces. "I beg your pardon," Jake asked in confusion.

"Jake, you're not handling this investigation anymore." Jake stared back at AD in disbelief.

Riya, baffled at the statement, sharing bewildered look with Jake.

Jake struggled to articulate. "I'm not handling the case anymore? But... why, sir?" AD had nothing to offer as an explanation.

"We're close enough to cracking the mystery and out of nowhere I'm informed that I'm not handling this case anymore?" Jake paused to see if an explanation was forthcoming and when it wasn't, he demanded, "What is this all about?"

"Its not in the scope of CBI anymore. We have orders from higher authorities to back off from the investigation." AD said, meeting his gaze straight on.

"Orders?" pressed Jake, demanding, "to back from the investigation?

AD nodded.

"What higher authority you are talking about?" Jake pressed.

AD exhaled loudly. "The Joint Intelligence Committee. They will take the case from here. Its better we leave it to them."

"But why?" Jake cried.

The Joint Intelligence Committee (JIC) was such a name that it held a powerful authority in itself. Tasked to work closely with the Intelligence community, this agency's prime function was sharing and coordinating information between different departments.

Now the question that really mattered was the name of the other agency they were jointly working with to investigate the murders. Before one of them could ask about the other agency, AD rose from his chair, dismissing them. "I suppose I've made myself clear."

Jake and Riya could not ponder on the reason for the sudden suspension of the case which was still ambiguous.

"Fine!" AD said sharply, adding. "Have a nice day."

CHAPTER 9

Katherine was in the grip of some enormous distress whose magnitude was impossible to be gauged by someone as young as Jake, who was only fourteen.

She had returned home drenched in the rain, her eyes red and puffy. From her drooping shoulders and her heavy and distant gaze, Jake inferred that something had occurred while she was away, something that had shaken her to her very core and shattered her from inside.

As she sat on the sofa, Jake inched closer to her and knelt before her, meeting her eyes. "Mom, what's the matter?" He looked at her eyes. "You wept. Dint you?"

"Nothing," she hesitated, wiping off her tears, "something seems to have gotten into my eyes as I was driving with the car windshield down. It'll be okay."

Jake watched her wipe her eyes with corner of her palms, knowing that she was lying, trying to conceal some pain behind the veil of pretense that she now wore on her face.

There was the sound of the door swinging open. Jake turned to find his father, George Stevens, walk in. He was drenched, too. And an intense agony had creased his pleasant features, making him appear no less worried than Katherine herself, as if both shared the same agony.

"Dad," Jake pushed onto his feet and walked to his father. He held his hands. "Look at mom. She's weeping."

When George looked at Katherine, he found her stare turn contemptuous. Then, she got up from the sofa, walked across to them and pulled Jake to the dining table.

"It's time for dinner, honey."

What is happening? Jake wondered as he let his mother drag him away from his father, disoriented and absolutely clueless about the whole situation that seemed otherworldly, an experience his parents had never gone through nor he ever been a part of.

Later that night, looking for his father, Jake had ended up on the terrace of their apartment where George stood with his head raised towards the sky, his gaze fixed upon the dazzling stars in the sky. He'd seen a travel bag resting beside his feet and understood that his father was due to take one of those official trips that had often kept him away from home for months.

He stood in front of his father and asked sadly, "You going again?"

George nodded, watching the stars.

Jake asked innocently, "For a treasure hunt?"

"Kind of," George replied, his voice sounding choked.

Treasure hunt: A response Jake had been receiving from his father since he was four, when George tried explaining to him about excavating ancient ruins in simpler terms. Of course, many in his profession would have described the task as a form of treasure hunting anyway. Jake grew up with that notion and always thought that his father was on a treasure hunt when he was away from home for months, onsite at a dig in some historical location. If only Jake had known that the treasure hunt his father was now about to embark upon would be the last one in his memory.

George knew that the treasure hunt had already begun. Only this one was nothing like what he'd undertaken so far. This was a quest that led the pursuer to a location where awaited a devastating secret about the origin of humanity, whose roots were buried back in the time of Genesis.

"And when will you return?" Jake asked with concern, following his father's gaze and staring into the starry night sky, knowing quite well it would be months before he would be back home.

George looked down at his son and knelt before him. He gave him a warm hug. "I don't know, son. I'm not sure even if this treasure hunt has an end."

Jake looked at him, a corner of his mouth turned down.

George whispered, "Perhaps, the next time when you're looking at these stars, I will be right next to you."

George then rose to his feet, picked up the travel bag and disappeared from his sight, forever.

For long after, Jake would run to the terrace and watch the stars, thinking his father's return was somehow tied to those stars. But he never returned. Neither had he been able to figure out what had really gone on between his parents that night. All he could recapture was a teenager's anticipation turning into desperation and then into a melancholy yearning for his father's return. Not long after that, his mother unable to endure the pain anymore, was afflicted with paralysis. She took her last breath in his arms, leaving him with a frightful memory that haunted him ever after.

Thereafter, life was a hell that took a devastating course, a path which led to nowhere but apathy. Under the guardianship of his maternal uncle and the care of his family attorney, Mr. Ravi Raj, he was admitted to a boarding school. Each day there, coping with his mother's untimely passing caused him great suffering. Deprived of love, his heart was filled with the agonies of the past until he found a new lease of hope on learning of his father's whereabouts. Yet again, destiny knocked him hard, engraving fresh pain on his heart when he learnt that his father was living with another woman: a widow his father was having an affair with, Eileen. A probable cause that torn open a rift between his mother and father that fateful night.

She was the woman he now hated the most. For she was the woman for whom his father had forsaken him and his mother, bringing disgrace to his family, revealing himself as a devious individual hidden behind a veil of impeccant innocence.

Fourteen years later, he was celebrating a very special event in his life with his friends—being appointed as a CBI officer when he had received a message that his father had passed away following a cardiac arrest.

That was another loss in his life which officially confirmed his orphanhood.

His father's funeral was performed in his presence. According to his mother's last wish, his father was buried far from her place of burial, as she desired not even the shadow of his tomb to be cast upon hers. It was at the funeral that he'd seen Eileen for the first time. Her disgraceful act had created such a massive rift between his parents that it extended even into their final resting place.

Sudden trills from his mobile pulled him back from his memories.

Jake, having drawn back in time, gazing at his mother's beautiful portrait on the table next to his bed, found his cell chiming.

He picked it up, puzzled. *Riya, at this time?*

She was someone who wouldn't bother him at this time of night, unless something really important had to be discussed. He answered the call. "Riya?"

"There is this…" She broke off.

Jake pressed the phone to his ears. "What's the matter?"

"A new officer has taken charge of the cases," she replied. "David Craig."

"David?"

"He's the chief co-coordinator of the JIC. A menace, they call him. A maniac, a lunatic and the list of names for his notoriety just goes on."

Jake pondered this for a beat. "What do you think is really going on? We have two back-to-back murders of scientists. Their accounts are wired with huge funds by an unknown organization they're supposedly working for just so they will keep silent about something confidential that they knew. And on the verge of cracking the mystery, we're pulled out from the investigation and the JIC steps in." He exhaled. "Does that mean something to you?"

Silence hung over the line before she replied. "I suppose, yes. These victims received a huge bribe to keep silent about a secret that would expose a massive political scam or corruption or even a classified document concerning a government agency or so the JIC now trying to cover-up."

Contemplating her views carefully, he corrected, "Half right. They both were guarding a secret that might've had to do something with the Intelligence agency."

"You say so only because the JIC has stepped in," said Riya.

"I wouldn't say no," Jake agreed. "If we consider splitting the whole scenario behind these two cases, it is lot easier to understand the unseen angle involved in these murders.

"Beginning with their background: both were professors who were forced to opt for voluntary retirement before pursuing the supposed research work that eventually got them killed. Apparently, the secret had something to do with their research, presumably, some kind of latest technology unknown to humans.

"Whenever any novel technology is in the nascent stage of development or say, nearing completion, the Intelligence agencies are the first to smell it. To see if that caters to their needs. And if it fits the bill, they instantly acquire the technology for their undercover operations.

"Now if you put these two halves together: these victims might've researched and invented some secret and mysterious piece of technology that drew Intelligence eyes and they traded millions to acquire it. Or say, to shut their mouth over their own invention. On one or more occasion, out of greed, they might've demanded more money. Possibly, they could have even threatened to leak their secret if their demands were not met." He exhaled contemplatively, concluding, "A reason strong enough to silence them forever."

Riya mulled over his statements for a long beat and agreed. "It makes sense."

CHAPTER 10

Tuesday, August 7, 2017.

9.30 AM.

CBI Headquarters.

What could have gotten them killed?

Rocking back and forth in his chair, Jake couldn't help going over the question again and again. The more he thought about it, the more baffled he was at the theories that enticed him into ideas that required thorough inquiry.

All of sudden, a thought struck him and he stopped rocking in his chair. He pushed to his feet and strode out of his chamber straight to the reception desk, where Ishita took a moment from her work on discovering him at her desk.

"You need something, sir?"

"I assume the artist's impressions of the suspect were not ready when JIC had confiscated the case files," he paused, noting her smile turning to one of those worried looks. "I was wondering if I could have a look at those sketches."

Jake knew she was aware that he had been pulled from the investigation the previous day. Now, the chances of her complying with his demands seemed bleak. Yet, he gave it a try.

After brooding over his request briefly, she said, "I'm not sure if I can do that for you. Those files have been moved to the confidential section."

I knew it. He recalled that the section housed files and records of a confidential nature, inaccessible without the permission of the head of the department. But he also knew that Ishita had maintained a close friendship with the senior clerk in charge of the section.

"But I'll give it a try," she said eventually, smiling.

"That's so sweet of you," Jake blurted, smiling broadly.

Ishita left her desk and climbed upstairs, heading for the confidential section. While Jake awaited her at her desk, he heard his cell buzzing in his trouser pocket. He reached for it, pulled it out and looked at the screen. *An unknown number?* He connected the call and held the phone to his ear.

"Jake Stevens?" a deep mysterious voice inquired.

Jake scrunched his brows trying to identify the voice. "May I know who this is?"

"Listen to me carefully," the caller said. "There's something more crucial for you to know than my identity."

Jake clutched his cell phone to his ear more tightly.

"Information concerning the investigation you've been pulled out of." That made Jake curious.

"Classified information that only Anurag Chopra, Ramanujan, me and...." the called paused.

"And who?" Jake pressed, drawing a sharp breath.

The caller's silence made Jake restless.

He is insane. "Now you listen to me," Jake replied disinterestedly. "Whoever you are, I don't like being trifled with when I'm in the middle of something important. And moreover, I'm not handling that case anymore. I'd rather suggest you get in touch with the concerned..."

"The fourth one was your father," the caller revealed. "Mr. George Stevens."

That name jolted Jake to the core. "What?"

"You heard me right."

The manner in which this caller had uttered his father's name made Jake go cold.

"It was indeed Mr. George Stevens," the caller ventured, "your father, the fourth of our brethren."

The world around him stilled for a second. "You mean, Anurag Chopra and Ramanujan knew my father?"

"Certainly," the caller affirmed. "There are more things that you're not aware of. Your father, Mr. George, formed a guild of four men that included us. We formed a secret guild to safeguard arcane knowledge belonging to the ancients. The one that was lost to time, recovered by your father."

This is lunacy. Jake's voice hardened. "What knowledge are you talking about?"

The caller's voice grew impatient. "Listen, we don't have enough time to discuss it over the phone. Come and meet me right away."

But Jake seemed disinterested. "Whoever you are, I'm sorry. I have no interest in knowing anything related to my father or the guild. He has long been dead to me. No matter how important it is for you, I'm out of it."

"Don't you wish to be privy to the secret that your father knew?" the caller said mysteriously, holding his attention. "A secret that if revealed could change the course of the world."

"I'm going to hang up," Jake warned, but before he could disconnect the line, the caller said something that swept Jake off his feet. Picking up a paper and pen from the desk, he spoke urgently, "Where are you?" Noting the address, he said, "I'm leaving right away."

Slipping the cell phone into his pocket, Jake dashed towards the basement in full sprint.

CHAPTER 11

A *swift* forty-minute drive off the highway on the outskirts of eastern Delhi channeled Jake through a network of small lanes to emerge before a splendid apartment of bourgeoisie standards that speared five stories into the sky.

Jake retrieved the paper from his pocket and crosschecked to ensure he had the correct address. Once sure, he pulled his car into the basement and parked alongside other vehicles.

He alighted from the car, glanced around to locate the way in and spotted an elevator at the far end of the basement. As he hurried across, he thought it was strange that although such apartments usually had at least two security guards posted at the entrance, he had not seen even one. The matter moved to the back of his mind once he stepped inside the elevator and rode it up to the fourth floor.

Stepping out of the elevator, he stood in the long deserted corridor. As Jake turned to his left, a strange premonition settled over him in the hollow space. He felt his heart pound as he moved ahead, looking for flat number 33, passing by flat 29, 30 and so on. With each step forward, the sound of a low human growling that seemed to emanate somewhere from the dead end of the corridor grew clearer.

Chills crawled along the nape of his neck as he found the door to flat number 33 open. *Something has gone wrong.*

He arrived at the door and saw a disturbing scene: men in khaki clustered at the center of the room. As he entered the flat, drawing closer, the men in khaki stepped back, giving him the first glimpse of what had caused the commotion.

Jake felt the ground beneath his legs nearly give away as he spotted a man lying on the floor, covered in blood.

Good heavens! Jake felt his head spinning. *This can't be happening.*

The dead body seemed to fit the voice of the man who had called him some time ago. Jake couldn't believe his eyes. He moved closer to the body and crouched beside it. His heart was reluctant to believe that a middle-aged man—the purported last survivor of the brethren and his father's friend and a guardian of some ancient secret—was no more. With his eyes looking like peas ripped from the pod, he now lay lifeless on the floor.

Jake committed the dead man's face to memory, cross-referencing to check if it matched any previously stored image data in his mind, but it yielded nothing.

"There you are," a voice said from behind.

Jake turned, rising from the floor to find a square-chested man with a roughcast face and cropped hair, standing a little over six feet tall, glaring at him with suspicious eyes.

"Mr. Jake Stevens," the man averred in a stern voice. "The chief officer, special crimes division, CBI."

He wore a brown leather jacket over a white T-shirt and denim trousers. Given the kind of authority he spoke with, Jake was sure that he was the officer in charge of this crime scene.

"Quite surprising to have you here though, CBI was never alerted on this crime."

Jake said nothing. He tried to sum up the identity of this man when, as if sensing it himself, the officer revealed it himself.

"They call me, David," he furnished with a tinge of pride to his tone. "David Craig, chief co-coordinator, JIC."

Memories came to his mind. *He is hardheaded and a sort of maniac…a lunatic.* Jake remembered Riya relating this man's idiosyncratic aspects last evening. That much was proven true when Jake held out his hand to shake but David refused it bluntly, brushing past his shoulder, halting at the feet of the corpse, observing it.

"I suppose you must be aware that I have taken over the investigations that you were heading before." He paused for a moment. "That being said about this case, too."

"Well," Jake said, turning to face him, "that goes without saying."

David assessed his statement for a beat. "What makes you say that? Are you thinking these murders are linked?"

"That's unmistakable," Jake replied with a suspicious smile, "now that your agency has taken over this investigation too."

"Mr. Jake," David said, rubbing a corner of his eye with his index finger, "you are being foolish making connections, trying to link these separate deaths that are obviously a mad man's work, a serial killer on the loose."

"Are they?" Jake smiled sarcastically staring back into David's eyes. "I thought I was only trying to make sense of the involvement of your agency. I was trying to figure out the mess they want to sweep under the carpet." He broke off with a suspicious gaze. "The mess that they've created, God knows for what, out of a loosely plotted conspiracy."

Jake's bold accusations irked David, but he pretended to be unfazed.

"If your accusations about JIC are true, what will be your next move?" David questioned with a snort. "Let me guess…" he said, "you'll flush these cases from your brain?"

Jake maintained his cool.

"I would say that's a wise option if your life and job are dear to you." David's tone was hard.

Jake observed his eyes which were blazing in disdain.

David came closer to Jake, affixing him with a contemptuous look. "If you try sticking your ass into these cases," he rasped, gritting his teeth, "then have a coffin ready for yourself."

"Coffin, yes," Jake met his gaze unflinchingly, "but in your size."

The corner of David's lips curled devilishly and he spread his arms wide open, as if inviting Jake to the battle. "Then, I'm here."

Ignoring David's wicked face, Jake took a moment to examine the corpse lying on the floor. One strange thing registered instantly with him—the pattern formed by the fingers on the dead man's right hand.

The thumb and the index finger pointed outward and the rest were coiled inward. Jake remembered that the pattern bore a striking resemblance to the one seen on the hands of Anurag Chopra and Ramanujan, which strengthened his suspicion that this strange fashioning of fingers really meant something crucial.

David carefully studied Jake's behavior as he examined the corpse.

Turning his attention from the corpse, Jake looked at David, saying with strong conviction, "My quest to uncover the truth behind these murders begins now. Use all the force you have. Employ as many men as you can and stop me from uncovering the truth, if you really can."

Throwing a fierce stare at David, Jake walked away, past the corpse, through the door and out of the apartment.

David had watched him leaving the place with a strong realization dawning upon him: *Jake Stevens could be a thorn in the flesh.*

Lifting his cell phone from his trouser pocket, he stabbed some numbers on the keypad and held the phone to his ear. After the fourth ring, he heard a voice.

"What's the situation?"

"Under control," he replied. "But I think we have a small problem, sir."

"Jake," the voice identified the threat almost instantly.

"Yes. He was here a while ago. He could be a pain in the ass."

"Did anyone raise an alarm to the CBI?"

David turned to the corpse on the floor. "No, not to the CBI, but to Jake. The victim had contacted Jake just before he was killed. I saw Jake's number in the call log of his phone."

There was a brief silence on both ends. Then the voice crackled back.

"Did he tell you what he knows about all this?"

David replied, "He's sure about our involvement."

Following a brief moment of silence, the voice concluded, "Keep an eye on him."

CHAPTER 12

I'm close to my fortune…

A thin, greedy smile creased his lips as he gripped the steering wheel of the SUV with one hand while letting the fingers of the other type in the message in his cell phone. Ensuring the image of the crime scene was tagged along the message, he hit the send button, tossing the phone onto the seat next to him.

OPERATION: THE LOST ARCANUM.
TARGET: JASWANTH SINHA.
TASK: INCOMPLETE.
TARGET STATUS: TERMINATED.

The message was through and the killer silently thanked the orphanage that gave him enough education to read and write, although he had abandoned his studies at early age. Strangely, where murders were performed with a skill leaving no proof of the crime behind, his hirer, on the contrary, had demanded an image of the crime scene to be sent after each killing as a proof to his services. *Or for another reason?*

Then a thought abruptly occurred to him about the man who had hired him. The manner of conduct of his hirer had taken an instant liking in him. *He's a Master.* He had an enigmatic personality and a clever individual hidden behind an intriguing disguise.

Some four days ago, lying on a craggy, undulating bed in a shack on the top floor of a wretched building, situated along the railway tracks close to Delhi city, he'd received a call from this unknown man. Over a brief conversation, the caller had lured him into a tantalizing deal worth lakhs. And shortly after, he had received a white envelope with photographs and written instructions.

The photographs you're holding belong to men who possess the supposed link—The Lost Arcanum. Confiscate that link. If need be, terminate them. But be cautious enough to cover your tracks.

A loud honk from the traffic pulled him from his reminiscence. He checked his watch, but his attention was instantly drawn to the rattling of his cell phone.

Master? The killer Soori identified the unknown number and connected the call.

"No word on The Lost Arcanum?" the caller asked in a troubled breath.

"I'm afraid that's true. They gave up their lives but not a word on the whereabouts of The Lost Arcanum."

The caller snorted in despair.

The killer added, "They were firm about their decision and audacious in the face of death. They took the link with them to their graves."

The caller gasped. "I'd rather call them a bunch of fools for concealing a piece of history that earned them no good but death ultimately."

The killer sensed a deep frustration in his master's voice over the failure to acquire what he had lusted—The Lost Arcanum.

The caller exhaled audibly. "Your fortune awaits you at a florist's shop, third stop down the main road. Meanwhile, stay put. Wait for my orders."

The killer hung up the call and whispered greedily, *my prize!*

CHAPTER 13

Do you not desire to know about the secret your father knew? A secret that if revealed would change everything we thought we knew about our origins? A secret so dangerous that if disclosed will rock all the world religions to their very foundations?

Quite desperately, Jaswanth Sinha had enticed Jake with these mysterious and perplexing questions when he'd tried hanging up the call.

Now, as Jake attempted to expel the thoughts from his mind and concentrate on the steering, the dead face of Jaswanth Sinha blurred his vision. His final disturbing words meddled with his composure.

"Thanks for calling," Jake had cut him off disinterestedly. But a stunning revelation had knocked him off his feet before he'd disconnected.

Would you still ignore me if I tell you your father was innocent and virtuous? Would you care to overlook the fact that your father's death was not due to natural causes but that he was killed ruthlessly like the other two?

Jake had felt a deepening chill through his body.

"He was conspired, Jake. Like we all have been. He feared his family was in danger as long as the shadows of enemies lurked around. That's when he broke family vows and left you and your mother desolate, to keep you both from harm. He had fallen prey to a cleverly orchestrated plot to acquire the secret we harbored for the welfare of mankind. The secret we called 'THE LOST ARCANUM.'"

Jake had instantly reacted to this revelation and had arrived at Sinha's residence, only to discover him splayed dead on the floor.

The digital clock on the dashboard buzzed the time, breaking his reverie. It was 7 PM. Outside his car, darkness had blanketed the sky.

He could not help but ponder again on the bizarre events he'd experienced in the past few days. Anurag Chopra had been stabbed to death. Ramanujan had been shot in the temple the very next day. On the verge of cracking the murder mystery, he had been pulled off from the investigation. And then a call from Jaswanth Sinha, relating a connection between those murders and his father before his own death, all pointing out to a single cause---a long-lost secret, one that was responsible for their horrible deaths, a secret they called *The Lost Arcanum.*

Jake found it all a puzzling jumble of conflicting information. Yet, it seemed comprehensible when the sudden involvement of the JIC was taken into consideration.

Jake looked out the window of his car.

The streets of Kingsway Camp were already washed with the vivid golden yellow of the lampposts. Deep in these illuminated lanes, within one of those posh societies, someone had been waiting for him for years. Someone whom, after all these years, he found worth his time and someone he thought might possibly hold the answers to all the unsettling questions concerning the murders. That someone was somebody he thought he disliked the most: Eileen, the woman his father had had an affair with.

Jake slowed his car and brought it to a halt in front a small house with a red-tiled roof. He got down from his car and walked through the unmanned gate, making it to the main door. He paused for a second and then buzzed the doorbell.

The door half opened a full minute later. Through the slit, a familiar face peeked out, flashing a dubious stare and then a surprised look. "Jake!"

Then, the door opened wide. "Goodness me," Eileen stared at him in disbelief.

Clueless, Jake was unsure how to react, but he still managed to find a half-smile in return.

She cupped his face in her tender hands and leaned forward, kissing him on his forehead. Then, she ushered him in. "Please, come in"

Jake fought the urge to turn around and walk away. Still he reminded oneself that he was here on another business. Not personal. Although reluctant and a little embarrassed finding it all happening so suddenly. He had hated her all his life, never wanting to meet or talk to her. But he'd never imagined destiny had other ways of bringing them together, landing him on her doorstep seeking answers to questions he hoped she knew.

Eileen walked him into a small cozy living room stuffed with Indian-style furniture and made him comfortable on the sofa, choosing a seat in front of him. She didn't look very different from when he had last seen her at his father's funeral. Her dark, kohl-lined and gleaming eyes were beautiful and her shimmering wheatish complexion was intact, indicating that she carried Manglorean genes, as people native to this part of the country had a facial profile that was so exotically defined as though God himself had designed their beauty to be at its best.

Eileen sensed that Jake wasn't comfortable. She saw him slide a glance around the room and then at her. The atmosphere was unnerving, as it went quiet, their gazes meeting a couple of times, unsure about where to start and who should begin first. The silence that had swept into the air was one accumulated over years of resentment.

Eileen, however, feeling the unfriendly aura broke the silence first. "I knew you would come one day, Jake. Despite your unwillingness, my heart was sure I'd get an opportunity to prove my innocence."

"What's the truth?" Jake asked calmly. For a moment, he forgot his anger against her that had built up over the years.

Eileen smiled. "Truth is stranger than fiction, Jake. And sadly, all you know is only fiction."

Jake looked at her stoically.

"The fact is that you know nothing about your father. Neither did your mother."

Jake said nothing. He realized he was here to find the truth about his father and something about the secret called *The Lost Arcanum*. He suspected that Eileen knew about the events that had occurred during the past few days.

"You never allowed your father a chance to prove himself," Eileen said, "nor did your mother."

"Look," Jake cut her short, "I am not sure what makes you talk so about my mother even though you know very well that you're the reason behind my parents' separation."

Eileen went quite.

"I was his only son." Jake vented emotions that had been suppressed for long. Despite his best efforts, he couldn't hold the barrage any longer. "He loved me. He loved my mother. Ours was a loving family. But you poisoned it. You pilfered a husband from his loving wife and a father from his loving son."

"It wasn't me, Jake." Eileen interrupted him. "It was your mother, who isolated her husband. She stole your father from you. She created the mess out of nothing."

Jake waited her to complete.

"I was working as a librarian at National Archives Library," Eileen began to narrate her story. "I was a barren widow. That's how society recognized me."

Eileen shrugged with a contemptuous grin. "It was sometime in 1992, I remember, that I first met your father. He was doing some research that often brought him to our library. He spoke to me on several occasions, seeking my help to locate reference books. I barely entertained any strangers, but your father was an exception. An extremely kind-hearted and generous person. It was for the first time in many years after my husband's death that I felt I had met someone who understood me.

"In no time, he befriended me. But our relationship was like that of siblings. There was hardly any instance when he hadn't spoken of your mother. He used to talk about her likes and dislikes and everything that made her the apple of his eye.

"I still remember the day I spoke to your mother."

That surprised Jake. "You spoke to my mother?"

Eileen nodded. "Several times."

CHAPTER 14

Eileen rose from the sofa, drifting across to the window on the far side of the wall like the cold sweep of a breeze.

"Speaking to your mother soothed me, made me forget all my sorrows. We often spoke at length, as if we had known each other for long, like we had shared the same womb. But that night, everything changed for the worse."

Staring at nothingness outside the window, Eileen teleported Jake to that fateful night, the same lamentable night his father George had left him and his mother never to return.

Sometime in January 1993,
8.15 PM.
Green View Restaurant

Eileen raised her glass of wine, sipping from it. "Thanks for this great evening, George."

"Thanks for coming," George winked, acknowledging the toast with his glass of wine.

Outside the restaurant, rain lashed the city streets with a roar of thunder, disrupting the power supply, plunging the streets and the restaurant into cave-like darkness.

The waiter had apologized for the inconvenience, arranged for candles on the table and had hurried off, assuring them that the lights would be back soon.

In the golden glow from the candles, George observed an unusual radiance lingering in Eileen's eyes and a smile so pleasant that he wondered if she were the same woman who barely knew any joy.

"By the way," Eileen said, "what's the occasion George? I think you called me here for a reason. What's that?"

George shook his head. He fished in his pocket, pulled out something and set it on the table in front of her.

Eileen brightened at the sight of it. It looked like a jewelry case. She placed the box on her palm and eyed it carefully. The box had a velvet finish and was some three by three inches with a tiny clasp.

"Jewelry?" she took a guess and looked up to him for the answer. "Am I right? It's a ring or a necklace?"

A playful smile escaped George's lips.

"Let me guess…it's for Katherine?" she tried, furrowing her brows inquisitively.

George let a chortle, sipping his drink. "It's for Jake." "For Jake?" She was amused. "Can I see what is it?"

"Of course," George replied in excited tone. "That's why you're invited here. And also for one more reason."

Eileen's brows crinkled in confusion. "I will tell you but open the box first."

Her fingers lingered a moment longer around the box, before she tipped the clasp and had it open.

Her eyes bloomed in awe. Perched atop a velvety bed was a golden chain, neatly coiled around a pendant at the center. Strangely, the pendant didn't look like one.

It was a key.

She glanced up at him. "A key?"

George exhaled staring at key forged out of cast iron, with a dull sheen. "It's not just a key. It's something whose power in indescribable. It's very precious."

Eileen still looked confused, wondering how that would be useful to Jake. Reading her expression, George explained, "This key unlocks a treasure of incredible worth. The treasure is not gold or some precious jewelry, but something far more valuable and potent than anything on earth made available to mankind."

He leaned over the table, whispering to her gravely. "This key opens the portal to a vast amount of mystical knowledge and a devastating secret about the origin of humankind."

Eileen was not buying any of it. "What mystical knowledge are you referring to?"

"Knowledge that is so powerful and prized and that was shared only among a few worthy people and has remained unknown to the world." George paused. "You're keeping this key with you. You need to preserve it for me. For Jake."

She lowered her gaze to the key, watching it in a new light and then glanced up at him, insisting, "Why me?"

George stretched back in his seat thinking for a long second and exhaled worriedly. "Because someone out there wishes to steal it from me. They could go to any lengths to retrieve it. It's too dangerous to keep it at my place. I'm scared they might harm my family."

Staring at the key, various questions rose in Eileen's mind, including how anything so small would lead anyone to uncovering a priceless treasure.

"It will be safe with you." George broke through her reverie. "And I trust you on that, Eileen."

She couldn't deny him. She felt honored to safeguard something for a man she deeply respected. But she had a doubt. "But why do you want to leave it for Jake?"

George shifted in his chair. "That you'll learn once you entrust it to him when the time comes."

"And when do you think it will happen?" asked Eileen impatiently.

"When he comes looking for it."

As if pricked by sixth sense, Eileen's gaze drifted to her side, picking up a dark silhouette in the distance. George recognized the form too, almost immediately.

"Katherine...?"

Katherine stepped out of the darkness into the candle light, her eyes lowered on the jewelry box in Eileen's hand. Then she glanced at her husband. "This was the important work that held you back?" she said with disgust. "That's shameful."

It was not until George had seen the entire scenario between him and Eileen from Katherine's viewpoint that it hit him that she had fallen prey to a misunderstanding, misinterpreting the occasion, their actions and their relationship.

"Katherine...it's..." he faltered as he tried to clarify.

Katherine ignored his plea and turned to Eileen. Tears welled up in her eyes as she spoke. "I trusted you. I took you as my sister. But you betrayed me."

Eileen hesitated. "What?"

Katherine ignored, sobbing, broken, shrugging as if she had something to say, then turning, she threaded her way out of the restaurant.

Eileen's mind was clouded, too dumb to react in defense. George, on the other hand, was caught up in grim despair, speechless, his mind in a state of deep unbearable unease. But he couldn't give up. Not when he knew he had done no wrong. He sprinted out of the restaurant after his wife Katherine.

Outside the restaurant, the rain had intensified, washing the entire streets clean, even of people; only the beaming lampposts stood bowed down in resignation.

George rushed after his wife and caught up with her near her car in the parking lot. "Katherine," he screamed over the battering sound of rain. He caught her hands, stopping her. "You've misinterpreted the scene. What you saw is not what you should assume."

"Oh really, George?" Jerking off his hands, she threw a fierce stare at him. "Is that how you sum up the whole issue and conclude it so simply?"

George ran out of words. "You..."

"George, you can't deceive me anymore. I should've listened to him when he told me about your illicit relationship with Eileen long ago."

"What?" George seemed shocked. "Illicit relationship with Eileen?

Jesus Christ!" He uttered in disbelief. "And who is this he?"

"There's someone who knew about your relationship. He told me long ago, though I didn't believe it."

George fired back, "Have you gone insane?"

"Yes, I have." Katherine cried out loud. Tears were trickling down her cheeks. "You have to leave us right away, George."

Those acrid words fell on him like a bolt of thunder. With great agony, Katherine repeated. "I want you to leave us before Jake gets to know about all this."

"Have you lost your mind, Katherine? You can't be serious."

"Yes," she exclaimed harshly. "I have lost my mind. And I mean what I said." She announced in a wavering voice, "You're leaving us right away."

George could not believe it. "No, no...no...you can't do this to me, Katherine. You cannot..."

"This marriage is over, George," Katherine declared with a heavy heart. "It's all over."

CHAPTER 15

"*George was innocent,* Jake," Eileen said in a gentle tone of reassurance, bringing him back to the present. "He had done no wrong."

"Then what held him back from visiting my mother on her deathbed?"

Eileen let his question linger until she returned to her seat from the window. Pursing her lips, she revealed, "He did often come to see your mother in your absence. They spoke at length on various issues, like your upbringing."

"If so, then why didn't he come to see me?" Jake pressed, letting out the line of questions that had been waiting long to be answered. "Where was he when my mother was laid to rest?"

"George was indeed at your mother's funeral," Eileen said, "concealing himself from your eyes and from everyone there. Katherine wished him to remain away from you, regardless of any predicament."

A distant sadness tugged Jake from within, constricting his heart.

"Katherine never wanted George to see you." Eileen informed him. "A penalty she imposed on him for a lifetime, for a sin he'd never committed."

For a while, Jake remained mute as he digested this. Settling back quietly, he weighed what she had said and thought about the unknown facts from which the veil of secrecy had finally been withdrawn. Still, some queries pestered him.

"Do you have any idea who might've called my mother that night?"

"No," Eileen shrugged. "Katherine said nothing when George insisted that she reveal the caller's identity."

Jake thought for a moment and asked, "Do you know my father didn't die of a cardiac arrest?"

Eileen's brows pinched in uncertainty.

"My father was killed," Jake said sadly. "He was murdered."

That shook Eileen to the core. "What are you saying? George was…" She drifted off for a moment in daze.

Jake shook his head. He gave her the condensed version of what had occurred, walking her through the chain of events leading up to the time that he was compelled to withdraw from handling the investigation of murders, the call he'd received from Jaswanth Sinha with a mention of a link that led to *'THE LOST ARCANUM'*, and finally the crime scene, where officer David Craig from JIC had warned him to stay away.

After hearing all of it, Eileen shook her head, saying, "I think, I know where the link to The Lost Arcanum is."

That made Jake curious. "You know about it?"

She nodded and excused herself, disappearing somewhere inside her home and returned shortly, holding something.

She set that something on a knee-high tea table before Jake.

Instantly, Jake's eyes went wide, recognizing what was set on the table: a jewelry box.

"This might be the link to *The Lost Arcanum*," Eileen declared solemnly, "the root cause of your parents' separation."

Jake was listening to her, but his eyes were on the box.

Eileen continued, looking down at the box. "George accepted a life of solitude to protect its contents. An obligation he believed was more important than his own life and his family. He couldn't turn away from it. No doubt he placed you and your mother before all material wealth, but at the same time, he had one more task of safeguarding this possession. He was forced to make choice between his family and this box. And what he chose is right before you. This box. Which I'm sure he did that for a reason, for a cause greater than his own desires."

Staring at it, Jake reached for the box and held it in his palm. With his heart pounding in his ears, he tipped the clasp and opened it, revealing a key of about two inches, snuggled on a velvet base with a gold chain coiled around it.

Looking at the key, Eileen voiced, "He never told me what this key opens. Except that it gives access to a vast amount of secret and mystical knowledge. Knowledge that is too dangerous to be revealed."

Jake found it hard to believe any of it.

"Letting this key fall into the wrong hands would push the world to the brink of disaster," Eileen added. "No matter what, this key should be concealed from the ones who are hunting for it. George feared that those who sought this key would wish harm to his family, which is why he left it in my protection, wanting me to hand it over to you the day you were ready for it, old enough to grasp the marvelous potential this key seems to hold."

Jake looked up at her.

"This was the last favor your father had wanted from me, just two days before his death."

"He met you before his death?" Jake was surprised.

Eileen nodded. Her voice was filled with pain. "He really looked worried. As if his end was near. He told me someone was after this key, someone who had threatened him and his three friends to comply with their needs or face dire consequences. Now, it all makes sense. They were never pardoned. They were killed. But surprisingly, everyone was adamant about protecting this key. All gave their lives, but none gave its whereabouts. That speaks about the dangers this key might unleash if it gets into the wrong hands."

Following a brief silence, Eileen said, "My task of protecting this key comes to an end. Now this key belongs to its rightful owner." Eileen smiled, looking at the box in Jake's hand. Then she raised her gaze to him. "You're the true owner of this key, Jake. Now it's your responsibility to protect what your father and his secret brotherhood protected in the past."

In a single breath, Eileen declared, "The key you're holding leads you to the *Lost Arcanum*. Go find it."

CHAPTER 16

Wednesday, August 8, 2017

9 AM. Secretariat Building,

New Delhi.

L*ocated on the* Raisina Hill, the Secretariat Building has two separate blocks, North and South, hunched on the opposite side of Rajpath, the stretch of road leading up to the Rashtrapathi Bhavan, the official residence of the head of the State—the Indian president.

The North and South blocks are crowned by central majestic baroque domes raised on a plinth thirty feet from the ground. From an architectural perspective, it holds one spellbound. Within these buildings are clustered some of the most important ministries of the Government of India. Each block, comprising four floors, has close to 1,000 rooms all together. The North Block is also home to some well-preserved paintings depicting various war themes and justice and peace. The South Block has canvases on different cities of the country and emblems of old kingdoms. Among the two, the South Block is the most important as it is also home to the Prime Minister's Office, popularly known as the PMO. In addition, it houses the offices for the Ministry of Defense and the Ministry of External Affairs.

Cramped in a maze of ministry offices and departments, number '137' is the address to the office within South Block Divisions A, B and C, reserved for the Director General of the Defense Intelligence Agency (DIA).

The office was currently presided by Balbeer Singh.

As the head of the entire organization, he was the chief adviser on Intelligence to the Minister of Defense and the Chief of Defense Staff. He was assisted by the Deputy Director General with the primary function of coordinating with the Directorate of Military Agencies, Directorate of Air Intelligence and Directorate of Naval Intelligence.

With his hawk-like eyes on the computer screen, Balbeer Singh poured over crucial data files from the DIA archives. He looked as serious as ever. His turban, his silver-streaked beard and his stocky nose stood testimony to his grave countenance and classy mannerisms that had remained unmarred through his decades of service in the Indian Army. For anyone with his caliber, moving up the ladder from Director of Mechanized Forces of the Indian army to the Director General of DIA was seemingly an easy task. It was a designation well-deserved. And experience on par with excellence.

He scrolled through the classified, treasured intelligence assets owned by the DIA, beginning with the Directorate of Signals Intelligence which acquired and gathered information on the enemy and deciphered their communications. Next was the Defense Image Processing and Analysis Centre (DIPAC), established to control India's satellite-based image-acquisition capabilities.

The list of classified files included several reports on electronic intercepts concerning the Defense Information Warfare Agency (DIWA) tasked with tracking psychological operations, cyber-war, monitoring of sound waves and warfare repertory. As he slid through the file names, his heart raced in excitement, knowing well that at the end of the list was a folder on a project tagged extremely confidential.

Acquired and fostered with great endeavor and caution, this project was deemed highly classified, access to which was restricted only to an elite few, indeed to a handful of individuals who had overseen its progress for over two decades, protecting and safeguarding, sworn to secrecy about its existence since its discovery. Since he'd got his first glimpse of the scrolls back in 1990, at its face value alone, he had gauged how valuable its content could turn out to be for the DIA. Its significant illustrations, mysterious content and never seen before depictions of uncanny renderings, held the promise of changing everything man thought he knew about science.

Exploring the contents of the folder himself a myriad number of times, now as he found the cursor resting on it, he felt the same wave of chill washing him all over again as it did for the first time.

Letting the excitement linger, he clicked open the folder to see a collection of Word, pdf documents and jpeg files collapsing beneath each other, forming a cascade of files. With excitement reigning in, he selected images and opened them one by one.

A smile appeared on his lips seeing the images that he'd been watching over and over since their discovery. The scanned image files of an ancient manuscript containing mysterious designs, illustrations and calculations that predated any known old civilization in the history was veiled in allegories and legends to serve a noble purpose. A purpose he had understood and had kept silent about ever since.

But now, in spite of maintaining silence over this top-secret project for over twenty long years, doing everything he possibly could to keep the secret contained, word on it had finally escaped to the world outside. The individuals involved in this heinous crime were dead, but their end had taken another turn, fueling his worries, surging it a hundred-fold once he had found out that Jake-- the chief CBI officer handling the investigation of these murders, was son to one of the victims George Stevens. One who was now suspected of having the link his father had bequeathed to him. With the link in his possession, Jake seemed a probable threat, far more dangerous than those dead ones had been when they were alive. Before events slipped out of control, it was immensely crucial to pull him off the case and hand it over to someone who ensured the link never see daylight.

That's when David Craig had been called in.

Balbeer Singh scowled thinking about David Craig's keen sense of curiosity. He still remembered the day when he'd walked into his chamber and sat opposite his desk, rifling through the case files, including information that reported the victims as a threat to national security. After careful consideration of the events and assessing sensitivity of the circumstances involved, David Craig had glanced up at him with eyes loaded with acute suspicion.

"I'm glad I've been chosen to take over this investigation. But what I don't understand is Jake." he paused raising his gaze at Balbeer, "a young, dynamic capable CBI officer is pulled out from this investigation, despite his best professional credentials in the entire CBI?"

"When assets become liabilities," Balbeer Singh said solemnly, holding his gaze at him, "it's better have them eliminated than let them thrive."

David Craig looked him in the eye, trying to get the gist of his statement.

Balbeer Singh leaned over the desk. "Jake is son to George Stevens. It won't be long before he discovers his father was murdered and start probing for the answers behind the murders than solving them."

"It means," David Craig stretched back in his seat, looking into the file. "You want me to windup the case files without investigating it at all?"

"Correct," Balbeer Singh replied tersely. "You're assigned the duty to take over the cases and close the investigation. But more importantly, you've been called in for another task."

David closed the file and looked at him squarely.

"You have to recover a link that Jake is suspected to hold. It's of paramount importance."

"What link?" insisted David.

Balbeer Singh sighed heavily, seeming miffed with David's attitude. Earlier when he had asked for top officers from JIC to be recommended, he was provided with a list of officers with decent track records. But he had liked dossier on David Craig, one that many among his interesting professional credentials, including his off the rules working style, had reported his offensively nosy attitude. Only because he found David Craig suitable to the task at hand had he decided to summon the man for the investigation, regardless of this annoying attribute.

"It all began in the year 1991," Balbeer Singh began to narrate. "When one of our military regiments, in hot pursuit of a terrorist who had crossed the border, stumbled onto a huge chasm in the Thar Desert where the ruins of a historical monument lay buried for over centuries." His eyes had gone distant, traveling back to the time.

"George Stevens, the senior head of the archaeological department in charge of dig had discovered some ancient scrolls from its ruins. I was offered a glance at it What I found in those scrolls was unlike anything I had ever seen. They were filled with elaborate illustrations and descriptions of a technology more sophisticated and complex than any scholars from even this generation can understand."

His explanation intrigued David Craig.

"Realizing that it was crucial, I confiscated those scrolls for further investigation at the Aeronautical Research and Development Board. The board commissioned a committee of four members to translate those scrolls. Each member was meticulously handpicked based on their specialization in different aspects of science and technology.

"George Stevens was well versed in multilingual translation. Anurag Chopra had a PhD in physics. Ramanujan was a specialist in fluid mechanics.

"All of them were summoned to a top secret location, where they pursued the research work for over a year. The research work was deemed highly classified. But they seemed to have double crossed us. Knowing the real worth of what they were researching, trying to recreate that ancient technology, they became greedy. To keep silent, they wanted us to make them filthy rich. They threatened to leak the documents to other countries."

David Craig nodded in understanding, recalling their bank account details which showed a huge influx of funds every quarter of the year.

"Lest the secret leak, we had to comply with their demands."

"What was the secret?" David Craig leaned forward, meeting his eyes curiously.

"The documents included details of an ancient weapon deadlier than any nuclear weapon ever designed."

David absorbed this silently. In his mind, Balbeer Singh smirked at having tricked David into believing his fabricated version of the secret. The secret, which in actuality had nothing to do with constructing an advanced weapons system; rather, it was more deadly and mightier than any nuclear weapon on earth could cause harm of that magnitude.

Once he was sure David was convinced, Balbeer Singh concluded, "You have to maintain a low profile over these murders. Close the investigation before the media gets wind of it and move on to the next task, that of recovering the link."

CHAPTER 17

10.30 AM.

State Bank of India,

New Delhi.

From the seat opposite the desk of the branch manager, in an enclosed chamber bathed in bright fluorescent light, Jake silently watched the man working at the computer.

Mr. Melkundi was of an average build, fifty something, with bulging eyes under steel rimmed glasses. To Jake's surprise, the branch manager hadn't seemed any different from what he remembered from his earlier visit. Regardless of the heavy workload, he had maintained his courteous manner rather than growing cranky with age.

Finding him busy, Jake took a moment to reflect on his relationship with this bank. His father had banked here for years. Fixed deposits, insurance cover, saving

s policies and safe-deposit boxes had remained intact since his father's death—a fact the bank manager had reminded him of several times in the past two years.

Jake knew that his presence here today was to serve only one purpose. To check the safe-deposit box for this prized treasure—The Lost Arcanum.

Jake's fingers felt the bulge of the key hanging from a gold chain under his shirt: *the key to The Lost Arcanum…*

"So, Mr. Jake Stevens," Melkundi turned from the computer, handing him an envelope. He rose from his chair. "Come with me."

He knew that the law required the bank manager to stay, view the contents and make a note of exactly what had been added or removed from the box.

As Melkundi led Jake through a maze of cubicles towards the vault, they exchanged a few sentences inquiring about the other's well- being. Then, suddenly, Melkundi said, "I forgot to tell you something important."

Jake listened as they walked.

"Two men from the Intelligence Bureau turned up at my desk, insisting on access to your father's safe."

"What?" Jake stopped dead in his track. "You allowed them to access the safe?"

"I'm afraid, I did," Melkundi said, motioning him to continue walking. "I had no choice. They had permission from higher authorities. And I would've faced legal difficulties if I had caused hindrance to their investigation."

Jake was rattled. He gave up any hopes he'd invested on finding something on the murder mystery and the ancient secret in the safe-deposit box. It was another mistake, he thought, an irrefutable blunder to ignore the safe for this long. It could mean a huge loss and a lifetime of regret if he failed to recover anything from the safe.

But something kept Jake going. Probably, it was his gut feeling. Then Melkundi stunned him with another statement.

"There was another person who also came with the same request."

"And you gave him the access too?" A shadow crossed Jake's face. *I'll blow your head if it's yes.*

"I showed him the exit," Melkundi replied.

Jake sighed. He felt like he was drowning in through a churn of surprising revelations coming his way.

"Who was he?" Jake asked, pressing, "what did he look like?"

"I don't remember." Melkundi said. "That was some two years ago. But I think I can recognize him."

They reached the vault where an armed security guard unlocked the metal door and let them in. Upon entering, Jake scowled at the sight of the vault. A massive iron frame holding hundreds of aluminum metal boxes, closely abutting each other, forged into one side of the wall.

As he furthered, the hollow space and musty stench of aluminum made his breath labored. His eyes assaulted by bright neon lights, making him feel as if he was entering a white box.

Reaching a safe-deposit box, Melkundi rummaged through a ring of keys, while Jake stood near him and closely observed the makeup of the safe-deposit box.

Forged of aluminum, each box was one foot in length and width, secured by an electronic keypad with a small digital display above it.

Melkundi inserted the key into the slot, turning it to the left. The digital display was instantly activated, glowing bright red, prompting:

Enter your four-digit PIN

Melkundi motioned to the envelope in Jake's hand. Jake opened it, found the four-digit PIN and punched the numbers on the keypad, pressing the enter button. There was a short beep, followed by a metallic click as the aluminum box slid on its hinges, throwing open its small rectangular door.

A knot formed in Jake's throat as the manager stepped aside and gestured for him to access the safe. His hands shook as he reached inside the safe and found some files, half a dozen scattered envelopes and a bunch of papers fastened by rubber band. He felt on edge, sensing the feel of the investigators' hands on it. Taking out the contents one by one, he shuffled through the envelopes of fixed deposit receipts, but found nothing to his interest.

Standing still in the hollow silence of the locker room, an odd sadness coursed over him. There was no trace to the ancient secret, *The Lost Arcanum. Whatever might have been pertaining to The Lost Arcanum, was now gone, and possibly taken away by the men from Intelligence.*

When the manager asked Jake if he was done, he stood there in silence, holding the contents from the safe and gave a nod after a long pause. It was only then when Melkundi was about to lock the safe that Jake's eyes were drawn to something unusual inside the box. He paused for a split second, disoriented by a glare from something inside the locker.

What was it? Jake was flummoxed. He wouldn't risk overlooking even a pin-point of detail on thing that could pave his way to the ancient secret. Almost instinctively, knowing what had to be done, he dropped the papers in his hands to the floor. As expected, Melkundi bent instinctively to pick up the papers for him.

"Oops...I'm so sorry," Jake apologized, relieved his plan has worked.

"That's ok. I'll get them." Melkundi replied, as he knelt on one knee and began to collect the scattered papers.

Jake reached inside the locker and skimmed his hands on the floor of the box. There was nothing. The locker was empty. He took a step back, letting more light from the neon bulbs overhead illuminate the locker space.

Then he saw it again.

Everything was so clear. A clear-cut vision of a shiny material reflecting from the locker floor caught his sight once again.

His pulse raced.

Stepping closer, he reached for the locker space and swept his hand against the side walls, feeling every corner, closely, and then the roof.

He froze.

His fingers nicked something cold and hard, stuck to the locker roof. *It is magnetic,* Jake realized. Holding it tightly, he pulled it with a jerk.

The magnetic box gave way.

Without even bothering to see what it looked like, he quickly slipped it in his trouser pocket, by which time Melkundi had risen from the floor, holding the assortment of dropped envelopes and papers.

"If you're done, shall we?" Melkundi said, gesturing him out of the safe vault.

On the way back to the manager's chamber, Jake couldn't help but think about the hidden contents of the box. He visualized his father and the three scientists concealing something in a place so unusual that it was possible that it could be that most valuable treasure of the ancients, *The Lost Arcanum*.

After completing several bank formalities Jake headed to the exit. At the door, he turned and informed the manager, "Keep my visit a secret. Let me know if someone drops by asking about my visit or something which might be of my interest."

ЖЖЖЖЖ

Outside the State Bank of India, at the corner of the street, David Craig sat inside his SUV watching Jake driving off from the bank.

He picked up his cell phone and placed a call.

"Yes?" General Balbeer Singh answered after half a minute. "He just left the bank. I'm afraid he's in possession of that link." "You're sure?" Balbeer's voice was full of worry.

"Quite sure, sir," David replied. "I have an informer in the bank. A security guard, tasked with escorting the clients to the vault. He noticed a prominent bulge in Jake's trouser pocket after he'd stepped out of the vault. Jake also seemed nervous. A natural reflex when something unexpected comes along."

"That's next to impossible, officer." Balbeer Singh said with conviction. "We had his safe checked thoroughly soon after George's death. There was nothing in the safe. Except for his will and other official documents, there was no damn trace of that link."

"But from what I've heard about Mr. George Stevens," David replied, "he was quite ingenious in handling such matters. He did every little thing with precision, meticulously. I'm sure he did likewise with the link, concealing it in the same safe, away from our eyes, in a place only his son could reach,"

General Balbeer Singh was silent, weighing the caller's speculation. Then, carefully considering the sensitivity of the issue and the possible consequences, he empowered David Craig with the authority to deal with the crisis, before hanging up.

CHAPTER 18

Locking the door from inside, Jake moved across his chamber and reached his desk. Shoving aside the files and papers to one side on the desk, he sank into the chair. He took a deep breath, pulled out the magnetic box from his pocket and set it squarely on the desk.

Under the bounty of natural light cast through the window behind his chair, he stared at the box for the first time. It was a grey-colored box, some four inches long and two inches wide and about one and a half centimeters thick. It had a brilliant sheen, casting a mesmerizing glare onto the walls of the chamber. On the surface of the box were carved mysterious symbols, some of which were astrological and some that he couldn't identify.

Jake recognized symbols referring to twelve constellations. There were more symbols, of patterns he had never seen. But at the center, Jake noted a script: A two-line verse engraved within a star.

As above…So below? Jake crinkled his brows, wondering at the two-line script. *What is that supposed to mean?*

He sensed those words, feeling deep respect for his father and for the rest of the brethren for everything they had suffered to conceal this box. They'd sacrificed their lives but not the secret, eventually leaving the key to this prized treasure with Eileen. Taking a curious breath, he reached for the gold chain on his neck, from which hung the key to The Lost Arcanum. He undid it from his neck and placed it next to the box. Then he picked up the box and searched for a keyhole.

To his surprise, there was none. Befuddled, he searched again. Right, left, top and bottom. Indeed, there was no keyhole at all. Neither had he found any gaps or hinges or clasps along any surface to conclude that it was a box containing something inside.

All it now appeared to be was a shiny grey slab. He felt anxiety creeping into his mind. *Is this not the treasure chest holding the ancient secret called The Lost Arcanum?*

Although the key and the magnetic box were on the table in front of him, it seemed that The Lost Arcanum was far from reach. He looked backed at the two-line verse engraved within the hexagram star on the surface of the box.

As above...
...So below.

It sounds cryptic. He reflected on it again, processing its cryptic meaning but his mind wandered over to other crucial matters such as the fact that the JIC sought the box he now possessed. He pondered their sinister intentions and the great lengths they'd go to acquire it and the consequences thereafter.

Strangely, he sensed a deep foreboding that they were coming to get this box. To confiscate it and to destroy whatever was locked inside it Before things veered out of control, he knew what had to be done. He rose from his chair, catching a glimpse of the two-line verse.

As above...
...So below.

Whatever secret was embedded in that two-line verse, he decided that it had to wait. First it was top priority to move the magnetic box to a safe location, out of harm's reach and that he knew had to be done right away.

Slipping the gold chain over his neck and grabbing the magnetic box, he rushed out of his chamber, stuffing the box in his trouser pocket.

CHAPTER 19

In the basement of the CBI headquarters, Jake hurried towards his car, ensuring that the magnetic box was in his pocket and darting cautious glances around.

Midway through, he stopped short, discovering a car roaring in from the other end. The car came to a screeching stop just a few yards in front of him.

Jake felt his skin prickle watching two men in civilian attire, climbing down from the vehicle and walking straight towards him, their eyes locked on him, vigilant. One was tall and hefty, while the other was short and plump.

Terror dawned on him as they neared, watching him suspiciously. Then, the short man thrust his identity card in Jake's face. "Mr. Jake Stevens, we're from the Intelligence Agency. We have orders to detain you."

Jake froze in his place. He tried to rein in his anxiety. Yet, he was helpless when his worst nightmare had shaped up in the form of two Intelligence officers, probably from JIC, standing right before him. Eluding them seemed nearly impossible.

"Detain me?" Jake asked, "but on what grounds?"

They glanced at each other and then the tall man took over. "You are being detained in the interest of national security."

Jake felt a shiver run through him.

The tall man stepped forward, adding ominously, "Mr. Jake. You have got to comply with us or I'm sorry to tell you," he paused pointing his thumb at their vehicle, "we'll have to wedge you in the backseat forcibly if you resist us."

Jake tried to maintain his cool, processing his escape route, now blocked by these two men from Intelligence, one standing right in his face and the other having taken guard behind him. Caught in this uncongenial situation, he thought it was best to comply with their demands. Still, he couldn't swallow the idea of being detained by these men—the ones behind the murder of his father and the other scientists.

And the magnetic box being confiscated by them was something he wanted last thing to happen.

As they came over and motioned him towards, escorting him to the rear of the car, Jake looked for an escape route, hoping for a miracle.

The short man held open the back seat door to usher Jake inside. A stealthy glance showed Jake that the tall man was settling into the driver's seat. Snaffling the opportunity, he hurled himself backwards on the short man, elbowing him in his gut and then in his chest. The blows were mighty enough to send him scrambling backwards.

This move earned Jake some time which he expended in tackling the tall man, who was half out of the driver's seat when Jake jammed him in between the door and squeezed him hard.

"You bloody…!" The tall man groaned, trapped between the door frame and the door, like a cat in a hunter's net.

Jake slammed the door repeatedly and then dragged the agent out by his collar, throwing him onto the short agent who was recovering from his off-balance state and was about to unholster the gun.

They went zooming back, crashing to the floor in a tangle of arms and legs.

Jake felt a rush of adrenaline as he finished mapping his escape path. He sprinted towards their car, tossed himself into the driver's seat and shifted the gear, thrusting the gas to full throttle.

The officers failed to gain their feet in time and found Jake behind the wheel, dashing ahead, leaving them behind at the loud squeals of tires that echoed in the basement.

Through the rear-view mirror, Jake saw his would-be captors chasing after the car, raising a cry for help on their walkie-talkies.

Breathing heavily behind the wheel, Jake knew that the quest had begun and at a price he would pay later. And grim realization dawned that more of such cat-and-mouse games were yet to come.

In fact, a hell of a lot, he thought, catching sight of the panting officers in the rear-view mirror.

CHAPTER 20

Bedtime stories had seemed extremely fascinating, when his granny's engaging voice and prodigious imagination took him across whimsical and adventurous lands. He had played a chivalrous Rama in the school play on the *Ramayana* and dressed up as the wise Krishna from the epic of *Mahabharata* for a fancy dress competition. If he'd imagined himself flying with Aladdin on his magical carpet, he'd also dreamt of steering Sinbad's ship through stormy seas.

Right through his childhood and into his adolescence, he grew up engrossed in such fanciful folklore only to realize that these stories were merely the product of one's imagination, conveyed down through generations.

One fine day, however, a head-on collision with a shocking truth had changed his perception forever, for that what he'd considered to be merely myth and fables from distant past became factual and the characters in it were all once flesh and bones.

Over two decades ago, some ancient birch bark scrolls had surfaced from the ruins of a historical monument in the scorching hot desert of Thar. The scrolls were abundantly filled with an advanced scientific knowledge and a devastating secret that held him spellbound, sending him through every library and archive across the nation, making him dig through piles of records to cross-reference and figure out if what he'd found was true, if there was a really a mention of that secret anywhere. To his great surprise, he found it nowhere else than the very ancient religious scriptures and in that of all world religions that spoke about the secret but in cryptic phrases, imperceptible to ignorant eyes but transparent to wise.

On that day, he realized that the only way to understand the ancient religious doctrines was by reading between the lines. This was followed by the stunning conclusion that the roots of this devastating secret traced back to an ancient secret brotherhood, old as time, which had carefully guarded the secret for millenia.

In an effort to keep the knowledge, which various religions had branded as forbidden, from the unworthy, this brotherhood began to disseminate it through mystery schools. Within a few hundred years, these mysterious schools had spread across the Asian, African and European continents, gaining widespread acceptance through various occult channels. The people initiated into these schools came from an elite class, who were made privy to a vast amount of mystical knowledge and the secret on the origin of mankind.

Rampant persecution of its members by religious orders forced the brotherhood into hiding. To keep the knowledge alive and out of harm's way, it was split into smaller divisions and each was sent off to a different part of the world.

Over time, however, several societies branched out of this brotherhood, corrupting the true essence of this knowledge for their own sinister ends. From performing bizarre and disturbing rituals involving animal and human sacrifices to distorting the original teaching of the brotherhood itself, these societies warped the knowledge, eventually becoming known as societies with sinister intentions.

The original teachings of the brotherhood were unfortunately lost and its purpose of salvaging humans from religious slavery remained unaccomplished.

Regardless, Balbeer Singh knew his keen interest in the brotherhood had only grown exponentially over the years. His relentless pursuit of truth had brought him in contact with a clandestine cabal, one of many that had evolved from the original brotherhood but still retained a fair amount of the original teachings. Further investigation had revealed that all the individuals in the cabal served in high ranks and elite positions in the defense departments in USA, Russia and China. Reaching its innermost circles was impossible; it was easier for a camel to pass through the eye of a needle than for a man like him to be initiated into the cabal.

It was his mentor-cum-friend, the then Director of Defense of the Indian Army, who had made his dream possible. Having chaired several powerful committees off the Indian shores and having been involved in various foreign matters, he had gained an enormous amount of influence and contacts on foreign soil. Using his potential influence as bait, Balbeer Singh pulled several strings to get in touch with a key figure Lukas Covitz from the cabal.

Being the Grand Master of the cabal, Lukas Covitz formed a prominent personality at the very heart of the brotherhood, taking the entire weight of the brotherhood on his shoulder. Right from handpicking its members who proved their worthiness to honing them to perfection, he had ensured their trustworthiness and ushered them into a cover cult union that carried the legacy of his forebear's of safeguarding the arcanum with utmost care.

Majority of members of the brotherhood had belonged to various military and governmental wings of different countries and Balbeer Singh was addition to the growing list of high ranking officials that also included Vladimir Gobarchev, the Director General of Defense, Russia, among others. In a secret meeting, Balbeer Singh had tabled his ancient documents. After being put through a rigorous screening to prove his trustworthiness, Balbeer Singh was introduced to the members of the cabal.

Unlike other secret societies that practiced bizarre and macabre initiation rituals, this cabal had welcomed Balbeer Singh by putting very elementary and simple procedures in place. In a secret crypt beneath an old mansion in Manhattan, New York, and before a small congregation of influential men from various domains of profession, his initiation into the cabal had come to pass with ease. He had sworn total obedience and loyalty to the secret he was made privy to, followed by a pledge that listed serious consequences in case of violation and absolved him from any allegiance to any nation or king or government or constitution. Even years after the initiation, he was under constant surveillance by the cabal, lest he betrays the society and leak the secret. But Balbeer Singh had proved to be like one of those virtuous individuals from the cabal, whose profound allegiance to the secret would continue until his death.

Feeling rather proud of himself, Balbeer Singh looked down at a ring on his middle finger with great admiration. The ring bore an ancient symbol that belonged to his brotherhood: a snake feeding on its own tail. The symbol signified infinite knowledge. And his initiation into this brotherhood meant he was worthy enough to receive that knowledge.

I'm the chosen one, he thought, smiling, *chosen to guard a secret as old as time…and to keep it from the world.*

Recently, he'd learned that there was someone out there, who for in greed for power and wealth posed a threat to the cabal and the very secret it guarded at its core. He had done all he could to protect it thus far. And now he was ready go to any lengths to keep it buried that way.

This is my solemn pledge, Balbeer Singh whispered with determination.

A trilling sound snapped him back to the present. Balbeer found his cell phone vibrating on the desk.

He reached for it and pushed the talk button. "Yes?"

"I have a bad news for you," said David Craig on the other end.

Balbeer Singh pressed the phone to his ears in apprehension.

"Jake got away."

Balbeer Singh exhaled loudly and closed his eyes as David filled him in on the escape.

"I don't know how," Balbeer barked, gnashing his teeth, "but stop that goddamn son-of-a-bitch, right now!"

He tossed the cell phone on the table and tried calming his nerves. He raised to his feet, lit a cigar and walked up to the window, feeling dismayed by the caller's information. As thin wisps of smoke escaped from the cigar, a thought abseiled into his mind: *Jake is a potential threat to the cabal and the national security.*

CHAPTER 21

Jake sat silently in the small compartment in the cybercafé, staring at the magnetic box resting on the computer table in front of him.

It gleamed under the fluorescent lights overhead, tantalizing him with the mysterious two-line verse inscribed within the star engraved on the top.

An hour ago, following his escape from the grips of two men from the Intelligence Bureau, he had loitered along the busy streets of the old Delhi, hunting for a safe location. He had abandoned their car in an old alley, boarded the metro-rail to Gurgaon city and landed in a cybercafé in a relatively isolated area on the outskirts. With his mind on edge, his urge to pry open the box and lay his hands upon whatever treasure it held was irresistible.

Jake held the box in his palm and caressed the engraving.

As above. .
...So below.

What in the world does that mean?

Whatever the two-line verse meant, he knew it pointed the way to unleash the contents of the magnetic box.

Since ancient times, the secrets that were held most precious and valuable were often embedded in plain sight, making it perceptible only to someone worthy. Jake had learned that from his father. Showing him the historical records and artifacts recovered from various excavations, George had taught his son Jake the ingenious ways the ancient people used to conceal their secrets.

Now, several thousand years later, in similar fashion, Jake suspected his father George had tread along the same path as that of the ancients, hiding a secret called *The Lost Arcanum,* within a small magnetic box, probably leaving the clue in the mysterious symbols or within the two-line verse itself, impressed on the surface of the box.

Jake glanced at the mysterious symbols etched on the box. *Do these symbols have anything to say?*

Then he read the two-line verse again

As above...
...So below.

Sometimes, the answers were hidden in plain sight, Jake recalled his father telling him.

Then it struck him like lightning, making him see the same two- line verse in a new light. His hands gripped the box tightly, reading the two-line verse again: ***As above...So below.*** Gradually, he turned the box to expose its underside.

Jake felt his body stiffen.

On the underside of the magnetic box, engraved intricately was a four-line verse, small and faint but legible.

On the hills of Nallamala lies a temple,
Engraved on its wall souls transcendental,
Seek what they possess privileged to someone worthy,
Its glorious power shall transform this box unto thee.

For a second, he was confused. Then he knew what he was looking at was a riddle.

The phrase *'Nallamala'* in the first line grabbed his attention, but the word *'hills'*, suggested some physical location. Curious, Jake launched the browser on the computer in front of him, brought up the Google search engine and entered the phrase *Nallamala*. Instantly, numerous articles filled the screen. Surfing through a few websites, he was astonished to discover that the term was, indeed, pointing to a specific geographical location—a cluster of hills regarded as one of the holiest places on earth.

CHAPTER 22

Thursday, August 9, 2017,

3PM.

A state of heightened security gripped the entire city of New Delhi, the nation's capital.

With the borders sealed and patrolling units tasked to scour all the check posts with ample details on Jake, a literal manhunt had begun in full sprint in the city. Thus far, from the thickly populated cosmopolitan city centers of the east to the trendy streets of the west, from the rustic stone-walled structures of old Delhi to the swanky localities of the south, Jake was nowhere to be found.

Serenely aloof from the chaotic capital New Delhi and from the mighty clutches of the Intelligence, Jake had covered seventeen hundred kilometers to board an air-conditioned coach that now snaked its way through the lush green forests of Andhra Pradesh in the Saiva Mountains of eastern Deccan, en-route to the holy shrine of Srisailam.

The previous night, Jake had learned from the web links that the hills of Nallamala mentioned in the riddle were located in Srisailam-- a revered and exalted place in Hindu tradition. Situated on the right side of River Krishna in Karnool district of Andhra Pradesh, this celebrated place has been the center for Shaivite pilgrimage for centuries. It is one of the country's ancient holy sites and its significance lies in the fact that every Hindu family performs their daily household rituals by specifying the location of their existence with reference to Srisailam.

On an average, the sacred hills of Srisailam draw close to half a million devotee every year, where the most devout temporarily retiring from their materialistic daily chores, take refuge at the holy resort of Lord Shiva. While some assume this journey as a mere retreat or a religious obligation, there are others whose faith alone is enough to steer them into the lap of these sacred hills.

Like a sore thumb, Jake found himself crammed between devotee in the pilgrimage bus, as his voyage to this cluster of sacred hills was more than in the pursuit of faith. His was a historical quest for something called The Lost Arcanum, a supposed treasure of ancient knowledge that was lost to time.

Immensely relieved that he was on his way to uncover the real cause behind his father's murder and probably even discover The Lost Arcanum, Jake inhaled a deep breath. He reclined into the seat, trying to put behind him the memory of the turbulent events of the past few hours.

Immediately after one of his contacts had provided him with air tickets, he boarded flight to Hyderabad—the city of Nawabs, closest to his destination. Getting down at the airport, he reached city bus stand and hopped into the bus destined for Srisailam

Now relishing the warm rays of the sun through the glass window. Jake pulled out the magnetic box and viewed its underside. The four-line riddle tantalized him with its mysterious sheen. Its labyrinthine phrases would've consumed him entirely if the sudden honking hadn't drawn his attention.

He leaned out of the window to see a flock of cows cascade down the bushy hills of Nallamala forest like a grand procession from heaven, choking the road ahead. This was unavoidable as the road to Srisailam was peppered with small villages, whose rusticity Jake had gauged from the smalls huts with thatched roofs dotting intermittently the green landscape of the hills.

Having gained enough information on the popular Nagarjuna Tiger Reserve, he felt unlucky at not having spotted any tiger walking the jungles. Even so, occasional sighting of monkeys, deer and wild boars along the journey to Srisailam had been a visual treat.

After an exhausting seven-hour journey, the last hour of which had been spent traveling a nauseating winding trail cut into the hills, the pilgrimage bus finally came to a jarring halt on the pinnacle of Nallamala forest.

Jake alighted from the bus with the pilgrims and found himself staring at an enormous statue of Sri Dakshinamurthy at the entrance to Srisailam. The statue had taken Jake's liking immediately at first go itself. Designed to hold a lofty *veena,* a multistringed musical instrument, in its hands, the statue of Sri Dakshinamurthy sat on a enormous pedestal facing south, under a banyan tree whose shoots spread behind like slender tentacles of a large ocean octopus. Small forms of *sadhus* were depicted around the main statue, in meditative poses.

After taking momentary pleasure from its sheer beauty, Jake traced a path that primly led all the way up to the threshold. In the distance, a classical *gopuram*, a pyramid-like structure towered against the blue sky. *The holy shrine of Mallikarjuna.* Recognition hit Jake instantly.

On the hills of Nallamala lies a temple... Jake's eyes glowed at the sight as he replayed the first line from the riddle. *This is the temple the riddle speaks of,* Jake realized staring at the structure.

It's marvelous.

He walked towards the temple.

The temple of Mallikarjuna is an astonishing six hundred and sixty feet long and five hundred and ten feet wide free standing structure surrounded by a vast stretch of thick green forest. Built in the Dravidian style, the main shrine is made of stone with a lofty tower, standing at the center of huge courtyard secured by iron gateways at the north, south and east ends. Its facade is an exquisitely ornate and intricate sculptural work that along with small shrines of various avatars of Lord Shiva dotting around the main shrine, adds to a distinct flavor of devotion that is beyond the material reach.

In Hinduism, this temple has great prominence as it is a Shaivite shrine, dedicated to Lord Shiva, and houses one among the twelve *Jyothirling as* spread across India and held in great veneration.

From its historical viewpoint, the origin of this temple can be traced back to somewhere around the Buddhist period, perhaps even earlier to the Mahayana school of Buddhism that emerged during the first century AD. This temple is mired in numerous legends whose imprints are exemplified in the bas-reliefs on the outer walls of the courtyard, particularly on the south and eastern walls, representing a museum and library of the past, fused into one.

With his gaze climbing up and down the length of the temple tower, he paced up the steep walkway. Soft devotional chants drifted into the air. Souvenir shops lined the sides of the walkway, replete with assortment of tiny idols of the presiding deity of Srisailam, photo frames of various Hindu gods and goddesses, incense, flowers and other ritualistic offerings.

Jake knew, people mostly picked up these devotional articles as a keepsake on their way back home, especially the idols which served as a memento of their visit to this holy shrine.

He hadn't even taken off his eyes from the assortment of idols when a thick swell of men in black, chanting hymns to Lord Shiva, rushed up from behind, pushing past him and other devotee, snaking their way towards the temple.

Garbed in black robes, with ash smeared foreheads and arms, these specific sect of devotee--worshipers of Lord Shiva, came from south India. They were hardcore devotee of the Hindu deity Ayyappa, son of Harihara, the fused representation of Shiva and Vishnu. And they took an arduous path to redemption, by following rigid practices of abandoning worldly pleasures and luxuries.

As this rush reaching farther, dissolving into the throng of people ahead, Jake's focus gradually shifted back to the ornate handiwork of the temple tower, the *gopuram*. By then, he'd stepped into the courtyard of the temple through the main entrance gate on the eastern side. This gate was flanked by two elaborately carved pillars with a bull atop and two small gates on either side. Avoiding a maze of mesh of iron security barricades leading to the entrance of the main shrine, Jake took a immediate left and arrived on the southern side of the temple, knowing exactly where it would take him.

In prior, Jake had done his homework quite meticulously, scouring through as many records of the temple as possible, given his delicate situation and the small window of time he had before he needed to leave this location. Now, equipped with enough details on the riddle, he moved towards the outer walls of the temple.

Engraved on its wall… the second line from the riddle thrummed in his ears, as he slowed down appearing before the outer wall of the temple.

Wrapped in a rich tapestry of artwork of history, the twenty-feet high southern wall of the ancient temple was constructed of pink sandstone and fortified with iron railings. Each block of pink sandstone formed a panel depicting a distinct tale, chiefly various popular forms of Shiva and legends connected to him.

Jake swept his gaze across the different panels, wondering that there were too many to be scrutinized minutely. Leaning over the iron railings, he first examined noteworthy sculptural images that included various lore, famous forms of Shiva and other Shaivite gods and goddesses, scenes from wars, hunting, *gandharvas* (skilled singers playing musical instruments), human forms in different poses and rich floral patterns. The rows at the bottom depicted elephants in rich trappings and anklets, as if in procession, some with their trunks twisting up trees. Other rows were devoted to cavalries, soldiers, dancing nymphs and musicians.

As he examined the carvings minutely, he was also mindful of his surroundings. He could sense people walking past him, pausing momentarily, staring at the wall and then at him, as if trying to make sense of what he was up to.

To the onlookers, he stood out like a sore thumb, the only one interested in the outer walls of the temple rather than the Shivalinga inside the main shrine itself.

Out of the corner of his right eye, Jake saw some movement, which drew his attention off to the side.

A *sadhu* resting on the ground, with his back propped against the barricade, was staring back at him, unblinking. He was garbed in an ochre robe with a turban head gear. With intense deep set of eyes and a crimson tilak marking his forehead, his obscenely unkempt long grey beard and moustache framed his ash smeared face making him appear no less than a Aghori Naga sadhu.

Jake's eyes lowered to the man's neck that was heavily burdened with sacred beaded necklaces, and then to his wrists, rife with bracelets, and the fingers bearing stone-studded rings, all adorning his ash bleached skin.

Sightings of ascetics at holy shrines were common, as they dwelt along such serene lands focusing on spiritual practices, secluding themselves from all that bound them to worldly planes. Yet, Jake had always felt that there was something very unusual about these men who appeared godly. Their subtle behavior, their bizarre and freakish appearance and their disconnect with their surroundings had always made him wonder about the force behind them choosing the path they were onto.

Shaking off the reverie, he found the *sadhu* still staring back at him sternly, as though rebuking him for trespassing upon his privacy.

Jake immediately looked away, turning his attention to the rich panels on the walls. He'd heard some freakish stories on Sadhus. Stories relating the curses they practiced, their bizarre rituals of consuming blood of animals, of gorging on human feces, as these macabre other worldly customs empowered them with some kind of mysterious force that could cause potential harm to those who looked upon them with disdain.

And Jake didn't wish to mess with them. Avoiding those thoughts as he continued to scan the images on the wall, midway through the length of the wall, his eyes stopped on some that were so unusual in nature that they seemed to have absolutely no relevance to any of the other images in focus.

The panel, one which he found strange, depicted a grotesque scene: human forms working on equipment that seemed to have come straight from a science laboratory, more precisely, a chemical laboratory.

Confused, Jake bent little more over the barricade, trying to get closer look at the panel when he heard a mellifluous voice.

"They were alchemists!"

As Jake turned, he discovered a gorgeous woman smiling back at him, endowed with a grace he'd never seen in anyone before.

CHAPTER 23

It would be her.

Jake was sure that was what he would say if someone asked him if he'd seen an angel walk the earth.

The woman who had almost instantly captivated Jake equaled him in height and appeared to be in her mid-twenties. She was elegantly dressed in a close-fitting floral print top and blue denim trouser, wearing her jet black, lustrous hair loose over her shoulder.

"I'm sorry for having bothered you," she said, stepping closer. Her accent was heavy American. "It appears to me you're quite confused by what you were looking at." She broke off. "I think I know what this panel portrays."

Her facial profile examined up close had convinced him that she was irresistibly attractive and charming. She had full pink lips and a sharp pointed nose, an exact fit for her long face. Noting her rosy skin and cerulean eyes beneath dark firm brows and long eyelashes, he suspected her ethnicity to be either Middle eastern or European region. She was exceptionally stunning and graceful, so much that Jake wondered Cleopatra would've envied her if she had lived in the twenty-first century.

Yet as alluring as she appeared, Jake recognized a pesky shade underlying her personality. He liked her candidness, but it was little too much to endure.

"Thanks. But I don't…"

"These sculpted forms are slightly extended," she continued, cutting him off and pointing to the images on the wall. "They are carved finely to stand out from the background." She faced him. "These are known as bas-reliefs, an early archetype of sculptures often cited in old temples."

Jake was puzzled at her candidness which he felt was too nosy. Arriving from nowhere or perhaps from one of the tourist groups, she had extended assistance he hadn't demanded without even bothering to check if he really needed her help.

Still, something about this girl constrained him from interrupting her. He watched her in deep silence, as if her intoxicating voice had incapacitated him.

She marched on, pointing out to the figures on the wall.

"These men in this bas-relief were alchemists, the masters who guarded arcane knowledge. And these things here," pointing out to the shapes that filled the background in the relief, she stated, "the crucibles, the alembics and the fire set-up was their apparatus. Like the ones you find in a chemical laboratory. They employed them to conduct chemical experiments." She broke off for a moment, before completing, "it's easy to miss them unless you're really looking for it."

"Alchemists?" Jake pursed his lips contemplatively. "You mean the ones who attempted experiments to convert inferior metals into gold?"

"Kind of," she replied, smiling. "That is the best known definition of alchemy in popular culture, although alchemy had another aspect to it."

Jake cast an uncertain look at her, clearly demanding further explanation, hoping she would reveal something more.

But she suddenly blurted out. "Oops-a-daisy!"

Jake looked at her, confused.

"I think that was a mistake." She flinched. "Now look what I've done to myself. You're already assuming I am your guide."

Jake was still staring at her clueless, unsure how to react, wondering what to make of her behavior when she burst into a naughty laugh, taking him by surprise.

"So be it," she said, casting an amiable smile.

Is she insane? Jake thought inwardly, making a face at her. But she wasn't. Jake understood it as he understood that she was lively and bubbly and didn't mind occasionally giving up her formal etiquette to behave childishly.

"From a physical standpoint," she stated, drawing a long breath and then continuing, "alchemy was all about transmuting base metals into gold and a vigorous attempt to create a substance called 'the elixir', a cure for diseases and a potion to prolong man's earthly span indefinitely.

"But on a much broader scale, alchemy was a philosophical and experimental science, more specifically, an art concerned with the purification of the soul. Its objective, however, is widely misunderstood. According to some it was perfection not in the physical but in the spiritual sense that alchemists sought."

Jake glanced over at the human forms in the bas-relief.

"They were real alchemists," she continued with her gaze fixed on the bas-relief, "possibly, the famous Nagarjuna and Veerbhadra, the two iconic and mysterious figures from the ancient world of alchemy, known to have existed in different time periods. They had mastered the art of alchemy with constant effort and had even accomplished successfully the transmutation of metals." Casting a look of reverence on the bas- reliefs, she noted, "So they came to be known as transcended souls..."

Jake sensed a deepening chill seep through his bones. He looked over at her.

"They possessed wisdom and spiritual insight beyond human understanding that enabled them to transcend to a state where they could perform God-like miracles."

Transcended... Jake remembered the phrase from the riddle. ***Engraved on its wall souls transcendental...***

That's it. Jake felt the hair on his neck stand on end. *That's the phrase I was looking for...* He touched the bulge of the magnetic box in his pocket. The riddle was pointing at this bas-relief. And the phrase '*souls*' in the second line was referring to Nagarjuna and Veerbhadra, the two alchemists who had transcended the ordinary, eventually becoming transcendental souls...

The souls transcendental...

"So you believe in that alchemy thing?" Jake asked, trying to sound casual.

"Absolutely," she replied confidently. "There is a popular legend. I wonder if you've ever heard of it. In times of famine and other natural disasters, the temples and religious relief organizations in ancient India received large quantities of gold from an unknown source."

"And you believe this too?" Jake pushed a little more.

"Of course, yes," she said. "This mystery intensifies further with the fact that the sheer quantity of gold throughout the country and that available with the kings could not possibly have tallied given that India had just one gold mine back then."

Jake digested this information. It sounded more like a fantasy rather than the historical facts her genuine tone seemed to suggest. Then, he glanced back over at the bas-relief.

Seek what they possess privileged to someone worthy...

In the bas-relief, Jake now began to seek what the transcended souls had possessed. Meticulously, he watched the two human forms in the image, straining to see their laborious task. The attention of the two men was completely on the experimental set-up. The apparatus, the fire source and the different forms of containers in the background, all seemed to remind him of a medieval foundry.

"The entire set-up in this bas-relief," Jake said, luring her into telling him more, "seems more like a fictitious tale with loads of grotesque imaginary instances interlaced in it." He glanced at her. "This picture reminds me of a gothic laboratory from the medieval period with an aged wizard in dark robes looming over a large boiling cauldron, trying to unleash a terrifying monster."

She raised her brows at his sardonic remarks. But surprisingly, someone else was displeased by his words.

"That's it!" a harsh tone sounded from somewhere around them.

Puzzled, they abruptly turned to discover that the voice belonged to the same *sadhu* who was seated on the pavement. H had risen to his feet and now stalked towards them, protesting in Hindi. His ochre robe hanging loosely from his lean profile, slightly bellowed behind as he marched towards them.

"What more can one can expect out of an ignorant, arrogant man like you," he stated gravely, arriving in front of Jake, "a man of prejudice whose ignorance knows no limits."

CHAPTER 24

Who else could have been privy to the ancients' and their mysterious secretive knowledge than the *sadhus* themselves, who preferred life away from the chaotic world and wandered in the wilderness, dwelt in caves and retired into the solace of monasteries, chasing what has eluded the great minds of the world for countless eons.

In the deafening silence of cold austere locales, they reflected upon their own mortality. Through meditation, they merged with the cosmic consciousness, seeking answers to the puzzling questions of life that innumerable men before them had pursued: who they really were, where they came from and what was the purpose of their existence.

Knowing what it had taken him and others from his clan to walk along that arduous path, the *sadhu didn't seem to spare any of those who dared speak disgracefully about all that he held sacred. Now* he was ready to fight Jake's remark on the bas-relief, which he considered sacrilegious.

"I wonder with what authority you speak so disrespectfully of these sculptures."

The female tourist took a step back, alarmed by the *sadhu*'s sudden burst of temper. Jake stood rooted, confused, trying to assess what the *sadhu* was getting at.

"A few academic degrees don't earn you the right to talk gibberish and make filthy, blasphemous statements about these sacred sculptures." He held Jake's gaze firm. "Knowledge is not what you learn within the four walls of any popular university. It is something you earn through your personal experiences and endeavors, like these great men here." He pointed to the men in the bas-relief.

It was then Jake understood that the sadhu had been irked by his remarks at the bas-relief, which he knew had been unintentional.

The sadhu walked closer to the barricade, looking over at the bas- relief. "These were *siddha* alchemists, righteous and determined. They acquired sacred knowledge on the art of alchemy not from any popular universities, but from their relentlessefforts and perseverance.

"Do you even know why our ancestors dedicated such a great deal of their time indulging in activities like painting, sculpting and rock inscriptions?" He turned to Jake. "They wanted to hand over their knowledge, their culture and their rich history to future generations. They wanted to usher them into learning their sheer wisdom and skill which enabled them to accomplish what now seems impossible to us.

"They were greater. Their knowledge was greater. And the heart beneath their flesh was even greater. It was the sole reason for them engraving their knowledge on the rocks, embedding excerpts from their own lives and their experiences on stones." The *sadhu* paused, his eyes trained on Jake.

"But I feel sad when I look at their future generations." He glanced at the female tourist and then at Jake. "The generations they long desired now heed to their stories with such disrespect, rudeness and ignorance and look back at their labors and their achievements with mockery."

Jake tried speaking up in defense, but the words dried up in his mouth. He hesitated, knowing he hadn't meant to hurt anyone's feelings.

"My apology for what I said, *guruji,*" Jake spoke at last, trying to sound as gentle as possible. "I'm really sorry. I never intended to hurt anyone's feelings."

The *sadhu* stared back at him.

"I respect these sacred reliefs as much as you do," Jake said. "If I were ignorant, why would even I go the trouble of flying down thousands of miles to this temple just to seek the blessings of Lord Mallikarjuna"

The *sadhu* smirked. His features appeared morbid against his ash smeared face "What I really don't understand is you urbanites. You educated people are trapped in two worlds. With one foot firm in the physical world bound to materialistic luxuries, you try to crease other foot in the spiritual world." He paused, "But be informed that the truth u seek is not that easy to be found. For what you pursue is far beyond your reach. " Throwing at them a serious stare, he motioned to the bas-relief. "Listen to the screams of these lifeless forms on the walls. Heed to their glorious triumph over the impossible rather than casting a glance for the pleasure of your eyes and walking away.

"Observe this picture not with the eyes of your flesh, but that of your mind. See the unseen they've overcome. Comprehend what they're trying to reveal to you about the arcane art that they've learnt and mastered by years of endeavor, inspired by a vision—a vision of the ascension of man to a level on par with perfection, standing God- like in realization and enjoying powers akin to His."

Gazing straight into Jake's eyes, he advised, "And so should your vision be. A vision like that of these sages. Then see for yourself, that what is below is like what is above," he said, his index finger pointing heaven-ward, "and what is above is like what is below," pointing down to the earth.

The *sadhu* glanced at them somberly and repeated his gesture, pointing his index finger up and then down, saying, "As above…So below."

Letting those words linger, the *sadhu* walked away.

In complete silence, Jake watched him disappear in the crowd of devotees rushing into the temple premises.

"He seemed really pissed off!" the female tourist told Jake, stepping closer to him. "I was afraid he would create a ruckus."

But Jake was barely listening to her. His mind was processing something that seemed hazy. Then suddenly, the cloud settled. And an understanding came to him: the words articulated by the *sadhu* were actually the same as those inscribed on the magnetic box.

As above…So below…

"Oh cripes!" With the realization piercing him like a spear, Jake took off in a sprint, in the direction in which the sadhu had disappeared.

CHAPTER 25

Caught in a flurry of devotees pouring into the temple premises, Jake lost the sight of the sadhu.

Normally, at this time of the day, with dusk setting in fast, the temple would witness a heavy influx of devotees mostly from the neighboring villages. With baskets of flowers and desires in their heart, they would pour down at the feet of Lord Shiva with deep obeisance.

Now jostling his way through them, Jake scanned his sideways, back and forth, arriving at the crossroads of the temple, coming to halt beneath the statue of Lord Dakshinamurthy, where he had got down from the bus upon his arrival. But there was no sign of the *sadhu*. He seemed to have vaporized from the temple premises.

The chimes of the temple gong rang out loud, punctuated by the murmurs of chants by the priests. A subtle aura of sanctity filled his being. In the distant corner of his mind, however, the four words uttered by the *sadhu* thrummed with striking lucidity.

As above…So below.

A disturbing thought took root in his mind—how in the world did the *sadhu* know about the two-line verse etched on the magnetic box? Had his father contacted him before his death or had he too been made privy to The Lost Arcanum? However, the *sadhu* showed no hint of recognition at seeing Jake.

"I know where we could find him," a voice broke through his daze.

When he turned, he found the same female tourist who only a while ago had trespassed upon his privacy and had him briefed on the bas-relief.

"We?" Jake eyed her with suspicion. "Why we? And why do you intend to help me?"

A composed smile crinkled her lips. She extended her hand, introducing herself. "I'm Taneez, from the University of Boston, Massachusetts." She paused, adding, "I'm here on research work."

Jake raised his brows.

"I'm student of occult arts," she furnished. "I am learning about the ancients and their world of mystical and esoteric arts."

"No wonder you knew so much about alchemy," Jake said, shaking her hand. "I'm Jake Stevens, a historian."

She laughed. "No wonder you were so focused on this bas-relief on alchemists."

Jake forced a smile in return, wondering what to make of her statement, whether to take it as a joke or as an indication that she was suspicious of his identity. Since being hunted down by the men from Intelligence, to maintain a low profile, Jake had decided to pull on the disguise of a historian, concealing his true self from anyone he'd meet on this quest. Now he tried his best to keep it that way.

"So," Jake said, "it seems we both are interested in the same thing."

"Quite so," she replied.

She told him where they could find the *sadhu*, describing the *matha*, a monastic educational center, located in close proximity to the temple. Ushering him to walk along one of the four roads that diverged from the crossroads, she briefed him on the history of *mathas*.

In olden days, these *mathas* were religious establishments that had served as primary educational centers supervised by disciplined and experienced teachers known as *acharyas*. Over time, however, it had turned out to be a rendezvous point for most wandering *sadhus*, who retired into its placid environs for as long as they wished, before setting off on another journey of self-discovery.

As they walked, they discussed their families. Jake chose not to reveal every detail about his family and Taneez too had not revealed much other than the fact that she was of Israeli descent and born in America, currently based in Boston, Massachusetts.

They passed through a sparsely populated village snuggled deep into the forest, scantily peppered with small huts and shacks.

Jake checked his watch as dusk began to set in, painting the horizon purple pink. It was forty past five. Once the thick blanket of darkness dropped on these hills, Jake had heard this forest will turn hostile. Nocturnal beasts wandered the jungle in search of prey.

"We need to find him before night falls," Taneez said, as if sharing his worries.

Her fear was palpable. Jake changed the topic, to keep the panic at bay.

"I don't get this," said Jake. "You don't understand Hindi. Then, how you do even know what the *Sadhu* said?"

Taneez replied, "I could only make out that your remarks on the bas-relief got on his nerves. That's all."

"But that's such an overreaction," Jake said, pacing ahead. "Don't you think these godly men too possessive and rude in defending their weird rituals?"

"Alchemy was not a ritual," Taneez sufficed. "It was an esoteric discipline meant only for the most adept. And why not be possessive about it when it took them a tremendous amount of effort, dedication and commitment to achieve their goals?" She let out a breath. "Despite many attempts and failures, it was their courage and perseverance that paved their way to success. They unraveled mysteries, the existence of which had been denied by various religious sects, and ended up bearing persecution and derision throughout history.

"Furthermore, these godly men are believed to be the keepers of the lost knowledge of the ancients. They guard the secret wisdom of all ages. And they always speak in cryptic phrases."

"As above…So below," Jake said, reminding her of the last words of the *sadhu*.

"An ancient and popular Hermetic axiom," Taneez clarified, "found on the *Emerald Tablet* of Hermes Trismegistus."

Reading from Jake's keen expression on her response, she went on to shed more light on Hermes, the most mysterious personality in the history of alchemy.

"Hermes Trismegistus was believed to be a greatest philosopher astrologer and a white magician. Records suggest that Hermes had mysterious and magical powers and was often found hovering between the divine and human world. And this axiom, 'As above…So below', is one of the thirteen adages inscribed on the Emerald Tablet that expounds the divine cosmic design. Hermes believed that it was in the heavens that the secrets of life were embedded.

"Every level of nature and creation on earth mirrors the cosmic design. From the structure of atoms in things which have no life to the biological cell—the basic building block in a living organism is a replica of the cosmic design."

The look of incomprehension on Jake's face made her realize that he needed an elaborate explanation. Taneez pulled out her cell phone and opened an image from an encyclopedia website: a biological cell of a living organism.

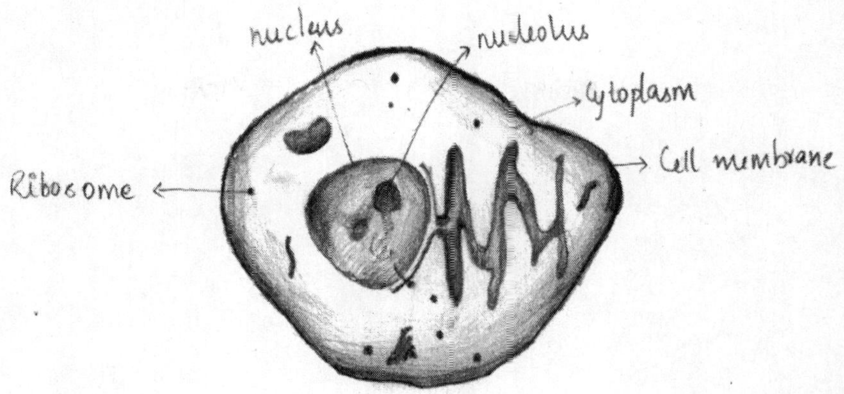

"This is the structure of a single biological cell. A basic building block of all life on earth," Taneez informed him. "And this is the structure of an atom," she said, showing him another picture, "the smallest indivisible component of any matter."

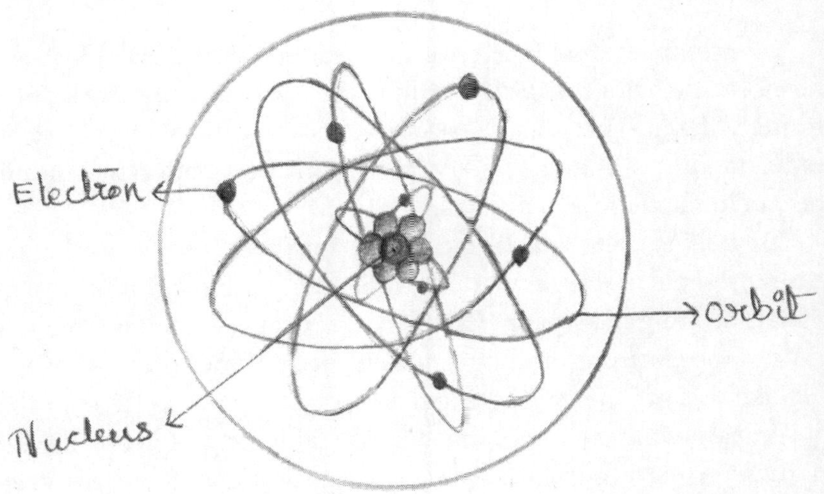

"Now if you compare these structures with the design of our solar system," she pulled up another picture, "what do you make of it?"

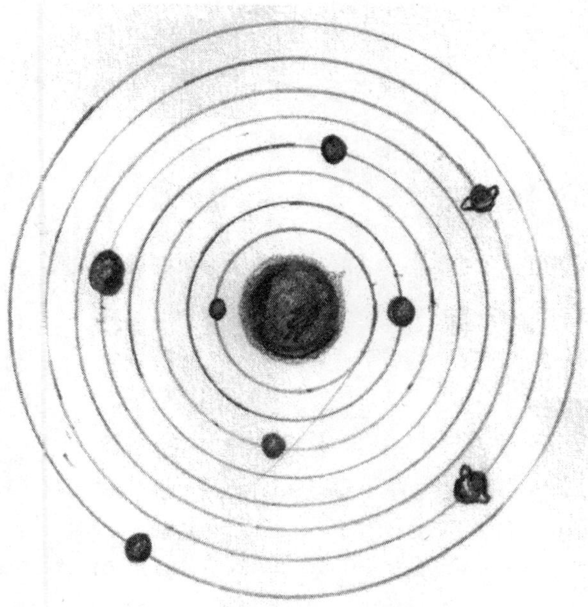

Jake compared the images of the structure of the biological cell and the atom and with the design of the solar system, going back and forth through them. Then he glanced up at her with a feeling of vague understanding. "They have a common nucleus at the center, similar to the sun in the middle of our solar system."

"Bingo!" Taneez smiled, motioning him to continue walking. "The sun represents the nucleus in an atom and in a biological cell. And the planets orbiting the sun are like those cell organelles from the biological cell and the electrons orbiting a nucleus in an atom."

Jake was gradually grasping her theory.

"Imagine if these forces, the centrifugal force that keeps the planets in their orbits around the sun or the Coulomb force between the electrons and the protons in an atom suddenly ceases to exist. What consequences would that have? Wouldn't it send the planets hurtling outward, out of their specific orbits and cause the entire solar system to collapse?

"In the same manner, a slight alteration in the biological makeup of a nucleus in the cell could lead to disorders in living forms and in the atom of an element could lead to a change in the physical configuration of matter.

"In nature, this cosmic design is a code of life originating from the nucleus of the universe, the place where all matter was created, where all life seemed to have originated from. The place we call the throne of God. And the axiom 'As above…So below' holds the key to the secrets of life. All these factual theories draw us towards a single truth. As it is above in the heaven, so it is below on earth."

Jake reflected on this, going over every detail of the theory surrounding the Hermetic adage, 'As above…So below.'

The distant growl of an engine snapped Jake to the present. He turned around to catch a glimpse of a strong beam of light dancing left and right through the thickets of the forest as some heavy vehicle made its way through sharp twists and turns up the winding track of the *ghat* section. Jake was informed that the *ghats section* would shut down as night set in. There would be no vehicular movement until the next sunrise.

Taneez was pacing ahead, her breath labored. Jake was close on her heels, still thinking about how long it would be before they reached the *matha* when they bumped into an elderly man herding some sheep and cows.

Jake took a moment to inquire with the old man the path to the *matha*, to ensure they were on the right track. Once this was confirmed, they resumed their journey, now striding a little faster.

The silence this deep in the forest was spooky, punctuated by the screech of crickets and insects and the occasional howl of owls and foxes. From behind the bushes, as they passed, Jake felt the eyes of predators, watching them in dead silence as if waiting for the right moment to strike. When he glanced at Taneez, he realized she too was spooked. To dispel the fear, he struck up another conversation with her.

"You're a student of occult arts." Jake kept his voice low. "So tell me, how sure are you that alchemists in ancient India had actually succeeded in transmuting base metal into gold?"

CHAPTER 26

Taneez *smelled something* fishy about his excessive inquisitiveness. Her instincts were suggesting that this man was not a historian as he purported to be. But the urge to answer his question pushed aside her suspicion for another time.

"I have enough facts and records to convince on that matter. But before I say anything further, being a Christian, how much do you know about the *Temple of Solomon*?"

Jake paused for a moment taking a quick flick through the pages of the reference book in his head. "It was one of the most spellbinding structures in human history, commissioned by King Solomon for preserving The Ark of the Covenant---a gold-plated chest known to contain stone tablets on which God had inscribed the Ten Commandments. The tablets had been handed over to Moses on Mount Sinai. Apart from that, the temple served as the primary center for Jewish worship."

"Can you recall anything on how and from where King Solomon might have got shipped the precious materials to construct the temple?"

Jake rubbed his chin, as he knew little about it. "He received cargoes of gold and gems from a place called Ophir, which was known for its riches. That's all I can recall. But why do you ask?"

"Hold on," Taneez said, "Ophir, right?"

Jake nodded.

"You know what Ophir means?" Jake shrugged.

"The Bible renders this Hebrew word 'Ophir' to 'Sophir', which according to Coptic--the liturgical language of the Coptic Church used in Egypt and Ethiopia written in the Greek alphabet, translates to India."

That intrigued Jake. Yet, it didn't validate the fact that alchemists in ancient India had been successful in transmuting gold from inferior metals.

"If India had massive wealth around that time," Jake added, continuing, "it still doesn't prove that King Solomon imported transmuted gold from India. It could be mined gold."

"Even though India had only one gold mine then?" Taneez hurled another fact. "Jake, what you are suggesting is unlikely. With all the sophisticated tools in place, it takes no less than a millennium to mine enough gold to account for the sheer quantity of gold available throughout the country, be that in temples or with the ancient kings, seeing that India had just one gold mine way back then."

Though it made sense to Jake, he still found it hard to believe. He was one of those skeptics who relied heavily on valid proofs rather than on folklore and legends. Coming from a background of science, he had a strong grip on how science would disregard this transmutation process as absurd. It was his turn to educate Taneez about transmutation from a scientific standpoint.

Jake cleared his throat to speak. "When you talk about transmutation, you're talking about converting one naturally occurring metal with a specific chemical composition into an entirely different metal with a different chemical composition." He glanced at her. "You know what that means?"

Taneez looked over at him, waiting for him to continue.

"At the atomic level, you're trying to alter the naturally available number of protons within the nucleus to level it to the required number of protons in the metal that you desire to obtain. And when you're doing this, you're basically attempting to introduce or knock off protons from the structure of an atom of a base metal to bring it up or down to the level to form gold. And this is not possible by any advanced means of chemical technology known to man. Science is still too young to push into the frontiers of that domain."

Taneez smiled at his theory. "I'm afraid I have to tell you that you're wrong." She pulled out a note application on her phone and fiddled with the screen, before flashing it back to him. "This is how far science has pushed into the frontiers of that domain."

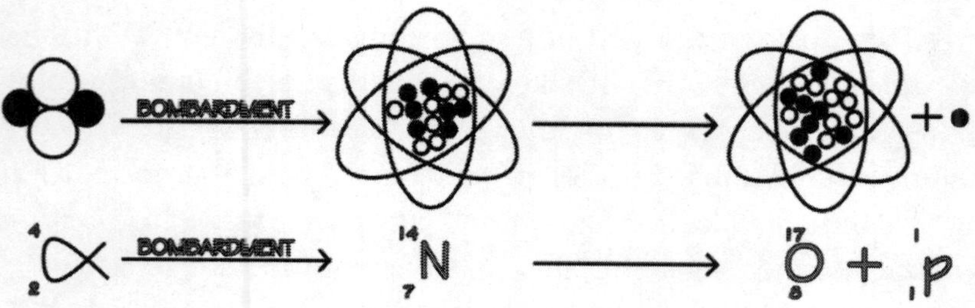

For a second, Jake was silent, deciphering the image. His brows rose in appreciation of her knowledge of physics. "Now you're talking about nuclear reactions."

"Nuclear transmutation," Taneez added, "to be precise."

CHAPTER 27

All naturally occurring elements are defined by the number of protons within the nucleus of an atom, which is also their atomic number. Jake had learnt that in high school.

Changing the elements required changing of the number of protons within the nucleus, an insurmountable task by any advanced chemical process known to man. But what he hadn't known was that physics can be used to add or remove protons from the nucleus and change one element into another by the processes known as nuclear fission and fusion reactions, the spontaneous reactions occurring naturally in highly radioactive elements.

Taneez, shedding more light on the theory of nuclear reaction, had told him that lead with atomic number 82 and a stable isotope of mercury 197 with atomic number 80, were the most common stable elements used by alchemists for conversion into gold with atomic number 79. By simply forcing out one proton from mercury or three protons from lead, by bombarding alpha-particles into the nucleus of their atoms, these elements were transmuted into gold.

"Do you even know what that means?" Jake chuckled at her theory. "You're trying to force a proton into a nucleus. This is an unattainable task. Protons are positively charged particles. And when you try forcing a positively charged particle against another positive proton, there is huge repulsive force generated.

"In order to get them past this repulsive force, you need a vast input of energy. Energy equivalent to that released from the explosion of an atomic bomb, to speed up the protons being introduced to the speed of light before slamming them against the nucleus of the atom and knocking protons from it. That is again impracticable unless you have a particle accelerator."

As he explained his theory, Taneez was busy with another drawing on her phone screen, which she now showed him.

On the mobile screen was an equation.

$$^{197}_{80}Hg + ^{1}_{0}n \longrightarrow ^{197}_{79}Au + ^{1}_{1}p$$

A pleasant smile stretched her lips, seeing him engrossed. "I suppose this answers your question."

"Neutron slamming mercury, knocking off the proton from it and turning it into gold?" Jake seemed surprised, staring at the equation. Then suddenly he recognized the phenomenon.

He gazed up at her in disbelief. "Neutron Bombardment!"

Taneez nodded. "Neutron, which is neutral in charge, is much easier to force into the nucleus of an atom to knock off protons from it."

Jake weighed it for a moment. "Neutron Bombardment must have been a viable option. Still, you miss the point here. What about the heat? How do you generate the tremendous amount heat required to conduct Neutron Bombardment?"

Taneez said softly, "That's where the catch is. These ancient alchemists seemed to have possessed a magical substance that generated enough heat to bring about the transmutation."

"And what was this substance?" Jake pressed casually.

"Lapis Philosophorum," Taneez furnished. "A Latin term for Philosopher's Stone. This magical substance when added in small quantity generated enough heat required to bring about the transmutation. It was more of a catalyst in the transmutation process. Apart from turning inferior metals to gold, this magical stone also seemed to possess powers to create elixir--a potion which when mixed in water and consumed, improved the lifespan of humans, making them immortal."

Seek what they possess privileged to someone worthy...

Jake remembered the line from the riddle wondering if this was what he needed to find. *The Philosopher's Stone.* That as claimed by the riddle, promised to transform the magnetic box in his pocket. He touched his trouser pocket, feeling the box, as the line hummed in his ears.

Its glorious power shall transform this box unto thee...

Even then, Jake sensed it was nonsensical. He wondered what he was chasing. A legend, a myth? That which held the promise of transforming the magnetic box in his possession? His thoughts on alchemy were still mired in ambiguity: was this arcane art only a philosophical experiment to perfect the human soul or was it really conducted on the physical plane to create gold out of worthless metals?

After passing many bends and twists in the forest, there still seemed to be no sign of the *matha*.

"What are you researching?" Jake suddenly asked her.

Taneez sighed and replied after a long silence. "There's an ancient legend that speaks of a mysterious place hidden somewhere upon these hills in Nallamala. The place, as claimed by the villagers' accounts, is a sacred portal that provides access to a secret chamber buried deep in the earth that holds a precious treasure hoarded by the ancients. This treasure, believed to be one of the greatest, is protected by some mysterious and dangerous invisible forces."

Jake looked surprised, wondering if she was really serious. "Are you kidding me?" Taneez gave him a blank expression.

"You're on a treasure hunt?" pressed Jake, his eyes wide.

"Treasure hunt, yes." Taneez smiled. "But, I'm hell-bent on proving that the amount of treasure the ancient Indians had amassed was the product of transmutation."

"The legend that you speak about could be just a treasure." Jake cut her off, exasperatedly. He explained to her that it was not necessary that whatever lay buried, hidden behind a sealed portal as it was rumored to be, belonged to the ancient alchemists. India was once called 'a golden bird.' The ancient emperors who had amassed massive wealth in the form of gold, jewels, gems and other precious artifacts, had it buried in secret vaults under temples. During invasions, foreign rulers had plundered entire kingdoms except for the temples. There were many such temples across India existing since ancient times that might hold treasures in their underground vaults, buried intact even to this day. He concluded by citing the recent discovery of a massive treasure in five secret vaults hidden beneath the Sri Ananta Padmanabha Swami Temple in Thiruvanthapuram, in south India.

"Well," Taneez said, "I appreciate your knowledge on that discovery. But what you're not aware is that when one of the gold artifacts from the treasure was subjected to scientific analysis on its quality, the results were incredible. The reports proved that the gold recovered was not mined gold. It was the product of physio-chemical metallurgy, a method of transmutation invented by ancient *siddha purushas.*" She smiled, adding, "*Siddha purushas* was a name given to ancient alchemists in India."

Jake shook his head just as the reason behind her assisting him to find the *sadhu* hit him. "You believe that the *sadhu* has knowledge of the location of that treasure?" He paused for a second. "Is that what makes you want to find him now?"

Taneez faced him almost instantly with a hint of uncertainty in her eyes. "Haven't you grasped the truth yet, Jake?"

"Truth? About what?" Her expression was one of disbelief. She tucked her loose hair behind her ear. "I thought you had accepted the invitation extended by the *sadhu*. I thought that is what made you look for him." Jake's expression was a mix of confusion and curiosity.

"Oh, I'm sorry," Taneez said apologetically. "You're a historian and rely on facts rather than on any signs of mysteries."

Jake stopped in his tracks, growing anxious and irritated. "Can you be plain and specific?"

"This..." Taneez said raising her right wrist high, with three clenched fingers and the index finger and thumb extended outward, pointing it upward and then downward, stating, "As above...So below..."

Jake eyed her silently. "What about that gesture and the verse?"

"It's a mystical invitation," Taneez revealed. "One who have knowledge of its meaning holds the map to the most coveted treasure on earth.

CHAPTER 28

As above…So below…

This axiom used in conjunction with the gesture, three fingers clenched and thumb and index finger outstretched, forms an old icon. Known as *'hand of mysteries'*, this gesture symbolizes an invitation to discover a prized treasure, the sacred teaching of all ages. Throughout history, this 'hand of mysteries' has been a secret icon, with simple variations across traditions with each finger bearing a symbol: a crown on the thumb, a star on the index, a sun, a lantern and a key on the rest. It was the most desired invitation extended exclusively by a master to an initiate deemed worthy to receive it, which ushered the recipient into a secret knowledge.

Jake remained silent, in disbelief. Was that why my father had left me with this gesture: *'As above…So below'*, which is a map that leads to a treasure? The treasure they called The Lost Arcanum? After a full minute, he had finished connecting the dots in his mind and looked straight at her. "You mean to say that the *sadhu* left us an invitation? His hand gestures, his stating 'As above…So below…' together is an invitation that leads us to a treasure?"

Taneez shrugged. "That's what the gesture signifies."

"But the hand of mystery gives access to treasure of knowledge," Jake pointed out, "not the literal physical treasure of gold that you're looking for."

"Its both," Taneez countered, "the literal physical treasure of gold created out of treasure of knowledge.'

As Taneez finished, they had entered a large courtyard with a huge banyan tree at the center, spreading out laterally. In the near darkness, its aerial prop roots branched out extensively, forming a matrix of trunks that appeared extremely spooky. Behind this large looming tree, at the foot of a mountain, a stone mansion jutted out from the earth.

Jake entered the courtyard, with Taneez keeping pace with him.

From the old wooden doors to iron-barred windows of the mansion, even the shoots of the banyan tree hanging like the hair of grizzly ghouls made the premises a ghostly set-up straight out from a Hollywood flick.

Taneez seemed afraid. Beside her, Jake was amused by her eyes that were soaked with fear, as if she wanted to turn around and run away from this place.

"This place reminds me of the mansion from the horror flick, *The Conjuring*," Jake whispered next to her.

Taneez frowned at him, knowing he was trying to scare her. She maintained her composure, as they made their way through the creaky iron double door and stepped into the mansion.

A dim electric bulb hanging from the ceiling lighted a narrow passageway that led them deeper into the mansion, into a large dark inner open courtyard. They took a moment at the threshold until their eyes adjusted to the gloom. With a sweep of curious eyes, Jake noted some doors along the courtyard, but these were closed. It was then that a shadowy figure stepped across their path.

Taneez stumbled backwards in fear.

Jake stood dead still. Taneez stepped behind him, gulping down a knot in her throat, looking over his shoulder.

The lanky frame silhouetted against the darkness emerged into the light, revealing a familiar ash smeared features with set of steady eyes, staring back at them.

"Now, what makes you both trespass upon my privacy?" the *sadhu* asked in grating Hindi.

"We're sorry again," Jake replied in Hindi. "But this," he made the hand gesture, his voice lower, "As above…So below…"

"What about that now?" the *sadhu* cut him off rudely, looking over his shoulder at Taneez.

Jake half smiled, unsure how to react. "It's…it's a gesture you made before you stalked off from the temple premises."

"How does that matter to you anyway?" insisted the *sadhu*.

"Jake, come to the point," Taneez whispered at his shoulder. "Tell him that we seek the treasure."

The *sadhu* looked at her fiercely.

"Stay quiet," Jake told her without looking back at her. "Let me handle this my way."

Half smiling again, he said, "We suspect you have knowledge about the location of a great treasure that lies buried somewhere beneath these hills."

The *sadhu* smirked. "You're wasting your time chasing a legend that eludes your comprehension. It lives not in reality but only on the tongues of the ignorant like you." He paused for a second. "And even if it exists, it will reveal itself to the chosen ones."

From his brusque denial, it was clear that the *sadhu's* anger would not simmer down anytime soon. He would not reveal any secret of the treasure. Jake had to spin another idea, to weave some story to get this man speaking about whatever he knew of the treasure.

"It's sad that you misunderstand us all over again." Jake let out a troubled breath. "It's not the treasure we seek. It's the knowledge, the sacred knowledge that we pursue."

The *sadhu* remained quiet, letting him talk.

"She has come from a distant land," Jake said, his thumb indicating Taneez, "looking for great men like you. To research and write about those men who have been guarding the secret knowledge for ages. Not that she desires the location of the treasure itself." He paused. "She's only interested in learning if the alchemists were really successful in transmuting gold. To confirm if the *siddha* alchemists were truly what they purported to be." Jake broke off and concluded, "This is the only chance for you to let the world know what the truth is."

For one whole minute, the *sadhu* said nothing. He continued to stare. Then turning abruptly, he walked into one of the abutting rooms, leaving the door wide open. Jake and Taneez followed him silently. Soon, they found themselves being offered seats on floor. The *sadhu* served them water to drink. Jake refused the glass of water, but Taneez was thirsty and downed the entire glass.

Jake's eyes wandered across the interiors of the room, picking up some paintings of deities nailed on the walls. A small cloth bag and two neatly folded blankets were laid on the far side of the floor.

The *sadhu* sat cross-legged on the stone floor in front of them. Like Lord Shiva, his eyes were half closed, basking in the eternal bliss of the astral planes while also aware of their presence.

Following a long spell of silence, the *sadhu* asked somberly. "What is it you want to know?"

They exchanged glances. Then Jake asked, "Among the legends that abound, there's a specific one that refers to a secret passageway on this hill of Nallamala, leading to a hidden chamber which has treasure of inestimable value hoarded by ancient alchemists." Jake broke off. "Some say, within the chamber lie tons of gold that the *siddha purushas* produced by the process of transmutation. There are also whispers about the so-called nectar of immortality hidden in there.

"But there has been a lot of misinterpretation about the true aspect of alchemy, as many believe that it was merely an art performed on a spiritual plane." Jake glanced at Taneez and back at the *sadhu*. "We believe you possess knowledge that can shed light on the ambiguity over the two-dimensional theory of alchemy." Choosing his words carefully, Jake pressed, trying not to give offense this time, "Alchemists gold? Or purification of the human soul in a spiritual sense?"

The *sadhu* uttered a thoughtful sigh and clambered to his feet, stating solemnly, "Mysterious as it appears, the truth…was not always so mysterious." Then he ordered, "Come with me."

CHAPTER 29

For ages, humans across different continents, civilizations, races and times, had relentlessly pursued mastery of the art of alchemy. But as the history has it, this art eluded great minds. It was one of the oldest and darkest aspects of science and also the most closely guarded secret discipline in the history of mankind.

For countless men in history, this art was both a laborious quest to uncover the secrets of transmuting inferior metal into gold and about seeking the most prized recipe: the secret to longevity, *the nectar of immortality*.

The chase, however, had been fruitful to those few righteous and virtuous ones whom destiny had proudly deemed pious and worthy. The endeavors of those lusting after materialistic wealth remained futile. However, they still continue their search through places rife with legends and myths on alchemists.

And the hills of Nallamala in southern India are, unquestionably, home to many such legends about alchemy, one of which speaks of a secret portal leading to a hidden chamber comprising massive treasure hoarded by the ancient alchemists.

Jake had tried cajoling *sadhu* into divulging the truth behind alchemy, wondering aloud if alchemy was truly a process of converting inferior metals to gold or simply a practical approach towards understanding the spiritual process of purifying the soul. In reply, the *sadhu* had walked into an adjacent room and made them stand in a corner.

Closing the door to the room, he had pulled a lantern from its wall mount and dispelled the darkness by lighting its wick, holding it against his ash smeared face.

Under the soft amber glow of the flames, they could see his gleaming eyes staring back at them. Crimson Tilak on his forehead was bright against bright background.

Jake felt Taneez pressing her shoulder against his, slightly scared.

The *sadhu* turned and crouched on the floor, setting down the lantern beside him. He shoved aside the mat on the floor, revealing a checkered floor of limestone. The square limestone slabs were laid out perfectly and cemented. But strangely, one slab in the center seemed odd one out, as if someone had tipped it from its place earlier.

The *sadhu* slipped his fingers in the gap, gripped the edge of the tile and tipped the stone slab, sliding it aside.

Jake felt his skin prickle at the sight, while Taneez had goose bumps finding a rusty square metal hatch underneath the stone slab. Jake inched closer and rounded up the exposed square metal hatch.

Taneez followed, her pulse racing.

Is this where the alchemists hoarded their treasure? Jake thought, as he stood directly over the hatch, with Taneez at his side.

The *sadhu* put his hand over the hatch and worked a small latch. The hatch shuddered on it hinges as he swung it outwards, exposing a dark hole of inestimable depth in the earth.

Jake's eyes went wide. Taneez, too, shared his expression.

Holding the lantern aloft in one hand, the *sadhu* raised his right hand, stating solemnly, with index finger pointed toward the sky, "As above..." and then pointing downward, "so below..." He moved the lantern directly over the dark hole, revealing something under the metal hatch that had been hidden in the darkness for centuries.

CHAPTER 30

This is scary…

Jake and Taneez had almost jumped in fright, noticing a flight of dusty stone stairs hewn out of rock, hidden beneath the square metal hatch, running deep down into the bottomless pit of darkness.

The hole was at least two square feet in size that can easily accommodate a well- built man through it. Holding the lantern in hand, the *sadhu* asked them to follow him, before he started to descend the steps.

Taneez retreated from the edge of the stairs, feeling a powerful urge to turn around and run. But Jake stopped her by her hand, pressing it gently, assuring her that it would be fine.

Trust me, his eyes seemed to say.

Taneez nodded and stepped forward, inching to the edge of the hole. Taking a deep breath, Jake stepped onto the first stair and began to tread down, gradually.

Taneez stepped on it in tandem and followed him immediately.

As they ventured down, gradually abseiling themselves into the dark pit, they discovered that the stairs were steep and narrow, with walls cramping them on either side. Soon, they had entered another world down under the ground.

Stepping off the final stair, they found themselves grounded in a long and narrow low-ceiling shaft, partially illuminated by the flames of the lantern. Floor underneath their foot was slippery.

Jake recalled seeing some eerie spaces before, but this one was rather spooky.

"Jake," Taneez whispered, squeezing his shoulder, motioning him to look forward.

A few meters ahead, the *sadhu*, who had led the way with the lantern, had stopped abruptly, dangling the lantern over his shoulder to reveal another piece of horror.

Not again, Jake prayed, *not one more.*

Ahead of them, a dark opening in the rear wall of the shaft, now flickering under the light of the lantern, beckoned them. It appeared to be a dark portal, like the mouth of a cave waiting to welcome them, as if inviting them to become a scrumptious bite for the tenebrous abyss beyond. Only on stepping up to its edge did they realize that the mouth of the cave opened onto another flight of stone-cut stairs.

"Mind your feet," the *sadhu* cautioned them and stepped onto the stairs. He set off down what seemed an alarmingly steep staircase that spiraled down into inky-blackness.

This time, Taneez was the first to follow the *sadhu*. Placing herself between the two men, she felt safe and secure, knowing that it would be either the first one or the last one in line who would be more susceptible to dangers, if they encountered any on the way.

The *sadhu* walked down the stairs, leaving behind to them a golden yellow trail of light from the lantern to illuminate the path. Jake followed behind Taneez, descending into the unknown depths.

He felt the narrow winding stairs leaning on them, breathing heavily on their backs. The air down here was cold and moist and an awful stench that he couldn't identify wafted all over. As they continued their descent, Jake felt a damp chill seeping out from the stone-cold walls and covering their body in a deathly embrace. The stillness was uncomfortably ominous and lasted until their melancholy path straightened out at the end of the stairs.

Stepping off the final stair, Taneez stood gathering herself.

Jake glanced at the ceiling, feeling the sheer weight of the mountain overhead, wondering what would happen if the entire section caved in, trapping them in this ghostly tunnel forever.

"I'm wondering," Taneez spoke, cutting through his pessimistic reverie. "If this is the same passageway that leads to the secret chamber that the legends speak of."

"Perhaps," Jake replied. "Even if it does, how will this *sadhu* set it free."

Taneez glanced at him questioningly.

"Ancient treasures were always guarded by some mysterious forces. They could be anything. Ghosts, snakes, deadly scorpions and so on, invoked by reciting certain powerful *mantras* such as Garuda Mantra to seal the door permanently," Jake broke off thoughtfully. "And rumor has it that the legend we're looking for is under the protection of a ghost."

Taneez wanted to stop him, but the words dried up in her mouth. She was too scared to react. She said hesitantly, "Yeah, but it could also be a mysterious force that guards the chamber.'

"Mysterious force is another name for 'ghost'," Jake replied flatly.

She gulped down a lump.

Jake smiled inwardly. He was enjoying her fear. "They are so powerful that they can be really nasty."

"But," Taneez said in a tone that seemed to be aimed at reassuring herself, "I'm sure this *sadhu* is capable of warding off the ghost. I trust him to do that."

"You can trust him on that," Jake said. "Still, you need to know something. Human intervention in releasing the sealed door has always proven to be fatal. Instances of mysterious accidents, illness and unnatural deaths have always followed whenever someone tries to pry open the sealed chambers, meddling with those mysterious forces.

"The sealed doors can be set free only by those powerful men who know *Garuda mantras*. And as per my information, there are only a few men left on the planet, mainly living in the Himalayan Mountains who know how to recite these potent *mantras*." Jake broke off, letting her digest what that meant.

Taneez clenched her fists tightly. Though she tried to ignore the thought, she sensed some malice lurking in the subterranean passageway.

Ahead of them, the *sadhu* had stopped abruptly and had turned to face them. Raising the lantern high over his shoulder, he moved it to his left, lighting up something behind him. The sight over the *sadhu's* shoulder left Jake and Taneez in awe.

Behind the lantern, illuminated by the golden yellow glow, lay a large and solid door that extended from floor to ceiling, as wide as the tunnel. Its surface was tarnished but it was unmistakably cast of wrought-iron. There were no bolts or nuts or latches. It simply seemed embedded into the rear wall of the tunnel, as if it had been hermetically sealed.

Eyeing the door in astonishment, Taneez guessed it was possibly secured by *Garuda mantras* or mysterious forces of some sort, which required the *sadhu* to chant the spells and set it free. Beside her, Jake shared her apprehension, earnestly waiting to see how the *sadhu* would go about opening the door.

The *sadhu* calmly rested his hands over its surface and exerted minimal force, slicing the door to one side, opening it halfway. When he turned, he found them with their mouths half-open, their eyes flickering in earnestness.

"Wait here," the *sadhu* instructed and then slipped into the half-opened door, disappearing into the darkness behind the threshold. Shortly thereafter, the space behind the door was bathed in a radiant amber glow and they heard the *sadhu* calling them to enter.

They glanced at each other anxiously and in unison stepped into the space, vanishing behind the door.

Beyond the threshold, only after their eyes had adjusted to the amber glow did they realize that they were currently afoot in the middle of the location that the legend spoke of.

CHAPTER 31

A*s the legend had it,* tons of gold jewelry, coins, precious gems, s the legend had it, tons of gold jewelry, coins, precious gems, valuable articles, hoarded by the ancient alchemists, lay stashed within the walls of the secret chamber.

This night, however, Jake and Taneez witnessed the spectacular sight of another treasure amassed by the ancient alchemists. The treasure being not gold or other valuable ornaments, but something rather unexpected and surprising, the existence of which gave rise to an entirely different connotation to the alchemists' treasure.

Under the golden glow of wall-mounted torches, they silently swept their glance across a cavernous chamber the size of an auditorium. Alembics, retorts, tubes, flasks and scorifiers were neatly arranged on a shelf beside a large hearth cut into the rear wall of the chamber.

This was the same apparatus, Jake recalled, depicted on the outer walls of the temple; it resembled modern-day equipment from a chemical laboratory.

Although it seemed like a letdown, they felt privileged to have set foot in a place the ancients had obscured for ages, under the holy shrine of Mallikarjuna: the secret laboratory of alchemists. It was in this laboratory, the *sadhu* revealed proudly, that Nagarjuna and Veerbhadra, the two popular alchemy experts, had succeeded in transmuting inferior metals into gold.

Taneez, although slightly dejected, managed to gather her thoughts and bring herself back to the chamber. Off to her side, Jake stood mesmerized by the sheer magnitude of the chamber's layout. He moved closer to the right wall which was impressed with strange symbols and mysterious inscriptions.

The *sadhu* walked across to the fireplace on the far side of the rear wall of the chamber.

Running his hand over some of the symbols incised finely into the stone wall, Jake pondered their meaning. Some of them, he realized, were also present on the magnetic box. Those connected to astrological signs. Most of them, however, were unusually mysterious. He wondered if the mystical symbols and the graphical depiction of what looked like experiments signified the prime interests of the alchemists who obsessively engaged in embedding their experiments in the form of art.

"What are these symbols?" Jake asked the *sadhu*.

Taneez, who was taking a close look at the retorts nearby, turned to look at him.

"Those symbols are astronomical signs," the *sadhu* replied.

I know that, Jake thought. *What about the others?*

"Symbols for planets," the *sadhu* furnished as he prepared to light a fire in the hearth. "Alchemy has its roots in astrology. The growth of each metal was believed to be ruled by one of the heavenly planets and under certain astrological conditions. Its influences, as held by alchemists, were necessary to carry out successful experiments."

He carried wooden logs to the hearth, explaining. "Seasons on earth, time periods, the four basic elements, alchemical compounds and esoteric symbols formed an integral part of their practices, which had the power to alter consciousness and connect the human soul to the divine."

Jake looked at the symbols, masking a confused look as he failed to identify any.

Taneez watched him from where she stood.

"Each alchemist, who was successful in accomplishing his goal, invented his own secret symbols associated with planets and processes and embedded half his experimental procedures in codes, by inserting them in between the recipes."

Jake found his hands caressing the symbols. Their unearthly nature made him want to know more about them. He started from a simple symbol engraved on the wall. "This inverted triangle," he said, "what does it signify?"

"Water," replied the *sadhu*. "It is one of the four basic elements. And the triangle pointing upward denotes the second element, fire."

Jake searched for it and found it a little farther away. He continued to track the symbols one after the other as the *sadhu* continued to shed light on the symbols and their meanings.

"The inverted triangle with a horizontal line slicing it midway denoted the third element, earth. The same symbol but with the triangle upright indicated the fourth element, air." He said, "*Earth, Fire, Water* and *Air*—the ancients believed that the universe was composed of these four basic elements, which contained critical energy essential to sustain life. Great philosophers and scholars have regarded these four elements as the altar of science. And these four elements came to acquire powerful symbolism across all cultures. *Earth* and *Water* being heavier were governed by the principles of gravity and had a downward direction."

Jake, being a novice to this discipline, had only started to realize its significance. But when he'd translated the *sadhu's* explanation for Taneez, she nodded, having understood immediately since she was well-versed with the symbolism of alchemy.

The *sadhu* approached the rack filled with ceramic jars and glass containers, as he spoke, "*Fire* and *Air* were lighter and were ruled by the principles of levitation, having an upward direction." Collecting some jars from the rack, the *sadhu* returned to the hearth, inviting them, "Over here."

CHAPTER 32

Different cultures, across different civilizations had different connotations for the four basic elements upon which alchemy was based: Earth, Water, Fire and Air.

Great masters from different time periods, those who were said to guard the secret wisdom of all ages, labored intensely to understand the significance of these four basic elements. They came to the understanding that the key to alchemy was indeed, buried in the essence of these four elements, deeply rooted in their inherent nature. These masters of alchemy traditionally passed on the secret to initiates whom they deemed worthy of this arcane art.

This night, however, for the first time in history, the invitation was extended to two undeserving people: a CBI officer desperately chasing the truth of his father's murder, and a student of occult arts for whom this was not only a great honor but a privilege that a master believed them worthy of the hidden wisdom.

"*Earth* and *Water* represented the feminine archetype, while *Fire* and *Air* symbolized the masculine archetype," the *sadhu* stated.

Jake and Taneez had settled around him, observing the apparatus, including ceramic container jars arranged on the raised platform next to the hearth.

The *sadhu* then opened a rectangular window cut into the wall just above the hearth, exposing a shallow chasm that extended not more than three feet beyond.

Jake walked up behind the *sadhu* and peered over his shoulder to discover a cylindrical furnace built into the stone wall. To his surprise, the furnace seemed to be lined with ceramic material. Equipped with an inlet and outlet valve, channels to drain slag and molten metal, this set-up had all the aspects of a modern-day blast furnace used in steel production.

Taneez's attention came to rest upon the bellow set up right in front of the hearth. She noticed that it consisted of a cylindrical ceramic vessel fitted with a flexible leather cover that had a flap. Recognition on the instrument hit her. Moving the cover up and down would draw in air through the flap and force it out through the nozzle. This type of device was commonly used by ancient metallurgists to stoke fires and increase the rate of combustion and output of heat.

The *sadhu* set the wooden logs on fire. As the flames danced, spreading among the logs, the otherworldly ambiance in the chamber, the loud characters engraved on the walls and the eldritch screech of the alchemist's struggle lingering in the air, all quietened to dead silence. The fire crackled with a thunderclap and then the clash of alembics and container lids took over the silence.

The *Sadhu* picked up a ceramic jar that contained some powdery material, dull metallic gray in color. Jake glanced at Taneez raising his brows, silently wondering if she recognized the material.

Taneez shrugged, not knowing what it was.

"*Earth,*" the *sadhu* said, drawing their focus as he scooped out the dull material with a large spoon and emptied it into a bone-ash cupel. "The first of the four basic elements corresponds to solidity. In its raw state, it is impure and reflects man's imperfect soul that is easily overcome by the temptations of evil."

He looked over at them. "Man is made up of three factors: the body which is the outward physical make-up, the soul which is the inward actuating cause of the individual's life and the spirit which is the universal soul of all beings. The alchemists believed the metals were similarly made up of three components: the body or the outward shape, the soul or its properties and the spirit or the essence of all metals."

Taneez handed over a shallow scorifier to the *sadhu* on his request. It contained some liquefied semi-transparent material she failed to identify.

"*Water,*" the *sadhu* continued, placing the scorifier next to the bone-ash cupel containing the dull metallic powder. "*Water* always held the power to cleanse. It symbolized healing and purification on a spiritual level, while referring physically to fluidity. It is essential in washing away impurities from the earth."

Jake gradually grasped that each ingredient the *sadhu* had used, represented one form of the four basic elements. The metallic dull powder referred to *Earth,* while the semi-transparent liquid symbolized *Water*.

Beside him, Taneez was curiously watching the sadhu as he produced a finely crafted ivory box, of about two square inches, from the upper seam of his breechcloth.

He opened it, exposing a chunk of a substance that resembled a glass, shiny, ruby red in color. "This is tincture," the *sadhu* pronounced, flashing a piece a little larger than a cumin seed.

They stared at the tincture blankly, showing no signs of recognition.

The *sadhu* dropped it into the scorifier containing the semi-transparent liquid. Then, collecting the cupel, he poured the dull metallic powder over the semi-transparent liquid, which instantly fizzed before turning into a dark green paste.

The *sadhu* lifted the crucible now containing the prepared mixture, walked to the hearth and placed it inside the furnace, closing the rectangular door and sealing it tightly.

Jake and Taneez followed the *sadhu* as he turned away from the furnace and crouched down to take a seat on a small raised platform in front of the hearth, just beside the bellow.

By now, the flames of the fire had grown intense, burning the wooden logs to a deep red. The *sadhu* hurled more logs into the hearth.

"*Air*," he said, blowing a blast of air into the hearth, "stood for communication and harmony. Spiritually, it was associated with spirit, soul. On a physical plane, it was breath, life." He trailed off, intensely observing the flames that began dancing fiercely, crackling, licking the base of the furnace. "It gives life in the same way it is now stoking life in the fire."

As the crackling of the fire steadied, a soft buzz began to emanate from the furnace, indicating the onset of both physical and chemical reactions.

Seated in the midst of the laboratory of the alchemists, witnessing what very few ever might have, Taneez and Jake found their attention shifting to the furnace.

The buzz of the furnace gave away to a sizzling sound, like a wave of water hitting a hot surface. It grew louder and louder. It continued for a good few minutes until steam escaped through the outlet valves. At this point, Taneez nudged Jake, drawing his focus to another outlet valve through which a molten metal flowed down the length of a long channel and emptied itself into a small crucible placed on the chamber floor.

The *sadhu* picked up the crucible and brought it to the platform, placing it delicately on the flat base. He waited for Jake and Taneez to appear beside him.

Once they arrived, he let them wait curiously for some magic to happen in the crucible.

But there was no change.

The molten metal accumulated in the crucible looked nothing like transmuted gold. Rather, it seemed like a slag, the impurities formed and separated out when a metal is smelted from ore.

The *sadhu* lifted his gaze and announced, "This was what the grand art of alchemy was all about."

They looked back at the *sadhu*, unimpressed.

"*Fire*," the sadhu stated solemnly, explaining the last of the four elements, "signified transformational power. On a spiritual plane, it stood as the guiding light. And on the physical plane it acts as the catalyst, burning away transient impurities from the body and bringing about the completion of the soul by transformation."

"God Almighty!" Taneez nearly jumped out of her skin, drawing Jake's attention to the crucible.

For a split second, Jake froze, trying to size up what he was seeing.

The *sadhu* watched them, taking in their excitement as they examined the crucible closely, their eyes now flickering to lump of precious, glittery metal in the crucible, one that every human on earth desired: gold.

"This is incredible!" Jake whispered, blown away by the sight. He gaped at the lump of gold, realizing a shocking truth, one as fascinating as the base metal that had been transformed into gold that the *sadhu* was an alchemist, who with mystical knowledge stashed underneath his rustic attire had achieved what every alchemist in history has striven for: creating a precious metal from a worthless substance.

The *sadhu* cut through the silence, declaring, "Alchemy is not a delusive art as many suggest. And the alchemist's life was indisputably occupied with performing chemical experiments on a physical plane, with a strong motive to transmute base metal into gold, just like what have you seen now.

"They were never defeated by difficulty or hard work. They persistently devoted themselves, spending whole nights at the mouth of the fiery furnace, putting in many laborious hours to harvest the fruit of their hard work."

The *sadhu* motioned for Taneez to spread her palms and then placed the lump of gold on it.

As Taneez caressed the lump of gold in her palm, Jake translated for her as the *sadhu* spoke of the transmuted gold symbolizing the redemption of man from evil, transforming his soul into spiritual gold. The realization was the spiritual transformation itself. The sacred science of ultimate human experience was used as a metaphor by the alchemists to conceal their gold-making recipe under philosophical allegories, parables and cryptic symbols to keep it from the unworthy. In the wrong hands, it was disaster. People would live wickedly in greed and the whole world would be ruined.

CHAPTER 33

Jake sauntered past the Sri Dakshinamurthy statue with Taneez at his side.

At night, to witness the lofty statue illuminated in shades of brilliant gold and brown, was a pleasant visual treat. Besides, stepping under the wings of deity had brought Jake a great dose relief he could not have explained in words, mainly after having been through a mysterious, inexplicable experience. The ghostly mansion, the gloomy tunnels, the secret laboratory, the transformation and more shockingly, the discovery that the *sadhu* was a real alchemist possessing the ultimate key to the art of alchemy, were too much to fathom. He could not help but revisit the events in his mind again and again.

Soon after they had left the secret laboratory and surfaced under the full-moon sky, they offered their final goodbyes to the *sadhu*, and set out for the Srisailam temple premises. Midway through the forest, a patrolling jeep had pulled up in front of them. The officer in charge of the patrolling unit had found out that Jake and Taneez, two tourists, had lost their way in the forest while trekking. Warning them against such recklessness of travailing on foot through a predator-filled forest in the dark, he had offered them a ride back to the Srisailam temple premises, more out of compassion than duty.

Jake glanced at Taneez as they strolled on the path to the temple.

She was quiet and pensive. An indication that she was overwhelmed by the recent events. His eyes assessed her looks; her pretty blue eyes were gleaming beautifully under thick brows that met just over her straight nose. Her rose-tinted lips were full and luscious. Jake had to conclude once more that she was a woman with charms any man would easily fall for.

Taneez looked at the gold piece in her hand. Placing it in her palm, the sadhu had asked her to share it among the poor, citing that the kingdom of God belonged to the needy.

"It's hard to believe that this is a genuine piece of gold."

"I agree," Jake replied after a brief moment, glancing at the piece as they walked. "He was in possession of something very precious that transmuted base metal into precious gold or could extend one's life on earth." Suddenly, he trailed off, as if something was not adding up. "Wait a minute...," he said staring at her in bewilderment.

Taneez looked at him, perplexed.

"Alchemy..." Jake stammered, "alchemy...it was a quest for a key that possessed powers to transform base metal into gold and to create the nectar of immortality, that which was believed to extend one's life span and give back youth."

A second later, he exclaimed. "Holy shit!"

After a beat, Taneez caught up with his reasoning. "My goodness! He's really smart!"

They remained looking at each other, enthralled at their own idiocy. The sadhu had skillfully manipulated and tricked them into believing that what they saw, the transmutation of base metal into gold was what alchemy was all about, which it indeed certainly was not. Transmutation of base metal into gold and concocting the nectar of immortality were just part of alchemy, an inconsequential component of the alchemical concept which could not be produced unless one held a substance, a precursor to accomplish the later.

The sadhu's sober and aggressive personality spoke of a wise man hidden behind his rustic attire, who had accomplished two goals in one shot: making them known to the fact that the transmutation of gold was not just a legend or delusive art or limited to books, was rather real, while keeping the real aspect of alchemy to himself—that he possessed a precious stone, a coveted substance without which the transmutation was impossible.

Thinking along the same lines, Taneez had instantly determined the substance.

"The Philosopher's Stone!"

Jake agreed with dull nod, recalling the glassy ruby-colored substance in the ivory box that the *sadhu* called a tincture.

They walked silently. Reflecting deeply over everything that had come to pass in the past few hours. Engrossed in their thoughts, they entered a maze of souvenir shops, in the narrow lanes of the Srisailam temple premises that were now brightly lit in colors of gold and orange

"The base metal was transmuted to gold," Jake reminded her. "But what do you think? Did that tincture possess the power to cure ills and extend one's lifespan, like say, curb the aging process and bring back youth?"

She thought it over for a second or two, before replying, "I think so. Since there are numerous tales that speak about men living for more than hundred years, and even thousand years, out of necessity of food and water. The nectar of immortality might have made it possible. These extraordinary men go aloof and spend their time in caves, forests or mountains. For years and sometimes decades, they stay there, occasionally showing themselves, say to coincide with some rare astronomical or celestial phenomena. This concoction gave them control over their own death."

"But science declares this concept ludicrous," Jake added.

Taneez shook her head in disbelief at his reluctance. "I haven't seen a historian like you who denies the evidence of his own eyes. You're a typical skeptic, Jake. You've seen what happened to the mixture in the furnace. What more do you want to believe that there are things in the universe governed by laws that defies science?"

Jake shrugged. "I don't know why, but that's how I am. I'm a skeptic and being one, it's hard for me to believe that transmutation of metals is possible by means of neutron bombardment. Or whatever processes the *sadhu* might've used."

Taneez chuckled. "If only you knew there was also something called cold fusion."

"I'm sorry," Jake made a face, wondering if she was trying to tell him that there was a process other than nuclear fusion that didn't require enormous amounts of energy to fuse protons into nuclei of atoms of different elements, or to knock them off, changing their atomic configuration.

Taneez explained, "In 1989, a leading British electrochemist Martin Fleischmann, reported that he had experienced cold fusion, a kind of low energy nuclear reaction at room temperature, in his experiment. This discovery garnered enough media attention as a new form of energy source, an alternative, free and abundant energy source that held huge promise to solve a lot of our energy problems. But owing to their failure to reproduce the same conditions in succeeding experiments, their discovery was branded a pathological science, funding companies withdrew their support and the experiment was shelved. Perhaps, by some fluke, they had stumbled across low energy nuclear reactions. That which was once fully understood by the alchemists. But what this experiment showed us was that there is some kind of energy or force that brings about nuclear reactions at low temperatures."

"Which in this case was brought about by the Philosopher's Stone," Jake concluded.

"Very much so," Taneez accorded. "The Philosopher's Stone is a magical substance that when added in a precise quantity, undergoes spontaneous disintegration under certain conditions, giving rise to an enormous amount of heat, which creates tremendous turbulence, speeding up the particle, slamming particles against atoms, knocking off or fusing protons into their nuclei, altering their atomic configuration and thus converting them to another element."

"The same as what happens in a particle accelerator," Jake added, walking ahead.

He turned in time to see Taneez had vanished from his side. Panicked, he looked around and spotted her approaching one of the souvenir shops off to their side. Jake raced after her and saw her staring at the image of an old man framed in glass and displayed for sale. Strangely, the old man in the glass frame had a close resemblance to someone with whom they had spent the last few thrilling hours: the *sadhu.*

Taneez lifted the glass frame and looked at it in astonishment. Jake took the frame from her hand and gazed at it before asking the owner in Hindi, "Brother, who is this man?"

"Vyalipa," the man replied, explaining that he was a popular late seventeenth century *siddha,* a sorcerer and powerful *siddha purusha.*

That sent a chill down their spines. Taneez knew that *siddha purushas* were alchemists.

"From the seventeenth century?" Jake asked, scared to the core. "He lived way back in 1790," the shopkeeper retold. "There are many accounts of people who have actually seen his soul wandering in the deep forest. Somewhere in these hills, there was a secret laboratory where he used to practice alchemy. It's where he guards his treasure."

Taneez barely understood Hindi, yet she could guess what the shopkeeper was saying. *Aatma…soul…*She felt her head spinning. She began to sweat.

Jake was swept away by the sheer intensity of this shocking revelation.

"But what is so great about him that people want to put his picture up on their walls?" Jake asked, suppressing his fear, knowing the answer well but still reluctant to believe it all.

"People look up to him as God for his victory over death," the shopkeeper replied. "Do you want to have one?"

Jake was still processing the information.

"Sir," the shopkeeper asked again. "You want it?"

"No," Jake replied. "Thanks, brother…"

Turning, he grabbed Taneez's hand and drew her away, blurting, "We've already seen him in real…"

CHAPTER 34

It had taken some good ten minutes for them to emerge from the impact of the shock.

Taneez had frozen in terror having learnt that the *sadhu, whom* they had encountered in the temple courtyard, hunting him down at his ghostly mansion and spending few thrilling hours as he made them privy to grant art of alchemy, was supposed to have died some two centuries ago.

Leading her by her hand, Jake had walked her into the temple courtyard and had her seated on one of the benches facing the main shrine. In sheer shock, she hadn't spoken since.

With the real identity of the *sadhu* revealed, everything appeared like a terrifying nightmare. The gloomy subterranean passageway, the secret laboratory and the *sadhu* appearing in human form was one of ghastly chain of events barely had anyone from their time had endured. It was appalling to believe that they had been part of a journey through the world of alchemy under the tutelage of a long- dead alchemist.

Watching the temple's shrine looming large in front of them, illuminated against the full moon sky, Taneez spoke softly, explaining to Jake that there were things in the world that science had no answers for. There were countless aspects of the universe that man was unaware of or unable to accept as real and possible.

"Science gives us space for inventions," Taneez said, "but at the same time, its prescribed guidelines constrict us from believing in anything that exists but cannot be accounted for practically. Anything that science cannot explain practically, it simply disapproves as hypothetical and conjectural."

Jake had to agree. Although he was a hardcore science guy, the transmutation of precious metal from what had seemed worthless elements had turned his belief in science topsy-turvy, which further was strengthened by Taneez's explanation of the Philosopher's Stone.

"Science was created by man," Taneez added thoughtfully. "Sadly, that's a fact man always tends to forget. Today, if science's perspective on alchemists is clouded, if science is reluctant to accept that alchemists were successful in transmuting inferior metals into gold, then it's purely ignorance. It's proof that this concept of Alchemy is beyond science's comprehension." She paused, before declaring solemnly, "In a way, science's prescribed guidelines are hindering inventions. If science wants to understand the laws of universe, it needs to push its boundaries."

After a moment of silence, Jake looked up to find Taneez lost in thought. "What is it?"

"Nothing," Taneez said, snapping back from her thoughts. "I'm wondering what to make of it."

"Of what?"

"Was the *sadhu* really long dead or did the elixir keep him alive?"

"There's not much difference, if you ask me," Jake said, beaming. Taneez looked at him, waiting him to continue.

"I don't know about you, but I have a different understanding of a ghost or a soul," Jake said looking at the beautifully illumined Gopuram of the temple. "Everything in the universe exists in a state of vibrations. Every living and non-living thing has a specific vibrational frequency that decides their dimensions and visibility. Amoeba, the smallest living creature on earth, is a two-dimensional organism. It cannot see us, but we can see it, as we are creatures of higher dimensions. The soul is the essence of life as it animates the human body. When we die, our souls leave our bodies and enter a higher dimension. A distinct dimension from where they can see us, but we cannot see them. They are now the entities of higher dimensions with different vibrational frequencies that make them invisible to us. But there's a point here..." Jake broke off, glancing at her, maintaining the suspense.

"What?"

"I'm only starting to comprehend that the *sadhu* was a spiritually evolved being. He had complete control over his spiritual existence, which gave him the ability to tune the frequency levels of the vibrations of his being and enter into any dimension at his will. Like we tune our radio frequency to the band of our favorite music stations. In the same manner, he would occasionally tune himself and enter our dimension at will. Like he did today."

"Hermes Trismegistus...," Taneez whispered. "He, too, was often found hovering between the divine and human worlds with his magical powers."

"As above...So below...," Jake whispered, finally getting the crux of the concept. It spoke of different dimensions, higher and lower dimensions where the secret of life was embedded.

They jumped at the sudden ringing of the cell phone. It was Taneez's mobile chiming in her pocket. She pulled it out, answered the call and hung up, turning to Jake.

"That was a call from my tour coordinator. They have arranged a night stay at one of dormitories here." She stood up from the bench.

Smiling, she extended her hand, "Time to part..."

Jake stood up and shook her hand, reluctant to let her go. Then again, he realized, it was inevitable. *That's life*...everything would come to cease, every moment, every second and the end to their short, unexpected rendezvous had arrived. One that was mysteriously sweet and memorable.

Waving goodbye, she walked away, making it out of the temple through the main entrance. Jake turned and gave one last look to the classical skyline of the Mallikarjuna Temple.

Its luminous tower now glowed in a white and golden hue, imposing great grandeur against the moonlit sky. As it soared in the sky towards the sublime source of illumination, so deep it descended below through a staircase that allowed man to enter the bowels of earth, where the greatest treasure of mankind awaited.

As above...So below...

Recalling the hermetic axiom, he bowed down in deep veneration and offered his heartfelt gratitude. For it had served him well, with all he needed and would continue to serve all those who sought true wisdom with a pure heart. Then he walked off, with a thought that this place held a great secret that very few men had ever known and even fewer had seen.

CHAPTER 35

It is incredible…

Witnessing the silvery magnetic box transform in front of him Jake's eyes nearly bulged out of their sockets.

Half an hour ago, after exiting the temple courtyard, Jake had entered a small tea stall on the sidewalk and had ensconced himself in a corner seat, away from the direct view of the main door, sipping coffee and pondering the last two lines of the riddle. Soon, his heart had raced as every word of the riddle began to unscramble, gradually making sense.

Seek what they possess privileged to someone worthy,
Its glorious power shall transform this box unto thee.

Without doubt, Jake could tell that the word 'what" in the sentence *'what they possess privileged to someone worthy'* referred to the Philosopher's Stone. Then he concentrated on trying to identify the next set of words:

'Its glorious power shall transform this box untothee.'

At that moment, a small boy who had served him his coffee ran past Jake in haste, nudging his shoulder and jostling the cup of coffee in Jake's hand. A few drops of the piping hot beverage got spilled on the box.

The boy had apologized immediately, but Jake gave him a *that's ok* pat on his shoulder and turned his focus to the magnetic box, only to be appalled discovering a small portion of it had melted under the heat of spilled drops of coffee.

Although he had initially thought that the meaning of words *'Its glorious power'* suggested fire or heat, he had assumed that more than two thousand degrees Celsius of heat would be required to melt this solid magnetic box. He hadn't expected the box to have such a low melting point as to transform under the heat of coffee, which could not be more than seventy degrees Celsius.

Finding it hard to trust his own eyes, he had picked up the magnetic box, touching the melted part to ensure that what he saw was true.

Once he confirmed it, he had asked the same boy for a bowl of hot water and had dropped the box into it.

For the first half minute, there was no change. Then the magnetic box gradually melted like butter in the hot water. Its thin silvery top layer peeled away from its surface, dripping off its side, settling at the bottom of the bowl, forming a silvery pool of molten metal, exposing a dark metallic grey box hidden underneath.

Recognition hit Jake like lightning. Staring at the transformed box, Jake realized what the coating was made of—known as Field's metal, it was a fusible alloy of Bismuth, Tin and Indium. It had a low melting point and was primarily used to solder metal onto glass and to make a metal-to-glass seal for vacuum.

Jake wore a pensive smile, when memories from his yesteryear came back as this wondrous fused alloy had become part of his science project back in school. His father, with all the necessary elements and technology, had guided him in making up the project. Though it had many commercial applications, but Jake had never imagined his father would use it in this ingenious way, for a distinct cause—to conceal something precious, of inestimable worth.

Feeling victorious, Jake fixed his eyes on the magnetic box that was now fully transformed into a metallic grey box with the pentagram star with the inscription **'As above…So below…'** still visible at the center.

Gingerly lowering his fingers into the bowl, he picked up the box and wiped it clean with a napkin. He could see that the first riddle inscribed on the underside of the box had vanished along with the fused alloy, serving its purpose. Now replaced by a tiny clasp, which appeared on one side, making the box look more like a small chest.

Taking a deep breath, Jake tried to settle his mind which was turbulent with speculation —had his father and his associates really harbored scriptures holding the secrets of alchemy, recipes for creating the Philosopher's Stone? If that had to be the case then the involvement of DIA in the conspiracy made no sense. There was no logical connection between the DIA and the recipe of the Philosopher's Stone. Answers to these perplexing questions, Jake knew, could be sealed within the box.

He reached for the clasp, tipped it and popped it open to reveal a small paper scroll. He plucked the scroll from its mount and placed it on the table. Pinning down the top edge of the scroll with a finger, Jake carefully unrolled the scroll until four lines which read like another riddle, appeared:

Rock Temple of Ellora holds a marvel of past,
From heaven it beholds an assembly on earth aghast,
Hidden deep within the mountain far apart,
Unleash the key, guards two voluptuous Ajantan art.

Beneath the riddle, there was something more:

Jake's eyes tried to make sense of what seemed like a very complex cryptic illustration—a circle replete with random English letters enclosed by a ravenous snake feeding on its own tail, devouring the two scripts of cipher text.

After staring at it for a while longer, he felt a deep anxiety thinking that the secret, *The Lost Arcanum,* was still far from his reach. There was one more riddle to be solved; he had to decipher the cryptic lines running the length of the snake's body.

Committing it to his memory, Jake re-read the riddle. He could easily identify two words: Ajanta and Ellora. These were the names of popular tourist attractions in India, world-class magnificent cave complexes in Aurangabad, Maharashtra.

Still, he needed some clarity on the text.

Entering an adjacent telephone booth, he placed a call to Riya. After the fourth ring, she answered, expressing her surprise over his call. Then they exchanged vital information, most of which he ignored but what she had to say about AD was disturbing.

"He's quite upset with what's happened yesterday" Riya said with concern.

"Any intel on David and his team?"

"Guess what," Riya paused for a beat. "You've put yourself on the most wanted list in Intelligence."

Jake exhaled loudly, knowing it was inevitable after making away with a link to a prized treasure.

He was helpless on that front. And against all odds, the presence of Riya on his side was the sole consolation amid this turbulence, when people dear to him, like AD, had locked horns with him. She was like a sibling to him, standing shoulder to shoulder with him through thick and thin. Now again, after Jake had revealed his next destination, she was backing him up with whatever information she thought he would need to keep up with the quest.

She was silent after Jake narrated the whole day's events. "Jake, I don't feel even close to understanding what's really the riddle is pointing at. But from what little I know about the names cited there, these are rock-cut mountains in the district of Aurangabad in the state of Maharashtra. That's all I know."

"Quite enough."

"When are you leaving for Aurangabad?" Riya asked. "Right away, if you can help me."

As he explained his requirement, she put him on hold before returning shortly.

"Jake, there's a flight at 5.00AM from Hyderabad to Chikalthana Exactly eight hours from now."

"What's that place like?" he asked her.

"Chikalthana airport. It's as close as you can get to those two caves. Some two hours to reach at the most. Perhaps, you should leave right away," she said before giving him details on where to pick up his tickets.

"Thanks, Riya."

"Keep me posted on your progress," Riya said, before hanging up.

CHAPTER 36

Friday, August 10, 2017,
11 AM.
Aurangabad.

Jake pushed back comfortably into the plush seat of a luxurious Volvo bus, as it pulled off from its source, en-route to the historical caves of Ellora.

He frowned, looking at his watch. The delay of an hour and fifteen minutes had got on his nerves. He had emerged from the Chikalthana airport and entered an apparel shop, where he had shed his dirty clothes and pulled on a pair of faded denim trousers and a dark brown leather jacket over a black collared T-shirt.

He was indecisive choosing between a taxi, which provided him the least security from the Intelligence people, and the tourist bus, which furnished him with the perfect camouflage among other passengers, finally opting for the latter.

He slid a casual glance to his side, at the window seat occupied by a lady whose features were obscured under the linen, with little curls of her long dark hair pushing through it. *Strange,* Jake thought, finding someone bundled in a sheet considering the humid weather outside.

Returning his attention to the task at hand, he pulled the scroll from the box and memorized the first line of the riddle.

Rock Temple of Ellora holds a marvel of past…

Rocks withstood the destructive forces of time, being both a livelihood to the sculptors and a medium to showcase the passions of the kings who commissioned their legends and everything of significance they wanted to convey to future generations.

Knowing this, Jake realized that the riddle was pointing to some sculptor who had chiseled on the surface of a rock—a narration in stone probably. Slipping the scroll back into the box, he relaxed in his seat, stretching out his body. He glanced sideways again, toward his neighbor who still seemed to be buried under the linen. Turning away, he discovered some magazines in a pouch at the back of the seat in front of him. Jake pulled it out and read the title.

A Complete Guide to the World Class Caves of Ajanta and Ellora

He felt relived since he knew this book would spare him from boring tour guides, while narrowing his search. Determined, he quickly flipped to the pages on the Ellora caves that read:

Thirty kilometers from Aurangabad district of Maharashtra, this historical site is a spellbinding, remarkable and unsurpassed accomplishment of man in the form of rock-cut cave monuments, dating back to as early as second century BCE. Abundantly filled with exquisite wall paintings and life-like sculptures, this site is considered a masterpiece of architecture, fusing three different religious arts: Buddhism, Hinduism and Jainism. It houses 34 caves in all. UNESCO identified this monument as a World Heritage Site in 1983.

The thought of thirty-four caves in Ellora was troubling. He flipped the pages of the guide book, skipping those that seemed irrelevant, such as the classification of caves as *viharas* or monasteries and *chaitya grihas* or temples, on the basis of the exalted purposes each one had served. He was still reading through the book, when a familiar voice calling him at his side in surprise.

"Jake!"

When he turned, he was equally stunned. "Taneez?"

"This is really surprising," she said, turning to him fully. "What are you doing here?"

Jake couldn't trust his eyes: it was Taneez again in the window seat next to him, suave and charming as ever, the same graceful smile and her gleaming cerulean eyes beneath her brows that suggested that she shared same exciting of seeing him again.

"Well, that's supposed to be my question," Jake replied beaming a wide smile.

Needless to say, he too was very excited to see her, not expecting her at all. After they'd parted last night, he thought he would never see her again. Yet, neither of them ever knew what destiny had planned for them. Taneez briefed him on how after she had left Srisailam yesterday, she had flown in from Hyderabad earlier this morning to Aurangabad and driven straight from the airport in a taxi to hop on board this Volvo bus.

Interrupting their discussion, a voice on the speaker announced the arrival of their destination: the caves of Ellora.

CHAPTER 37

The epitome of grace…

Jake whispered to himself, gazing at Taneez. He could not help but closely observe Taneez as she cast a dazzling smile before alighting from the bus and heading towards the cave entrance with her fellow tourists. She looked stunning in a pair of brown leggings and off-white printed sleeveless kurta, with a maroon leather handbag slung over her shoulder.

Mesmerized by her looks, Jake's footsteps slackened, capturing every bit of her sparkling being in his memory. It was a feast for his senses with her mellifluous voice like a symphonious tune from a flute. It took him a minute to emerge from the spell she seemed to have cast and step aside from the tourist group, into the fresh aura of nature seeping from every element of the lush green environs surrounding the cave complex of Ellora.

He rejoiced and savored the tranquil ambiance of this secluded piece from history. The place had instantly appealed to him. The large basaltic formation of hills as a backdrop, a pleasant vast landscape to the rear and the tremendous craftsmanship of the Ellora caves in the middle. The caves, carved directly from the rock face of the staggering cliffs surrounding the site, were an outstanding and breathtaking visual.

He had never imagined that his life would take such a course. Suddenly airlifted from the busy lanes of Delhi, he had landed in the middle of intriguing and mysterious Srisailam, from where he had traveled to this historical monument that was emblematic of religious harmony.

Coming out of his reverie, Jake channeled his attention back to the task at hand. He stopped momentarily at the entrance of the cave complex from where he gauged the length of the largest single monolithic structure of basaltic hill. It trailed north and housed different caves, each cut from the vertical face. The Buddhist caves, the oldest ones, began at the southern end. And if he was right he was standing at the southern end, which was the starting point.

But the riddle points to some temple at Ellora.

Unsure of whether it was a Buddhist, Hindu or Jain temple, he rifled through the travel guidebook, narrowing down his search. What he discovered was that except for cave ten, the others were *viharas*—monasteries.

Cave ten was a temple.

I should be looking for the answer there…

Accordingly, Jake threaded past cave one, two and so on, up to cave nine, stealing brief glances at each one. Some caves were small, while the rest were larger and adorned with sculptures of deities and of Buddha. Coming to a stop by the foot of cave ten, he scrutinized its entrance for a few seconds.

This cave was popularly known as the Vishwakarma cave; once flanked by a large wall, it was now in a partial ruin.

Vishwakarma cave is the most famous among the group of Buddhist *chaitya grihas* or temples. Built around 700 AD, it has a multi- storied rock-cut court entrance. Beguiled by the other worldly charm, he stepped into the courtyard of the Vishwakarma cave, glancing at two pillared porticos on the either side on the back walls housing chambers and sanctuaries that were never completed. His attention was drawn to the facade on the gallery that consisted a three-lobed opening with beautiful triads—each composed of a male and two female celestials converging over the axis of the arch. The railings of the gallery and the roof were embellished with bas-reliefs of deities and several other figurines, rendering it more expansive, although only some appeared intact while the others have been scourged by time.

Taking a narrow flight of stone stairs, he ambled into the main, large elongated hall that held a few tourists. The hall was impressively colonnaded. It had a central nave divided into two side aisles, separated by massive twenty-eight octagonal columns with plain bracket capitals.

With each step that took him deeper onto the hall's stone floor, an austere air of Buddhist virtues filled his senses, insinuating the ambiance this place might have once served the hermits who took refuge here, desiring a solitary life, while dedicating their entire time to the contemplation of their deeper essence.

Once deep inside, Jake found some tourists captivated by the interior visuals of the cave. With raised heads, they absorbed the vaulted roof of the main hall, which bore incredible rib-like structures resembling wooden architecture, and the massive rectangular columns supporting the hall and adorned with beautiful vases and foliage.

In the middle of this grand historical set-up was a stupendous three-and- a-half meter statue of the Buddha at the apsidal end of the hall, in *vyakhyana mudra*---teaching posture, inside a *stupa* on a lion throne. Flanked by two standing attendant *bodhisattvas* and two celestial couples on either side with the *bodhi* or *pipal* tree, it forked out over Buddha's head, forming an arch and enclosing the entire scene.

Jake began to survey the hall with great interest. But to his surprise, he felt someone brush past his shoulder and walk ahead.

It was Taneez.

She was seemingly charmed by the place and surveyed the gigantic space, turning on her heels in a slow circle, in wonder. "This place is incredible." Her voice echoed in the hollow of the cavern. "Exactly how I was told it would be!"

Jake puzzled. "Who told you what?"

"These caves in Ellora and Ajanta complex," she began sweeping her gaze to the roof, "are significant because of their careful positioning around the cliffs. Its arrangement reveals an unusually advanced understanding of celestial activity."

"The layout of these caves is aligned with the position of the stars?" Jake rephrased her sentence and asked suspiciously, "Is that what you mean?"

"Precisely," she answered, lowering her gaze to meet his, smiling. "These caves are oriented in various directions. Some face the south and some the west. But the *chaitya grihas*, which serve as temples, are mainly oriented towards the east, facing the rising sun. Like this one where we're standing right now."

Jake reflected on it.

"These conclusions are drawn by a researcher at our university," Taneez explained. "He found that ancient people in India had a strong fascination for the universe and the relationship of heavenly bodies. Some caves are oriented towards winter solstice and some towards summer solstice. It's said that on the morning of these solstices, the first sunlight filtering through the large windows in the facade illuminate the stupas in these caves."

Jake turned, glancing over his shoulder towards the three-lobed opening at high with beautiful triads and traced the imaginary path of the sun's rays entering through it and illuminating the Buddha in the stupa. The pattern of rib like structure created to mimic the rays of the sun.

Solstices are astronomical events occurring twice every year when the sun reaches the highest or lowest annual altitude in the sky above the horizon. In a broader sense, the days on this event are either the longest (summer) or shortest (winter) of the year. In many cultures across the world, these events are celebrated as festivals marking the beginning or the midpoint of winter and summer. In India, people mark this event by celebrating the festival Makar Sankranti.

What Taneez said seemed credible to Jake as this cave had the name of Vishwakarma, the son of Brahma, who was thought to be the presiding deity of craftsmen and the architect of whole universes and had designed palaces, flying chariots and weapons for gods. This meant that the positioning of this cave of Vishwakarma aligned along one of those solstices was highly likely.

"Look at the roof," Taneez said, elevating her eyes at it. "These rib-like structures resembling wooden architecture are actually created to mimic the pattern the sun rays take upon entering through the opening in the facade."

Jake observing the ceiling, could not deny the fact. However, he found it irrelevant to the riddle he was trying to solve. Ignoring it for the present, he walked up to the stupa and observed it meticulously, wondering if there was any possibility of the riddle pointing to this set-up.

Taneez intervened again, appearing by his side. "You know something, Jake? The stupa is symbolical of the power of flight. Stupas were always used by Buddha as a means to ascend into the heavens."

He turned to her and frowned. "Now you say that stupa is some kind of a spacecraft?"

She pulled out the travel guide from her leather handbag and tapped on the pictures of cave nineteen and twenty-six. "Look here, the Buddha is placed inside a stupa just like the one in front of you. These works suggest that Buddha was going into space manipulating some type of control inside the stupa."

Jake exhaled exasperatedly. "That's your understanding which is conjecture. Not that it is true."

"Then what do you think, Jake?" She looked at him. "What do you have to say about these intricate artworks of stone? These high elaborate ceilings built and tunneled by chipping inside a solid rock. Don't you think it is a difficult task unless you have some sophisticated high-tech gears and equipment to make it perfectly oriented towards the solstices?"

Jake was considering the implications of her questions.

"It's quite evident that there was some highly intelligent race involved in the construction of these caves," Taneez said with conviction, "some unknown entities…"

"Cut the crap!" Jake cut her short. "Your theories present a whole new dimension to these caves, inviting conspiracy theorists to pick on these ancient subterranean spaces that have remained unmolested for thousands of years."

CHAPTER 38

Ellora Caves is the largest megalithic rock-hewn monastic temple complex in the world. Shaped out of a volcanic basaltic formation of Deccan trap--a part of the Sahayadri mountain range that runs parallel to the western coast of the Indian peninsula, these stone structures dates back to the cretaceous era on the geological timescale.

According to historical sources, the thirty-four caves of Ellora were built by the Rashtrakuta dynasty, a royal lineage that ruled most of the Indian subcontinent between the sixth and tenth century. This stone complex is more than two kilometers in length, chiseled out of hills rising abruptly from the surrounding plains on the south and west side bearing witness to three main religions prevalent in the Indian sub-continent during the period: Buddhism, Hinduism and Jainism--A testimony to great Indian spirit of tolerance and religious harmony that allowed religions to co-exist and flourish.

The first twelve Buddhist caves trail successively from south to north, having been commissioned between the fifth and eighth century. Of these, only cave ten is a temple while the rest are monasteries. Caves thirteen to twenty-nine are devoted to Brahmins. Constructed around the sixth century, these are undoubtedly the best known. Most important and spectacular of these are cave fifteen, known as the Cave of Ten Avatars or Dashavatara, and cave sixteen, the Kailasanatha Temple. Caves thirty to thirty-four belong to the Jains.

Owing to its location, in close proximity to the ancient trade route connecting the western ports of the Arabian Sea, the Ellora caves were never deserted. Many royal dynasties extended their patronage to religious establishments and countless imperial personages and ardent travelers visited this place on a regular basis.

This afternoon, however, Jake, who belonged to neither of the two social classes, imbibed all this information from his guidebook and paced ahead, banishing all that Taneez had implied in cave ten.

Taneez simply moved away from the tourist group and followed him from caves thirteen to fifteen, cross-referencing the exquisite carved friezes with images in her travel guide.

Jake was getting desperate. He scurried down the blocks of caves feeling dismayed as the answer, though somewhere nearby, seemed to be getting farther away with each step he took. Besides, he was starting to worry about his strange interactions with Taneez. He realized that she had started to wonder if he was really who he claimed to be. It was evident from the way she seemed to be testing him.

"Jake, I was wondering, you're a historian," she said in a hurried tone, keeping pace with him. "A camera and notes are a historian's equipment, or say basic tools, so he'd never forget to carry them on visits to historical sites." She paused, casting a suspicious glance at him. "It's strange that I see none with you."

Jake continued to walk. Although her inquiry was like a bolt from the blue, he had maintained his composure. He was not one who would waver when questions like these were hurled at him.

"My two eyes make up a camera," Jake replied coolly. "And my mind is a memory unit where everything gets recorded."

Taneez made a face.

He continued, "Besides, you should ask this question of yourself as well." He lowered his gaze to her handbag on her shoulder. "I never seen a researcher with no camera or any notes."

Taneez's face turned ashen. She had not expected her questions to backfire. She fumbled as she replied, "Actually…the real stuff is…"

Before she could complete her explanation, she found Jake's attention drift and pause at something in the background. He then strode off, that soon turned into a sprint.

Taneez stuffed the travel guide in her handbag and ran after him, coming to halt before a gigantic structure that extruded from the ground, as if breaking free from the womb of Mother Nature and reaching skywards, defying all laws of science.

Jake stood still, seemingly taken aback by sheer splendor of its large imposing structure. As such is the magnificence of the brilliant architecture of Kailasanatha Temple, whose sheer magnitude would leave everyone short of breath.

CHAPTER 39

The Kailasanatha Temple at Ellora is a colossal structure and the most lavishly elegant, refined rock-cut temple in the world.

Built as a replica of Mount Kailash--the abode of Lord Shiva in the Himalayan mountain ranges, this multi-storied free-standing complex was commissioned under the reign of Rashtrakuta King Krishna-I, circa 756-766, which took more than a hundred years for completion.

This enormous temple is chiseled on a staggering cliff from a humongous rock and detached by digging huge trenches on the north and south ends of the hill. The ingenious sculptors and architects, surpassing all designing standards went on to create a full temple, carving vertically down into the face of a living rock, achieving both, architectural grandeur and sculptural wonder. With its dimensions almost twice as that of the Parthenon of Acropolis, Athens, measuring an astonishing thirty-six meters in height and eighty-six meters in length and fifty meters in width, makes it one of the spell binding rock cut temple in the world.

The main entrance forms a high *gopuram* with a recessed balconied tower, which serves as a curtain, obscuring the direct view of the temple. The exterior facade is adorned with several contrasting themes of Hindu deities on opposite walls. The north wall has sculptures of Shiva, his different forms, Vishnu and Brahma, seeking the beginning and end of the flaming *linga* and ultimately turning out to be Shiva in the ultimate form. These scenes summarize Shiva as the supreme deity, encouraging unity among other deities for the pursuit of knowledge in order to achieve *moksa,*--release from the cycle of rebirth. The south wall portrays, in almost epic proportions, Vishnu in his dwarf form, Vamana, defeating the demon Bali and claiming the universe for God.

For history buffs, this monument is an absolute visual delight, forming a crowning glory, a peerless centerpiece of Ellora standing as compelling evidence to the accomplishment of ancient Indian artisans and architects. Taneez had to admit that even she was enthralled by its splendor. By the time she had collected her thoughts, she saw Jake entering the temple through the high entrance gate. She raced after him. Although she knew it was none of her business, she believed she had to unravel the mystery surrounding this man who called himself a historian.

As she made her way through the entrance with other tourists and strode past them, she appeared under the rock bridge attached to the porch of pavilion. Few steps to her left was a massive rock pillar. She hastened onward with her head raised to take in the loftiness of the pillar, carefully climbing a wide stone staircase that raised her to the floor level of the courtyard.

It was a U-shaped courtyard with three-storied galleries that opened up on all sides. And in the center, an impressive edifice spearing the skyline was the main shrine, a thirty-meter high, three-tiered, pyramid-like structure resembling a south Indian temple, supported on a lofty plinth sculpted to give an effect of life-sized elephants and lions seemingly holding the structure aloft. Adding to the grandeur, it was flanked by two hundred feet tall grand and lofty monolithic pillars known as *dwajastambhas*.

The interior of the temple is a pillared hall with sixteen square pillars. In addition, the shrine comprises gathering halls, inner and outer rooms, alcoves, recessed balconies, with an enormous lingam at its heart and adorned with finely crafted pilasters and images of deities on the walls. The ones to the left of the entrance are Shaivite and those to the right are Vaishnavite. Staggering scenes from the epic *Ramayana* are carved on the north wall of the temple and from the *Mahabharata* on the south wall, providing a visual feast to ardent devotees

Mesmerized by the structure, Taneez moved deeper into the courtyard, looking this way and that. The vivid sculptures on the outer walls of the temple captivated her imagination. But in the midst of this, she felt herself being pulled away by her curious case --Jake, whom she spotted standing in a corner on the north side of the temple.

His gaze had crept higher on the outer wall of the temple, closely analyzing something that she couldn't quite make out until she had covered the distance between them and found out for herself that what had his attention riveted was a beautiful rock carving.

CHAPTER 40

Using her hand to shield her eyes from the mid-afternoon sun, Taneez lifted her head to look at the sculpture on the outer wall of the Temple Jake was investigating.

Confused, Taneez pulled out the travel guide from her handbag and riffled through page after page until she found what she was looking for. "Here it is," she tapped on the page. "This carving you're looking at, depicts one of the instances from the Hindu epic *Ramayana*."

Jake turned to see what she was showing.

"It portrays the fight between Ravana and the vulture called Jatayu," Taneez furnished, furthering, "Ravana is in a close tussle with the bird Jatayu en-route to his kingdom Lanka, in his flying chariot after abducting Sita."

Jake thought about this, knowing it did not seem to be connected to the lines in the riddle.

"And it says," Taneez continued, "that the flying chariot was a modern-day aircraft and the vulture was an unmanned drone."

"What?" Jake felt it preposterous. He reached for the travel guide in her hand and looked through it himself. "Where does it say that?"

Taneez allowed him to look at the book and waited. After a while, he glanced up at her suspiciously.

Taneez chortled. "Actually, that's my take on the scene."

Jake breathed out in disbelief. "You are insane."

"I am," Taneez replied accepting his comment with a sincere smile. "That's what people tell me when they get a fist of reality in the face of their ignorance."

Jake shook his head at her. "She's correct," a polite voice informed.

When they spun around, they saw a well-groomed, middle-aged man in blue denim trousers, a white T-shirt and a cowboy hat walking towards them.

Now, who is this? Jake wondered, tired of intruders.

Flashing a genial smile, the man looked at Taneez. "She's right about the flying chariot."

"In fact, if you look carefully..." the man pointed to the scene carved high on the temple outer wall.

Jake and Taneez glanced up to where he was pointing.

"Ravana is using a flying device known as Pushpaka Vimana. Not a flying chariot as the epic narrates. That device is attached to his back which is fastened around his waist by a safety harness. It has all the functional units of a modern-day jetpack. It has propellers. It has a safety roll. It has a thrust nozzle, through which heat was pumped out as needed for the jetpack to take off."

Jake wondered at his identity. Taneez, too mirrored her concern, turning back and looking at the man.

The man seemed to sense this and introduced himself. "I'm Arun Kumar, an art historian."

"Wow.." Taneez said, excited. "Then meet, Mr. Jake," she said, inviting him towards Jake. "He too, is a historian."

Arriving closer, Arun Kumar extended his hand which Jake shook hesitantly, glancing at Taneez with a frown.

Taneez ignored him and said to Arun Kumar. "I have been trying to convince him that all the carvings here on the walls, half-animal half-god, flying angels and all the flying machines shown in the background had at one point in the past existed for real. The ancients carved what they saw. But Jake is a bit of a skeptic. A modern historian who prefers to bolster his research on the basis of credible scientific proof."

The art historian beamed at Jake.

Jake hesitated, unsure how to tackle the situation. "Actually..." he trailed off, trying to gather his words. "This idea that a flying machine existed back then leaves me in serious doubt. Did the ancients really possess the profound scientific knowledge that would have enabled them to build flying machines millennia before the Wright brothers?"

"They actually did," Arun Kumar said with conviction. "They had constructed a powerful flying machine known as 'Vimana.' It was a fast aerial vehicle that matched the speed of the modern-day aircraft. There's a whole mass of fascinating information about these mysterious flying vehicles lying intact in ancient Indian epics and other sacred scriptures."

"Indeed," Taneez took over, "the Wright brothers borrowed the design of their airplane from the ancient Indian epics of *Ramayana* and *Mahabharata*."

"To be precise," Arun Kumar interjected, "they borrowed their design from Talpade."

What in the world was he saying?

As a matter of fact, Arun Kumar explained, most Indians are oblivious to the fact that the design of the modern-day airplanes was heavily borrowed from a model first invented by Shivakar Bapuji Talpade: a Sanskrit scholar and Indian scientist in 1895, some eight years before the Wright brothers. This unmanned flight, which served as the archetypal model later for the Wright brothers' invention, took off on a test ride before a large audience, including some noted personalities like Maharaja Sayajirao Gaekwad-III of Vadodara and Bombay High Court Judge Mahadeva Govinda Ranade, at Chowpathy Beach, Bombay. It flew about fifteen hundred feet in the air for seventeen minutes before it crash landed.

"Okay, but what source corroborates this event?" Jake asked casually, not attempting to offend the art historian.

"The Kesari newspaper of Pune," Arun Kumar replied. "Edited by renowned freedom fighter Bal Gangadhar Tilak himself. He reported this event."

"In that case," Taneez said, "Talpade is the first creator of the aircraft."

"Of course," Arun Kumar agreed. "His aircraft design was entirely based on the exemplary texts of the great Indian sage Maharishi Bhardwaaja's *Vaimanika Sastra*."

The revelation left Jake and Taneez in wonder. Their reactions though were nothing new to Arun Kumar, as this piece of information was lost in the pages of Indian history.

"It is aeronautical science from the *Rig-Veda*," Arun Kumar explained "discovered in some ancient temple. It formed the basis for the design of his aircraft, which describes in detail the construction of what is called the mercury vortex engine."

"I read about this mercury vortex engine recently," Jake said, trying to recall where he had come across it. "Some scientific organization is employing this technology."

"Yes, you're right," Arun Kumar concurred. "One of the world's foremost, richest, most powerful scientific organizations is endeavoring to re-create the same technology." He paused for a few seconds thinking they recognized it. "NASA. They are using mercury bombardment units powered by solar cells for developing aircraft for future use.

"This ancient document, the *Vaimanika Shastra*, probes into metals that were used in these crafts. It talks about electricity and power sources. It talks about the pilots and the clothing they have to wear. It talks about the food they eat during the flight. It talks even about the weapons that were loaded on these airships. This flight manual is synonymous in every respect with what we find in modern-day aircraft."

Our ancestors were extraordinary, Jake thought. The world owes them so much.

"But surprisingly," Arun Kumar continued, "despite their best efforts, NASA had failed to replicate the experiment that Talpade managed hundred and eight years ago."

"Then why praise the Wright brothers instead of Talpade?" Taneez asked earnestly. "Why did his invention go unrecognized?"

Arun Kumar explained that it was a sad truth that the Indian government had showed total negligence in this matter. The success of the Indian scientist was envied by imperial rulers. And according to some sources, Maharaja Sayajirao Gaekwad-111 of Vadodara was forced by the British Government to stop lending financial assistance to Talpade's future experiments. After his wife's death, Talpade also seemed to have lost the will to continue with his research. Following his death, the aircraft was sold to Rally Brothers--a leading British exporting company operating in Mumbai. They seemed to have transported the machine to Britain for further research and development. And unfortunately, the aircraft was never talked about or seen since.

"Talpade was an unsung hero," Arun Kumar declared solemnly, "a pioneer whose greatest invention went unacknowledged, failing to make it to the pages of history."

Arun Kumar quietened. Another such personality, he recalled, was scientist Jagadish Chandra Bose, as the world had no idea that he had laid the foundation for the technology that enabled wireless communication across the globe, by inventing a wireless of a millimeter wavelength.

"However," Arun Kumar resumed, walking up to Jake, "the mention of flying machines occurs throughout the Vedic texts. *Ramayana, Mahabharata, Rig-Veda, Yajur-Veda, Athar-Veda* and other classical Vedic scriptures like the *Satapathya Brahmana, Markandeya Purana, Vishnu Purana, Bhagavata Purana,* all make mention of *vimanas* that are identified with eloquence and marked out with different shapes: cylindrical, circular, triangular, double-deckers with portholes and domes, and saucer-shaped."

Jake's gaze grew distant, his thoughts suddenly drifting to another matter: the riddle.

He had believed that the riddle was not pointing to this specific carving. It was speaking of a marvel, another carving entirely, definitely not the one now being discussed. The whereabouts of which, he thought, this art historian might be able to provide.

I need to hurry up. Jake decided to lure the art historian into divulging more.

"That bird in the carving there," Jake pointed back at Jatayu, the bird pecking at Ravana's legs in mid-flight. "You agree it's the equivalent of a modern-day unmanned drone?"

Arun Kumar nodded. "It's the same bird that even in the state of injury had debriefed Rama on what had transpired following his intervention to thwart Ravana from taking Sita to Lanka."

"So technically speaking," Jake said calculatingly, "it was a kind of reconnaissance drone that was part of Rama's advanced surveillance system, loaded with weapons and disguised as a bird."

"Rightly said.," Arun Kumar replied. "That is what it means if you can read between the lines in the *Ramayana*."

"Do we have anymore carvings with the same theme in this temple?" Jake asked.

Arun Kumar paused for a few seconds before he replied, "Come with me. I'll show it to you."

CHAPTER 41

A *fleet of flying* chariots, steed maneuvered celestial cars, winged vehicles and floating aerial cities may sound like rip-roaring action scene from a science fiction movie, but these were all once real and their design come from ancient Indian texts. This explains how Gods and humans battled out their indifference's in the sky. The machines they used were called *vimanas*.

Vimanas are evidence of the existence of advanced civilizations in the distant past. Although many consider them a myth, several scholars and historians continue to draw interpretations from references to flying machines in ancient Indian and other older texts around the world. Rational historians continue to dismiss these texts, calling them excerpts of pure fiction. This debate, however, is likely to continue unless someone unearths hard historical evidence or an ancient flying machine itself, to support these passages. There are modern scholars who look beyond the myth. Images found on the ceiling beams of a three thousand years old New Kingdom Temple, located several hundred miles south of Cairo and the Giza Plateau at Abydos are reminiscent of modern-day aircraft, submarines and hovercraft underlining the fact that the early Egyptians knew about technology far more sophisticated than we are using today.

Likewise, various depictions of flying machines on the wall of the Kailasanatha Temple at Ellora serve as testimony to a staggeringly advanced technology practiced in India in the remote past.

Expounding on this, art historian Arun Kumar, had walked Jake and Taneez to the north side of the temple, where another carving on the similar theme was located.

The carving portrayed a cluster of men and women on the ground, some clambering over a mountain and some riding horse-drawn carts, all looking skywards at a airborne couple in a flying chariot. This unusual piece of art was carved out intricately on the face of the rock.

'Rock temple of Ellora holds a marvel of past...' Jake recalled the riddle, looking at the carving. ***'From heaven it beholds an assembly on earth aghast'***

To his understanding, the word *'it'* was referring to a flying machine, while the word *'assembly'* definitely implied the cluster of men and women, who did seem *'aghast'* at the sight of a flying machine.

The haze from the riddle lifted. *This is it*, Jake thought, knowing that the second line of the riddle fit the narrative on the carving perfectly.

Beside them, Arun Kumar quietly waited to shed more light on something specific he thought was important: a flying chariot.

"Can you see that flying chariot?" Arun Kumar asked Jake.

Jake nodded, thinking that it had wings like a bird.

"Some scholars have termed it a 'mechanical bird'," Arun Kumar informed them.

Taneez lowered her gaze from the carving to Arun Kumar, as he explained.

"References to *vimanas* in the *Mahabharata* compare their appearance to highly beautiful birds. The grotesque elements in the machines are closely interpreted as turbines and expansion chambers similar to those found in modern jet engines. Since ancient people allegorized fantastically, their narration made it much more cumbersome to understand the propulsion systems from a scientific viewpoint. *Vimanas* were often cited as being drawn by celestial steeds, elephants, swans and donkeys. It's because the ancient people had intentionally designed the encasing of the propulsion systems to resemble these animals."

"So when seen from the ground," Taneez interrupted, "they appeared real and full of life. And ancient Indians recorded these instances in the scriptures, because that is what they saw."

"Exactly," Arun Kumar agreed, excited that she had understood what he wanted to convey. "They used incongruous animal look-alikes to conceal the real nature or form of the propulsion system lest the techniques of manufacturing the *vimana* be compromised."

"Why did this have to be kept secret?" asked Jake.

"Because these flying machines were meant only for a special class of individuals, say for people from within the elite circles, who were intelligent. In the wrongs hands, it would be disaster. That's where our wise ancestors saw the danger and disguised the mechanism."

That's really great…but what about the key the riddle speaks of? Jake couldn't ignore the question blooming at the back of his mind. He was desperate to figure out the riddle and was growing anxious with every passing minute.

Hidden deep within the mountain far apart,
Unleash the key, guards two voluptuous Ajantan art…..

The lines kept clawing at him from inside.

Only a second later, he realized there were more worries lined up than he'd imagined, when a muffled sound of a bullet fired from somewhere within the courtyard of the temple, splintered the stone wall near him.

With slack-jaws, Taneez and the art historian's terror stricken gazes lowered down in unison to the discharged bullet lying only inches from the foot of Jake.

CHAPTER 42

S*hards of stone* lay scattered near the spent bullet on the floor.

As Taneez tried to recall last few moments, all that could conjure was just a sharp pain in her wrist.

What is going on? Taneez wondered, rubbing her wrist. Jake had grabbed her by her wrist and ushered her to the back of the pilaster wall of the temple, where she now remained squatted, safely, breathing heavily. All because some unknown men had shot at them.

She gripped her handbag tightly and glanced at Jake to see if it were a dream. It wasn't. The sound of breathing was loud in the silence. She realized that it was her own. The dark basaltic cliffs soaring high in front of her and to the sides of the temple, stared down at her menacingly, as though moving closer to swallow her into the gloomy colonnaded gallery at the base.

The sight was chilling. She tried to shake its sting away. But the stone cold elephants supposedly holding up the temple aloft seemed to bristle against her head with their long snouts, like a spooky urban legend greeting her with its deathly embrace.

Taneez shivered. *What is this all about?* The more she endeavored to flush out the fear gripping her thoughts, the more apprehensive she became. Never had she imagined that she would end up in such a situation, stuck in a labyrinth of stone-cut monuments where bullets were being fired without warning.

She was still dazed by what had erupted around her only minutes earlier. *Who had fired the bullet? At whom and why?* She knew the answers to these questions lay with two men: one, the art historian, Arun Kumar, who had already fled the scene for his life and the other, the man huffing at her side, darting his head out to peek at the shooters.

When Jake turned to face her, he noticed the wary look on her face. Her eyes were suspicious and loaded with questions he had no time to answer.

"Jake, what's this all about? Who are these people? Why are they shooting at us?"

Suddenly, she heard what sounded like another bullet ricocheting off the edge of the stone wall, missing Jake by a hair's breadth. She saw him duck and the next thing she realized were that her arms were being yanked out of their sockets again, with Jake forcing her to the rear end of the temple.

Once behind the rear wall, Jake drew a long breath, cursing. *They're here again*… implying those who had tried to detain him in the basement of the CBI office.

Adrenaline flooded his veins as his mind rewound what he had seen: four field-operation specialists from Intelligence, all in civilian attire, cautiously heading in their direction. One of them had obviously fired after spotting them.

The whole scene was horrifying. Pushing the thoughts from his mind, Jake let out a troubled moan and glanced over at Taneez. She seemed stunned. Her expression horrid. He knew, behind those terrorized eyes, more questions were swamping, which he hoped would be answered once he found a way out of this hellish predicament.

ЖЖЖЖЖ

With crisp agility, a field operative clutching a silencer gun in hand, took a cautious position along the edge of the exterior wall of the temple. He had fired two bullets. Both had missed the target. Reloading the gun, he patiently waited for the perfect moment to fire at his target, speaking into the microphone clipped to his throat.

"He's right in the scope. He's unarmed. But he's got company."

He glanced over his shoulder to ensure his three associates were in precise positions behind him, near the pillars, with guns tucked behind their backs, trying to draw as little attention as possible.

They waited patiently, eager to act upon his orders.

"Eliminate them," the voice at the other end ordered in a grave tone. "No other casualties. Keep it low profile.'

"Affirmative," the operative signed off.

He peeked over the edge at the rear wall of the temple. He knew, his target had taken cover there, with his companion .

He glanced back at his associates and signaled them a go.

ЖЖЖЖЖ

Hugging the rear wall of the temple, Jake peered into the corridor and was surprised to see it empty. Most of the tourists were inside the temple, which was a bad sign. He had planned their escape route hoping to seek cover among the tourists.

Jake worried over it. This was going to be his loss and his enemy's gain since it would give them the stealth they needed.

Emerging from his thoughts, Jake found Taneez's lips quivering, probably fumbling over a fresh set of questions.

"For God's sake, Jake," finally, Taneez broke her silence, insisting, "tell me, who are these men?" She gazed into his eyes. "Why are we being hunted?"

Jake saw that her cerulean eyes now burned with fear. He wanted to console her but knew this was not the time. It would have to wait.

He looked ahead, thinking of heading towards the entrance. But he realized the points would be sealed with more field operatives guarding the exit. The only cover he could think of was the door to a small shrine a few yards from the massive pillar. A while ago, he had seen a swarm of tourists flock inside. And this, he guessed, would restrict their hunters, buy him sufficient time to find an escape route.

Deciding on this course, he took a deep breath and glanced back from the edge of the rear wall to track the location of his hunters.

ӜӜӜӜӜ

Blending with the tourists, the four field operatives briskly moved towards the rear wall of the temple. Their hands were resting on the automatics inside their trouser pockets, tucked there to avoid detection by the tourists.

Until yesterday, this operation had been low profile, set to low priority. But with Jake having eluded the Intelligence officers, the stakes had been raised. The higher-ups had set the priority level to high and orders had been changed from simple detainment to execution on sight.

The operation's leader concentrated ahead. He had left three of his field operatives to guard the entrance which was also an exit. Even if the targets succeeded in escaping from the courtyard, there was absolutely no way they would make it out of the caves.

Cautiously, he kept pace with the rest of the operatives, approaching the rear wall of the temple. With each step forward, he felt the pressure building on his shoulder. The orders blurted out by his superior officer reminded him of his duty, *Eliminate him. No other casualties. Keep it low profile.*

A good few meters from the rear wall of the temple, the leader glanced back at his operatives and nodded. Then, like a flight of birds taking off from their perch on a tree, the four field operatives, with automatics in position, flew down in a wide curve to converge at the rear wall of the temple.

ӜӜӜӜӜ

"Jake, I'm talking to you." Taneez grabbed his hand. "Will you, for God's sake, answer my question?"

She insisted, but her words seemed to hang in the air.

Paralyzed at the sight of field operatives converging at the rear wall of the temple, he simply caught her hand and hauled her away, blurting, "This way…"

As they bolted forward, Taneez's handbag bobbed in her hand. Halfway through, they stopped dead, finding the tourist group, their supposed cover, pouring out from the same entrance they were about to enter.

Damn it! Jake thought as he paused. *Now where can we run?* One wrong step would bring about his defeat. He would lose the magnetic box and the ancient hidden mysteries would remain buried. The thought of it sent tremors down his body. Besides, there were lives at stake. Taneez was in danger and he didn't want to put her life at risk at any cost.

He grabbed Taneez's hand once again and scooted down the corridor, away from the rear wall of the temple, hoping this was the right move.

CHAPTER 43

Taneez felt the air vacate her lungs. Her pulse raced as Jake forced her down the bustling corridors, along the south wall of the temple. As they ran, the colonnades to their side receded faster. Yet there was no looking back. They had almost been nailed. But Jake felt fortunate because as he had anticipated, the crowd was still dense enough to camouflage their run.

This afternoon, however, the tourists remained oblivious to the cat-and-mouse game that was now taking place within the walls of the cave complex.

Jake and Taneez sneaked inside the colonnaded gallery along the south end of the temple. Hollowed out from the cliff's base, the gallery was enormously large but empty and poorly lit. Life-sized images of deities clung to its walls wore grim expression and appeared darker than they seemed to be.

Taneez, stepping inside, felt a strong urge to turn around and run away, from the gloomy space, from Jake and from all those who now seemed to be chasing her. Instead, she stood still. Seeing this, Jake pulled her behind one of a series of large pillars inside the gallery.

"What is this all about?" she asked again, feeling drained.

"It's a long story," Jake informed her, casting an apprehensive glance over her shoulder. "First, we need to get out of here and then, I'll explain everything to you."

Taneez winced. "Then you better find your way and let me find my own." She turned to leave, but catching a glimpse of a field operative entering the hall, Jake pulled her forcefully behind the pillar nearest to them. Stunned, Taneez tried to scream but found one of his hands already resting tightly over her mouth. He gestured for her to calm down.

"Good heavens," Taneez said, jerking off his hands. "I'm going mad with what's happening. But for your kind information, let me make one thing clear to you." She broke off, breathing heavily. "I'm not a part of this cat-and-mouse game. So, please spare me and let me go."

She took a step intending to walk out but Jake grabbed her, wrapping one hand around her waist and drawing her closer to himself. His other hand was over her mouth again. She tried to twist away, move, free herself, but she was no match for his size and strength. Her tired body was now a slave to his rigid clasp.

Jake snuck a look at the lone field operative in the hall. He assumed the rest could be looking for them in other colonnaded galleries.

The field operative with automatic in hand, scanned the hall. Step after step, he was now advancing nearer.

Turning away, Jake encountered Taneez's fear-filled eyes but he was angry. She could feel the warmth of his breath when he leaned down and placed his mouth next to her ear and whispered, "You want to know the truth? Then listen. I'm a fugitive. And the ones who're chasing us are from Intelligence."

Her eyes went wide at the revelation. She tried to react but he was still holding her mouth shut.

"They're after something I have. Something they think is a threat to national security. Now, as far as you're concerned," he broke off, "you've been spotted with a fugitive. Undeniably and inevitably, you've invited trouble for yourself."

Jake glanced back at the field operative and ensuring that he was still far off, he looked back at her. "So, stay back and stay calm. One single mistake and you will end up in a cell with hardheaded Intelligence men interrogating you."

Taneez's eyes were wide and staring at Jake.

"Now it's up to you to decide," he told her. "Either listen to what I say or simply show yourself up and do as they want." Pausing for a second, he announced, "The choice is yours."

Jake released his hands from her mouth and Taneez gasped. Her lungs were burning and she took long gulps of air. She looked at Jake, who was now eyeing every move of the field operative from the edge of the pillar. His words replayed in her mind. *You've been spotted with a fugitive!* It left her troubled.

I can't stay quiet. I'm innocent. She wanted to protest, but the words dried up on her lips. She took another deep breath and tried to calm herself. The forms of humans and deities carved on the stone walls in front of her seemed to stare at her gravely, as if enraged over the invasion of their sacred space. Sometimes, from the wall they appeared full of life, mocking at their helpless state of being caught in a deep trouble, and sometimes, they peered down at them threateningly to expose them of their hiding place to their onlookers and while also seemed unstirred by their presence, lost in the glory of the magnificence of their own era.

She closed her eyes and tried to purge the images from her mind but they re-materialized when she opened her eyes. She turned to find Jake behind the pillar to her left.

Jake had his back to her; he was closely following the movements of the field operative from behind the pillar.

The man was lean with cropped hair. He seemed nimble, with an air of proficiency and professionalism. Eluding him seemed difficult as he was not alone and he had the company of others with his strength. Jake also realized that although he himself was not alone, the woman with him would be no match for these operatives.

Jake heard the field operative cocking his gun closer to him. He swung his gun in all directions, his ears perked up like that of a wolf's, ready to pick up even the sound of a pin dropping to the stone floor. And his vision like that of a hawk's, exploring every cranny of the colonnaded gallery with acute focus.

Then something caught his trained eyes. Portion of a hand bag exposed from behind the nearest pillar. He drew a sharp breath took a shot.

The sound caught Jake off guard. Shocked at the thought of having their cover blown, first thing that struck his mind was Taneez's safety. Reaching for his trouser pocket on a sudden impulse, Jake's fingers closed around something that he was sure would divert the operative's attention.

CHAPTER 44

The *operation leader* twisted to face a sharp tinkling sound behind him. He shot a round in the direction of the sound. But there was nothing for the bullet to hit. *Oh damn!* He realized he had opened fire at a few coins rolling on the floor.

The next moment, he discerned from the corner of his eyes someone leaping over him. And then, blam! He took a sharp blow to his side, flying sideways in the air. The blow tossed his gun to the floor. Everything blurred for a split second, followed by pain spurting through his body as he took another punch to his torso.

As he fell back, he saw the man who was inflicting the pain: it was their target, Jake.

The operation leader evaded the next blow as Jake hurled himself onto him. Instead, grabbing Jake's arms, he rammed his knee into Jake's chest and threw him against a pillar.

Jake's face crashed into the stone pillar. The collision set Jake's jaws rattling. He struggled to overcome the discomfort.

The operation leader was reaching for the gun lying on the floor within arm'sreach.

Reacting on impulse, Jake leapt onto the man's back, taking him crashing down to the floor. The operation leaders' face bumped into the stone floor, sending a jarring ache up his skull. He convulsed on the floor, his hands to his head. The anguish was acute and to his misfortune, it intensified as he received a violent thrust in his ribs that seemed to crush his lungs, leaving him gasping for breath. Even under the effect of excruciating pain, he pig-headedly managed to hold onto Jake's leg as he tried to reach the gun.

The hold was so firm that Jake could not move even an inch. Enraged, Jake threw a hard punch at the man's vertebral column that loosened his hold and then jabbed a fist into his chest. Pulling him up from the floor, Jake hoisted the man up and charged him against the stone pillar.

The operation leader groaned as the pillar's sharp edges poked deep into his back, leaving him momentarily breathless. He twisted and contorted, battling to breathe, to subdue the excruciating asphyxiation.

Jake took a moment to catch his breath. Then he walked over to where the man was convulsing on the floor. There was no blood marking his injuries. Jake analyzed it standing over him. The injury, Jake suspected, was internal and nasty enough to leave him gasping for breath for good few hours.

Jake massaged his head to get rid of the pain. His eyes fell upon the microphone hanging loose from its mount on the operation leaders' shirt. He bent over him, plucked the microphone and adjusted the mouthpiece, clipping it over his ear.

Cacophonic voices of the man's fellow operatives erupted, call-outs of status updates.

Jake felt a hand resting on his shoulder. When he glanced over, he found Taneez offering him the gun she'd snared while he was wrestling with the operative. He snapped it up and turned back to the injured operative, who was still writhing in pain.

Holding the gun directly over the operative's temple, Jake cocked it and fired.

Thud!

CHAPTER 45

The Sun loomed overhead.

Taneez stole an anxious glance at her watch. It read 1.10 PM. And the sun outside the car window loomed lazily overhead, burning the hilly landscape into brazen hue as the car cut right through the undulating terrain of Sahyadri mountain range.

She was quite comfortably settled in the backseat of a city taxi they had hired the moment it had crossed their path after they surfaced from the Kailasanatha Temple.

She tamed her vexed mind, looking out the car window, reassuring herself that she was safe and out of danger. Even so, her thoughts turned back to some disturbing moments. The stunning temples chiseled out of the rocky cliffs, the gloomy caverns with spooky sculptures adoring the walls, bullets peppering around them unwarily and the most disturbing, the combat between Jake and the operative in the colonnaded gallery.

The last thought sent shivers down her spine. She tried to shake off its sting, but couldn't help reflecting on that scene of her peering over Jake's shoulder as he aimed the gun at the operative's chest. For a second, she had been terrified, but she soon heaved a sigh of relief when the bullet hit the stone floor, splintering chunks of stone around the operative.

Jake had intentionally done that, as a warning to stay out of his affairs and not cross his path again.

Taneez glanced over at Jake seated beside her. As she had suspected, he was not what he had claimed to be. She couldn't deny that the mysterious and action-filled, adventurous side of his character was fascinating. She hadn't met anyone like him before in the tranquil academic waters she usually navigated. But there was also something gloomy and guarded about him, that, while also somewhat charming, was a little scary. Especially given the cunning he had employed in eluding their hunters in the cave complex.

Having got hold of the injured operative's microphone, he had cleverly deceived the other operatives using protocols and diverting them from the exit towards the colonnaded gallery along the north end of the temple while himself speaking from south end of the temple.

"All points!" Jake had yelled into the radio. "I have him. In the gallery along the north end of the temple." He glanced at Taneez. After a split-second's pause, he shouted, "Converge!"

His efforts had bought them ample time to carve their way out of the complex. A tricky move, appropriate at a critical point.

Jake turned from the window and noticed Taneez in deep thought. *You're safe,* he told her silently.

She looked at him, managing a half-smile, as though uncomfortable with the moment. Her smile was as graceful as it would otherwise be and her lips parted to mouth a question that he'd been suppressed all this while.

"What is it you're after?"

He couldn't deny her this time and he didn't put in too much effort to ward it off either.

"I'm after uncovering something," he told her staidly. "A secret that's been buried for over two thousand years."

She looked at him, her expression a mix of confusion and disbelief.

He nodded strongly. "I stumbled onto a link to this secret while was working at an archaeological dig due north of Rajasthan, a couple of years ago."

She listened keenly, unaware that she was hearing a fabricated version of his story aimed to lead her astray over again.

"Link?" She pressed, mystified.

"Yeah, a link those people are after." He slid a glance at her, adding, "I chanced upon this box." He produced the box from his pocket and placed it on her lap.

Baffled, she lifted the box, taking in its magical and mysterious appearance. Jake picked it up and placed it upside down on her palm, giving her an abridged version of how he had stumbled onto the riddle that was once inscribed on the underside of the box, which led him to Srisailam. Then he pulled out the scroll and handed it over to her to look at. "This is was locked inside the box. And this riddle, one of more such, will supposedly lead us to that secret lost for two millennia."

Taneez went through the riddle and looked down at the picture of a snake feeding on its own tail, enclosing a circle marked with random set of letters rimmed by astrological and alchemical symbols.

She looked up at him. "But how does this link serve the interest of the Intelligence people? Why are they involved in it?"

"Their involvement is quite plausible, Taneez." He glanced out the window before turning back to her. "I have something that is very crucial and sensitive. A key to information that if unveiled would pose a threat to national security." He quietened for a second. "They have every reason to stop me and seize it."

As Taneez contemplated on his version, her sight was resting on the box. She glanced at the riddle in the scroll.

Jake regretted for having to lie her again, in spite of gaining her trust. But there were some things he thought was best remained unsaid. Especially one on the link that which had gotten his father killed and the rest who were guarding it. He wanted that to remain hidden for a while longer.

Taneez scrutinized the riddle as Jake mentioned its significance to the carving on the Ellora caves, also pointing to the key that would decipher the puzzle.

Unleash the key, guards two voluptuous Ajantan art.

"The key to the cipher is hidden back there?" Taneez asked him, sounding slightly alarmed. "Don't tell me you're thinking of going back to Ellora again?."

He let out a soft grunt. "Not required."

Then how? She thought to herself. "We're going to another place." Jake furnished. "To a place where I'm sure answer can also be found."

He paused before revealing, "*The History Museum.*"

CHAPTER 46

The History Museum at Aurangabad, in the vicinity of Dr. Babasaheb Ambedkar Marathwada University, is one of the finest museum in India with a staggering collection of the most amazing artifacts from various time period.

From ancient Indian paintings, coins, fabrics, handwritten codices, to jewel-encrusted daggers, sculptures and images of Brahmanical, Jain and Buddhist significance, everything of significance from the seventh-century to the twelfth-century dynasties of Chalukyas, Rashtrakutas and Yadavas are here on the grand exhibit.

Its large galleries and halls, in addition to plethora of antique artifacts, exhibit a robust collection of miniature paintings; arms and armor; copper, gold and silver coins and marble sculptures from different eras.

Right through the day, the museum witnesses a heavy throng of tourists ambling through its vast galleries, taking in the sheer pleasure of exquisite collection of antique paintings and artifacts from diverse time frame.

This afternoon, however, Jake and Taneez, added to the growing number of visitors to the Museum. As they brisked into the museum hall, skimming through the collection of paintings, Jake silently thanked the taxi driver. Certain that he would find the key to the cipher here, Jake had given the taxi driver their destination. The taxi driver, ferrying them to here, dropping them at the entrance to the museum, had then driven off. Jake had ensured he had tipped the driver well, both for his generous drop and to keep mum about their whereabouts if someone had inquired on his way back.

Making their way through the long corridor, they arrived in a gallery replete with images of the carvings from the Ellora and Ajanta caves. However, even after twenty minutes of meticulous inspection, they had found no image of the bas-relief in the collection. That concerned Jake.

“Let me see the riddle again,” Taneez said. She took the scroll from Jake and read it.

"Unleash the key, guards two voluptuous Ajantan art," she read the last line aloud and then looked at him. "The carving we saw depicts devotees on the ground amazed at the divine beings airborne in a flying machine. It also depicts some devotees climbing over the mountain seemingly to take a close look at the flying machine, while a horse driven cart, a few shacks and trees are portrayed in the backdrop. That's it. I don't recall seeing anything else."

"Look at these phrases," Jake pointed at the last words in the line. "It says something about the art, a voluptuous Ajantan art." He glanced at her and added skeptically, "It corresponds to the physical beauty of a female. One that is erotic."

Taneez held his gaze for a moment before turning to navigate through the gallery once again, minutely examining the images on the wall. Jake showed her a couple of images that were slightly erotic in nature. The first one was a sculpture from cave eight of Ellora complex, on the antechamber wall. The image showed Goddess Mahamayuri with a peacock. A sage was reading a book, while flying dwarfs and female attendants were seen in the background.

Taneez inspected the picture. "This appears erotic to you?"

He knew it was a carving and not Ajantan art, but he still argued with her. "Isn't it erotic? Two women in the picture are skimpily dressed, with their firm things poking out..." he said holding his hands over his chest, mimicking the shape of breasts.

Taneez winced in embarrassment, watching him doing so.

"I mean..." Jake faltered, embarrassed himself. He immediately dropped his hands from his chest. "It's...it's their firm things...you see..., which I thought appeared more prominent."

His indecent gestures though, unintentional and impulsive, added to her disgust.

Shit! He exclaimed under his breath. Uncomfortable and wanting to avoid stretching the awkwardness any further, Taneez drew her attention to the next few image.

In the next picture, male and female forms were depicted in intimate positions. The figures were named *mithunas* The term epitomized male and female figures, passionately making love in sensual postures.

Mithuna, also known as *maithuna*, is a Sanskrit term used in *tantra* to refer to a sexual union between a male and female, an act of copulation. It is significant in the rituals of *tantra*, where the female *shakti* and the male *shakta* transferred energy through their bodies to attain an exalted state of divinity.

Watching the amorously entwined couple featured in the carving, Jake was more guarded on his take on this one, as it was a carving and not Ajantan art. But a hint of embarrassment had already tinted Taneez's expression and she tried to obscure it, adding instantly, "Ah… this is quite an erotic and obscene."

"Obscene?" Jake was puzzled at her statement. "I'm sorry to say, I detest your opinion on its nature. That's an inappropriate phrase to define these carvings."

Taneez's brows scrunched incredulously.

"I agree these carvings are bold and explicit," Jake said. "Yet, they are not vulgar. In fact, they depict an exalted art of making love to create a heightened awareness of intimacy." He paused. "These carvings are just a candid dissemination of the carnal knowledge that was otherwise restricted within the closed walls."

Taneez raised her brows at his defensive statement, one that she suspected originated of cultural patriotism.

"Then, Jake, tell me, what are these luscious, sensual and bold carvings doing in temples?" She gazed at him accusingly, putting another point across. "These are the only Buddhist sites in the world that has defined femininity with such interest. And If I'm not mistaken, Buddhism is a religion merely populated by bastion of male monks." She broke off. "Then why have depictions of sensual carvings and paintings of women in their dwelling places that they have deemed sacred?

Jake cleared his throat to elucidate. "Where else is a better place than the temples itself, to remind people of their religious obligations?"

Her brows furrowed in incomprehension.

"Sexual union is a spiritual transformation of the male and the female, which allowed them to be incarnated as gods and goddesses, while their own self was diminished."

Intimacy, Jake elaborated, had its own significance deeply rooted in ancient Indian cultures, as this art of making love was treated as a divine union. In a broader sense, it was the *'science of love.'* Ancient Indians pioneered sexual education, imparting it through art and literature. Themes of romance and nudity are beautifully presented in frescoes and sculptures in temple complexes like Khajuraho, Ajanta and Ellora to remind people of their amorous obligations; married couples needed to abide by these as a part of Dharma.

They moved to the next image on the wall. It was of a nymph, a beautiful carving of a woman with pleasing curves and bosom, in a dancing posture.

"You're sure the last line in the riddle is pointing to these erotic paintings?"

"Certainly," Jake replied. "But at the paintings of Ajanta."

CHAPTER 47

Jake faced her. "Let's begin the whole thing again."

The hope was that by examining everything they would come across something, a hint that would throw light on the cryptic nature of the art mentioned in the last line of the riddle.

Unleash the key, guards two voluptuous Ajantan art

"It speaks of two voluptuous Ajantan art," Taneez read from the scroll and returned her gaze to Jake. "Which means, we should be looking for two different paintings that depict voluptuous figures."

Jake read it too for a long moment and then said, "The word *'two'* in the line seems to be referring to a plural. Strangely, though, the line mentions Ajantan art and not as Ajantan arts."

Taneez re-read the line. "Maybe it is misspelled."

"Or misspelled for a reason?" Jake wondered aloud, implying a veiled meaning within the word *'two.'* "Say, purposefully?"

Taneez did not agree. "I don't find any valid reason for the need to misspell the word Ajantan art instead of Ajantan arts. The riddle is anyway a message encoded in a cipher. So why a cipher within a cipher?" She shook her head "It seems to me a basic human error, nothing more."

Jake could not agree with her reading of the riddle. For some reason, he felt the word *'two'* served a different purpose. It seemed to him that it signified another meaning entirely, one that was not making any sense presently.

Moving forward, Jake began to survey the Jataka paintings from the Ajanta caves. "What more do you know about these nymphs and *mithunas*?"

Taneez observed the nymphs depicted in the Jataka Tales."The little about the *mithunas* that I've learnt is from you. If you ask me about nymphs, yes, I can tell you something about them." She explained, "Nymphs as curvaceous and gratifying women find mention in classical mythology where they symbolize a minor nature goddess, usually depicted as a beautiful maiden and admired for being attractive, charming or intelligent. According to Greek mythology, nymphs inhabited forests and water bodies. In European and Arabian mythology, they were known as sirens, portraying beauty at its best."

"In ancient Indian scriptures, they were known as *apsaras*, the angels," Jake adding to her explanation. "With their physical beauty and tender and shy nature, they fascinated men across civilizations and cultures. Their sensual charm was an inspiration to artists and poets, who with their gifted powers, painted, sculpted and penned beautiful literature on their graceful attributes and consecrated their femininity."

"And men from all ages have ruthlessly treated them as a mere object of lust," Taneez interjected sensing that his tone was one of a male chuvanistic. "From the beginning of time, kings and great monarchs desired every beautiful woman within their courts and territories. Regardless of whether they were married or virgins, they became an object for the gratification of those monsters. They treated them as sex-slaves." Indicating the nymphs in the Jataka tales, she concluded harshly, "Which is quite evident from the erotic carvings on the temple."

"Hey, hang on." Jake countered. "You're leading us back to square one. I've already taken you through the nature of those carvings. The painting purely describes the art of making love and is not vulgar. Indeed, Indians had a broader approach towards lovemaking than the West or any other country in the world. treating it as nothing but a science. And from these carvings, if the woman's bosom appears sleazy to you, then you must for a moment step out from the occult shoes and try to perceive, these beautiful carvings from another point of view.

"You should know that the depiction of nudity and romance in art was acceptable in ancient times. Owing to the fact that some part of India fell under tropical regions, men and woman from those regions felt the need to cover only the lower parts of their bodies." He paused and glanced at the paintings, continuing, "the excerpts of historical events are what you see illustrated in these paintings and sculptures and carvings on the walls of temples."

Jake looked at her. "There are various accounts of philosophical treatises in Sanskrit which portray this art in accordance with Hindu laws."

"And that, if I'm not mistaken, is the *Kama Sutra*?" asked Taneez, raising an eyebrow. "A philosophical treatise that emphasizes and explores intimate human desires, involving hundreds of techniques from seducing to pleasing a sexual partner in bed, scripted with utmost importance."

Jake smiled at hearing a woman well-versed with this manual on the conduct of human sexuality. That was unusual, yet not unbelievable.

"Why are you smiling?" Taneez asked, frowning.

"Nothing," Jake replied with a demure smile. "I was wondering at your wisdom, which is quite abundant in this *Kama Sutra* thing. Seems as if that's your primary area of interest."

She stared at him exasperatedly. "Jake that was a very cheesy line. Besides, if you're really serious about solving the riddle then we better get going."

Jake chuckled. He thought about how the age-old Indian treatise on human sexual behavior had made its way into most foreign lands. Some used it to spice up their bedroom fun, while some, grasping its true gist, made love in ravenous abandon and others used it as a pornographic magazine whenever their libidinal impulses drove them wild. But barely had anyone have grasped its true potential that it was more than just an exaggerated cognizance of sexual union recommending women to study different arts and crafts, known as *kalas* in addition to ten chapters exclusively dedicated to the stimulation of sexual desire.

For a moment, Jake was in deep thought, like something was not adding up. Then abruptly, he spun on his heels and bolted for the exit blurting, "There it is."

Taneez found herself responding instinctively, pelting after him instead of trying to infer anything from his impulsive action. She followed him out of the museum and into the university campus, covering a few furlongs in a matter of minutes. And when she stopped short, catching her breath, she discovered herself standing under a gate with an arch over it, that announced: *UNIVERSITY LIBRARY BUILDING.*

CHAPTER 48

Located within the university campus of Sonehri Mahal, the modern structure of Dr. Babasaheb Ambedkar Marathwada University Library building surges in prominence against the ancient historical setting with Bibi- ka-Maqbara due south-east and the rock temples known as Aurangabad caves to the north-west in the sylvan surroundings of the Sihyachal ranges.

The building's most prominent feature is the arch over the entrance gate that replicates the Great Ajantan arch, bringing to mind the intimate affiliation of Marathwada with a great historical past.

Jake wound down the spiral staircase that led into the basement of the building with Taneez following him close behind.

The air in the basement was damp and stale. The entire space was a maze of iron shelves, crammed with close to ten thousand books on various subjects, including a collection of rare books.

Surprisingly, the library was not very crowded. On the mezzanine, two stories above, Jake had spotted some university students near the shelves that displayed a collection of old and new periodicals. Some thirty-odd students were on the ground floor, seated in cubicles with their heads bent low over books that held their interest. In the basement, however, only book-filled shelves greeted the two curious individuals, Jake and Taneez.

Ambling past various shelves, Jake halted near the cabinet on Literature. He sighed, although he was a little apprehensive since he had had to compromise his official Identity card to get the librarian to allow him access to the library.

"Jake," Taneez snapped him from his reverie. "Paintings from Ajanta were what we were interested in. Now it's books? What book are you looking for in here?" Without uttering a reply, he ran a finger down the long shelf of leather-bound books. Lingering over some subjects, his finger came to rest upon one. Reading the title on the spine carefully, he eventually pulled out an old dusty tome, showing the title of the book to her.

She read the title and stared at him in disbelief. "*The Kama Sutra* by Vatsyayana?" Jake smiled.

"Huh!" She sounded frustrated. "You've still not given up on that sex thing?"

A sense of déjà vu struck Jake. "So tell me, sir," the lady librarian has said to him politely at the reception desk, some two minutes ago, soon after he had stormed into the library, dashing straight to the reception center. "How can I help you?"

Jake was huffing, trying to catch his breath. "I need to access a book."

She wondered at his exhaustion and flashing a weird look at him, she pressed, "Can I have your ID?" After careful thought, Jake produced his driving license.

The librarian made note of his ID card and handed it back to him, asking politely, "What book are you looking for, sir?"

"*Kama Sutra*," Jake had snapped instantly. "Will you be kind enough to let me know where I can find this book?"

The librarian cast a startled look at him at first and then recoiled with a slight modesty, withdrawing a bit, feeling uncomfortable.

Oh no way! Jake got the gist of her reaction. He knew she'd misinterpreted his intentions and desperation.

No, no, my exhaustion doesn't imply that I'm desperate for sex tips…

Giving him a weird look, she pointed him to a spiral staircase on the left corner that led down into the basement.

"Hello!" Taneez drew his attention once again. "I'm asking you something. Why this sex thing again? We've already discussed that issue to death."

I wish you could have seen that librarian react to my query, Jake thought, chortling to himself. *Her reactions were just too funny.*

Taneez saw him smiling to himself. "Have you gone insane?"

He did not respond to her. Rather, he felt the comfort of holding the book of Kama Sutra in his hand. He leafed through the ornately printed table of contents and then flipped to the forty-fifth chapter. Proudly, he showed her the name of the chapter.

Taneez was skeptical until she read the title of the chapter: **'Chapter 45: The Art of Secret Writing.'**

CHAPTER 49

The Kama Sutra is a Sanskrit work formulated by Vatsyayana, a Brahmin scholar. Regarded as one of the greatest literary works on human sexual conduct, this ancient Indian Hindu text is a compendium put together between the third and fourth century AD, inspired by a manuscript dating back to third century BC.

Kama, a sensual or sexual pleasure, is one of the four goals of Hindu life according to some Indian philosophies. Sutra meant a cord or thread that held things together. The complete phrase is a metaphor, referring to a set of principles or rules.

These texts, essentially narrated in prose and interspersed with poetic diction, is considered a classical curriculum that enunciates the use of this work not to be only for the purpose of satisfying carnal desires, but also to preserve Dharma and Artha--worldly health.

Besides consisting of sixty-four secret arts or *abhyantara kalas* of sexual intercourse, it also includes sixty-four different *bahya kalas* or practical arts. These are required study for cultured persons and discuss the nature of love, family life and other areas related to the pleasure-oriented facets of human life.

The arts and skills mentioned in *The Kama Sutra* were exclusively recommended for women so they could please their lovers. From flirting and romancing to techniques on seducing a man, the texts formed a concise but comprehensive summary of practical methods that though non-religious were designed for the ruling class to balance and enjoy their sensual appetites within their social and spiritual confines. Some of these instructions were necessarily professional skills required by women to earn their livelihood.

The skills discussed included singing, dancing, flower arrangements, personal grooming, the art of tattooing, the art of making a bed, making perfumes, learning magical chants, martial arts using swords or sticks or bows, jewelry making, carpentry, architecture, cooking, poetry, gardening and horticulture.

The forty-fifth chapter is specifically devoted to writing and understanding ciphers and is known as *mlecchita-vikalpa*. It refers to the ancient art of secret writing that originated in the ancient land of Meluha. It was used to encrypt messages intended for lovers to help conceal liaisons from prying eyes.

Popularly known as Vatsyayana cipher or Kama Sutra cipher, this is a classic monoalphabetic substitution cipher described in the forty- fifth chapter of the erotic manual. However, this encryption method has long been abandoned and rarely used since.

Until now.

Taneez grabbed the book from his hands and dutifully studied it. "This cipher is an ancient encoding technique?"

Jake didn't respond. He was pondering how magnificently the coding technique had served his father in the most honest way, guarding his secret.

They continued to examine the contents of the chapter. The solution to the cipher was very clear. The rules for decoding were mentioned in detail, enticing them to uncover its dark might that had been lost to history.

Taneez, unable to bear the weight of the heavy tome, strode to a nearby reading table and dropped it on the surface.

Jake appeared at her side and spoke, "This is a simple substitution cipher that involves randomly pairing letters of the alphabet and then substituting each letter in the original message with its partner." Jake looked up from the book at her doubtfully. "But our cipher is composed of the English alphabet, which contains twenty-six characters. This means…" he paused as he gave it some thought, "with twenty-six letters, we obtain twenty-five different likely cipher combinations, where A can be paired with any of the remaining twenty-five letters." Jake squinted into distance, assessing. "The total number of permutations is 25× 24×23…×1. That equals to…"

He asked for her mobile and calculated. When he was done, he showed the figure to Taneez: 7, 905, 853, 580, 625.

Taneez grew anxious. "That's over seven trillion possibilities."

Jake shook his head. "Even though this is a simple cipher algorithm, it involves shifting letters by a number of positions. And that number is the key here." He thought for a beat. "Code breaking is focused on discovering the key that defines the shift. This can be any number between one and twenty-five."

This cipher was simple to crack if one knew the key.

Taneez focused on the cipher method seriously.

Beside her, Jake fell silent. *The key should be mentioned somewhere in the riddle,* Jake thought, reading the last line of the riddle again and again.

Unleash the key, guards two voluptuous Ajanatan art.

Suddenly, his eyes focused on a specific word from the riddle that had seemed irrelevant. A little nudge to his brain and there he had it, the key to the cipher coming to light from darkness.

Jake looked up at Taneez and cast a triumphant smile. "What?" Taneez asked, wondering.

"Key that defines the shift," Jake answered. "You got it? What is it? Where?"

Looming his slender index finger over the lines from the riddle in the scroll, he pointed to a word in the last line: two.

Taneez was bewildered. "Two?"

Jake smiled. "As I told you earlier, the word *'art'* in the last line was not an error. It was not misspelled either. It was there for a reason. To point to another word in the same line which is key to unlock the cipher. And the word *'art '* point to word *'two.'* It is not used as plural, but as a key that defines the shift to decipher the code." He took a pause. "This riddle is ingeniously crafted. Cipher within a cipher."

Marvelous! Taneez was awed by the ingenuity of the one who had devised the riddle.

Examining it for a beat, Jake pointed to a pen stand on the table. "Give me a pen and a paper." From the corner of his eyes, he noticed her glaring at him. "I know, you're wondering I'm a historian and have no pen."

Taneez scowled, handing him a pen and paper, blurting, "You're disgusting."

Jake began jotting down the English alphabet on the paper. When he was done, he showed her the substitution cipher.

A B C D E F G H I J K L M N O P Q R S T U V W X Y Z
Y Z A B C D E F G H I J K L M N O P Q R S T U V W X

Taneez stared at the letters on the lower line of the substitution cipher which had been shifted two positions to the right. It seemed perfect.

Beneath it, Jake noted down the cipher text from the puzzle on the scroll, the one marked by the snake devouring its tail.

```
HTQOGVGTPCMEKVWTQYGFDADGTPKPKUQCTCPFFQYPJKOCNCACUVJGOAUVKE
GNGOGPVTQCT

RCVJVQUCNXCVKQPKUNCKFVJTWUCETGFRQTVCNUGGMVJGGNKZKTCPFVJQUV
CTIWKFGUVJGUVCTIWKFGUVJGOQTVCN
```

Once this was done, Jake carefully began substituting each letter with the corresponding one from the cipher key, until the decoded message became legible.

```
FROMETERNALCITYROWEDBYBERNINISOARDOWNTHEHIMALAYASTHEMYSTIC
ELEMENTROAR

PATHTOSALVATIONISLAIDTHRUSACREDPORTALSEEKTHEELIXIRANDTHEST
ARGUIDESTHEMORTAL
```

Examining it closely, Jake carefully began inserting a space after each meaningful word, transpiring the cipher to its entirety.

```
FROM ETERNAL CITY ROWED BY BERNINIS OAR DOWN THE HIMALAYAS
THE MYSTIC ELEMENT ROAR

PATH TO SALVATION IS LAID THRU SACRED PORTAL SEEK THE ELIXIR
AND THE STAR GUIDES THE MORTAL
```

Once it was finished, they both gazed down at the transformed message. A wave of confusion swept over their faces as they studied the deciphered text.

The decoded message was another riddle.

The third riddle in the quest. *And hopefully, the last,* Jake wished.

Jake's thoughts drifted to his father and his ingenious and painstaking efforts to conceal the key, the Vatsyayana cipher, in the life-size sculptures representing the legacy of *Kama Sutra*.

He was rudely pulled from his thoughts by a sound. He hushed Taneez, motioning to her to listen as faint footsteps seemed to be making their way down the staircase, guardedly, as if to unleash an ambush in the basement.

CHAPTER 50

In the nick of time, Jake hauled Taneez behind one of the iron shelves. The same field operatives they had confronted at Ellora caves were now pouring into the basement, guardedly. Jake glanced over at Taneez at his side. Her eyes reflected her terror. Jake turned away, pulled out a book from the shelf and carved a space through which he could get glimpse of whoever had made their way down to the basement. He was just in time to see three field operatives fan out around the staircase, with their automatics in position, alert.

"What do you see?" Taneez asked, fear burned in her eyes..

Jake was barely listening to her. He was calculating an escape route. He was reasonably familiar with the area and he knew their options to decamp were limited. There was only one way out and that was through the spiral staircase ascending to the ground floor, the same one that had brought them down into the basement. The staircase was fifteen meters away from where they were hiding and right now, it was under the control of an army of three.

Just then, he saw one of the operatives adjusting his microphone, mouthing something and then turning to his fellow operatives and nodding.

Jake turned to face Taneez.

"What?" Taneez asked fearfully.

"Our cover is blown." He let out a pained sigh. "They know we're here. They have backup arriving soon."

Lines of fear etched themselves on the skin on her graceful face. Jake glanced back at the field operatives through the niche. The three operatives had moved away from the staircase and were now moving around the basement, randomly, their guns in position.

As Jake kept a close watch on their movements, he couldn't help but wonder what in the name of God he possessed for which he was being hunted to be killed.

He stared down at the scroll in his hand. *Is this scroll, its coded message, so devastating that to protect it costs lives?* Jake asked himself in a moment of horror. *Is it worth more than my life and that of innocent Taneez, who has been unknowingly sucked into this game of life and death?* They were questions he didn't have an answer for.

Shaking off the distracting thoughts, he pushed the scroll into his trouser pocket and watched a field operative arriving closer.

"They're closing in on us," Jake whispered to Taneez.

She grew extra cautious, rising on her toes, ready to run if Jake told her to. Jake observed her with a deep feeling of concern. *No matter what, she'll walk out of this place and situation alive and safe.* Burning the thought into his memory, he pulled out the gun from his leather jacket and held it out to her.

"For me?" Taneez was puzzled, looking at it.

Jake nodded. "It has just one round. Keep it for your safety. And fire only if necessary."

Taneez grabbed it, recalling that it was the same gun she had recovered from the floor and handed over to Jake an hour ago, while he had pinned an operative underneath his sole, back at the caves of Ellora.

Jake sealed the niche, placing the book back and glanced ahead at a maze of shelves, now waiting to serve them with cover. He motioned Taneez towards an array of shelves that was farther and ran deeper into the labyrinth of the basement. Ducking low, they moved ahead guardedly, muffling their footsteps. Now arriving amid crisscrossed book shelves, he faced Taneez.

"We must not hide for long. The sooner we tackle them, the faster we can vacate the building."

Taneez nodded in understanding but a grim fear had taken up residence in her cerulean eyes.

Jake wanted to pull her close, hug her tightly and whisper his apologies for drawing her into this terrible situation. Then again, his gut willed him to cling on to hope.

He sensed an operative rustling close behind the shelf he now had his back against. Realizing there were two operatives moving in tandem, he inching ahead cautiously.

He turned to Taneez and signaled her to take a position beside him, guiding her about her role in this game.

Guardedly, Jake held his breath and moved to the edge of the shelf where the operatives would arrive at any moment.

As the rustle of the operatives grew louder, Jake grabbed two heavy tomes from the shelf. He hurled one over the shelf onto the other side and launched himself from behind the shelf onto the open pathway, throwing the other tome at the first operative.

The operatives were initially distracted by the heavy tome crashing onto them from above. Then, one of the men took a tome to the face and staggered backward, disoriented.

Falling into a crouch on the floor, Jake kicked out at the first operative, sending his gun hurtling. He moved quickly, hoisting the man to his toes and tossing him down to the floor. The operative went crashing into the shelf behind Jake.

Jake gained his feet and turned back to a loud thundering crash! Relief swept over him. On instructions from Jake, Taneez, mustering her full strength, had quite efficiently brought down caving an entire shelf onto the second operative in line.

It earned Jake sufficient time to react. He winked at Taneez appreciatively. Then almost instantly, he twisted out of the way of the bullet that shot past him by a whisker and struck the books on the iron shelf, spewing tattered pieces of paper into the air.

The third operative approached rapidly from the other end. He was about to fire again when something heavy slammed into his hand and sent the gun skittering out of his hand onto the floor.

"My handbag!" Taneez groaned, recognizing the object that had slammed into the man's hand and had slid onto the floor.

There was a rustle of movement near the staircase. Taneez and Jake watched as a dark silhouette leapt over the railings of the staircase and came up behind the operative. Within a second, the stranger had crashed into the operative, launching him forward to dash into the second operative who was about to gain his feet after being trapped under the fallen shelf.

The operatives went crashing into the rear wall of iron shelves, hurtling books onto the floor. Although the operatives wondered who the newcomer was, this stranger was quite familiar to Jake and Taneez. The man was tall and slender and had conveyed them from the caves of Ellora to the museum safely. The man stepping in again to protect them from danger was the taxi driver.

Grabbing the opportunity, Jake threw himself on the first operative who was clambering to his feet and had tried to lunge at him.

Taneez collected her bag and ran for cover behind a shelf. Once safely hidden, her eyes followed the two operatives ramming into the driver and pinning him against the shelf. One punched the driver on his jaw repeatedly while the other held his hands behind his back. His sturdy physique, she realized, wasn't just for show. She saw his knee rising up to ram into the groin of one of the operatives. The operative moaned and collapsed to the floor, his hands covering the source of his agony. The driver elbowed the other, punching him so strongly that the man went zooming backwards in the air, twisting out of his way.

To her left, Jake was in trouble. The third operative had locked his powerful arm around Jake's neck. And Jake's efforts to free himself were in vain. Mustering his strength, Jake thrust his elbow into the operative's gut, which loosened the man's grip a little Exploiting the opportunity, Jake swung around and his fist exploded into the man's ribs. The operative fell, crumpling onto the nearby desk, sending the books on it flying off its edge. Writhing in pain, the operative coughed, struggling to breathe.

On the other side, just as the driver bent to pick up the dropped gun, one of the operatives ran into him, thrusting him into the nearby shelves that shuddered at the impact. The driver, however, recuperated quickly to see the other operative rushing in from the opposite direction while the second rounded on him from behind, attempting to strike.

He leapt back and snap-kicked the attacker behind him in the chest, knocking him over. Immediately regaining his momentum, the driver charged forward, sidestepping the first opponent but grabbing his arm and twisting it around with enough force to snap the bone. He then dropped the man to the floor.

The blows were severe enough to leave them in pain for at least a few minutes. Taneez emerged from where she was hiding, picked up the gun from the floor and joined Jake. The driver arrived next to them.

Giving a quick once over to the grievously injured operatives writhing on the floor, Jake motioned to Taneez and the driver and scooted out of the library building.

CHAPTER 51

A *good sixty* miles from the library building, the black Fiat taxi moved smoothly, past the tranquil backdrop of hillocks and dry fields.

Ensconced in the backseat with Taneez, Jake had directed the course, avoiding from taking highway road on security reasons. He had expressed his gratitude to the driver for his efforts in rescuing them in the nick of time. The taxi driver had come to the library to return Taneez's handbag which she had forgotten in the taxi. That in itself was commendable. But seeing them in trouble, he had fearlessly stepped in, risking his life. It was his naivete, Jake thought, which made the driver so generous, a trait that very few people exhibited these days.

In the backseat, Taneez noted that Jake was lost in the cryptic figure of the snake eating its own tail.

She let her gaze drift from the interior of the taxi to the beautiful scene outside where a murky sky was preparing to envelope the orange fireball on the horizon. Her heart yearned to reach out and touch that lovely orange hue as she loved to drench herself in exotic landscapes. That way often she felt close to nature and its bounty. Under the wings of such pleasurable eye-catching scenes from nature, she had resolved crucial affairs in her personal life in the past. Strolling past the swooshing waters on the seashore or along serene paths, she had softly endured the great distress and disappointments of life.

But ruminating on the events of the past few hours, her mind was besieged by agitating scenes from the caves and the library building. She tried to still these troubling thoughts and calm herself, settling into the subdued normalcy of the comfortable backseat of the taxi. But there were too many unknowns, too many variants for her to switch off.

One specifically related to Jake's identity, to something she had recovered that belonged to him while he was busy manhandling the field operatives back in the library building. She pulled it out of her bag and tossed it onto his lap.

Confused, Jake took a second to gather that it was his personal property: his wallet and his CBI ID card. Suggestive that Taneez had had a good look at it.

When he turned to face her, Taneez was already looking at him furiously.

"Taneez, I'm sorry…" his voice wavered as he fished for words. "Look, I can explain."

"Explain what?" Taneez erupted. "That you aren't a historian but a CBI officer?"

Jake remained quiet.

"Now, everything makes sense," she said and looked away, out of the window. Her face was sullen with anger. "A man from Intelligence flies the coop with an ancient puzzle that he allegedly recovered from a dig. Stupid me, believing his story agreed to join him in the quest." She quieted down. "It's my mistake. I put my trust in you."

Jake's mind drew blank, wondering what to say and how to convince her. Just a little while ago, he had managed to get out of a difficult and unpleasant situation. And now once again, a different kind of problem was in front of him. He opened his mouth to clarify, but she raised her hand to stop him.

Adding to the worry just then was the driver, who spoke for the first time since they had emerged from the library building, when something trailing behind their taxi rushed into the rear-view mirror.

"I think we have company."

Alarmed, they spun around to catch a glimpse of a dark shadow rushing ahead, accompanied by the strained growl of an engine and a roaring screech of tires. Within a blink of eye, it rammed the taxi from behind.

CHAPTER 52

The driver's grip on the steering wheel tightened as the taxi lurched forward as a result of a jarring collision.

The impact rocked Taneez and Jake in their seats.

With a cursory glance through the rear-view mirror, driver knew the vehicle had rammed into them. A dark SUV dropped behind as the taxi disengaged from its predator, the momentum of the hit propelling it forward. Before he could press the accelerator to try to outrun the SUV, it pitched forward and rammed the back of the taxi again.

The force was greater this time, the SUV hitting the taxi at a slight angle and smashing its tail light. It sent the taxi veering wide and out of control.

The hillocks flashed in the windshield in a kaleidoscopic blur as the taxi slid a few meters before the driver wrenched it back on track and thundered ahead of the attackers.

"They're back," Taneez screamed as she recovered from the collision, her hair ruffled over her face.

Stunned, with his vision blurred and ears ringing, Jake tried looked through the rear windshield. He guided the taxi driver, "Look, don't stop. Just keep driving." "And my taxi?" the driver asked, worried, throwing a nervous glance at him and another at his rear-view mirror.

"The tail light is already down. I can't bear more damage."

Oh gosh! Jake squinted at him in the mirror. "You're worried about the tail light?"He informed in a hurried tone, "I'll get you a brand new one. Just keep going and do as I say."

Jake struggled to get a clear picture of the vehicle chasing them and the men inside it through the dusty rear windshield. He could only pick up the vehicle's model: a Mercedes M-Class. In the fading light, except for a faint outline of a man in the driver's seat, nothing was discernible. He could check on the occupants of the SUV by peering out the side window, but that would put him at risk of becoming a victim to their mini-projectiles.

No, I can't take the chance.

Less than a minute after the second attack, the driver spotted the SUV racing towards them, threatening to charge again. This time it veered away from the mangled tail light and closed in from the right side. The driver, while keeping tabs on their pursuers, also had to check the limitations of the road. The road was not wide enough to accommodate two four-wheeler's running parallel and it had a rough craggy surface ridden with potholes, giving the feel of a mountainous trail rather than a smooth-paved drive. More terrifying was an irrigation trench running along their left side that posed a serious threat.

It was only when the SUV headed in from the right that the driver inferred their intentions, to nudge the taxi into the deep trench on the left. He became nauseous as he played out the scenario. He knew they had only one option left to extricate themselves and only a few seconds to act. Despite his best efforts to keep the attackers at bay, the driver had failed to outrun them. The SUV was speeding ahead to match their pace. Jake saw the silhouettes of the occupants from the sun-tinted glass windshields. He could only approximate their number to four, two each in the front and backseats.

From the manner in which the SUV swooped to their side, his instincts indicated that it was going to be the beginning of another ominous event in this isolated place. If they were shot and thrown into the deep trench, they were unlikely to be picked up by any vehicles on this isolated stretch, especially with the night closing in. The thought of it caused serious discomfort to Jake.

The driver's courage did not falter as he pulled into final gear and floored the pedal to its full throttle. The speeding SUV menacingly matched its pace, moving parallel to the taxi, as though scoffing at their low-powered engine compared to their powerful one built on the chassis of a truck. The very next moment, the driver's heart pounded in his throat as he saw the front window panels of the SUV gradually sliding down and automatics protruding out of it.

Holy shit! Jake went cold in terror.

CHAPTER 53

Taneez ducked in her seat, as a volley of bullets rained down upon on them, splattering into the taxi. A couple more strafed the driver's side of the car in rapid succession, shattering the driver's side window glass.

Finding the road up ahead empty, an adrenaline rush through him made the driver pressed the gas pedal all the way to the floor. The engine revved hard and pushed him back in his seat.

Another string of bullets took out the rear windscreen, sending shattered glass showering down on Jake and Taneez in the backseat.

Jake glanced at Taneez, who seemed shell-shocked, but luckily, unhurt. To his surprise, the driver had maintained his cool, seemingly cautious and soaking in the moves of their pursuers through the rear-view mirror and trying his best to keep them far behind.

Most of the bullets hit the road, while some whizzed past their taxi and some drilled the tailgate, but the tires were so far, intact. The driver had skillfully parried many of the bullets, using the empty road to his advantage and driving in crazy zigzags. With each swerve, Taneez and Jake in the backseat of the taxi had tumbled and tossed. Their heads collided. Their bodies squashed against each other and then against the inside of the car. Their bones ached with the constant battering.

Jake motioned to Taneez to crouch down when she craned a little over her seat to catch a glimpse of the attackers.

"Stay low," he yelled over the sound of bullets.

She ignored him, seemingly still angry with him over his lie about his identity.

With a jerk, he pulled her back down to crouch in the leg space.

Taneez fumed. "Why do you care what happens to me? Show your concern for this poor man," she voiced over the ricochet of bullets, motioning to the driver. "He's sucked himself unknowingly into this sinister plot, the way I did, without even knowing your true identity and whatever you're after."

She flinched away angrily and craned again over the edge of her seat only to have a bullet fly past her head, lodging in the seat in front of her, spraying wood and cotton stuffing.

Infuriated, Jake hauled her down, "Have you gone insane?"

"Yes, I have," she said, tears welling in her eyes. "I have gone insane since I've embarked with you on this journey." She shrugged. "God knows why I trusted you." She rubbed her temple and said, "Anyway, there's no point regretting anything now. I better concentrate on getting myself out of this situation. And you better focus on your ancient puzzle to save it from them. From their tenacity, they're not going to stop firing anytime soon."

She's true. Jake realized. *She's in danger and so is the taxi driver.*

There were several lives at stake. *And all because of me.* Jake felt a pang of guilt. Rescuing them was the only aim in his mind now. He wanted to make sure the driver was safe. The driver had already staked his life to rescue them in the library building. Seeing him getting involved in the battle that was not at all his, Jake realized it was unfair.

I won't allow this anymore. Jake decided. *I'll put an end to all this.*

"Hey, hold on." Jake sprung up from his cover to face the driver. "Move aside. I'll drive."

The driver was puzzled at his demand and glanced over his shoulder at him, screaming over the sound of the bullets. "I hate letting anyone drive my taxi."

CHAPTER 54

The rain of bullets came to an abrupt halt after the men in the SUV had fired another couple of rounds that hammered their way into the taxi's trunk, entirely destroying the tail lights.

Ducked low in his seat, Jake felt his jaw muscles tighten wondering why the bullets had stopped raining: they were probably reloading their automatics. Whatever the reason, Jake was now primarily concerned about his fellow travelers. One who was angry with him and another behind the wheel, who clung to vague principles of not letting anyone drive his taxi, even when his life was at risk.

Jake's thoughts were interrupted when the SUV suddenly rocketed ahead from the side.

The driver's vigorous effort to block them from veering to their right was in vain. The SUV slammed into the side of the taxi sending it careening sideways.

The driver gripped the wheel tightly as the taxi zigzagged a good fifty meters until it regained its balance. Once it steadied, the driver shifted gears and floored the accelerator, launching the taxi forward, leaving the SUV behind.

The constant battering had left both vehicles with huge dents, but the passengers were safe and relatively unhurt. The shocks from the collision, however, had painfully rattled their bones. After each impact, Jake turned to check on Taneez. She was fine, crammed in the compact space of the leg room.

Besides, the taxi was not faring well. It had been worn out of shape with the constant battering. The engine lid was wrecked. The dent with every collision was caving in, just inches away from the main engine, which was worse. From its poor shape, it seemed likely to give up soon if the process continued.

As he struggled to keep his worries in check, the driver heard the meek growl of an engine in his ears. For an instant, panic surged in him as he suspected the sound was coming from his taxi's damaged engine.

But as he strained to hear a little better, he discovered that it was not coming from his taxi but from their attacker's SUV.

At which point, the growl turned to an ear-splitting roar.

Shocked, Jake and Taneez rose from their crouch to look through the shattered rear windshield of the taxi only to find a huge Ashok Leyland haulage truck looming behind like a giant bulldozer.

The truck seemed poised to ram into them, about to crush and bulldoze them under its huge set of wheels Surprisingly, however, in the next moment, it took a wide curve around the taxi's tail light, before it slammed its solid nose into the back of the posh SUV.

The impact was deadly and sent the SUV skittering on its wheels on the road, past the taxi, in a spinning motion, scattering dust and smoke, punctuated by the squeals of brakes, before it came to a gut-wrenching stop.

The driver slowed down the taxi, wondering if it had been an accident. Then, in the next moment, he realized that it wasn't, as the truck stormed past them towards the SUV and battered it all over again.

There was a loud bang like an explosion in some chemical factory. Smoke spiraled upwards from where the SUV stood.

Terrified at the sight, the driver hit the brakes and brought his taxi to an abrupt stop, putting a safe distance between them and the collision site. Through the front windshield, past the billowing, fiery smoke and dust, the trio in the taxi watched in grave silence as the truck regained its momentum and stormed towards the wrecked SUV, thrusting it wildly to its left and shoving it into the deep trench by the roadside and then speeding away.

With their slack jaws and eyes wide open, the trio in the taxi couldn't help but watch the horror unfold to its entirety. Jake felt sudden deep foreboding. That indicated a dangerous game and now seemed to involve another force, one that seemed more dark and malicious than he could imagine, suddenly emerging into the light from the shadows.

CHAPTER 54

Riya's cell phone warbled.

She reached for the phone on her desk and found an unknown number on the screen.

It can only be one man.

She answered the call. "Hi, Jake!"

Puzzled, Jake replied after a second of silence. "You smell humans by their numbers?"

"Yeah," she replied. "To be precise, I am well-trained to sniff fugitives on the run."

Jake laughed. "Ok. I need some money urgently. It would be great if you..."

"I'll have it wired right away," she answered, cutting him off.

Jake expressed his gratitude for her support, also briefing her on the day's events. Soon after he hung up, Riya called another number and passed on the information.

"I hope he hasn't grown suspicious about your involvement?" the voice on the other end inquired.

"Not a chance," replied Riya.

"Good. Keep me posted if anything important comes up." "Sure,"Riya said and hung up.

I'm sorry, Jake. She whispered a silent apology for betraying the man who had always trusted her, been her friend for years, standing by her and done her no wrong. But deep within, she knew she was doing no wrong. She was only sorting things on Jake's end.

ЖЖЖЖЖ

Steaming hot air whizzed out from the engine, as the car mechanic forced lifted the jammed front lid of the taxi with a crowbar to fix the source of damage.

Taneez had refused to disembark from the car and remained in the backseat, still sullen. Off to one side, Jake was seated on a metal chair and gulping down bottled water.

For the past half an hour, soon after they had pulled into a garage into the nearby village off the road, he had been trying to purge his mind of the frenzied images of the whole incident. One aspect of it, however, pestered him: the truck that came unheralded and thrust the SUV mercilessly into the deep trench by the roadside.

He also wondered how the people from Intelligence had managed to track his moves, realizing that there were unseen dynamics at play, unaware that he had someone from his own foster family who was acting as an informer to the Intelligence.

Pulling him back from his daze, the driver passed him a bill. Jake accepted the bill and checked it. It included costs for replacement of damaged parts and service charges. Jake smiled taking note of it and motioned him to the empty chair next to him.

"Where are you from?" Jake asked him in Hindi.

"I'm from Mumbai," the driver replied.

Over a long conversation, Jake learnt a lot about the driver. The serious man had not always been that way. Rather, weathered by the struggle to keep his poverty-stricken family afloat, he had transformed into a robot, a living machine that had long forgotten happiness, running errands far across from his territory.

After a brief pause, the driver asked, "Who were they? The people after you?"

There was certain information that was too sensitive to be disclosed. "Ah… that's a long story," Jake countered lightly, brushing off the matter.

Saying nothing, the driver rose from the chair to leave. Jake rose too and stopped him, placing his hand on the man's shoulder. "Hey, I'm really grateful for all your help."

"You don't have to be," the driver said coldly.

ӜӜӜӜӜ

A long single file of vehicles were queued up for clearance at a checkpoint connecting to the Nagpur-Aurangabad-Mumbai Express Highway. In the stark gloom of the night, the police force had beefed up security fourfold, vigorously probing into the identities of the occupants of each vehicle with flashlights, to ensure they didn't miss in the dark.

Keeping a close watch on the ongoing activity from afar, leaning against the lofty trunk of a tree by the roadside, David Craig, chief coordinator of the JIC, took a long puff of his cigarette and let thick swirls of smoke issue from his mouth.

His calm and optimism had helped him tackle critical situations with ease in his tenure with the Intelligence. While his fellow officers were aggressive in dealing their cases with, he preferred the alternative, which many perceived as mere stupidity. His theory was very elementary. Let the criminal loose for as far as one could go and then pull the string. That's how his mind was programmed to work, to devise plans that deprived the criminal of options.

Great brains for the clever fugitive, David sneered.

Even so, Jake's unusual course through ancient locations and the presence of dark and shadowy forces behind his escape justified one thing: that the link was not concerned with any nuclear weapon as General Balbeer Singh had suggested. It was cock and bull story. He had now begun to suspect that the link had to do with something else entirely. As he took another long puff on his cigarette, his commanding officer Balbeer Singh's, voice hummed in his ears.

"Kill Jake on the spot." David smirked at the thought.

He knew that Jake was a hard nut to crack, someone who was immensely skilled and able to plot his moves with caution. Something David had first learnt about him at the crime scene in the Noida apartment. He knew Jake would explore all avenues for safe escape, even if it had to be in daylight. And tonight, breaking out from under their watchful eyes would be child's play for Jake.

Now standing in the midst of this chaos, David flicked his cigarette butt in the air, dug his hands into his pockets and studied the activity in front of him closely.

He's somewhere far away now. David smiled. *Safe and far, perhaps, planning his next move.*

The quest was only getting wild and David loved the thrill. Their paths had crossed once, David recalled. And he knew it would cross again.

Very soon. He flashed a devilish smile.

CHAPTER 55

In the dead silence of the night, the taxi tore past the tranquil wooded National Highway 79.

High up in the sky, a cluster of clouds had gradually engulfed the waning moon. Frigid breeze flowing in through the half-closed window woke Jake. He blinked his eyes adjusting to the gloom and glanced over at Taneez next to him in the backseat of the taxi, to ensure she was protected by her sweater. She was next to him, asleep. A thin curl of her hair was gently assaulting her left cheek, as though desperately fondling it, which occasionally seem to be stirring her sleep. He raised his hand to tuck it behind her ear, then he stopped. Remembering that she was still angry with him, he withdrew his hand.

It had been almost four hours since she had last spoken to him. She had remained silent over dinner they had in Dhaba, and over the tea break. She refused to respond even when he addressed her, making it obvious that the rapport between them had been severed. The moment she had stumbled upon his true identity, her trust in him had shattered. Any effort to convince her had backfired, making matters worse. Taking this into account, Jake arrived at a solution that he knew was good for the well-being of both of them.

With that thought, he looked away from her, lowering his gaze to the cryptic drawing in his hand, that of a snake feeding on its own tail. The application of the Kama Sutra key to the cipher surrounded by the snake devouring its tail had unleashed another riddle. Jake was sure that solving this riddle would reveal the secret.

He returned the scroll to the magnetic box and slipped it into his pocket. Turing to the car window, he felt the soft, silvery moonbeams caress his face. The aroma of moist leaves emanating from deep woods, soothed his fatigued senses and eyes soon slipped shut in a dreamless slumber.

ӜӜӜӜӜ

Taneez woke up groggily from her sleep and looked out the window. The sun was glorious, having risen from the pillow of the horizon, punctuated with the squawks of flying parrots that filled the fresh morning air.

It's a lovely morning, she admitted to herself. With a quick sweep of her eyes, she discovered that the taxi was stationed in front of a rustic hotel by the side of the bustling highway. On the far side, she spotted the driver having tea and a cigarette.

Then her eyes instinctively swiveled to her side seat that was occupied by Jake the previous night and registered a note lying there. An alarm rang in her mind. She instantly picked it up and read.

"Taneez,

As you read this letter, I'll probably be somewhere far away. I'm really sorry but I had to do this. We had to part ways. I deeply regret keeping my true identity from you. I had to do it as I have reasons of my own that I believe you understand. I wish I could tell you. Then again, I can't stake your life anymore. I have already done enough of that. I can't drag you along with me on this perilous journey of mine anymore.

Forgive me if you can...

Jake Stevens"

As Taneez folded the letter closed, the taxi recounted her what transpired while she was asleep. From his gestures and his Hindi, which she barely understood, she deduced that Jake had left in the dead of the night, directing the driver to safely ferry her to the closest airport, which was in Indore City.

As if struck squarely in the chest by a lance, Taneez felt a piercing pain in her heart. She realized she had been too hard on Jake, which had brought about this separation. With a tightening in her chest, she reclined in the backseat, closing her eyes, as the taxi entered the bustling highway of Indore city.

CHAPTER 56

Saturday, August 11, 2017 8AM,
Gulmohar Park, South Delhi.

Seated comfortably on a park bench beneath a canopy of royal poinciana, popularly known as gulmohar trees, a man in his late sixties, in a white and black tracksuit, stole an anxious glance at his wristwatch. *More than fifteen minutes.*

Committing to memory, he shifted on the bench, letting his eyes sweep across the wide stretch of the lush green park in front of him, occasionally interspersed with flamboyant gulmohar trees that from afar gave an effect of flaming tree. Under these fiery tree, life thrummed with elderly couples walking briskly on an oval jogging track, and the health freaks indulged in some warm-up exercises.

From this park every morning, his little and not-so-hectic routine would begin. A thirty-minute walk, a short break on the same bench and a brief stop at the nearby supermarket to pick up groceries on the way back home. But this had been suddenly disrupted recently. Thanks to a mysterious phone call from an unknown source that had presented him with an opportunity, a once-in-a-lifetime chance, to settle some scores from his past he'd been hoping for such a moment for a decade.

His interest in life had suddenly been rejuvenated, veering him on to his dream path, one that held the promise of vengeance. Vengeance for the devastating event that had wrecked his life as consequence of an offense he had never committed.

He reclined his head on rim of the bench, closed his eyes and went back to reliving the nerve-racking incident that kept floating up from the deep recesses of his mind.

All seemed so beautiful that day. His wife and seventeen-year- old daughter had set out with him for a picnic, unaware that the trip would turn into a nightmare, their last journey together as a speeding truck rammed into their car from behind, sending it tumbling over and over.

The terrified screams, the painful cries, the blood and bile of his dear ones spreading out—the images jolted him upright on the bench.

The man let out a painful gasp, looking around. Taking a long breath, he gathered himself, shrugging off the memory. He glanced at his watch again, before he rose to his feet and walked out of the park, recounting the car accident, which in actuality he knew was not an accident that he could accept as the will of God and forget. It was, in fact, a grave repercussion for supposedly violating a secret clause surrounding highly confidential information that threatened national security.

He had not gone far when he felt a stinging pain in his right leg. He stopped and pulled up his right leg trouser to reveal the end of the prosthetic extension was chafing against his soft deformed knee.

A gift of life. He grimaced looking at his crippled leg. Having his right limb crushed in the accident hadn't been as painful and heart- wrenching as beholding the chilling sight of his own family's corpses.

He reached for his knee and readjusted the prosthetic extension, easing the pain.

It had all taken shape almost a decade ago, when he had newly risen to the rank of major in the Indian Air Force (IAF) and was tasked with closely monitoring and ensuring the safe shipment of highly confidential consignments in the warehouse. One fateful day, unexpectedly, he had stumbled onto something unusual that had changed his life ever after. The event reappeared with striking lucidity in his mind's eye and he heard once again the voice of his corporal, his second-in-command. The man had fumbled with one of the consignments in the warehouse that were to be shipped somewhere out of the country.

"Officer!" In a loud tone, the major rebuked the corporal. "What is wrong with you? Why are you so negligent with these crates?"

The corporal motioned him towards one of the crates, "You won't believe this."

"What are you talking about?" the major said, now stiffly striding across to him. He appeared beside him and took a look into the crate, asking, "What's in there?"

The corporal pointed to a crate with an open lid. There was no need for the corporal to say anything else. The major drew startling breath analyzing the opened crate. The crate contained something the likes of which the major had never seen before. At first he thought it was a delusion, a product of stress or some hallucination stemming from his late night shifts, but in urgency after quickly reading through the paperwork and army intelligence documents accompanying the crate, he was dead certain that what he saw really existed.

Finding twenty more crates with the same label affixed on top and stacked against the corner of the warehouse, the major quickly helped the corporal repack the crates and said with startled looks, "You never saw this. Nor you'll tell anyone of this."

That was the last he had seen of it.

Never again did he desire to see the crates or their strange contents or even hear about them.

But he never expected corporal couldn't remain mum about the crates which set in motion series of gruesome events that transpired soon after. Before long, corporal was shot dead by the Intelligence, but not before the major was embroiled alongside him as being privy to the secret, as a result of which the major's family was killed. Destiny had slapped a penalty right into his face for an act of dishonesty towards his profession that he had never committed.

Now it's payback time, the major reminded of oneself, gritting his teeth.

He continued his morning walk and entered a supermarket. Along one of the long racks stacked with confectionery, he spotted someone waiting for him, someone who apart from sharing his professional background had also shared both, sweet and bitter memories from his yesteryear.

The man tossed a microphone into the food trolley he was pushing and motioned the major towards a secluded corner, where they wouldn't be overheard.

"My friend, how are you?" the major asked clipping the microphone to his ear.

"In trouble unless you realize what you're up to," the man replied taking a look at the rack housing toiletries.

"I'm glad to know you're on my side, although you refused in the beginning."

"You know?" the man insisted, "you're as stubborn as a mule. You leave no stone unturned to get what you want."

The major picked up a packet of a ready-to-eat something and showed it to the man. "Ever tried it?"

The man smiled at him, making soft eye contact that assuring his support also conjured up the wonderful times they'd shared together some two decades ago: From family get-togethers to picnics and social gatherings, the bond of friendship between them, forged out of sharing a common profession, had not fizzled out even after they had parted ways owing to duty call in different regiments of Indian army.

Now though, things had changed.

"Is it not possible that you forget your past and start a new life?" the man asked the major. "I'll be by your side like I always have been."

"You say you're my friend and yet you don't get what concerns me the most?"

"I'll place your well-being before your needs, Major. You know that well. But what you don't you understand is the sensitivity of the issue. The stakes are high now. The DIA won't care who crosses their path. History shows that they've silenced all those who've dared to cross them. And what worries me the most is having you counted as one of their victims."

"If you have forgotten, then let me remind you. I was a major in the Indian Air Force for seven years," the major reminded his friend. "I know their ins and outs like the back of my hand."

"And don't forget that it cost you and your family."

"I will never," the major replied with pain in his voice. "Not unless I avenge them for the harm." He paused briefly. "It's payback time, my friend." The man sensed acrid retribution in his voice.

"Why does your opinion sound biased to me?" the major pressed. "As if pleading with me to abandon a task I've already decided on."

Encountering silence, the major turned to the man. "If so, you may leave now."

The man walked past the major, staring at him. The major thought he was leaving, but the man didn't. To keep their close bond anonymous, the man himself had demanded that they meet in public, acting like they were strangers, to avoid drawing the attention of prying eyes.

"What's the progress on your deal?" the man asked.

"Fairing as expected. I owe it to you," the major replied. "But Jake's random destinations have made me skeptical about the possibility of him ever making it to the secret. I'm confused by his trail."

"I'm not even getting onto that," the man said. "He seems to be obsessed about ancient mysteries, which are nothing but a myth."

"I disagree," the major snapped, sounding defensive. "Don't forget that some fragments of myths and legends were true. Like the one I witnessed in those crates in the warehouse that afternoon."

Despite the major having experienced hell for no reason, he had never uttered a word on what he had actually seen in those crates that day. Proving, he had lived by his oath from the time he had sworn as Major in Indian Air Force. Even the man with whom he now conversed had never persuaded him into revealing anything about it.

"I'm running late," the man informed the major looking at his watch.

The major glanced at him and bid him adieu.

He watched his lone and dear friend, leaving the store, who had been backbone through thick and thins in his life. Even after his retirement from Indian Army, his passion for serving his nation hadn't fizzled out. An evidence, Major saw, when his friend instantly grabbed an opportunity to serve his country as Additional Director, Special Crimes Division at Central Bureau of Investigation. Who went by the name Rajath Singh.

CHAPTER 57

Drawing a long relaxing breath, assured that he was safe for now and that Taneez would be safe as well, Jake pulled out the scroll from the magnetic box and studied the final riddle he had scribbled beneath the puzzle in the scroll.

Now where does this lead to?

From the eternal city rowed by Bernini's oar
Down the Himalayas, the mystic element roar
Path to salvation is laid thru sacred portal
Seek the elixir and the star guides the mortal..

After abandoning Taneez last night in the taxi, he had hitched a peaceful ride to Mumbai in a passing truck, making it to the thickly populated suburb of Andheri in the wee hours. Feeling disgusted for smelling like a rat, he had picked up a black collared T-shirt from the streets and had entered one of the hotels in the crowded lanes, had a shower and changed his shirt keeping his denim trousers and leather jacket, before getting something to quench his hunger and then later visiting a cybercafé.

Only a little while ago, he had called Riya on a VoiP phone for security reasons. She had assisted him in solving the riddle. But except for shedding light on two phrases, the *eternal city* and *Bernini*, her analytic skills were hardly facilitative.

Jake recalled each term and its meaning.

Eternal city referred to the ancient holy city of Rome. The largest city in Italy and also its capital, Rome was situated on the banks of the River Tiber. Although it once was the capital of the Roman Republic and the Roman Empire, it was now the seat of the Roman Catholic Church. And *Bernini* was a famous Italian sculptor and an architect of the Baroque period in Italy. He lived between 1598 and 1680 and had designed plenty of churches, chapels, fountains and tombs.

The riddle was indisputably pointing to a location in India with possible connections to Rome and Bernini. And the lines that followed had something more to offer on the place where the clue to solve the snake puzzle must have lain.

Jake stared at the computer screen summoning the combination of words to type into the Google search engine.

ЖЖЖЖЖ

Additional Director, Rajat Singh, pensively stared into space over Riya's shoulder, losing himself in the strange world that Jake had been exploring: the creepy subterranean tunnel underneath Srisailam, the eerie caves of Ellora and now Riya's input on Jake's recent developments had left him utterly confounded. First of all, George embedding the secret in the cryptic illustration of a snake feeding on its own tail, leaving clues in various unusual places was strange. Then there was Riya's suggestion that the riddle was connected to Rome, Bernini and the Himalayas.

AD was still struggling to fathom any of it. He peered at the computer screen which showed the results of Riya's search.

"It's still the same," he informed her. "I can't infer anything from these phrases. Rome, Bernini and the Himalayas..." he trailed off. "What makes you even think they are connected?"

She remained silent. Cobwebbed in confusion herself, she was not in a position to make any logical deductions as of.

As AD struggled to make connection between the phrases, he saw Riya's spirits rising.

And she announced proudly, "It's Bernini who'll guide us further now."

"Did he ever come to India then?" AD leaned forward, asking eagerly, "Or did he live on the Himalayas, after retiring from his profession?"

None of that. Riya smiled, shaking her head. Chasing a string of words, she hit enter. In a fraction of a second, a dozen files materialized on the screen.

Strangely, the string of words entered in the search space made AD go disarrayed: Piazza Navona.

CHAPTER 58

That's perfect.

Athar Khan assured himself, staring himself a moment longer in the mirror as he finished tracing a thin line of kohl under his tiny set of eyes. Then he straightened his white khadi kurta, ensuring it hung loose enough to conceal his fat-bellied profile gracefully. He lifted a traditional skull cap from the table next to the mirror and placed it over his head.

I'm ready to come into your presence, he whispered raising his head to the Almighty. *Once the meeting is over.*

Just two years ago, his life had been rather different. Making his livelihood by smuggling, racketeering, trading drugs and extorting money, he thought of himself as God, thinking that only he had the power to control his destiny.

But after all, he was just human. A realization that dawned only when he was pathetically sticking to the dark corners of a dingy prison after being sentenced to life imprisonment on charges of homicide.

One night, though, it all had ended....a new life had begun.

Deprived of all hope, as he sat hungry, cold and staring helplessly at the thin wisps of light lancing through a lone window of his cell, a brisk sound of footsteps had drawn his attention at his door cell. A dark silhouette of a mysterious man had turned up at his cell with the promise of a life beyond this ignominious incarceration.

"I'm wondering how helpful it would be for you to fret on your fate instead of realizing that there's a new life out there, waiting with arms wide open." The man with his face hidden in shadows had spoken in Hindi

"Who are you?" Athar Khan asked, demanding, "What do you want?"

"That question is one, I suppose, you should ask yourself," the man answered and waved out to the jailer, who unlocked the cell, let him in and offered him a chair.

The man took a seat in a dark corner, his face concealed, making it obvious that he preferred to be anonymous.

"You believe in Islam," the man said from the shadows. "Does your religion insist that you walk along the felonious path for fulfilling your earthly desires?'

That statement speared through his ego, infuriating him. Yet a sentence of life imprisonment was more humiliating and it had mellowed him.

"Why don't you take up tasks that are legal and permitted by your religious principles?" the man asked.

Athar Khan smirked. "I think you're not aware that I'm serving life imprisonment."

"How about if I get you out of here and you work for me?"

At first, Athar Khan hadn't wanted to believe. Still, the man's unwavering voice of assurance held a promise he strongly wanted to trust. Saying nothing more, the man had silently stood up from the chair and had walked out saying, "Start dreaming big again."

The man's voice still rang clear in his ears. And as promised, within days of his visit, Athar Khan was freed from all charges and given work that was purely legal—although he was required to implement his network of thugs to orchestrate some issues—and came with the prospect of earning a large fortune.

Strangely, the mysterious man never showed up again, preferring to remain in contact over the phone and work behind the scenes. It was why Athar Khan called him *'Master.'*

Not because he never disclosed his identity. But rather, he was someone with consummate skill who could deal with any complications or consequences with ease, the way he had pulled Athar Khan out of confinement.

Now, his life had changed. He was transforming. From a notorious convict to a middle-class orthodox Muslim. And the Koran he had memorized by heart was going to be testament to his transformation.

A sense of guilt would sometimes commove his feelings calling into question his faith: were his attire and deeds merely for show or were they really in sync with true principles of Islam and whether did he really abide by what it meant?

He had finally decided to give up all his immoral doings and follow the true path of Islam, once he was done with the ongoing deal.

I'll be transfigured soon. He cast a joyous smile in the mirror. *Once the deal is through…*

He hurried towards the mosque.

The deal his master had arranged would earn him a fortune. It would suffice to buy all the luxuries he had dreamt of—a plush home with attached swimming pool, a sedan and a few fixed deposits in his name. He had already been paid a chunk of the money in a meeting conducted during a flight a few days ago.

But oddly, the true nature of his task had been kept from him. He had been told nothing except that he was required to co-ordinate with Rabindranath, a former major in the IAF, in executing a plan using his network of thugs and other resources.

Everything was shaping up smoothly until recently, when an unavoidable incident had become a major cause of concern. Expressing great rage over this, the major had called him.

"Have you lost your mind?" the major hollered in Hindi. "Listen, Major..."

"No, you listen to me, Mr. Khan," the major had interrupted, "Your men have grievously injured four Intelligence officers, plunging them into a deep trench. Do you even have any idea of the consequences of locking horns with the Intelligence?"

Athar Khan fell silent.

"This is a covert operation, Mr. Khan," the major fumed. "Not a case of extortion, where your goons are at liberty to do as they please. One single mistake and we all are screwed."

"Understood," Athar Khan replied and hung up.

CHAPTER 59

Piazza Navona is an extremely popular and beautiful city square in the entire of Rome. Situated at the center of Rome, west of the Pantheon, it is one of the liveliest city squares, replete with outdoor cafes, restaurants and night clubs.

As an example of Baroque architecture. Piazza Navona is known for its elaborate and extensive ornamentation, specifically the exterior characterized by dramatic central projections, forming an outstanding piece of artwork that includes the Church of Saint Agnese in Agone and three magnificent fountains.

The southern end of the square is adorned by the Fontana del Maro, which has a basin and four tritons, sculpted by Giacomo della Porta in 1575 and further embellished by Bernini, who added a statue of a Moor wrestling with a dolphin at the center.

Towards the northern end lies the second fountain, the Fontana Del Nettuno or the fountain of Neptune, created by Giacomo della Porta again, in 1576. The statue of Neptune surrounded by sea nymphs was added later.

The main attraction of the Piazza Navona is, however, the famous fountain that sits perfectly at the center of the square, forming a masterpiece and the largest fountain called Fontana Dei Quattro Fiumi--the fountain of the four rivers.

Another important structure that stands prominently facing the square is the church of Saint Agnese in Agone, commissioned in 1652 by Pope Innocent X. This church was designed by Girolami Rainaldi and Francesco Borromini.

This morning, however, it was neither the church nor the two fountains at the north and south ends of the square that had Riya engrossed. It was rather, the largest and famous fountain situated at the center of the square, that went by the name --the Fontana Dei Quattro Fiumi.

Riya smiled proudly at AD, having figured out the location the first line in the riddle was pointing to.

ӜӜӜӜӜ

Giovanni Lorenzo Bernini, famously known as Bernini lived between 1598 and 1680. A leading sculptor in Renaissance Italy, he was endowed with a peculiar talent for capturing both the real essence of a narrative moment in marble and where the sculpture would be situated, rendering himself a peerless artist of his time. Owing to his strong religious beliefs, he embodied light as a key metaphorical element in designing the setting for his work, making himself stand out from rest of his contemporaries. He believed that it was the hidden light source that intensified the focus of religious worship or enhanced the dramatic movement of the sculptural narrative itself.

Amongst many of his accomplishments, one of his popular creations is the Fontana Dei Quattro Fiumi, the fountain of four rivers, erected right opposite the Church of Saint Agnese.

After reading the search results, Jake clicked on the hyperlink to the History of Fontana Dei Quattro Fiumi. The webpage began to load. Meanwhile, Jake glanced at his watch and noted that it was 11 AM.

I must soon get in touch with Riya. Jake read the now opened webpage.

The Fontana Dei Quattro Fiumi is the fountain of four rivers, designed by Bernini in 1650. The history of the design of the fountain unquestionably deserves mention as it recounts an interesting tale of victory of Bernini's talent over his rivals and of his artistic brilliance over obstinate minds. When Pope Innocent X planned to set up the great Obelisk brought to Rome by the Emperor Caracalla, he had designs made for its adornment by the leading architects of Rome except Bernini, since his rivals had influenced the Pope against him. But the wife of Prince Niccolo Ludovisi, the Pope's niece, persuaded Bernini to prepare a model, which she later secretly installed in a room in the Palazzo Pamphilj that the Pope had to pass. Struck by its beauty and magnificence, the Pope stopped to look at it closely. After admiring it, he said: "This is a trick… It will be necessary to employ Bernini in spite of those who do not wish it, for he who desires not to use Bernini's designs, must take care not to see them."

Jake found nothing of relevance to the clue. He skipped a few paragraphs and read on.

The fountain features four figures, each representing four great rivers from four great continents of bygone times:

The Nile,

The Ganges, The Danube,

And the Rio Della Plata.

His eyes quickly zapped back, seizing on the name of the second river: *The Ganges?*

For a fleeting second, Jake was surprised to find a reference to the River Ganges, the holy River Ganga of India, in a medieval sculpture of ancient Rome, which was amazing in itself. He continued to read:

Designs of each god are semi-prostate and surround the Egyptian Obelisk, having a symbolic importance pertaining to the significance each continent and the river carried at that time.

Jake magnified the high resolution image of the fountain.

All the sculptures in the fountain supported the Egyptian Obelisk. On the flanges of the reef were personifications of the four rivers, supported by lions, other animals and plants, each carrying its own identification, allegories and metaphors connected with it. Together, it appeared like a spectacle in action that could be seen by circling around it. He browsed images of each side one by one, taking in the short narrative under them.

The first image emphasized the river Danube, touching the Papal coat of arms, signifying its location which falls in closest proximity to the holy city of Rome.

The second one was the Rio Della Plata, a semi-prostate god sitting on a pile of coins, symbolic of the riches America could offer Europe and scared of the snake, implying the rich man's fear of his money being stolen.

The third figurine's head was draped in loose cloth, representing the river Nile, implying that no one at that point of time knew exactly where the Nile's source was.

Jake's mind started firing swiftly as he came to the last image on the fountain.

The fourth sculpture was in reference to the Ganges. The figurine was holding an elongated pole like structure that dipped into the water of the fountain, signifying the river's navigability.

That's an oar… Jake recognized the instrument used for rowing the boat. *'Bernini's oar…'*

He grew eager as the first line of the riddle unscrambled. And the word mystic element, Jake realized, was referring to *'water.'*

The river waters of Ganges...***'rowed by Bernini's oar... down the Himalayas, the mystic element roar...***

The second line disentangled.

But that rendered him a little anxious, as the river stretched thousands of miles down the Himalayas making it arduous to figure out what exact location the riddle was pointing to.

Jake looked at the third line from the riddle.

Path to salvation is laid thru sacred portal.

Salvation...sacred portal... Jake tried linking these two phrases with the Ganges.

According to age-old beliefs, River Ganga, also known as Ganges, was the path to salvation, Jake recalled. And the water of the Ganges was a divine element that flowed through several holy cities down the landscape of north India. Every Hindu was required to make a pilgrimage to the river's banks and bathe in its waters to purge their soul of sins, before they died.

But sacred portal? Jake was still clueless about that. *Portal is a gateway... What am I missing here?*

He re-read the last line of the riddle.

Seek the elixir and the star guides the mortal.

This line, he knew, was referring to something that had to be looked for. *But where?*

He looked at the phrase *'sacred portal.' Sacred portal...River Ganga.* All he could guess was that the phrase *'portal'* was referring to some location on the banks of the River Ganga.

Wondering over this, he called Riya over the VoiP phone.

CHAPTER 60

Power always comes at a cost.

Ajeet Awasthi, an opposition leader in Indian Parliament, sat ruminating deeply over this line. Garbed in half-sleeved linen shirt, even in his late sixties, he had charm for tactics that many from his age and profession would lack.

In his remarkable political career, he had grown old tasting only success, repeatedly being re-elected, a massive record in itself. People had often speculated that he had all the lucky planets on his side, favoring him with great fortune. Politics, and all his followers, had known him only by one name: The Invincible, the man who could never be defeated.

As in name, so in fate, Ajeet Awasthi thought, letting a proud smile bloom on his lips; Ajeet—the one who was invincible.

It was from his strengths that he had learnt to draw great pride, which had not only kept him abreast of the fast-changing facets of Indian politics, but had also helped him navigate the landscape of hardships in his staggering four decades of political career.

Knowing that he was now on the cusp of a breakthrough in his career, he glanced at his wristwatch and then back again out the window of the train coach, looking for any sign that the wilderness outside was giving way to traces of urban life.

But only bare fields greeted him.

He was looking forward to a discreet and an unofficial meeting due shortly with a party whose members were to board the train from one of the upcoming stations. Meanwhile, his thoughts turned to the travails of his past.

In the general elections five years ago, his political party had suffered a massive defeat. Loosing seats across all major states of the country, even in regions where their foothold was strong, they failed to secure even a mere sixty seats in the total five hundred and forty five seat in Lok Sabha parliament.

It was a great letdown for the independent parties who had planned forging an alliance with his party. As the storm in the political waters grew fierce and turbulent and most of the old politicians succumbed, he remained an exception, managing to keep his head above water. One serious problem, however, was that their supporting political parties had decided to split and withdraw from a political alliance.

Seeing it as another could be defeat, he sought ways to mend the alliance in all possible ways. It was around this time that a mysterious call, like a ray of hope, changed the fate of his political party for the better.

Spreading sheets of research data on the table, this mysterious man, who demanded secrecy over his identity, had explained in a secret meeting how his political party was sure to win the elections if Ajeet signed a pact with him. The pact, more of a business deal, apart from pinpointing the reasons behind the recent setbacks of his political party, also promised to entrust him with a powerful secret so devastating that if revealed would not only shake the foundations of all the religions in the world, but also bring down the ruling Indian government on its knees.

Having realized its potential, Ajeet Awasthi had instantly locked a verbal deal worth millions of dollars with the man in exchange for that powerful secret.

Over a confidential meeting with his allied parties, Ajeet Awasthi had brought up the matter, citing its bright prospects in the forthcoming elections. But to his surprise, he had several brows raised at him doubtfully when he had tabled his proposal to keep the alliance.

One of them had reacted almost instantly, sarcastically. "I wonder how devastating the disclosure is that it would topple the ruling government in the coming elections."

"I agree," another political party leader said,. "The whole country is humming the songs of the success of the ruling government. In such times, I believe that the so-called disclosure will only have a minimal impact on its performance."

After a long pause, Ajeet Awasthi had said, "I'm certain of what I have told you. This secret was born at the time when our ruling government last came to power in the early nineteen hundred. Ever since, even after the government was off the charts until now, the secret was protected and made privy only to an elite group. To those who serve high ranks in the government. It showcases the dark side of our government, its old ties with countries like USA, Russia and China to deceive people for decades, keeping the greatest truth from the mankind."

"What is the secret after all?" one of the politicians asked, as if he wanted to put an end to the argument, the meeting and the alliance itself.

"I'm afraid you'll have to wait a little longer to learn that," Ajeet Awasthi replied.

"Fine then," one ill-tempered member from the party said, rising from his chair to leave. "You'll also know very soon about our decision on whether we're still interested in keeping the alliance with your party."

He found all the members about to leave.

Saying nothing, Ajeet Awasthi had walked up to each one of them and handed them a data sheet. They paused as they read through the paper. Soon, they were slipping back into their seats in shock.

Striding up to the video screen on the wall, Ajeet Awasthi had brought up a slide of a bar graph, depicting party-wise early election projections from different states across the country. It was the same projection, all the political parties remembered, that had instigated them to end all ties with his political party.

"These projections were released by the media," Ajeet Awasthi elaborated, "and the ones in the sheets in your hands have come from an inside source. The inside source, as you all know, is more accurate, reliable and credible than that released by the media."

All the political leaders looked down at their sheets and felt a deepening concern as the figures mentioned in the sheet were not even close to half the mark they were expecting. It was a pathetic projection, which indicated that the ruling government was clearly on the upswing, while their parties seemed to take a big hit once again. Irrespective of the fate of this alliance, the data showed that the ruling government was sure to retain power for the next five year term. Besides, they couldn't risk ignoring his estimations as he had banked his entire career on his projections, winning back-to-back elections.

The information left the members in great tumult.

He eyed them seriously, confident that his plan had worked. "I suppose, now you know what choices to make."

After that, he had walked out of the conference hall while the party members were still glued to their seats, yet to emerge from their dismay.

But the same evening, he heard from all the political leaders, promising to keep their alliance and provide whatever support he needed.

Since then, there was no looking back.

A soft commotion snapped him back from his daze.

His assistant escorted two men into his compartment and made them comfortable in seats opposite him.

Ajeet cast a genial smile at them. He remembered their names well: Former Major Rabindranath, IAF, and Mr. Athar Khan, whom he'd seen at a confidential meeting during a flight a couple of days ago.

Over a short period, they mulled over the operation, *The Lost Arcanum,* that they were a part of, its developments and its future outcomes. Ajeet Awasthi expressed his deep concern over the grievously injured Intelligence officers, citing it as an act of negligence and warning them against such future recklessness.

Once finished, he turned to his assistant and signaled him. The assistant produced an attaché case stuffed with wads of cash and handed it over to them.

The major accepted the attaché case and looked into it.

"Ten million dollars," Ajeet informed the major. "The second installment as per the deal."

The major nodded, closed the attaché case and passed it on to Athar Khan.

"And the rest once I get the link," Ajeet said, concluding the meeting.

CHAPTER 61

"*Jake this portal* you're looking for is a figurative one," Riya assured him, "a metaphorical gateway that doesn't exist in reality."

She continued, scrolling through pages on the computer in front of her. "Probably based on one of the legends that state that the Ganga was a celestial lady dwelling in heaven. Her service was required on earth for the benefit of mankind. She was persuaded to descend to earth through the matted locks of Lord Shiva, who allowed for a controlled flow, lest she flood the entire landscape with her powerful currents."

Riya could not imagine what the metaphorical portal was referring to, but she suddenly realized something.

"The riddle suggests up towards the sky, Jake," she said. "Towards heaven, the term portal is pointing to heaven."

For the past few minutes, AD had seen his chamber turn into the home of legends, drawing him into a maze of ancient mysteries where myths were being brought back to life. He couldn't help but sit back and watch.

Jake responded, "Riya, the phrase 'portal' is, of course, a metaphorical term. But it occurs to me, it's not essentially heaven. It's something more. A physical location, also revered figuratively as a sacred portal. It may be a holy place along the shores of the Ganga " Jake paused. "Like Varanasi, Rishikesh or Devprayag?"

Riya was silent as she scrolled back to the top of the page, tracing the names of the locations he had announced. Then she paused finding something and her face was aglow. "There you go, Jake," Riya said excitedly. "You're correct. The term *'sacred portal'* does refer to a precise location along the shores of the Ganga, but none of the places you've mentioned."

Jake held the phone to his ears tightly. *Then, what is it?*

Riya moved the cursor to the top of the page.

AD leaned over the table, reading what her cursor was pointing at and looked at her in surprise.

She smiled, reading the name aloud. "It's Haridwar."

"Jesus!" Jake was taken by surprise. "You're right, Riya. It's Haridwar. Dwar refers to a gateway, a portal, and Hari is Lord Vishnu, which would make it sacred." He paused in awe. "That's absolutely what it is…Haridwar is a sacred portal."

The path to salvation is laid through sacred portal…Haridwar.

"And the last line in the riddle?" Riya demanded. "What do you think it means?"

"Not sure," Jake said thoughtfully. "The waters of the Ganga will reveal."

"Jake," Riya said, "I know someone who might be able to help you in this regard."

CHAPTER 62

10.50 AM.

The hum of the airfoils of the Boeing 737 Jet Airways flight en route to Haridwar, deepened as it banked high over the clouds.

Inside its plush interior seating and bright lighting, Jake adjusted in his seat, his brown leather jacket lying across his lap with the magnetic box stuffed in a pocket.

He thanked Riya for arranging a seat in this Mumbai-Dehradun outbound flight in the nick of time. With the final riddle almost cracked, he had set out to unscramble whatever the last line in the riddle guarded, one which possibly was hidden within the waters of Ganges flowing across the ancient holy city of Haridwar. The ancient city which was only fifty kilometers from Dehradun, an hour and half by road.

Jake looked out of the window at a bird's eye view of the city beneath. From this height, the hundred kilometer radius of the urban Mumbai had scaled down to only a few meters. His pulse raced at the scary scene below, fueling his acrophobia.

Then suddenly, he felt a tightening in his chest when he heard a familiar voice.

"Good to see you, Mr. Jake." A voice erupted from sideways.

Jake turned abruptly to find the JIC's chief coordinator, David Craig, slipping into the empty seat beside him. He wore a brown jacket over a white striped cotton shirt and dark blue denim trousers.

Damn it! Jake cursed under his breath.

"You know what I really like about this job?" David said, smiling derisively as he adjusted into his seat. "I love to see the faces of the hunted. A blend of fear and worry that runs deep."

How in the world had David known that he was aboard this flight? Was someone snooping on him? Or David was keeping close tabs on his whereabouts, wanting to pick on him alone.

Jake was still wondering, when the air-hostess appeared with drink for David. A plain soda. Thanking her with a bow of his head, David turned back to Jake.

"But, I'm impressed." He sipped his drink. "Despite stealing the link from under the watchful eyes of the DIA, beating up top Intelligence officials for crossing your path, your composure is intact."

Jake was jolted getting an official confirmation for the first time, from another official, on the involvement of the DIA. Keeping his surprise to himself, he met David's gaze.

"I have no 'link', contrary to what you and the DIA believe."

"And you want me to believe some jack shit story of yours?" David's voice was now grating. He sipped from his glass. "The link which your father bequeathed to you belongs to the DIA. And things that belong to the DIA are confiscated, first on request and then by the use of force, if necessary."

"And if I deny to comply with DIA?" Jake ventured.

"In that case," David said, "it'll be my pleasure to manhandle you, Mr. Jake. But before I do the honors, my profession obliges me to brief you on some crucial information which I think you're not aware off."

Jake raised his eyebrows. Like?

"It's apparent your father shared the information with someone before he hid that link for you. And that someone has conspired against him and his team members, further coaxing you to take up this mission."

Jake thought about this for a moment. "So you think I've been manipulated?"

"Unquestionably," David replied with a smirk. "I'm afraid you're part of a conspiracy that got your father and his team killed. They saved you by chasing our men into that deep trench yesterday." He paused staring into Jake's eyes. "They are aiding you to so that you will reveal what we are hell-bent on keeping buried."

As David sipped his drink, Jake thought about what he had heard. He thought back to witnessing the truck roaring up behind the SUV and pushing it into the deep trench. The idea of an external agency being involved made sense and seemed credible. But he preferred not to jump to conclusions at this point.

"So what have you decided?" David's voice sliced through his contemplation. "Just do as I say. Give me that link and I'll ensure that you are acquitted of all charges."

Jake said nothing. He wondered whether this theory about third-party involvement in the quest a real fact or a cleverly presented drama to trick him into surrendering? Any which way, he realized he was left with just two options: one, to surrender himself and the link, which he would not do after coming so close to completing the quest. Second, to break loose from David's clutches and complete what he had set out for, which again seemed impossible considering for the limited options in the flight.

Either way, his quest seemed to be screwed.

"Link…" David pressed, tabling his glass and spreading his hands.

Jake remained quiet. He continued to stare at David, clearly not ready to comply.

"Then, I'm sorry," David said, sliding his hands into his pocket. "I'm not in a position to compromise national security."

Producing handcuffs, he clasped one around Jake's hand and locked the other on the armrest of his seat. "This is the only option you've left me."

"Is there any problem, sir?" The hostess intervened seeing the handcuffs on Jake's hand.

"Can I have another soda?" David flashed her his ID card.

Still, her eyes glanced quickly from the handcuffs to Jake and back to David, before she nodded reluctantly. "Sure."

When the air-hostess disappeared, Jake reminded David. "This is your second glass. And too much of anything is bad, Mr. David. It could knock you unconscious."

"Poor choice of words," David could afford a sympathetic smile in return. "I suggest you prepare yourself to overcome the discomfort when you have a bunch of intelligence guys swarming over you once we hit the tarmac."

Jake discounted his remarks, turning away and looking out of the window.

"However, I'll have a short nap," David told Jake. "Your quest has cost me many sleepless nights. Don't I deserve a short nap at least?"

David stretched in his seat and closed his eyes.

Desolate, Jake helplessly stared out the window.

CHAPTER 63

David felt powerful arms jerk him from his sleep.

Groggily, he opened his eyes, to find himself surrounded by his officials, as if they were doctors and trying to revive him with CPR in an operation theater.

With more effort, he tried to shift in his seat, but an acute heaviness throbbed in his head, pinning him back into his seat. He tried to shake its grasp with the hints of awareness now breaking through his ache, bringing back a tangle of blurred images from the last thing he remembered. The images of him cornering Jake, followed by an argument and then handcuffing him before he slipped into a short nap.

With sudden instinct, David twisted to his left at the seat next to him, only to discover it empty. *Damn!* David closed his eyes. "I handcuffed him."

The official flashed him the same handcuff, holding it high. "We found this locked around your wrist, hooked to the armrest of your seat."

Enraged by the news that Jake had escaped, he attempted to rise from his seat, but a hammering pain pinned him back in his seat. David moved his hands to his head, trying to locate the source of pain.

"The heaviness will fade away soon, sir," one of the official said. David glanced over at him with a look of uncertainty.

"It's a mild sedative," the official replied. "It will last for an hour at the most."

"I was sedated?" David asked in surprise.

The official nodded and produced the glass from which David had sipped his drink. He was also handed a note which they had found tucked beneath the glass. David reached for the note and read it.

"As I told you, too much soda can have side effects, including this one. Anyway, better luck next time."

"Son of a bitch!" David cursed under his breath.

His officials explained how they had arrived as soon as the wheels hit the tarmac and checked each passenger before letting them exit; Jake was nowhere to be found.

Having listened to the story, David took a moment to get his bearings. He glanced at his officials and instructed, "Locate the air-hostess who served me the drink."

"She's missing too, sir," the official replied. David shook his head in disbelief.

His head was hurting acutely, not as much from the sedation as it was from the news that Jake had escaped right from under his nose, questioning his very ability to take him into custody even when he was within arm's reach.

Now in this silent moment of impuissance, David pondered that Jake was his personal foe more than a threat to national security. He swore he would nab Jake, to settle his own scores, and then wipe any trace of the man from the face of earth.

CHAPTER 64

12.15 PM.

CBI Headquarters.

AD returned to his table with two mugs of coffee and held one out for Director General Balbeer Singh, who sat opposite him, apparently lost in deep thought.

As if sensing his turmoil, the aroma of freshly brewed coffee swirling inside the chamber, diffusing through his olfactory senses, snapped him out of his ruminations, returning the critical issues that he was here to discuss.

There was silence as both men sipped their coffee.

Balbeer Singh was the first to speak. "We've known each other for several years. But we have barely spoken." He grinned. "And I'm glad that you're assisting us in our mission."

AD smiled, quietly sipping the coffee.

"Your input on Jake was of paramount importance. Otherwise, tracking his unpredictable moves would have been cumbersome."

"I place my country before any other bonds," AD clarified, making clear his filial affection for Jake was second to his profession.

Balbeer concurred with a smile.

At that point, Riya gave a soft knock on the door and entered the chamber. She gave a firm handshake to Balbeer before she took a seat next to him.

"I appreciate your assistance," Balbeer offered to her. "Your updates on Jake are really helping us a lot."

"It's my duty, sir," she answered impassively. .

Balbeer nodded.

"But despite our efforts, I'm confused about why he is still missing?" AD interjected.

Balbeer let out a troubled gasp. "We have information that suggests the involvement of some shadowy organization that has been responsible for our failures. They're aware that Jake possesses the link. Now they're using him to recover it for themselves." He said seriously, "In other words, he's been manipulated."

AD and Riya exchanged uncertain looks.

Balbeer looked at them. "I thought you might have some clue about this. That's another reason I'm here."

They met his gaze blankly.

"Anyway, we won't let him slip away this time," Balbeer continued. "Once he's been nabbed, the link will be confiscated and buried forever. It has been a threat to our national security since his father first uncovered it some two decades ago." As Balbeer spoke, he could sense their curiosity building. "Our nation is safe as long as the secret is buried. If it becomes public knowledge, the repercussions would be terrible. It will trigger hostile conditions across the country and elsewhere in the world, calling into question our very own beliefs in religion that any nations stands upon."

Balbeer paused knowing he wasn't at liberty to divulge any more information.

AD did not press the issue. Silence reigned in the chamber for a few moments. Their silence was an assurance to Balbeer that they too shared his concern about the country's security.

"We're here to serve our country and ensuring its safety is our duty," Balbeer stated somberly."Even if we have to go to any lengths to guarantee this safety."

Allowing his statements to sink in, Balbeer pushed himself up from the seat to leave, when Riya stopped him.

"You might want to know this."

Scribbling something on a small fragment of paper, she handed it to Balbeer. He instantly knew what he was looking at:

29° 54° North 78° 07° East. The geographical coordinates Jake was now heading to.

CHAPTER 65

About *twenty-five* minutes into his drive from the CBI headquarters, General Balbeer Singh, resting in the backseat of his chauffeur-driven limo, checked his cell phone to ensure he hadn't missed a call. Something was bothering him more than the absence of the call he was awaiting.

Jake's unusual course: From Srisailam to the caves of Ellora, and now to Haridwar.

None of these locations made any sense to him, as they seemed irrelevant to the link. He seriously doubted if these places were in any way connected to the classified information itself.

What else does he know? he pondered, going back to a time in December 1992…

Lieutenant Colonel Balbeer Singh of the Indian Army with other officers from the IAF and the team of scientists—Anurag Chopra, Ramanujan and Jaswanth Sinha—were seated around a desk, listening to the archaeologist George Stevens earnestly expounding on the researched ancient scrolls, a year after they had been recovered from the ruins of the two thousand years old monastery north of Rajasthan in the desert of Thar.

George's intense voice and distinctive facial expressions were imbued with a mysterious quality that was unforgettable. Balbeer Singh remembered it more thoroughly.

"It's been such a great honor to be a part of this research committee," George said with a firm voice. "I'm overwhelmed, Mr. Balbeer Singh. Thanks for allowing me this privilege."

Balbeer Singh accepted his compliments with reserved nod, calling to memory the altercation that had sparked up between them at the monastery as to who would keep the discovered ancient scrolls, with Balbeer seventually confiscating it in national interest.

George swept a glance at everyone. "The scrolls that we've recovered from the ruins are not any ordinary. They bear intricate, mysterious illustrations and descriptions that are elaborated with great eloquence in Pali, one of the oldest languages known to ancient Indians.

"When the contents of those scrolls were unscrambled with the help of our scientists," he motioned towards his research team, "the results were incredible. We were amazed at what seemed to be the extraordinary ability of our ancestors to produce sophisticated and advanced technology as far back as 300 BC."

Even though Balbeer had seen those scrolls before, he felt his pulse throb as George advanced towards a display wall.

Holding the remote, George said, "Gentlemen, I take great pride in presenting to you some of those technologies whose sheer magnitude surpasses all the frontiers of advanced science known to us today."

The moment George lit the display, the officials gasped in awe at the complex illustrations. He saw recognition flickering in their eyes as they absorbed the intricacy of the diagrams and their detailed descriptions.

George let out a chortle. "You've guessed it right, gentlemen. The Wright brothers weren't the first ones to fly airplanes."

Officials watched in stunned silence as George continued.

"These are ancient flying machines that were used in olden times." Balbeer Singh watched in awe too.

"Flying machines," George said, "that we once thought were a fantasy and relegated to mythologies or legends, really did exist at some point in history. And this ancient Indian document is proof of its existence.

"This is the most ground-breaking document ever to be found and researched. Which gives us knowledge of everything that happened five thousand years ago on this planet." George glanced at them with a sense of pride. "It'll provide deep insight on the fact that there was a world here before our own. Populated by a technologically advanced race that used flying machines known as *vimanas*." He paused, letting the statement sink. "If some of you can remember, these are the same vehicles referred to in Vedic literature."

"Like the vehicle in which Ravana abducted Sita?" one of the officials asked earnestly.

"Exactly," George replied, excited. "But to elaborate, I have to go back in time to when Rama's empire spanned the continent of Asia."

The officials listened to him with keen interest.

"Many serious scholars deny the existence of such an empire. But these documents speak of all those dramatic episodes as factual events and prove its historical validity."

Archaeologist George Stevens explained to them about Rama-Empire.

Known to exist some five thousand years ago, Rama-Empire grossly spanned across north India and Pakistan on the Indian sub-continent and had many large and highly advanced cities. The ruins of many of these can still be found in the deserts of northern and western India and Pakistan.

The officials sat completely engrossed as he further detailed the seven greatest capital cities known as *saptah rishis* that belonged to the Rama-Empire. Ancient Indian texts reveal that the people from this era had owned sophisticated flying machines. Their designs varied from double-deckers, long cylindrical ones to cigar-shaped airships, circular aircraft with portholes and domes, very much like a modern-day flying saucer. These craft flew with the speed of wind and emanated a melodious sound.

George pulled up another illustration on the screen.

"There were these aerodynamically designed structures that flew in mysterious ways and were believed to have been made by some intelligent entities, as mentioned in ancient texts such as the *Rig-Veda*, the *Ramayana* and the *Mahabharata*, having many features similar to that of Unidentified Flying Objects or UFOs."

The officials crinkled their brows, exchanging amused glances at each other, while some chuckled derisively at the mention of UFOs.

George frowned at their reactions. "I'm not a UFO buff," he said, "who stays awake all night in the paddy fields, hoping for a glimpse of some strange unidentified lights creating a crop circle."

The officials remained silent, assuming George had taken offense.

George clarified seriously. "I'm just drawing some similarities with features attributed to UFOs." After a second, a thin smile broke out on his lips. "Who knows, I might find one while doing so..."

The officials broke out into laughter, appreciating George's humor midst a serious lecture on ancient technology.

George went over the next set of illustrations. "The technology used to fly these machines is a propulsion system based on a combination of gyroscopes, electricity and mercury. Mercury is a unique element and it is also a metal, a liquid and a conductor of electricity. It was placed into an enclosed gyroscopic arrangement and made to spin around it. And when electrified, it produced the effects of levitation and anti-gravity and emitted bright light."

"Essentially," George continued, "the *vimanas* were powered by a combination of gyroscopes placed inside a sealed liquid mercury vortex. The machines were very powerful. It is mentioned in the scriptures that during takeoff, elephants and other creatures went berserk at the sound of exhaust, that which was produced when gas was thrown out with pressure from these engines."

Balbeer Singh sat alert in his seat, intrigued by what he was being told.

"In addition, the flying machines were equipped with specialized devices known as *yantras*, accommodated in various parts of the vehicles."

George clicked on the next picture and detailed different types of *yantras* that served special functions, starting with *darpanas* (lenses or mirrors), *manis*(crystals) and *nadis* (channels and outputs), all of which were operated in combination for harnessing energy from various natural sources, including sunlight.

As George lectured, Balbeer Singh watched his officials, who seemed impressed with George's knowledge and presentation skills. His unwavering voice, Balbeer realized, also contributed to keep his audience engrossed.

"Among the yantras, mirrors were the most substantial component. They performed light-related functions By reflecting, deflecting, redirecting, attracting and amplifying light and energy beams, these mirrors were used as primary weaponry systems for attacking and for defense.

"Let's ponder on one specific type of mirror," George said, pointing to a diagram on the screen. "It worked on a principle akin to television technology where the device captured high-resolution images of activities around the *vimana* and then projected it onto the screens inside for the crew."

"It sounds to me like advanced surveillance cameras!" one of the officials said in amusement.

"Very much so." George gave an appreciating nod. "The second one is a weaponry device, consisting of a special redirecting mirror that harnessed energy from the sun and winds and then used the combination to disable the enemy."

He paused, observing everyone in the room. "Basically, it is a directed energy weapon, similar to laser guns from the famous Star Wars movie."

Murmurs rose among the officials at the mention of the Star Wars movie. A popular science-fiction series, it portrayed characters using futuristic weapons like laser and stun guns. The franchise went on to become one of the best motion pictures to be ever produced and directed in the history of Hollywood.

"Star Wars borrowed heavily from the ancient Indian arsenal.. " Colonel Balbeer Singh added, diffusing a little humor which garnered everyone's laughter.

George was enjoying every minute of his demonstration on the researched ancient Indian documents. The response of the officials encouraged him to go on.

"But," George said, "the third type of mirror is more interesting. It performed operations akin to cloaking technology."

The officials waited.

"A cloaking technology, in which enemies were confused by projecting battlefield images and changing the appearance of the *vimana* with special deflecting mirrors. Much as today's optical stealth or holographic technology."

"Stealth technology?" one official repeated, slightly puzzled. "But I remember you saying that this technology was restricted to ancient Indian documents." The official paused glancing at his colleagues and back at him, before he pressed, "So your proposition is that USA has plagiarized this technology from these documents found in India?"

Serving in the defense forces for decades, the officials in the room were well equipped with knowledge of latest technologies being implemented by different military forces across the globe. Especially, the mysterious stealth technology, which evolved between the 1930s and 1940s when rapid worldwide development in radar systems fueled the need for stealth planes in times of war. These were the advanced crafts that defied radar systems and penetrated enemy lines, undetected. Post World War-II, the CIA had worked on different classified projects, developing advanced reconnaissance spacecraft, of which U-2 spy planes was exceptional. Then, suddenly, the CIA shifted its interest from U-2 spy planes to another ambitious project, called *Have Blue*, in collaboration with the US Department of Defense, keeping the development a secret until 1989, when it thrilled the world, unveiling its most successful stealth aircraft till date: F-117.

Having done a fair amount of research on stealth technology himself, George answered the official's query.

"Not actually. There's more to the story. Since these documents were discovered in our country, so my explanation about the history of the technology is restricted to the Indian sub-continent. Otherwise, these types of flying machines, in addition to India, were also used all over ancient Egypt and in Atlantis--the legendary island in the Atlantic Ocean which was believed to be swallowed by an earthquake.

"The aircraft used by Atlanteans was known as *vailixi*. Technologically more advanced than that of the Indians. The Atlanteans find mention in the ancient Indian texts as *asvins*. Although no ancient texts on *vailixi* are known to exist, some information has managed to survive through esoteric and occult sources, which describes flying machines that were cigar-shaped, identical to *vimanas* and could maneuver underwater, in the atmosphere and in outer space."

George noted that everyone was listening to him attentively. With his extensive research on the documents and his knowledge of history, he'd furnished them enough sources for corroborating all the facts he had put forward.

Cell phone vibrated on the seat next to Balbeer Singh, propelling him back from the past to the inside of the limo.

He reached for his cell, connected, listened to the voice and yelled. "I knew that son of a whore was double-crossing us."' He steadied his anger and steadied his breath. "Anyway, you get me more updates on the issue." He disconnected the call and tossed the phone on the seat next to him. He tried to calm his frayed nerves. Yet his mind was dazed with the caller's worry that introduced a whole lot of acrid possibilities.

He quickly pulled a laptop from its bag and turned it on. Shuffling through his suit buttons, he detached a small gadget and connected it to his laptop. He hit some keys on the keypad and transferred the data from the gadget to his laptop and then to his phone memory. Once this was done, he sent the data to a contact and leaned back in his seat, trying to relieve his stress.

As he watched high-rises pass in a quick blur outside the window, he couldn't help going back to playing the remaining episode of George's research on scrolls.

Towards the end of the lecture, George and his team of scientists were surrounded by the officials, who showered them congratulations and applause for their contributions in the research they thought was marvelous.

But Balbeer Singh stayed away, sticking close to the display, taking a close look at the illustrations. Seeing which, George excused himself from the group and walked up to Balbeer and stood beside him.

"It's a staggering accomplishment by the ancients," Balbeer said sensing George next to him, without taking his eyes off the illustrations. "It's incredible, unbelievably marvelous."

"Staggering, of course," George agreed after a brief moment. "Marvelous, of course, again."

Balbeer turned to him. "But not as dark and mysterious a secret your organization has been hiding from the world for decades."

George eyed Balbeer suspiciously, as if accusing him of a serious crime. "I'm sorry," Balbeer Singh tried to grasp his implications, although he realized what George might be hinting at.

"I know what you're hiding there somewhere." George repeated somberly.

Before Balbeer Singh could say a word, George had stalked away, leaving him with an acute sense of foreboding that would later, with time, multiply thousand fold.

His cell beeped again, bringing him back into the limo from the past. Balbeer picked up his cell and hit the answer button. "I hope you got the message. Keep it. And I assume you know what to do with it."

As he signed off, the words spoken by George way back in 1992, returned with frightening clarity. *Not as dark and mysterious a secret your organization has been hiding from the world for decades.*

His voice seemed unmistakably clear, pointing at a secret that, indeed, DIA was hiding from the world for decades.

CHAPTER 66

Since the beginning of time there have always been places on earth, in every continent, that have been revered as holy and divine, where special forces sprouting from the navel of Mother Nature are believed to provide access to some kind of mystically miraculous powers. Sacred mountains, healing springs and caverns, to name a few, that captivate millions of devotees with their charismatic dimensions.

Undeniably, one such place, in the very heart of the Indian subcontinent, is the River Ganges. The very name of the river seems to inspire might and sanctity, just like its turbulent streams, echoing from the dawn of history to the present times, from the pristine realms of heaven to the vast expanse of the earth, evoking a profound veneration in everyone's heart.

Considered sacred, River Ganges is one of the prime rivers of India, laced with powerful religious, historical and mythological significance. Worshipped as Mother Ganga or *Ganga Maiyya,* it has been witness to different human civilizations and has been a symbol of the great Indian culture.

Emerging from a stunning eleven thousand feet above the mean sea level—from the icy caves of the Gangotri glaciers, which resembles the snout of a cow and is called 'Gaumukh'—it melts into life as Bhagirathi River, which is thirty kilometers long and four kilometers wide. This tributary then flows downwards, gushing, tossing and gurgling to join with River Alaknanda before it transforms into the mighty Ganga. Its powerful currents, cascading down the Himalayan terrain, become navigable and tranquil as it reaches the shores of Haridwar at the foothills of the Shivalik Range.

Haridwar, the ancient city nestled along the austere banks of the River Ganga, is a pilgrimage site of great significance for Hindus, drawing millions of people into its embrace. Along its shores, a congregation of tourists and devotees bathe in the waters to wash away their sins and perform major religious rites associated with birth and death.

The name 'Haridwar', stems from Sanskrit, connoting *dwar* or gateway of Hari, where Hari refers to Lord Vishnu. The city is a gateway for three important pilgrimage destinations—Rishikesh, Badrinath and Kedarnath—and is considered one of the seven holiest places in the world by the Hindus and a starting point on the journey to the sacred source of the River Ganga that one must undertake before death.

Every morning, the rising sun impregnates the temples on the shore with its scarlet beams of divine light with a distinct flavor and magnetic charm meandering over the sacred river that which had entranced Jake, the moment he stepped across the threshold to the Ghat of Hari Ki Pauri

Hari ki Pauri is one of the sacred *ghats* of Haridwar and a prime religious center that gets its name from one of its stone walls that bears the impressions of the feet of Lord Vishnu. It was constructed by King Vikramaditya during first century BC to commemorate his brother Brithari, who used to meditate along the banks of Ganges. According to popular legend, it was in this place that the nectar of immortality was accidentally spilled when the celestial bird Garuda was flying overhead with the pitcher containing the nectar.

The *ghat* now teemed with ocher-robed *sadhus, pundits* and pious pilgrims.

As Jake bolted down the *ghat*, the fragrance of incense milled and swirled in the air around him. The chimes of *mantras*, temple bells and cymbals filled the air with mystic rhythms all that appeared surreal and heavenly. Behind him, vast stone works and marble terraces rose generously, and the endless stairs running down into the waters and ornate shrines lining the river were crowded with devotees indulging in ablutions and rituals that involved scooping the water and offering it eastward to the souls of their departed ancestors.

Absorbing the spectacle along the shores, Jake's mind was emptied of all thoughts. He slowed down, his vision imbibing the serene stretch of the grayish green river. With the soft ripples of the Ganga, he sensed the layers of his consciousness receding. All that was left was the guilt he had nursed since he'd realized his father's innocence, which reminded him that like every human on earth, he too was a sinner.

His sin was misunderstanding an innocent man, his father, whose deeds had been a means of keeping his family safe from harm.

Standing in silence, Jake offered his heartfelt prayers to Ganga, hoping she would absolve him of his sin against his father and convey to his father his apologies and all the love he felt for him. Then he slowly let his eyes open to the water of Ganga calling him into its arms.

Enchanted by its warmth, he walked to the edge of the *ghat* and peeling off his clothes and dropping it to the side, he trudged down the steps in his boxers. He stood directly over the surface of the river water, staring at his reflection dancing in the soft rippling waters.

In that moment of introspection, burdened in the world of *karma,* his soul clambered as if trying to dive out from the confinements of his mundane flesh into the river water, to purge itself from sin. He felt a strong spiritual affinity with the depths of the water, as though it was coaxing him to plunge into the realms of divinity.

As he gradually lowered himself into the holy water, a sublime emotion suffused his inner-self and a great joy, an exalted feeling, sprouted from deep within. The gloomy world of deception and ignorance around him faded into oblivion as he immersed himself into the water, with the divine water covering his being. His superficial attachments to the world detached and he felt the waters cleanse his sins and purge his soul.

To Jake, it was another world down there, so far from chaos, from misery. An indefinable experience for the first time in his life. Overwhelmed, Jake rose from the river. The water trickled down his body, leaving his soul sanctified, in a state of bliss, with an out-of- the world delight.

It's an amazing experience, Jake whispered to himself, standing there for a moment, feeling endowed with pureness and reinvigorated with a subtle power that was beyond his understanding.

With sublime devotion for Ganga, Jake climbed back the stairs of the *ghat,* donned his clothes and picked up his leather jacket. He slid his fingers in the side pocket and pulled out the magnetic box. He opened it, took out the scroll and read the third line of the riddle silently.

Path to salvation is laid thru sacred portal

It now seemed credible that the riddle was hinting that this *ghat* was the sacred portal, an unseen gateway to millions of devotees coming to her from all cultures and races across the world in search of a path to salvation for their sins.

It had finally dawned upon Jake that this leg of the quest was also one of spiritual cleansing and of rebirth. The river was a vital force of life, its flowing water was, unquestionably, replete with some kind of special energy, a gravity of divine power bestowed by the Almighty himself, as a salutary contribution consecrated for sinners.

With her fresh waters, the beautiful Ganga with a solemn promise to wash away one's transgressions embraced everyone who came to her with remorse. Like a child in the arms of its mother, so are sinners in the bosom of Mother Ganga. Tangible, ever approachable and all accepting and all forgiving, with her generous heart, she erases all the sins accumulated over a hundred lifetimes.

When Jake raised his gaze, he noticed a man watching him silently from a distance. He was in his early fifties, dressed in a maroon shirt and beige trousers, staring back at Jake with a flicker of recognition in his eyes.

Instantly, Jake knew that this was the man whom Riya had arranged for him to meet at Hari Ki Pauri.

Subrutho.

A Professor in Hydrology.

CHAPTER 67

"*The water of* the Ganges is amazing," Jake said solemnly, glancing at the swift flow of the river water.

Soon after a formal introduction, Subrutho had asked him if he was seeing the Ganges for the first time. Jake had replied in the affirmative, his reverence evident.

Learning that the Ganges had won Jake's profound veneration at first glimpse, the professor had to mention something of great significance.

"If you've liked the Ganges, then you will be glad to know that the spot you took a dip in is known as Brahmakund."

Jake turned to the professor with a flicker of wonder at the name. "Brahmakund," the professor repeated, "is the most sacred place in Haridwar. According to Hindu scriptures, this is one of the four precise spots where the drops of nectar of immortality fell from the sky while being carried in a pitcher by the celestial bird Garuda-- the vehicle of Lord Vishnu. In commemoration of this event, once in twelve years, this place has a huge influx of devotees, in the millions actually, to take a dip in the waters and cleanse themselves of their sins."

Jake had already discerned that the professor was referring to the great Kumbh Mela--a mass pilgrimage of Hindus. This is the most sacred, largest and the most peaceful gathering of Hindus in the world, which is held once every three years at one of four places: Haridwar, Allahabad, Nashik and Ujjain, in rotation.

As per Hindu scriptures like the *Bhagavata Purana, Vishnu Purana,* the *Mahabharata* and the *Ramayana,* the Kumbh marks the episode of *samudhra manthan,* the churning of the ocean of milk. The scriptures tell the story: the *devas* who had lost all their power owing to a curse from a Durvasa *munni* implored Lord Vishnu and Lord Shiva for divine intervention to help them regain their strength. Lord Vishnu asked them to churn the primordial ocean of milk to seek the nectar that would restore their power. To perform this laborious task, they called upon their arch enemies, the *asuras,* with an agreement to share the gains equally. When the *kumbh* or pitcher or urn, containing nectar emerged, a war ensued. For twelve years, the *devas* and *asuras* fought in the sky. Finally, Lord Vishnu ordered Garuda to fly away with the pitcher of nectar. It was during this flight that the drops of nectar were spilled at these four places.

After the professor had walked him through the event called *samudra manthan*, Jake wondered if this was a myth or one of those factual accounts that countless ignorant minds had overlooked as popular lore. But considering the episode of transmutation, the *sadhu* hovering between heaven and earth and the clues on the walls of Ellora that spoke of advanced aircraft in the ancient past, he realized that if the riddle had brought him to the shores of this sacred *ghat*, then there was definitely some element of truth behind whatever had been said of Brahmakund.

Jake glanced at the spot once again and imagined the heavy throng of devotees during the Kumbh Mela, rushing all around him towards the river water. He sensed millions of hands joining in obeisance to the river water, offering silent prayers for forgiveness of sins.

He shook off his thoughts and turned to the professor, who held out a set of papers. Jake remembered Riya saying that this professor had recently completed jotting down his years of research and findings on the miraculous properties of the waters of the Ganges. It was why she thought his knowledge would be helpful. But what Jake was reluctant about pretending to be an editor from a major publishing company, interested in publishing the professor's work, as Riya had suggested.

Jake leafed through the papers and realized there were approximately two hundred pages.

Huh! Jake was frustrated, knowing it was difficult to look for an answer in so many pages.

"It takes a great deal of effort to pen such a work," Jake said, trying to lure the man to talk about his work. He thumbed through the pages, adding appreciatively, "Collecting water samples, conducting laboratory tests, a systematic investigation to establish facts and once the results are confirmed, comparing established facts with existing contradictory opinions and finally validating the facts of the research in unbiased fashion."

The professor took over, "Certainly. The papers you're holding are the product of five years of my dedication and hard work that explores the Ganges purely from a scientific viewpoint. It includes results obtained from experimental observations and evaluated against older researched facts."

"Older researched facts?" Jake was puzzled. He flipped the pages to find the information on older facts hoping they might be relevant to the riddle.

But the professor saved him the tedious job of pouring over the papers. He explained that this sacred river was known to have brought thousands of curious minds to its shores, who came to its banks in search of the secrets hidden deep in its waters. There's little documentation available on the identities of those investigators and their research work before the eighteenth century. But the first modern observation was reported in 1896, when a French journal, the *Annales de Institut Pasteur,* published an article by British physician Ernest Hanbury Hankin who wrote on the Ganges after testing its water.

"In his experiment," the professor continued, "he was thrilled to observe that the bacterium Vibrio Cholera, which induces the deadly cholera disease, when put into the waters of the Ganges was destroyed within three hours."

That fascinated Jake.

"And there are numerous accounts," the professor ventured, "that speak of foreigners who on their way back to their lands collected the water of the Ganges from the dirtiest mouths at Hooghly. To their surprise, it remained fresh throughout the journey when compared to water from other rivers, which over a period of time would putrefy due to lack of oxygen and promote the growth of anaerobic bacteria, leading to a stale odor."

Why read a book when he's a repository of information? Jake thought as he stopped thumbing through the papers.

"Word of this remarkable quality of the water of the Ganges reached the Western world and piqued the curious mind of a French-Canadian microbiologist named Felix D Herelle. After subjecting the river water to a series of laboratory tests, he concluded that there was a special kind of life form inhabiting the water of Ganges that gave it an anti- bacterial nature."

Jake closed the file and looked at the professor.

Professor revealed. "A virus known as Bacteriophage."

CHAPTER 68

The river Ganges, personified as a goddess, finds recurring mention in the *vedas* and the *puranas* and the *Ramayana* and the *Mahabharata*.

Its water has been used from olden times for remedial purposes, as it does not putrefy even after being stored for lengthy periods. Many theories have been suggested to explain this unique self-cleansing ability of the river. The phage activity is one such theory.

Bacteriophage is a parasitic virus that enters a neighboring bacterium's organic structure and uses its machinery and energy to produce more phage until the bacterium is destroyed and the new phage is then released to invade the surrounding bacteria. Felix D Herelle was the first man to coin the term Bacteriophage, meaning 'bacteria-eater', after observing the anti-bacterial nature of the water.

Subrutho had walked Jake to a secluded place some few furlongs away from the chaotic Brahmakund and had him settled on the stairs of the *ghat*. Once seated comfortably, he continued to elaborate on this theory, facing Jake.

"This Bacteriophage found in the water of the Ganges led to the revolutionary innovation of phage therapy. Scientists who manipulated its properties made ground-breaking discoveries in the field of medicine for which they were honored with the Nobel Prize."

"Was that the conclusion then?" Jake asked. Then, recalling that he was pretending to be an editor, he changed his question to suit what editors might say. "I mean, there might be other issues you examined before you came to the conclusion that the presence of this Bacteriophage made the waters of the Ganges anti-bacterial."

Subrutho thought about this query for a few seconds before he replied, "I did face challenges. The contribution of the Bacteriophage in scavenging disease-causing bacteria is corroborated by considerable research. But what they failed to substantiate was how and when this virus had originated."

The professor gave another brief account of research that was conducted in recent times. A research team from the National

Environmental Engineering Research Institute (NEERI), an apex research organization under the Indian Council for Scientific Research, investigated the impact of the Tehri Dam on the purity of water. Over the course of their study, they came up with new theories on the self-purifying ability of the Ganges. According to them, the sediment of the Ganges showed remarkably higher concentrations of radioactive compounds than any other river in the world. Sediment of the Ganges releasing copper and chromium in negligible quantities are not only within safe limits, they are also bactericidal and proliferate phage activity.

"That was what others had analyzed," the professor said. "But in my exhaustive study about the properties of the Ganges, I came across an interesting factor that substantiates a remarkable self-cleansing ability of the waters of Ganges."

Jake waited patiently.

"It is the presence of a high level of oxygen in the waters."

"You mean dissolved oxygen?" Jake guessed, with little knowledge about it.

"Yes," the professor replied, excited. He explained that the organic life in water usually depleted available oxygen in a river and as a result, water would start to putrefy. But the Ganges possessed the unique ability to reduce its biochemical oxygen demand much faster, leading to oxygen levels twenty-five times higher than that found in any other river in the world. It can also clean up suspended waste twenty times faster than rivers elsewhere. In addition, when the water of the Ganges is added to any other water in adequate amounts, the Bacteriophage in it quickly multiplies in the new environment and destroys deadly foreign bodies in it.

This account of remarkable properties of the Ganges stunned Jake. While he was a little acquainted with the sacred nature of the Ganges, he had not known of this aspect of the river water, much as people of this generation were unaware of what made the water of Ganges *amrit*-- an elixir.

The professor pulled Jake from his thoughts. "For this very reason, the tradition of carrying the water of Ganges back home to clean local water is still being practiced in some places, although many are blind to this custom and its benefits."

The soft ripples of water lapping against the stairs drew Jake's eyes. Fascinated by its astonishing history and mysterious attributes, Jake instinctively stood up, descended the steps of the *ghat* and scooped a palm-full of water in his hands.

The professor silently watched him doing so.

Jake experienced the same magical feel, all over again—a profound sense of devotion from within. It was just a handful of water, so clear and beautiful, yet with miraculous healing properties. Gulping down the water, he turned to the professor."So, it's the high level of oxygen that gives the water its unique properties?"

The professor shook his head. "There are two major factors that act collectively to give the river its incorruptible abilities. One, is the presence of the Bacteriophage that has anti-microbial attributes and the other is the higher level of dissolved oxygen that keeps the water fresh for a long period."

"There's also a third factor," the professor said with a cryptic smile, as though he was enjoying apportioning the information sparingly, bit by bit.

"There's this unknown component, a mystery factor that forms the basis for the other two to perform their functions in conjunction."

Jake eyed him over eagerly. *Seek the elixir and the star guides the mortal*. The line hummed in his ears. "Mystery factor?"

The professor rose to his feet, wound down the steps and stood next to him, meeting his eyes, averring, "What better term can be designated for the trait that baffles human understanding? It's that mystery factor which for over centuries has inspired and drawn a great number of scientists and myth-makers to its shores, who skimming along its course have spent their lives trying to decode the secret of this holy river."

"You're saying there's no one who has figured out this mystery factor?"

The professor cast a mysterious smile, mysterious like the secret dwelling in the water of the Ganges.

CHAPTER 69

From the earliest times, great civilizations had endured the devastating effects of plagues that struck mayhem. It led to the belief that the disease was a punishment from God—an idea that still exists among many today.

However, scientists have confirmed that almost every living thing can contract a virus, be it animals or insects, emphasizing its beneficial outcomes in balancing the ecosystem by ensuring that the population of animals and insects remain under control.

If all viruses were to vanish from the face of earth, a global catastrophe would ensue, unbalancing ecosystems and the world would collapse under the burgeoning population of insects and animals.

An examination of the mystery of the grand old Vedic civilization would definitely amaze one, given their secrets of immunity and great strength that defied the deadly effects of pathogens.

'When the going gets tough, the tough get going', the popular proverb seemed to fit ancient *rishis* and *Ayurved acharyas,* medical practitioners of Vedic culture, who used their yogic powers to master the art of living by encompassing *richas, mantras* and *slokas* for Dharma, also integrating Vedic microbiology.

This suggests that concern for health was integrated as a significant part of Dharma. Some Vedic principles on hygiene are still being practiced in rural regions. Blowing on the conch shell, ringing bells in temples, performing severe penances, using cow dung and urine and adding anti-microbial spices to food preparations are a few such practices. Most prominently, the sacred water of the Ganges was used as vaccination against various kinds of microbial infections, including diarrhea.

Over time, researchers had tried to crack the mystery surrounding the exceptional healing properties of Ganges. They had looked at the river's source in the Himalayas, where wild plants and radioactive rocks made the river bed. Some attributed the unusual medicinal properties of the Ganges to the medicinal secretions of herbs and the mineral content that gets mixed with the water, but that theory was discarded later owing to insufficient evidence.

The knowledge on this *'mystery factor'* had stirred Jake. From his expression, the professor had deduced that this editor seemed convinced and would publish his work.

Feeling very excited, Subrutho went on, "Our great seers and *yogis* from Vedic times performed severe penances and acquired great supernatural powers. They imparted spiritual training to disciples in centers like *ashrams*, once believed to be located on the banks of the Ganges. Their bodies were known to have transcended material necessities of food, water, air, time, space and could travel unfettered to any corner of the universe as per their wish and manifest in any form. Under the tutelage of these great seers, their disciples excelled in knowledge of natural sciences like solar science, astronomy, astrology, ethereal science, lunar science and exhaustive bioscience."

Jake listened carefully as the professor continued.

"It's believed that a vast accumulation of knowledge in the science of microbiology besides containing arcane knowledge also included answers to the mystery factor of the Ganges. Sadly, however, this was passed down into the care of chosen ones deemed worthy of it.

"The mystery factor was hidden by the seers and was lost to future generations. But from time to time, for the benefit of mankind, the seers contributed generously by passing down the secrets of microbiology to the most adept. There is an account of a historical invention in the field of medicine that if it had not been designed would have brought the world to the brink of disaster, bringing the human race on the verge of extinction."

And what was that? Jake mused on it.

"The antiserum for cholera and plague," the professor revealed.

"Indians are behind its invention? I mean…" Jake's expression was one of surprise and disbelief. "I thought it was someone in the Western world who'd invented the vaccine for those deadly diseases."

"So the world thinks," the professor replied. "But the truth is that it's a boon from Indians to the world."

Like many others, this invention too was a contribution from Indians to the world. Jake took pride in the realization, but also felt distressed that it had gone unacknowledged, like many others inventions.

"Have you ever heard of the Invisible College?" The professor yanked him out of his daze.

"Is it some kind of secret society?" Jake guessed.

"You're partly right," the professor said, as he sat on the stair. Jake settled next to him.

"It was," the professor continued, "an Europe's premier institution called the Royal Society of London, formed by an elite group of scientists. Englishmen Sir Francis Bacon, Robert Boyle and mathematician-cum-mystic John Dee were all Rosicrucian. You know about Rosicrucians?"

Jake had a vague memory of reading about Rosicrucians. From what he knew, it was some kind of secret society, popular for practicing alchemical lore. But he didn't want the professor to know he knew on it. The professor was definitely a database of knowledge and would be helpful as long as Jake pretended to know nothing.

The professor, deciphering Jake's expression, explained briefly that the Rosicrucians formed a seventeenth century secret society of philosophers and scholars, who were well versed in mystical, metaphysical and alchemical lore. The society still exists and its members appear everywhere with pseudonyms.

The professor continued, "The Royal Society of London comprised the world's smartest brains like Sir Isaac Newton, Benjamin Franklin and more, who began meeting in secret to discuss the philosophy of science and all the arcane information related to it. Their basic concept behind forming the society was to acquire knowledge by mystical work rather than by scientific declaration, by exposing themselves to ancient wisdom. This society was later brought under the patronage of the British Government for the improvement of natural knowledge and renamed 'Britain's National Academy of Science.'

"It exists to this day. And being the world's oldest scientific academy, it has always been at the forefront of inquiry and discovery since its inception. In the year 1890, a French bacteriologist from this society, Alexandre Emile Jean Yersin, had come on a secret voyage to India. He was a student of Louis Pasteur and the closest collaborator of Pierre Paul Emile Roux. It was on his undisclosed journey to India, in Madras—Chennai now—that he was supposed to have acquired mysterious skills and instructions on certain biological secrets from seers, as a result of which he was able to prepare the antiserum for cholera and plague."

"Your claims imply that Indians had established a good rapport with the scientist from that secret society," Jake stated.

"Claims?" The professor laughed. "It's a well-grounded truth. Don't forget that India was under British rule for centuries. Scientists and philosophers from Britain frequently came to India. They were intrigued by the abundance of mystical knowledge available with the sages. And they came here in pursuit of that knowledge. Nonetheless, most of them could not receive what they desired."

That's incredible, Jake thought, feeling immensely proud of having been born in a land whose history, unlike any other, had acted like a beacon—a guiding light to the whole world, disseminating across the globe all branches of knowledge from pre- and post-Vedic ages, through the altruistic endeavors of the sages. He also had to agree that it was such a disgrace that despite hailing from this land, its people had turned a blind eye to its glorious past and failed to acknowledge the bygone times when ancient religion, science and philosophy empowered the evolution of not only a great Indian civilization, but also of world civilizations.

While this was interesting information, the mystery factor in the waters of Ganges remained obscure.

Jake turned to the professor. "And the mystery factor?"

CHAPTER 70

"*The river and* its properties are beyond the purviews of science. They belong to the unconventional realms of mysticism and religion."

The professor stated with immense fervor, his eyes on the wonderful stretch of the flowing water of the Ganges.

Jake struggled to make sense of his statement.

"One has to break free from the shell of ignorance to explore the mystery factor of the Ganges." The professor turned to Jake to shed some light on his words. "I'm a scientist and belonged to a class of wise men who practice atheism. And this research was my endeavor to explore the mystery factor from a scientific outlook. But, I failed too, like countless others."

"You aren't an atheist anymore?" Jake asked with slight surprise. "There are numerous questions science has no answers for. One of these is the mystery factor in the water of the Ganges." The professor paused in thought. "Religion lend a helping hand when science stumbles. It has answers to all that science fails to explain, just as I failed to sum up the mystery factor from scientific experiments."

Jake's hope of extracting clues to solve the riddle diminished as the professor continued.

"This sacred river," the professor eyed the Ganges, as he continued, "which has absolved sinners and purified the dead, from a time beyond even recorded history, has transformed my life to something it never was before. Turning my ignorance to reverence, making me believe in a higher power, a universal source of knowledge that is beyond the reach of science." He paused. "That which is not measured in any laboratory, but by a subjective state of mind."

Jake sensed something wrong with what the professor was telling him. "It sounds confusing when you try to base your conclusions on mystical grounds with a shade of religion to it."

The professor responded, "That is what it is. The mysterious dimensions of the Ganges and its essence of sanctity can only be comprehended by mystical experiences from within religious confines."

Jake felt like scratching his head.

"Of course, religion and mysticism are entwined, but it's religion, its prescribed traditions and customs that brings about the experience of mysticism."

The professor pointed out that the external expressions of religion, its concern for the observance of divine commandments, rituals and great festivals shape a moral society obligated by religious laws. This worked best when driven by inner experience and devotion of heart. Which is what mysticism was all about. Communicating with the divine by personal inner experiences, subtler practices, more intensely than made possible by law or rituals. This would help gain true knowledge of what alone is ultimately real.

Casting a long, brooding look over the shimmering river water, the professor said solemnly, "The secret of the Ganges is embedded in its history. And in the way it's been made to flow."

By now, Jake had a fair idea that the history of the Ganges was replete with legends that marked God's hand in its design with great passion, ensuring that it became the lifeline of civilization. But there was something he hadn't understood.

"The secret lies in the way it's been made to flow," Jake repeated. "What do you mean by that?"

The professor clarified, "Pure, natural and unpolluted water is structured water. Its molecular structure under standard conditions is not amorphous. But when exposed to changing conditions, it forms pseudo-crystalline structures, affected by parameters such as surface tension, dielectric constant, ultraviolet and infrared spectra and some biological properties. When exposed to electromagnetic fields, pressure, temperature and other chemical pollutants, substances or the synchronous action of more than one of these factors, the water molecule is restructured, resulting in the elimination of oxygen from the water" He broke of for a beat. "This won't happen with the waters of the Ganges due to its ability to retain a high oxygen capacity."

Why is this so? Jake was frustrated.

As if sensing his turmoil, the professor furnished, "And this is because the Ganges flows through Haridwar. Then through Devprayag, Varnasi and so on, navigating through different landscapes and reaching shores that are deemed holy."

For the first time since they had begun talking, Jake felt that the professor was offering him a weird assortment of answers. And what followed was even more puzzling.

In the majestic presence of the water of Ganges that lapped at the stairs of the *ghat*, the professor revealed somberly, "The crystalline structure of water molecules responds to the positive and negative vibrations of their external environment."

Before Jake could infer anything from the professor's statement, he saw the man's eyes widen in panic at something behind him. Jake knew someone was nearing them. Before he could turn, a sturdy leather sole struck him in his back with great force, sending him tumbling over the stairs into the river water.

CHAPTER 71

Jake sank like a wrecked ship.

He tumbled over himself, momentarily disoriented about which way was up. The man who had knocked him into the river dived into the water after him, caught hold of his hair and thrust him underwater as Jake tried to resurface.

Jake had a glimpse of the man who continued to pin him down under the surface of the water: David Craig, chief coordinator from JIC.

Rendered immobile by panic, the professor stood with his eyes wide open, watching the ongoing tussle between Jake and the other man who had arrived unannounced. David turned to him and gave him a threatening look, motioning for him to leave. Frightened, the professor collected the scatter of his research papers strewn across on the ghat floor and scurried away, disappearing from the *ghat*.

The outside world faded into darkness as Jake strenuously fought to hold his breath under water, channeling air through his mouth. His lungs burned, and he struggled to loosen the firm grip David had on him.

David pulled him back to the surface for a fleeting second, and in very next moment, Jake found himself back in the water, battling again for oxygen. "You, son of a bitch," David cursed, thrusting him underwater.

He wrapped his powerful arms around Jake's neck. Water rushed in through Jake's nostrils. The cold water raced down Jake's throat, gushing down his entering his windpipe. He felt a sharp burn in his chest, as the terrible and excruciating prospect of death neared. Jake wondered if there was any chance he would survive. Terrifying though David's stranglehold seemed Jake struggled to survive, pushing away any thoughts about death.

I have to free myself and stay alive.

Jake circled his hands to grasp David, trying to hold him, his clothing or something, but his hands returned empty. On the verge of losing consciousness, he suddenly felt a strong pull and moments later, a piercing pain in the back. On the edge of his consciousness, he realized that he had been yanked out of the water onto the stairs of the *ghat*, its edge hurting his back.

Jake coughed up water, lying on his back on the stairs. Incapacitated, like a defeated emperor on a battlefield, he felt drained of energy and burdened by his water-soaked clothes.

In the feeble light of the setting sun, a demonic face reappeared in his line of sight. A scowl followed by a jeering smile formed on his lips as he said, "Come on, you whoreson! Come on! Come and get me, you bastard!" He punched Jake in the abdomen ferociously.

Jake let out a pained moan, before slumping to one side, writhing and tumbling down a few steps. Jake lay where he fell, on his back although his senses were alert to David's movements.

This portion of the *ghat* was too far away to draw the attention of the devotees. Only the ripples of water hitting the *ghat* stairs were audible.

David closed in on Jake and pinned him under his hard leather soles. Then, producing a gun, he brandished it menacingly over Jake.

"I won't let you die before I show you something that you deserve to see," David said, reaching into his pocket and retrieving his cell phone. He tapped a few keys and held the device up for Jake to see.

Jake, lying on his back and trapped under David's leather shoe, realized he was watching a video. As the clipping progressed, David saw the change in Jake's expression.

In the video clipping, AD and Riya were in conversation with another man he had never seen before. David knew it was General Balbeer Singh.

"This is the real face of your beloveds. And this footage has been shot exclusively for you," David said, recalling Balbeer Singh informing him about a spy camera he'd affixed to his suit button prior to meeting Rajat Singh and Riya at the CBI headquarters this morning.

After watching the whole video and listening to the conversation, Jake turned to look at David.

David enjoyed the unmistakable pain of betrayal in Jake's eyes. Glaring at him, he mocked, "As I told you before, the people who you think are assisting you are conspiring against you. Riya, your closest friend, and Mr. Rajat Singh, the man you respect like a father, have stabbed you in the back, chalking out your entire plan for us. They are the ones who kept updating us on your moves."

The disclosure pierced Jake like a poisoned lance. He had never imagined that two of the people he cared for above all others would betray him. For a moment, he wished it were a dream, a nightmare or something that would vanish when he opened his eyes. But sadly, it wasn't. Discerning Jake's emotional state, David told him, "They have done no wrong in betraying you. You deserved to be treated so. You are a threat to the very nation that has sheltered you."

Jake took his eyes off the mobile screen but the pain caused by the image was difficult to shake off. With his chest pinned hard under David's sole, his eyes shifted to the gun barrel that rose to his temple, David's fingers curling over the trigger.

"CBI will be sad to lose you." David's smile was sinister.

Jake closed his eyes as David pulled the trigger.

He heard a muffled shot. The years of his life, the days of his pursuit of The Lost Arcanum all came to an abrupt end, with the bullet drilling into his skull, splattering blood and exiting from behind his skull. The world around him collapsed. Or at least that was what Jake had assumed would happen.

Oddly, however, he felt no pain. Puzzled, Jake opened his eyes only to catch sight of David's sturdy frame collapsing into the water of the Ganges like a razed pillar.

At the far side of the *ghat*, a silhouette appeared, gripping a gun with both hands. Jake blinked to get a clearer picture of the silhouette. When he did, his eyes went wide, finding someone whom he thought he would never see again but who had shown up suddenly and saved his life. Overwhelmed by the emotion of surviving death, Jake screamed out in surprise and relief.

"Taneez!"

CHAPTER 72

Taneez wasn't alone.

She had company. The driver, who'd been of great help in rescuing them in the library at Aurangabad and had then been involved in a dramatic chase, was surprisingly still at her side.

Scampering down the stairs, Taneez helped Jake, while the driver quickly pulled the body of David from the water and laid it on the steps of the *ghat*.

"I can't believe you're back," Jake told her, as he slowly clambered to his feet. He sensed a throbbing pain in his head as he balanced himself. His body was battered. "How did you even know I was here?"

"I solved the first three lines of the riddle," Taneez replied. "It pointed here to Hari Ki Pauri."

Jake's attention was suddenly drawn to the gun in her hand. "And this gun? Where did you get this from?"

She smiled. "Someone who really cares for me gave it to me for my protection."

Jake recalled that that someone was none other than himself, who had given it to her in the library building when the operatives had attacked unannounced.

"He's dead," the driver declared from the steps below, after checking David's pulse.

"Dead!" Taneez rushed to join the driver, kneeling beside the body. "That's impossible!"

Jake joined the duo, squatting by David's dead body on the other side.

"I shot him in the legs, only to disable him temporarily." She gaped at Jake. "Then how come he's dead?"

Jake ripped David's clothes, exposing his chest, at which point Taneez reeled back in disbelief, placing her hand on her mouth, spotting a hole drilled into David's chest.

"My God! I can't believe my aim is so inaccurate." Taneez's voice was laced with fear.

"I'm sorry, but it is." Jake said curtly, a little worried. He looked at the entrance of the *ghat*, seeing the surge of devotees with dusk fast setting in. "We have to do away with this corpse before it draws someone's attention."

ЖЖЖЖЖ

After a while. after disposing David's body in a secluded corner at the dead end of the *ghat*, the trio of Jake, Taneez and the driver were scuttling away from the scene when Jake stopped dead in his tracks.

"What?" Taneez asked, following his glance, which was taking in the sight of their footprints on the *ghat*. Wet soles had left a trail from the spot where David's body had been dumped.

The driver had seen it, too, and he spoke in Hindi, "Those footprints will evaporate in no time. It's untraceable like those of fish in the water."

"That's not my concern," Jake said, still gazing at the footprints. "I think giving the dead body to the water of the Ganges is better option than having someone spot it. This is unsafe and will draw somebody's attention very soon." He paused thoughtfully and said, "you two hurry on outside the temple. I'll do the rest on my own and join you there."

Jake guided them over to the exit and went back to complete the work.

ЖЖЖЖЖ

Away from prying eyes, the trio had retired into a roadside tea stall that overlooked Hari Ki Pauri. From here, they had a clear panoramic view of the *ghat*.

Dusk had almost set in. And there was no commotion near the spot where they had disposed the body of David Craig, which meant the murder was yet to come to light.

Taking solace from it, settled comfortably on the wooden table Taneez had given a brief description to Jake on what had happened after he had abandoned her in the dead of the night. With the help of the driver, she had reached Indore and then driven non-stop to Haridwar.

Jake glanced at the driver who stood on the far side of the stall relishing tea and a local cigarette.

Jake furnished his own tale, revealing everything he had kept from her. He spoke of everything that had occurred right from the beginning of the quest. The three back-to-back murders, about him having been forced to back off from investigating the cases, the discovery of a conspiracy behind the murders, discovering that his father's death had been a murder and recovering the magnetic box concealed in his father's safe that had set him on a journey in pursuance of the secret, *The Lost Arcanum*.

For a minute, there was an unsettling silence between them, as both pondered over each others story.

Taneez glanced at the driver who was inhaling a long puff from his cigarette and sipping tea. She remembered she owed him immensely for all his help, from saving their lives in the library building to that dangerous shootout on the road and accompanying her here, only seconds before Jake had almost died.

Taneez then turned her gaze to the flowing river that seemed to be suffused with golden light, reflected from the sparkling glow of the temple on the bank.

The secret of the Ganges lies in its history…and the way it's been made to flow. She recalled Jake relating this cryptic statement uttered by the professor before David's ambush. She also wondered at the origin of the Bacteriophage in the river water of the Ganges that had baffled scientists for ages. Gazing at the beautifully illumined Hari Ki Pauri temple in the backdrop, Taneez mulled over the line again: *The secret of the Ganges lies in its history.*

"What specific history was he referring to?" she asked Jake, turning to Jake. "Its history is steeped in rich legends."

Jake thought of it himself. "It could be anything." He rose to his feet and moved closer to the railings on the river bank. "Or rather, those legends itself could be the history and we should be looking for an answer there." He was quiet for a few seconds. He then turned, facing her, resting his back against the railings. "Maybe the legend that speaks about its birth and origin. It is repeatedly invoked in the *puranas,* the *Ramayana* and the *Mahabharata*. But each of these scriptures tells a different story about its origin."

Taneez looked at the last line of the riddle.

Seek the elixir and the star guides the mortal.

Elixir, Taneez whispered the word. "What is the other legend that you mentioned? The one that talks about the nectar spilled into the river water from heaven?"

Jake walked her through the entire scene from Samudra Manthan, of the nectar being spilled from the pitcher being carried by Garuda, the vehicle of Lord Vishnu, also relating to her the significance of the Kumbh Mela. When he was finished, she took a moment to think. Then she looked at him with a victorious smile.

"What?"

"I found the elixir," Taneez said with excitement.

"What is that?"

"The Virus," Taneez furnished, adding, "Bacteriophage."

"It can't be." Jake disagreed. "The riddle speaks of an alchemist's elixir. That was concocted using a mixture of extracts from various herbal plants known to cure all ills and extend the earthly span of humans."

"Jake, you're not reading between the lines here. The history of the episode of *samudra manthan* narrates a mythical bird Garuda, which was a vehicle for Lord Vishnu."

"What about it?" Jake asked, unable to understand what she was implying.

"It has features reminiscent to Jatayu, the archetype of the modern-day drone that attacked Ravana while he abducted Sita."

Jake was beginning to see where she was taking this all.

"Don't forget that all the mythical birds were in actuality mechanical and had the power of flight. These machines were disguised as birds and other animals to conceal their mechanisms. Along those lines, Garuda was a drone too, a remote-controlled aircraft without a pilot that spilled the nectar from the pitcher into the water of the Ganges. Whether that was a predetermined act or just an accident, Garuda served its purpose, spilling the nectar."

She rose from her seat, walked to Jake and smiled. "The nectar that was spilled into the water of Ganges contained the benignant virus."

CHAPTER 73

In the sacred doctrines of every religion and civilization, the concept of nectar was a recurring theme. It appeared under various names. In ancient Greek mythology, it was *'ambrosia'*, the food and drink of gods. In Hindu mythology, it was *amrit* or *soma rasa,* a ritual drink of importance in the Vedic age. It featured as *'peaches of immortality'* in Chinese mythology and as *'elixir of life'*, a potion of immortality among alchemists.

With sound knowledge of the concept of nectar, Taneez, a student of esoteric studies explained to Jake how history had misinterpreted its ingredients and functions over millennia.

"Nectar need not be a concoction of the extracts of plants or a sweet-tasting juice that is pleasant to consume. Anything that serves the purpose of being beneficial to life is a nectar. If we consider the functions of the virus Bacteriophage carefully, we can see that it was nectar. When it was spilled from the pitcher from heaven, it thrived in the water, multiplied to billions and destroyed disease-causing bacteria, making the water of the Ganges clean and pure. Thus, turning the water into nectar," she said, "an elixir and the supposed drink of gods that granted immortality to anyone who consumed it."

Jake could sense that they were now reaching a point back in the history when myth was a true instance, whose status eventually, due to the sheer ignorance of educated minds, was relegated to a popular fable.

"The ancient seers had enormous knowledge in microbiology," Taneez said, now facing him, with her back leaning against the railings. "They had a fair understanding of microorganisms. Their structure, classification, evolution, their ways of infecting by exploiting host cells for reproduction, their interaction with host organisms, the diseases they caused and the technique to isolate and culture them to manipulate them in research and therapy. It's analogous to modern day viral therapy."

Somehow, Jake was reluctant to accept her theory that Bacteriophage was the elixir the riddle was pointing at.

Taneez held out her hand, asking for the scroll. Jake produced the magnetic box, took the scroll from it and handed it over to her. When she began to look into the random letters, he stopped her.

"No use. Like I said, the elixir is not the Bacteriophage," he squinted into the distance, "It's something subtler, intangible, out of our grasp, like a spiritual elixir."

She glanced up at him anxiously.

"Or we have to figure out what the professor meant when he said 'the secret lies in the way it's been made to flow.'"

Consumed by these thoughts, she turned to face HariKi Pauri Ghat on the opposite of the bank, watching the temple glowing magnificently. For a few silent minutes, they pondered the words uttered by the professor.

Soaking up the vivid background of the temple, Jake said softly. "In the depth of her waters, she guards her secret, as she's done for over thousands of years and still continues to... provide enough for everyone's need but not for everybody's greed."

"Why do you feel so, Jake, about the Ganges?" asked Taneez watching the *ghat* on the other side of the bank.

Jake exhaled. "The Ganges is the most treasured river in India. It brings a smile on the faces of farmers, enriching their fertile fields. It brings joy to the eyes of the sick, caressing them with its medicinal properties and it waits with its arms wide open to embrace those who are remorseful, to purge them of their sins and help them seek salvation."

He broke off as he looked affectionately at the meek current of water slapping the bank close to him. "This river, in some way along its course, besides closely associating with spiritual and religious beliefs of millions of lives, has also become an important source for people's joy and their livelihood." He went silent for a beat and told, "But I'm not getting into what the professor meant by 'the water of the Ganges responds to its environment.'"

Taneez said nothing. A few seconds later, she erupted all at once. "He said that to you?" Her eyes suddenly lit with surprise.

"Yes."

After a second or two, she spoke. "A few years ago, I read about research conducted by the HADO Research Institute in Japan. It was found that the crystalline structures of water respond to the positive and negative vibrations of their external environment."

Taneez pulled up a picture from the HADO Research Institute website on her phone.

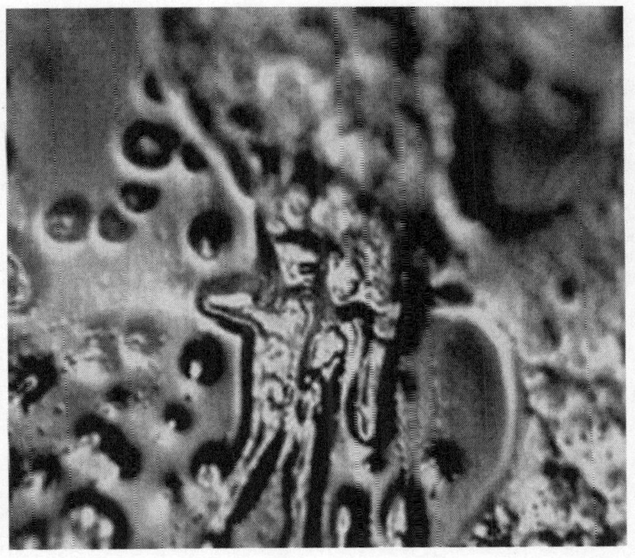

"This is how the structure of polluted water appears under the microscope," Taneez informed him.

"And this," she said showing him another image, "is the structure of the water molecule after prayers has been offered to the water. It turns hexagonal and symmetrical, arranged in harmonious patterns."

She also emphasized that the positive vibrations enhanced the arrangement and energized the water so that the molecules returned to their original life-giving state, known as super-moisturizing state, which allowed maximum moisture absorption into the cells of living beings.

"The arrangement of water molecules is the key to retaining a high level of oxygen and to healing."

Jake considered her information, wondering about the answer to the final riddle without which the cryptic puzzle was incomplete. One thing did not add up. "How does this place, Haridwar, or any other holy place along the river's banks, contribute to this?"

She thought for a while and shrugged, implying that she had no idea.

All of sudden, their attention was drawn by the faint chimes of bells that swelled from the other side of the river bank.

What they found was swell of devotees, close to two hundred had gathered on the HariKi Pauri Ghat, at Brahmakund. Priests held large fire bowls in their hands, gongs were rung in the temples in the background and prayers were chanted in praise of the holy Ganges.

"That's an amazing panorama," Taneez exclaimed, mesmerized by the view.

Jake was moved by the sight, looking over at the temple *ghat*. It appeared brighter and resplendent. Like some grand ceremony offered toward heavens. Shortly thereafter, they spotted lamps floating in the river, making it a spectacle of sound and color.

The man who came to serve them their tea saw them marveling at the ritual taking place on the *ghat*. Assuming that they were seeing it for the first time, he explained that the ritual being performed on the *ghat* was called the *aarti* ceremony. It was offered to Goddess Ganga every evening at dusk followed by devotees and pilgrims floating floral lamps and incense to commemorate their deceased ancestors. He observed that everyone who came to Haridwar made sure to attend this ceremony.

As the man hurried off, they watched the spectacle, sipping their tea, enchanted by the sight of hundreds of little lamps now floating in the river. They couldn't take their eyes off the captivating scene ahead.

Suddenly, something occurred to Jake and he drew a startled breath. Angling at her, he concurred, "I think I know the secret."

CHAPTER 74

The revolution in science known as quantum physics has been around for several centuries. Only recently—the past two decades to be exact—has it been considered the subject of serious study and pursued ardently by scientists and scholars across the world.

Quantum theory explains the laws of energy at the quantum level, where a 'quanta' or 'discrete particle' can be an atom, molecule, nucleus or micro particle, each posing a subtle vibrational energy. These 'vibrations' form the fundamental basis of quantum physics and exist in everything. Humans, animals, plants and all substances in the universe vibrate. Quanta have its own frequency of vibration unique to itself, like a fingerprint or genetic code to an individual.

Dr. Max Planck (1858-1957), German physicist and Noble Prize winner in Physics, said:

"Everything is a vibration and its effect. In actuality, no physical matter can exist. All physical matters are composed of vibration."

In the recent years, the discipline of quantum theory formed an elementary premise for the Institute of Noetic Sciences and the HADO Institute in Tokyo for addressing the interplay of consciousness and the physical world, proposing how beliefs, thoughts and intentions affect surroundings. Science relies heavily on external observations and focuses on objective evaluation and experimentation, as Dr. Masaru Emato, a leading HADO scientist and scholar, pointed out in his profound discovery of interaction between conscious mental activity and the physical world itself. His detailed research into the effect of human consciousness on water is encapsulated in a book, *Messages from Water*. It notes that water quality is reflected in its crystalline structure and the consciousness of water can be affected by exposure to positive and negative environment like pollution, words, music and prayer.

Specific research was also carried out on the waters of the Ganges and it was found that harmonious patterns exist in its crystalline structure.

Taneez had read the article some years ago. But Jake based his explanation on his knowledge of the discipline of Noetic science.

"The crystalline structure of water molecules of the Ganges responds to positive vibrations in its external environment," he repeated the lines. "Haridwar is the first place on the banks of the Ganges and the positive external environment is right before your eyes," he pointed to the ongoing procession on the Hari Ki Pauri Ghat.

Taneez now watched the procession in a different light, illuminated by Jake's idea.

Beside her, Jake kept clearing the haze from the secret.

"As sound has vibratory power, so do thoughts. Prayers, chants and *mantras*, every word and character of which has a precise meaning and distinct vibrational amplitude and frequency, form a unique vibratory pattern when recited with intense emotion that can build or destroy a subtle structure in their immediate environment. Likewise, when powerful emotional desires from the heart are concentrated in the mind, fine electrical vibrations of thoughts that escape from the mind are converted into mechanical waves that interfere with the object in focus. That is exactly what is happening here. Devotees are the source and the object in focus is the Ganges," Jake said, now speaking fast in excitement. "As the devotees come together with love and gratitude and focus in shared reverence, the output, the oneness of this shared experience, the coalescing of emotions of those many committed minds renders the waters of the Ganges harmonious."

"This theory sounds synonymous to Noetic science," Taneez said after a brief moment. "Rather, it supports the secret you've identified."

"I know it," Jake replied.

The word 'noesis' comes from ancient Greek where 'nous' means 'mind', 'understanding' or 'intellect.' It is a branch of metaphysical philosophy concerned with the study of the mind and intellect. The theory states that human thoughts have the potential to affect the physical world. They have weight and like every weighted material on earth, they are affected by gravitational forces, but to a lesser degree than other materials, transforming the physical world.

After reflecting on this, Taneez pondered aloud, "This reminds me of an episode from the New Testament, where Jesus cursed the fig tree."

"Yes," Jake instantly remembered the episode in the gospel of Mathew, Chapter 21, verse 18-22:

"Early in the morning, as Jesus was on his way back to the city, he was hungry. Seeing a fig tree by the road, he went up to it but found nothing on it except leaves. Then he said to it, "May you never bear fruit again!" Immediately, the tree withered. When the disciples saw this, they were amazed. "How did the fig tree wither so quickly?" they asked.

Jesus replied, "Truly I tell you, if you have faith and do not doubt, not only can you do what was done to the fig tree, but also you can say to this mountain, 'Go, throw yourself into the sea,' and it will be done. If you believe, you will receive whatever you ask for in prayer."

"The mind has the potential to alter matter," Taneez noted. "It can manifest any particle as per one's desire. Positive thoughts manifest positive results. Likewise, the converse is also possible, just like in the episode of Jesus and the fig tree. It's the concept of mind over matter." She trailed off, squinting into the orange-tinted water of the Ganges.

"Science has just begun to unravel things that our seers long back had profound insight into," Jake said watching the procession on the *ghat*. "They had deep knowledge of the concept of mind over matter and had predicted that one day, this magnanimous water body would become the prime source of joy for millions of Indians. Which was the reason why they composed hymns, *mantras* and chants simultaneously designing rituals that were required to be performed in mass meditation here on the *ghats* of the Ganges, to render it harmonious, in a life-giving state. It is certainly a lifeline for our nation."

He broke off for a long beat.

"Indeed, the secret of the Ganges lies in the way it's been made to flow. It's a river of miracle that flows from beyond the unrecognizable."

Jake quietened to hear the soft sound of the Ganges thrashing against the river bank.

He pondered on the last line of the riddle.

Seek the elixir and the star guides the mortal...

"The elixir..." Jake whispered to himself. "What is the elixir in the water of the Ganges?"

"Besides this Bacteriophage," Taneez said, "there are these positive vibrations that restructure the water molecules. And this vibration is 'energy' and there must be this 'force' that binds them together."

"You're correct," Jake agreed. "By nature's law, the flow of life 'energy' is always toward the outward world and its effects are reciprocated back to life by the 'force.'" He looked down to the water of the Ganges, glinting golden hue. "Vibration is the smallest unit of energy and the water of the Ganges is filled with sublime emotions of devotees."

Jake glanced at her. Deep in his eyes, she saw a flicker of a unique deep glow of reverence. His voice grew humble, as though what he was about to divulge was not coming from his deduction but was directed through him by a divine grace, from Ganga Maiyya herself from heaven above.

"This unseen 'force' is God that keeps 'life' and 'energy' united. The 'life-force energy' is Ganga Maiyya."

"Life-force energy," Taneez repeated, shaking her head.

Jake grabbed the scroll from her hand and scanned the letters inside the belly of the cryptic snake feeding on its own tail. In the next moment, he glanced up at her with a victorious smile. "Yes, the elixir in the water of the Ganga is indeed 'life-force energy'... the spiritual elixir."

Jake produced a pen from his pocket and chalked the letters in the grid, handing it over to Taneez.

Taneez looked at the scroll.

"Goddess Ganga, her waters are the *'gateway to heaven',*" Jake told her as she studied the transformed cryptic snake. "Her pristine water guards the vital 'life force' and 'life energy' of the universe necessary for every living form in order to maintain health and wellness, mentally, physically and emotionally."

Ganga Maiyya's waters are *soma,* the bliss, the 'nectar' of immortality. It is the stream of honey that brings about rejuvenation of body, mind and soul and carries the essence—the *rasa,* the delight hidden in everything

CHAPTER 75

Hanging up the phone, Jake walked out of the cybercafé and joined Taneez and the driver, waiting outside on a street bench in a sprawling commercial complex.

Jake had just finished making a VoIP call to his office secretary, Ishita, with a request to send him the same information he had asked of her some two days ago that he forgot to grab in the wake of Jaswanth Sinha calling him out of the blue. His secretary had hung up with a promise to deliver the information within fifteen minutes.

"He wants to leave," Taneez informed Jake motioning towards the driver.

Jake thanked the driver, giving him a large tip. The driver waved goodbye and then disappeared, mixing into the crowd along the broad walkway.

"He's been so kind," Taneez told Jake, watching him dissolve into the crowd far ahead.

Jake didn't respond. When she glanced at him, she saw him lost in the orphic layout of the cryptic snake puzzle. She noted that he was making some modifications to the grid of letters inside the snake's belly, shading the grid along certain letters.

Following a brief moment, Jake had managed to give a new perspective to the cryptic snake puzzle. Taking the modified scroll, Taneez observed the changes he had made.

"X?" Taneez wondered aloud looking at the X mark having emerged in the middle of the circle following Jake's modifications. "That is all there to it?"

"It's not a perfect X mark though," Jake said, pointing to an arm on the upper right that was long of all the four. Save for the alphabet 'I' from the outer most circle, the rest of alphabets were excluded from the shaded region he had drawn.

"Does that mean anything to you?" Taneez asked, looking at the alphabet 'I' in the puzzle. "Is it significant?"

Jake shrugged. "The alphabet 'I' is used instead of 'E' to complete the word Energy. Other than that, I don't think there's anything else left out. Not unless we're missing something here."

Following a brief moment, Jake stated, "Star guides the mortal," reminding her of the words from the last line in the riddle. "We're missing the 'star' here…that which guides the mortal, which refers to our mortal being." He broke off to give this some thought and said, "We should spot a star hidden somewhere within this circle that guides us…"

"True, I don't see any star either," Taneez said, scanning the cryptic snake puzzle. "There are astrological and alchemical symbols inscribed around the rim of the grid. But, I don't see any of it making any kind of reference to a star…a guiding star, precisely."

Jake had to agree with her. Although the rim of the cryptic snake puzzle was replete with mysterious symbols, alchemical and astrological, there was nothing that referred specifically to a star. Then Jake saw something that piqued his interest. He took the scroll from her and carefully observed the words that now introduced a new prospect to him.

Taneez realized something had intrigued him. "What is it you're looking at?"

"These letters," Jake pointed to the letters that had been left out of the 'X' mark. "U, R, and V." He tapped the letters as he explained, "I wonder if these letters make any sense since they top the four arms of the symbol X with 'I' already touching the rim of the circle."

Taneez considered Jake's explanation. Then she grabbed his pen and extended the remaining three arms until it touched the rim and shaded the boxes containing those letters, before holding it out to him, motioning him to look at it.

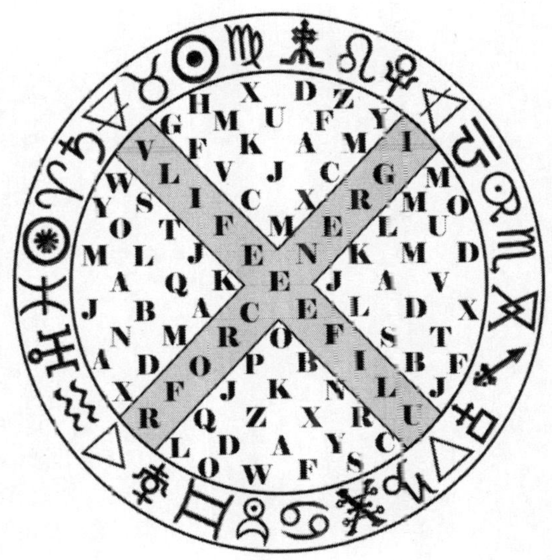

Jake saw that she had extended the shaded portion to touch the rim of the cryptic snake puzzle.

Apparently, there was not much of a difference in the pattern. "You don't get it?" Taneez asked, excited about something she thought was relevant and that Jake seemed to have missed.

"It's still the same symbol." Jake shrugged.

Taneez smiled softly. "Sometimes, a shift of perspective is necessary to spot a secret hidden in plain sight." She winked at him and holding the scroll, she turned it forty-five degrees and motioned for Jake to look at it again.

CHAPTER 76

Staying low and alert, Jake and Taneez pressed forward through Haridwar's popular Moti Bazaar.

Situated on the road north of Hari Ki Pauri Ghat, this bustling market is a favorite destination for tourists. A one-stop shopping center for those who like brass ware, stone idols and religious knick- knacks, colorful glass bangles, woolen garments, pickles and Ayurvedic medicines.

Making their way through the bustling market, they discussed the cryptic snake puzzle, taking care to occasionally look into shops, pretending to be potential customers. Now, huddling inside a small clothing shop, Taneez looked for some *kurtis* while Jake intently gazed at a symbol that had transformed into another symbol, one that had emerged when Taneez had turned it forty-five degrees.

The figure was a well-known one, that of the quartered circle.

Taneez scanned the racks of *kurtis*, as Jake asked, Is this a symbol for clinic?"

"Actually, you're correct in a way," Taneez said. "Although, this quartered circle is used as a modern symbol to indicate a medical center, it's been around since 3000 BC. Over the passage of time, different civilizations had various connotations for this symbol of the circle stamped with a cross. Pagans used it as their sacred cross. Others thought it indicated the fourth element, earth."

She paused for a beat and said, "But in actuality, the four arms of the cross represent four cardinal directions—North, East, South and West."

"In that case," Jake said, looking into the symbol, "are we looking at some kind of a compass?" He glanced at her, his eyes brimming with anticipation. "A cryptic compass that also acts as a map concealing a secret location?"

"Not precisely," Taneez replied. "Although this appears to be a compass or a map, it's only metaphorical. The one that supposedly speaks of a location but not specifically, unlike a real map that provides geographical coordinates."

Jake had to concede with her. Real maps always gave geographical coordinates for a location. This one was simply, a figurative map.

However, there were unsettling questions jostling up Jake's mind. He could not help but go over both the connotations of the symbol of the quartered circle. If the symbol in question was a pagan cross, then why would his father go to such lengths to hide the secret unless his father was a pagan himself or the secret had something to do with a pre-Christian cult, which was a preposterous idea

But even so, Jake couldn't stop asking himself: *What's next?*

He also had another concern weighing down upon him. Night was fast approaching and they needed to get shelter somewhere in the city. He had already had an argument with Taneez who wanted to lodge at a five-star hotel; he thought that was risky. The best place, according to him, would be a service apartment or room in some rundown area nearby.

For the time being, he decided to put the cryptic snake puzzle on the back burner and asked the shopkeeper to recommend a service apartment for a one-night stay.

The shopkeeper rubbed his chin as he thought of options before he spoke in Hindi, suggesting a few names. After thanking him, Jake and Taneez were about to leave the shop when the shopkeeper added in Hindi, "And sir, close by is a decent hotel which goes by the name Urvi."

Jake froze in surprise and spun on his heels. "What hotel did you say?"

"Urvi," The shop keeper replied. "Its pretty descent and quiet economic."

Taneez puzzled, giving a *what happened?* reaction.

"He's suggesting another hotel which goes by the name Urvi." Jake added with Bingo smile.

Taneez started at him blankly.

Without saying a word, Jake spread the scroll on his palm and using his long fingers, he pointed four letters topping the four arms of the cross, clockwise, starting with the letter U, then R, V and then I.

When Taneez understood what he was pointing at, she glanced up at him from the scroll and let out a smile of triumph. "That's deadly!"

ӜӜӜӜӜ

The edifice of the Hotel Urvi was lofty, with a brightly illuminated creamy-white facade. It sat in the middle of a square compound, with a sprawling lush green lawn near the entrance.

What in the world is hidden here? Jake asked himself, as he entered the porch and then the foyer, thinking about the four letters, U-R-V-I, inscribed on the top of each arm of the cross in the cryptic snake puzzle.

"Jake," Taneez clutched his hand tightly as they walked towards the reception area, glimpsing the plush interiors of the foyer and the grand chandelier that loomed low over them.

"Are we on the right track? Do you think this symbol truly represents the name of this hotel?" She insisted uncertainly. "Will this hotel serve us the answer we're lookingfor?"

"I'm not certain," Jake replied, unsure himself. "The quest ends in this city. And the answer to the last riddle when fed to the cryptic puzzle blossoms like a flower, revealing a symbol of a quartered circle which in turn points to the name of a hotel, Urvi. The symbol showing up in this city and having a connection with some hotel in here is more than a coincidence." He looked at her anxiously. "Whether or not this place holds the secret, this hotel has some story to tell about The Lost Arcanum. And in the worst case, even if it doesn't, it will at least serve the purpose of sheltering us for this night."

The foyer was large, illuminated in a golden hue by the huge chandelier suspended from the high ceiling. A luxury sofa was placed at one corner and at the other corner was a male receptionist seated behind a marble desk. He received them and after some formalities, a waiter led them to a double luxury suite on the third floor of the hotel.

Earlier, Jake had alerted her that reputed hotels allotted accommodations to men and women separately unless they were in wedlock, to avoid allegations of prostitution. Surprisingly, they acquired a double bedroom with ease, and he appreciated Taneez for her perfect acting skills that convinced the staff that they were espoused. Inside the luxury suite, there were two separate bedrooms with one leading into another. The first one was well furnished and adorned with the latest interior designs and plasma TV facing the bed, while the other had a luxurious bed attached to a plush restroom.

CHAPTER 77

Jake logged into his Gmail account and waited patiently as the webpage began to load.

He had left the hotel room for a cybercafé close by and had chosen a compartmentalized work station. As soon as the webpage loaded, an unread message from Ishita beckoned.

Quick as flash, Jake clicked on the e-mail and read the message. Ishita had responded to his query with two attachments. Both JPEG files He had clicked on them immediately.

As the images loaded, Jake recalled requesting his office secretary Ishita to send him the photofit of the prime suspect in Ramanujan's murder case. The man who was probably behind murders of all those who were harboring the link to -*The Lost Arcanum*.

Jake squinted at the screen, his fists clenched as the image gradually materialized.

Then, boom!

The photofit image was an eye opener. The side profile of the suspect exactly resembled the person Jake was having doubts about. He clicked on the second file and opened it.

The ground beneath his legs seemed to give away, as this one more clearly showed features that formed a facsimile of someone Jake knew.

Jake could not help but drop his jaw in shock. "Holyshit!"

ӜӜӜӜӜ

The male receptionist in the lobby of Hotel Urvi glanced at Jake, alarmed when his demand which seemed more like a threat than a request.

"I'm sorry, sir. I need to take permission from higher authorities before I let you access the customer's record."

Jake appreciated his loyalty and pushed a five hundred rupee note on the desk. "Your fee."

The man stared at Jake, still reluctant to proceed. "As I told you, I can't help you with this…"

Then, Jake pulled his CBI identity card and slid it on to the desk.

The man scanned it and then looked up at him, troubled and anxious.

"I guess that's enough to get you going," Jake said. "This is a CBI investigation. And I'm sure you're aware of the consequences if you cause hinder in the investigation."

The man gulped a knot in his throat and helplessly nodded.

Only a while ago, Jake had extracted information from a waiter who had explained how their hotel, moving away from the traditional method of managing records, had adopted a digitized database management system that archived even older records. Now, standing behind the male receptionist, Jake peered at a computer screen, thanking the advancement in technology, confident that the information he required would be available in a matter of seconds.

The receptionist, noting down the required name from Jake, prepared to pull up the record, opening the database console. Jake was trying to concentrate but his mind was a jumble of thoughts. The photofit images of the suspect his office secretary had mailed him was troubling. The suspect's facial features, Jake remembered, were nearly identical to what he had seen in real life.

It's unbelievable, Jake thought.

"Sir, George Stevens?" the receptionist's words drew his attention.

The man looked at Jake to ensure he had spelled the name correctly.

Jake nodded.

As the receptionist hit the enter button, the console pulled up only one record with the name Stevens G. The receptionist turned to inform Jake about it, but found that Jake was already jotting down the details from the record onto a paper.

"That's the right one," Jake assured the receptionist, as he finished noting down the details. Once done, he pushed another five hundred rupee note on the desk. "This is to keep your mouth shut."

The receptionist glanced up at Jake, stammering, "Understood, sir."

Pinning the receptionist with a grave stare, Jake stuffed the paper into his pocket and walked away.

CHAPTER 78

Is this it? Taneez kept wondering, looking at the piece of paper in her hand. Half an hour ago, Jake had passed onto her the details he had extracted from the hotel's customer records, which proved that his father, George Stevens, had stayed at the hotel, making it likely that the scroll was leading them to Urvi.

The record, dated January 17, 1993, had included details like personal information of the customer, type of suite selected, food and entertainment charges and overall expenses. Of these particulars, Jake had shown her one specific item, something very crucial that looked like it guarded the secret his father had concealed decades ago.

Now, having bribed the waiter and coaxed him to join their mission, they were passing through several rooms in the corridor on their way to the top floor of the hotel. Once they reached there, Taneez waited patiently with Jake as the waiter fumbled through a bunch of keys to unlock the door to a chamber where the valuable listed in the record could have been resting for decades.

Taneez lifted her eyes to Jake. "You think the secret your father harbored lies in this video disc?"

Jake's gaze drifted as he thought of the movie that was billed under entertainment charges in the records relating to his father's stay.

"Possibly." Jake replied, his heart racing in anticipation.

The waiter turned on the lights in the room and invited them inside.

Jake stepped in with Taneez. Although the room was large and cavernous, it was strewn with broken chairs and furniture as if it was the hotel's dumping yard. Near the rear wall, several wooden shelves were placed haphazardly. All of these held cardboard boxes containing video discs.

Jake held his breath as the smell of dust and wood hit him. Taneez was already sneezing.

The waiter motioned them further in, snaking through the assortment of broken chairs and furniture, complaining how with the arrival of the digital era, satellite cable system had unseated the movie video library. It was no longer in use and was relegated to this chamber on the top floor of the hotel.

Arriving near the shelves, the waiter started digging through the cardboard boxes, saying, "Can you repeat the name of the movie, sir?"

Jake lowered his gaze to read the name of the video mentioned in the details. *Dad was an ace,* Jake thought admiringly. Like the name of the hotel 'Urvi', which was an ancient Sanskrit term for earth, the name of the movie, 'Dharti', was also an old Sanskrit term for earth. Thus had his father concealed the secret.

Dhar, dhrithri and dharti, all these Sanskrit terms referred to the element earth, meaning that which holds everything. Now the video disc held the supposed secret. He let out a sigh and glanced at the waiter. "Dharti."

The waiter, after rummaging through the cardboard boxes, retrieved a pouch and held it out for Jake. "Here, it is."

Jake's felt his skin prickle as he received the video disc. Taneez peered over his shoulder at the video disc.

"I'm not sure if it plays," the waiter informed him. "It's not been used for years."

As Jake worked his hands through the pouch, it fell apart like a book, with two discs secured safely under the spongy side covers. Inserting his fingers inside, he felt something that he gripped it between his index and middle finger and pulled it out.

My God! Taneez could now make a sense of what she was looking at: it was a mini compact disc.

Jake felt overwhelmed, wondering if the compact disc really held the secret, The Lost Arcanum, then his father's crusade to conceal its whereabouts would be victorious and the whole idea was simply too brilliant to comprehend. At which point, a coarse voice emerged from somewhere behind them, declaring, "That belongs to me."

Startled, Taneez turned to discover someone in the doorway. It took only a split second for her to recognize the person who stood pointing a gun at them, wearing a wicked smile across his lips.

"You?" Taneez exploded in disbelief.

But Jake turned nonchalantly. "I knew he was coming for this."

CHAPTER 79

"*What your interest* in this disc?" Taneez asked, bewildered at the sight of taxi driver now holding them at gun point.

He had never seemed like a stranger, until now.

"He actually deserves it," Jake told her. "His endeavors to obtain this disc have gone beyond the limits of mine," he said, eyeing the driver. "You've seen only half of it."

"I don't get it, Jake," she replied hesitantly, casting fearful glances between him and the driver.

"This link has long interested him."

"You knew about him?" She sounded baffled. "You knew that he was coming for this?"

Jake nodded, staring at the driver. "Not until this evening."

She swallowed a lump in her throat.

"Do you remember, at Hari Ki Pauri, after disposing David's body in the water of Ganges I was looking at the wet footprints on the *ghat* floor?"

Taneez recollected the event.

"You thought I was worrying over it. And this man," he looked at the driver, "he said, 'those footprints are like those of fish in the water, untraceable.' What he didn't know was that sharks hunt their prey by the smell of their blood, not by tracing their footprints."

"His footprints seemed like a match for those discovered near Ramanujan's dead body, near the poolside." Jake glanced at the driver, telling her, "Do you remember, I went back to David's body telling you that giving his body to the water of Ganges was safer?"

Taneez listened to him anxiously as he spoke.

"That was to confirm my suspicion. You said you had shot David in the leg and the bullet pierced his chest," Jake said. "We thought you had aimed poorly. But that wasn't what happened. The bullet you shot had indeed skimmed past his right leg with minimal damage to the skin. And the one that pierced David's chest was shot from this man's silenced gun."

Taneez was too numb to react. She couldn't digest the true identity of the driver.

"This added to my growing suspicion and I decided to cross-check it. I called my office and got the photofit impression of the killer mailed to me, which matched exactly with this man."

Violent anticipation was spinning through her head, as she tried to digest the fact that the man who had traveled with them as a taxi driver was a murderer in disguise.

"But like every criminal, he failed to cover his tracks."

The killer burst out laughing. "It's great to see that you've done good homework on me. Now cut the crap and give me the disc."

Taneez was not at all surprised to hear him speak fluent English. Jake slipped the disc into his pocket.

The killer stared maliciously at him and opened fire. Splinters of wood erupted when the bullet exploded into the wooden rack as Jake ducked down.

Taneez moved out of the way.

"Damn you! You can't stop me from getting what I want!" the killer cursed, reloading his automatic and sprinting toward Jake, squeezing out several rounds, all of which bit into the wooden chairs and furniture. Jake, dodging the bullets, kept low as fragments of chipped wood and smoke rained down upon him, before he crashed into a wooden stool.

Terrorized by the sudden fire, the waiter huddled against one wall. Finding the killer distracted by Jake, he pressed his back against the wall and stealthily slid out of the room.

Taneez slid her hand into her purse and withdrew her gun, only to be brought down to the floor by driver's gunfire.

She gawked at the driver in fear as he gave her with a terrifying smile and turned to Jake. His lunatic grin turned into serious frown as he spotted Jake hurling something heavy at him.

It was too late to fend off the crash. The wooden stool rammed into his body, hurling the gun from his hand and throwing him off balance, against the wall.

Despite the impact, the driver tried to crawl to the gun which had skittered a little farther on the floor. Jake anticipating his action, kicked him in the chest throwing against the wall with a thud, lifting off his feet.

The driver hollered, crumpling to the floor. His head swayed uncontrollably and blurred images of Jake looking at him with disdain danced in front of his eyes. Even in this pathetic condition, his sight moved to the gun, which was within his reach if he could stretch a little.

As he reached for it, his fingers were pinned under Jake's shoes and he was kicked again in his side. He curled up in pain. Jake kicked and punched the driver in his spine and a punch at the jaws, landing heavy blows. But it seemed that was not enough. The driver grabbed a broken chair and hurled it at Jake.

It hit Jake squarely on his shoulder. He staggered backwards, yelping as he crashed into the wall behind and slid to the floor.

Climbing to his feet, the driver rushed to collect the gun and found Taneez had grabbed it and was leveling it at his face. She inched backwards as he moved towards her with vicious intent in his eyes.

"One step more and you'll meet your death," Taneez warned, backing up.

The killer uttered gravely, "This is between me and him. You stay out of it."

Taneez discounted his warning and looked around for Jake. He lay still on the floor, writhing. From his helpless state, she realized he was not going to be able to make it on his own. "Stay away. One more step and I'll put this goddamned bullet in your dirty flesh!"

The driver didn't seem to mind her warnings. He crept closer and closer.

She gripped the trigger and squeezed it.

"Shit!" she cursed.

The gun was empty.

The driver smiled devilishly and grabbed her by her waist and locked his powerful arm around her neck. Taneez tried to wriggle from his grips, but his strong hold constricted her muscles. With one arm wrapped around her neck, he let the other slide into his pocket and pulling out a sharp knife, which he brought up against her soft skin.

The killer spread his hands for the disc, bargaining with Taneez's life.

"No, Jake, don't do that," Taneez pleaded. "Just leave the place right now."

The driver nudged the knife against her throat.

"Leave her and take this," Jake held out the disc.

"No, Jake…," Taneez implored.

"Shut up, you bitch!" the driver blurted, tightening his hold around her body. "I'll slice your throat if you speak again."

The driver eyed the disc. Forcing her to walk ahead of him, he crept the distance to Jake and grabbed the disc from his hand.

"Leave her right now!" Jake warned allowing him to take the disc.

The driver shoved her aside, letting her crash to the floor.

After giving them one last terrifying look, the driver sneaked out of the door.

Panicked, Jake immediately crossed over to Taneez and helped her up from the floor, only to have her fall in his arms, unconscious.

Terrified, he screamed, "Taneez!" shaking her, trying to revive her to consciousness. But his heart almost came to stop the moment he saw her wrist, that was now bleeding copiously.

CHAPTER 80

Sunday, August 12, 2017,
10.30 AM. Haridwar.

Her wrist was hurting with a stinging pain.

There was also a mild pounding in her head. Regardless, Taneez kept pace with Jake as they threaded their way through the bustling Moti Bazaar, despite she had absolutely no idea where she was now being taken.

The previous night, after the driver had escaped with the video disc, Jake had carried Taneez to the hotel suite and bandaged her wound. Staying awake all night by the side of her bed, he had tended to her injury and used ice packs on her forehead to lower her temperature that had shot to a 102 degrees Celsius. Although she was barely conscious, in her waking moments she had felt his warmth towards her. A strange affinity had bound them like soul mates even if it was only for the time being.

Taneez snapped out of her thoughts and glanced at Jake.

He walked stoically. He was still not responding to her repeated queries. She couldn't take the silence anymore. It was killing her.

"Jake, I need the answer. That disc was so precious to you. How could you do this? How could you let him take it away?"

Jake replied as he kept pace with her. "You're valuable to me. This quest was possible only with your assistance. You're genuinely more precious to me than that disc."

For the first time ever, she felt a strong affection for him. His words had the gravity that would pull any girl into his arms. His voice imbued with a subtle warmth that was pleasant to ears and soul. She couldn't take her eyes off his, which held her fixated.

"And the other reason is that the cryptic snake puzzle is still incomplete."

His statement was baffling.

Sensing which, Jake elaborated, "The cryptic snake still hides a secret in its womb." He then produced a paper from his pocket and held it out for her.

She eyed at it and found an image of star.

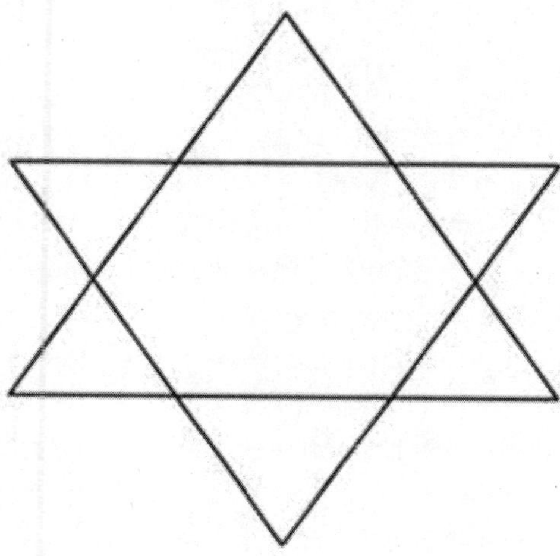

She looked up from the paper at Jake, puzzled. "A Jewish Star of David?"

"That is one of the names it goes by." Jake appreciated her knowledge, motioning for her to keep pace with him as he strode ahead. "The riddle talks about this same 'star' in the line *'the star guides the mortal.'*"

ЖЖЖЖЖ

OPERATION: THE LOST ARCANUM
TASK: ACCOMPLISHED
LINK: RECOVERED

One hundred and fifty kilometers from the holy city of Haridwar, the driver Soori, seated in the backseat of a hired taxi, sent an SMS to his master. When he looked at the taxi driver, he smirked at the thought that only a day ago, he had donned the same disguise. And now, all of sudden, he had switched back to his real profession: from taxi driver to real time killer.

No transformation has ever been permanent in my life, the killer thought.

Pushing the thoughts out his mind, he was enjoying the groovy beats of desi music on the taxi's speakers when his cell phone warbled in his pocket. He pulled it out and found an unknown number blinking on the screen. *Master!*

He connected the call and heard the voice of his master guiding him to collect his prize from a mason at a deserted construction site thirty miles north-east of Haridwar National Highway, in exchange for the recovered link. With those words, the deal had come to an end. And the killer felt overwhelmed.

I have emerged as a winner. The killer laughed wickedly.

ЖЖЖЖЖ

The six pointed star, Taneez remembered, had various interpretations across different cultures of the ancient world, but it was most popularly known as the Star of David.

The non-Jewish Kabbalah identifies the hexagram as the divine union of male and female energy, where the male is represented by the upper triangle and is referred to as *'blade'* and the female energy by the inverted triangle, is *'chalice.'*

"The hexagram," Taneez ventured, "supposedly appeared on the shield that David carried to battle Goliath. And later his son, King Solomon, used it in his seal called the Great Seal of Solomon."

Jake agreed. "This hexagram star was also the same star that seemed to have guided three wise men to Bethlehem where Jesus was born to Joseph and Mary in a manger." He smiled at Taneez, as they navigated the alleys. "Today once again, after two thousand years since it was first seen, the same star will guide us, the mortals, to the secret The Lost Arcanum."

"But how?" Taneez was still not clear on that front.

Noting which, Jake flipped the paper to the other side and handed it over to her to see. He explained as she scanned the image on the other side. "The Star of David is formed by an upside-down triangle overlapping an upright triangle. When you separate them we have these two triangles."

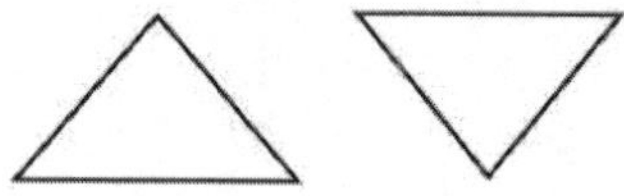

"A 'blade' and 'chalice'," Taneez interjected, "as per the Hermetic Kabbalah."

Jake had knowledge on those phrases. 'Blade' was a male force and symbol of fire, purely phallic in nature, while 'chalice' referred to female divinity and was symbolic of water, a representation of female genitalia. He provided the Hindu representation of those symbols.

"As per the Hindu version, they are the Lingam and Yoni, referring to the divine generative energies of Shiva and Parvathi, symbolic of their sexual union which is thought to have brought the universe into existence. Add a horizontal line to each and we will have four triangles."

He produced another paper for her.

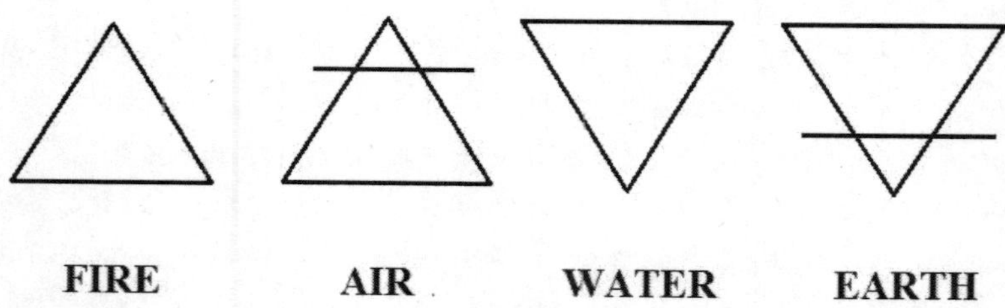

Taneez glanced up at Jake from the paper.

"Fire, water, air and earth," Jake declared, adding, "each representing four basic elements and," smiling playfully, he continued, "they also represent four cardinal directions—North, East, West and South."

"Don't tell me that you are assuming this cryptic snake puzzle is a map?" Taneez asked him incredulously.

"Bingo!" a thin smile escaped Jake's lips, "the star guides the mortal..."

CHAPTER 81

The driver Soori looked down at the crisscrossing lines on his palms. If the ancient saying was to be believed, these lines would transform with one's deeds over a lifetime.

So will mine, he thought, staring at palms that had suffered more than they were destined for. From gripping pencils between his tiny fingers in school to mopping tables in a restaurant, to cleaning utensils and washing lavatories, these were the same hands, he remembered, that trembled uncontrollably, gripping the blood-smeared knife after he'd stabbed to death his guardian, the man who had adopted him.

But now, they seemed rock steady, even after claiming many lives and with the prospect of more such assignments. He was remorseless. Instead, he seemed to have become tougher and more resolute in the face of difficulty. Nonetheless, he had now decided against such inhumane activities. Once he was in possession of the prize, he would retire to a dignified life, away from the world of crime.

As he emerged from his thoughts, his attention had suddenly drifted off to a panel attached to the roof of the car's cabin. Discerning it was a video disc player, he pulled out the disc he had captured from Jake and showed it to the taxi driver, asking if it could be played. The taxi driver seemed to he amiable, who agreeing on his demand, accepted the disc, inserted it and hit 'Play.'

I must see what it contains, the killer thought. *After all, I have gone to great lengths to recover it. I deserve to see what it holds that's worth such a hefty price my master had paid me to recover it.*

The panel swung on its hinges and aligned flat. A moment later, it sprung to life with crackling static and remained so for a few seconds, before the screen glowed with forms of an arcane nature.

At first the lines on his temples creased deeply, as he tried to make sense of what appeared on the screen. Then a cocktail of terror and amazement washed over his face. *What the hell?!* The killer started sweating in his seat, having seen nothing of the kind that was now being projected on the display screen. The forms were extremely unusual and shockingly repellent.

"Sir?" the driver said in Hindi, wondering at his silence. "Is everything ok?"

"Just turn off the video."

"I'm sorry?" the driver said, perplexed.

"I said turn off the video and give the disc back to me," the killer said aloud.

Taken aback by his passenger's sudden temper, the taxi driver abruptly ejected the disc and handed it to him. Over the rest of journey, he tried to assess what had caused such a reaction in his passenger who now seemed half-dead, as if he had seen something terrifying.

ЖЖЖЖЖ

As Taneez pressed forward with Jake through the ancient alleys of Haridwar, she asked him to prove that the cryptic snake puzzle was an actual map.

Jake had given her a sensible explanation, one that seemed to ring true.

"All night, while you were down with fever, I was trying to make a possible connection between the places mentioned in the riddles. I could not find a plausible explanation for the significance of each location or whether they were related. Although the places we have been to have no association with one another, the secret that we learnt from each location was based on the concept of one of the four basic elements. Alchemy was predominantly based on the element of *'fire'*, which brought about the transformation. The flying machine carved on the walls of the temple of Ellora was a testament to how the element *'air'* held secrets to produce anti-gravity technology. And the element *'water' as* in the water of Ganges nurtured power to change into an elixir."

"Fire, air, water and now, it has to be 'earth.' The final element that I'm sure has something to tell us about the secret hidden in the earth."

She still seemed reluctant to accept his theory. Jake then presented one last piece of information that he was sure would make her accept his conclusion about the cryptic-snake puzzle.

"Urvi and Dharti," Jake told her, breathing faster, as they kept pace through the bustling market place, "these words, one of which is the name of the hotel and the other the name of the video disc, are also Sanskrit terms for the element 'earth.'" To substantiate his assertion, he showed her a paper.

"As we've seen before, the rim of the cryptic snake puzzle actually works as a dial here." Jake reminded her turning the rim until the 'X' mark changed to a '+' sign, which was eventually a symbol for earth. "And the symbols within the rim, which we earlier thought were placed at random, for adornment, were actually placed there to serve a purpose. And the symbols of the four elements—fire, air, water and earth—serve as a marker here."

Jake produced another paper for her to look at.

Taneez accepted it and went through it, finding that the four triangles symbolizing four basic elements were shaded.

"The symbol for 'earth', the inverted triangle with a horizontal line slicing through it, marks the cardinal direction North." Jake began to shed light on it. "The upright triangle with a horizontal line cutting it marks East. The simple upward triangle marks South and the inverted triangle marks West."

"Even then, this map is not a map unless we have geographical coordinates." Taneez discarded the theory outright. "This cryptic snake puzzle is composed of letters, not numbers that give us a precise location if this puzzle is really a map."

Jake chortled and said, "Flip the paper."

When Taneez did, she looked at him in disbelief. "How?"

Jake peeped into the paper, studying it deeply.

The previous night, reclining by the side of her bed, on the carpeted floor of the hotel, he had worked out the cryptic snake puzzle. His instinct somehow didn't let go until he had unraveled the final missing piece of the puzzle. His efforts paid off and the path to victory was illuminated.

Now, he looked down at the cryptic snake puzzle once again.

The cross arms in the puzzle that were once filled with English alphabets in answer to the final riddle had now been replaced with numerical values. Just beneath the transformed cryptic snake puzzle, Jake pointed out to something more. Taneez clearly understood that what she was seeing was a simple substitution method of decoding the numerical values for the letters.

1	2	3	4	5	6	7	8	9
A	B	C	D	E	F	G	H	I
J	K	L	M	N	O	P	Q	R
S	T	U	V	W	X	Y	Z	

Taneez nodded in complete understanding and looked back at the fully transformed cryptic circle.

Her eyes squinted to make sense of the geographical coordinates marked along the cross-arms of the symbol, reading the number upward in the first arm as 34 degrees North and right arm as 79 toward East.

34^0 N

79^0 E

"34^0 North and 79^0 East," Taneez finished confirming the coordinates and looked at Jake. "It points to some location in the north-east region of India." Jake nodded.

"And what made you form this assumption that it points to the North-East other than this puzzle?"

Jake huffed. "Because the path we have trailed so far, from Srisailam to Ellora and now here to Haridwar, is north-east."

Taneez raised her brows, appreciating his intelligence.

As they had discussed, Jake looked for a cybercafé and eventually, found a small shop called Internet Zone, in an open market place. Upon entering, they found several workstations with single chairs, all crammed into a small space. Hiring a workstation, Jake took a seat, while Taneez stood behind him, looking over his shoulder.

Bringing up the Google Earth application and entering the coordinates, Jake drew a long breath and hit the 'Enter' button. He gave an anxious glance over his shoulder at Taneez wondering what place the coordinates would point to.

On the computer screen, they saw a rotating globe with an yellow pointer skimming over a revolving earth bisected of longitudes and latitudes, skipping across the continents, finally slowing down over the Indian sub-continent.

They exchanged anxiously curious looks at each other and then at the screen zooming in on the peninsular part of the Indian subcontinent, that swiftly moved diagonally across to the upper reaches of the Himalayan region of north-east India. There, it seemed to hang in the place, pausing for a long second, hovering momentarily over the India-China border and then in the blink of an eye, it zoomed closer and locked the coordinates at a specific point that was marked with a red icon.

Reading the name registered below the pointer marked by red icon, Jake and Taneez couldn't help but share a startled looks as it was not only the location least accessible to human but also, it was concealed in the cryptic snake puzzle for decades, the one supposedly holding a secret kept from the world for over two millenia.

Completely engrossed, they read the name aloud in unison.

"Kongka La!"

CHAPTER 82

2 PM.

Jolly Grant Airport,

Dehradun, Uttarakhand.

Thirty-six kilometers from Haridwar city, Taneez settled into the leather-upholstered seat in the luxurious cabin of the airborne King Air 90 turboprop. She whispered her silent gratitude to the amazing air-charter service that in little over an hour and half, within two hours of the discovery of the last clue from the puzzle and following their quick security checks at the airport with forged ID's Jake had arranged, had them airborne, now banking in wide circle, heading right for Ladakh.

When Jake had arranged for the aircraft service owned by his friend who not only summoned it to them in such a short span, but had also exempted him from airfreight, Taneez was quite impressed by the quality the contacts he maintained.

A favor returned in for a favor. Jake had quoted the line to her, informing about how his friend, whom he had helped him few years ago with his profession, was awaiting to show the beneficence in manifold that which he now returned.

With all going well, Taneez now realized that they would reach Leh, the capital of Ladakh, hours before dusk. From there, the distance to Kongka La was only a few kilometers.

Peeling her eyes from the window, she looked over at Jake, seated in the posh leather seat opposite to hers and looking out the window. From his placidity, she guessed that he was going over the secret his father had witnessed a decade ago at Kongka La, before encrypting its whereabouts in the snake puzzle and passing it down to him. Whatever was in there, she told herself, it was arcane, which was evident from his father's painstaking efforts to conceal it behind riddles and ciphers.

ЖЖЖЖЖ

At a deserted construction site off the main famous Yamuna Expressway, on the fifth floor of an unfinished building, the mason recoiled in fear when the driver Soori brandished a sharp knife, demanding that he handover the prize, a briefcase.

After watching the contents of the video disc, the driver Soori's intention had changed to one that of cunning. On his way to collect the prize money, he had decided that he would also keep the video disc. *I could keep the disc for myself and dispose it off to someone else at a price higher han what I'm now being offered.* He was mindful that there were plenty of them out there, wanting to acquire it for an incredible price. Ruled by an insatiable greed, he motioned the mason back with the knife, repeating in Hindi. "If your life is dear to you, then give me that briefcase."

Out of the blue, the knife went hurtling off his hand in the air before it fell to the floor. And a searing pain burnt his palm.

Panicked, Soori gaped at his right palm only to have it discover a hole drilled right at centre by a bullet, spraying flesh and blood on the floor.

I've been shot. Soori screamed in excruciating pain, bringing his left palm over the bleeding other, trying to stub the flow of crimson fluid. But his eyes scanned the surroundings, trying discern the source of his agony, at which point, as if sensing his turmoil, the entity conjured itself sending echoes of heavy footfalls to rebound from concrete walls.

As he faced the door, a grim figure walked into his line of sight. The man was tall and in sunglasses with a long black coat perfect fit for his average built. The figure walked in with a hefty gait, waving off the mason, who was stunned with what had erupted before his eyes a while ago.

Wincing in pain, Soori's sight lowered to the gun in man's hand. "Why did you shoot me?" Soori pressed in rage.

The man smirked, taking off his sunglasses. "Who are you?"

"I'm someone whom you have longed to meet."

"Master?" Soori wondered.

"Mastermind, precisely," the man let a cunning smile escape his lips, adding, "I'm the mastermind behind the operation the Lost Arcanum."

"You employed me to fulfill your task," Soori reminded him, "then why did you shoot me?"

The man drew a long breath. "You tried to double-cross me."

Realizing that the game was up, he's intention of keeping the disc to himself exposed, Soori attempted to pounce on him. But the man fired at both his legs and brought him to his knees. "This is for watching that footage without my consent."

"Motherfucker!" the killer groaned in pain as he came on his knees.

The man arriving closer, kicked Soori squarely in his chest and flattened him on the floor. Then, pinning him under his leather sole, he leaned closer to him, hissing, "Mr. Soori…"

The name left the killer shuddering. It was his name…his childhood name…a name given to an orphan two decades ago, an identity long forgotten. How on earth would he have known that?

"Twenty years ago, if you remember," the man reminded him, "a gentleman picked you up from an orphanage and brought you into a wealthy, loving family." He paused and rasped, "But you killed him."

Soori was astonished, wondering how this man, who'd hired him for a dangerous task, had gathered information that was privy to no one but himself. *How does he knows so much about me?*

"I killed him for the pain he caused me," Soori croaked. "He adopted me, promising education, but he made me his slave. I gave him what he deserved. He was a monster."

As Soori struggled under the gravity of his sole, the man forced the gun muzzle down his throat.

"And this is for killing the man who adopted you," the man leered, cocking the gun in the killer's mouth, blurting, "for the man who was my father."

The revelation tore through Soori's mind like a knife ripping through flesh. It was too bitter a truth to accept that the man who hired him to accomplish the mission *The Lost Arcanum* was none other than the son of the man who had adopted him, a man he had killed two decades ago.

Now helplessly, feeling pity for his fate, Soori stared into the fiery eyes of the man as he pulled the trigger in retribution, leaving him dead on the spot.

Blood splattered from the killer's throat, drenching the area where he lay.

ӜӜӜӜӜ

Quickly, recovering the vide disc from dead Soori's pocket, the man tossed some money to the mason to dispose off the body and vacated the building and hurried towards a limo stationed far from the building. Once he was seated in the backseat, the car took off to the main road.

He sat back with relief flooding to every pore and cell in his boy that twenty years of complete silence had finally paid off. He looked out the window, reflecting on the time while he was pursing his studies abroad when his father had called him, informing him about his decision on adopting an orphan. At first, it sounded like a noble cause that he then as a boy, approved without a second thought, unaware that within a year of the adoption, his father would be murdered at the orphan's hand.

The incident had shaken him to the core, leaving him deeply wounded and giving many sleepless nights. Right from then, he had nursed vengeance for this betrayal, but he waited for the right moment to vent it out. Fortunately, the time for vengeance came along with the opportunity to work for a covert organization. Because of his remarkable skills, he had become part of this organization. Using the killer Soori, as a prime tool along with the former IAF major Rabindranath and Athar Khan, he had finally recovered the link to the Lost Arcanum for opposition leader Ajeet Awasthi and for the covert organization, in return for an enormous fortune.

Soori, however, in this mission, was more than just a tool. An old score that had to be settled. He had accomplished two objectives: Recovering the video disc and eliminate his father's murderer.

Killing two birds with one stone, the man whispered, smilingly, self-satisfied.

CHAPTER 83

5.45 PM.

Kushok Bakula Rimpochee Airport, Leh, Ladakh.

Kushok Bakula Rimpochee Airport in Leh, Jammu and Kashmir, is situated at a staggering height of ten thousand six hundred eighty eighty feet above mean sea level, surrounded by beautiful mountain ranges.

Named after the venerable Kushok Bakula Rimpochee, whose nineteenth incarnation was thought to be that of an important Indian and Ladakhi statesman, the airport terminal is nondescript with a handful of reservation counters. In the wake of terrorism around the Indian border, baggage checks are given utmost importance and the airport is secured by the local police and patrolled by the Indian army around the clock.

At this astounding height, the afternoon mountain winds are nasty. Owing to this, all domestic flights are scheduled to take off and land in the mornings.

Today, however, unfettered by nature's inevitable, unpredictable moods, the wheels of the King Air 90 turboprop hit the tarmac, kicking up wisps of smoke, coming to a halt on one side of the aerodrome.

The door popped open and unwound into stairs.

Jake stepped across the threshold only to be blown away by the dramatic view of the snow-capped mountain ranges that emerged all around him as he climbed down the stairs and landed in the open.

"Oh my gosh!" Taneez moaned in awe, arriving behind him, gripped by the scenic beauty of the endless icy mountain ranges. "This is heaven on earth!"

That's exactly what it is. Heaven on earth. Standing on the tarmac, imbibing the warm rays of the sun, Jake and Taneez couldn't help but shake their head in wonder, sweeping their gaze over the dramatic vista that nature projected before their eyes in all direction.

"Sir," an airy voice intervened, pulling Jake back from his distraction. "Mr. Jake?"

A short, stout man, garbed in a woolen jacket and denim trousers was standing nearby. He wore a woolen cap, pushed down to cover his ears. "I'm your host this evening, sir." The man spoke decent English and smiled as he shook Jake's and Tanzee's hand. He motioned them toward a Land Cruiser, parked to one side on the tarmac. "Please."

As they walked along the tarmac towards the vehicle, Jake took a moment to appreciate the generosity of his friend who had not only arranged the aircraft at no cost but had also kept his promise of having arranged a host cum chauffeur meet them, who had promptly arrived on time and was now ready to ferry them to their destination.

It didn't take them long to clear the security check. Flashing fake ID's to the security officials and letting other supporting documents for scanning, they had patiently complied to all the necessary airport security formalities to have themselves signaled through.

Jake was elated that news of his new identity, that of a fugitive on the loose, hadn't reached this far to Leh.

Raising his head towards heaven, Jake thanked God and settled into the front passenger seat while Taneez climbed into the backseat, before the Land Cruiser veered off the airport and roared onward.

"These are your permits," the chauffeur said, handing over two documents to Jake as he drove.

Jake accepted them and read through the documents that his friend had arranged from the district magistrate's office at Leh.

As essential as a passport, the permit was necessary for all visitors to Ladakh, a mandatory even for Indian citizens. Furthermore, as this region is close to the border, visitors have to produce their permits at all checkpoints that diverge in different directions.

"Thanks," Jake said to the chauffeur and glanced at Taneez in the rear-view mirror. Settled in the backseat, she had raised the windows to ensure the nasty evening wind did not reach her. The weather in

August was usually hot and and at this astonishing altitude it was even worse. Mindful of such malicious climatic conditions of this mountainous terrain, Jake's friend had also arranged for convenient clothing and food for them.

Jake gazed down at Taneez's mobile screen. The coordinates obtained from the cryptic snake puzzle had already been fed into the GPS application on it. Now, using the directions from it, he guided the cruiser on to the Leh-Manali Highway, which wound up the starkly barren landscape of Ladakh.

In the background, the lofty peaks of the beautiful Zanskar mountain range diminished. Jake looked out the window at the gigantic, snow-topped mountains, some, however, were completely barren, bald and brown, rising and falling in sharp succession.

Occasionally, he turned from the window to glance at Taneez in the rear-view mirror, ensuring she was safe and comfortable. He had warned her about the unfriendly weather conditions that in combination with altitude and cold winds would make her sick. Unfortunately, she was already showing signs of a mild headache and general uneasiness, which, Jake knew, would only worsen with further climb.

As far as it was concerned with himself, Jake had been accustomed to trekking on higher altitudes from his college times. That way, he knew it would not be much of a problem for him to get acclimatized to this dangerous weather high up these mountains as much Taneez could.

ЖЖЖЖЖ

Turning off from the main Leh-Manali Highway, the Land Cruiser, now cruising peacefully at fifteen thousand feet above mean sea level, hit the tar road in the direction of Tso Kar, a salt lake situated in Rupshu plateau in the southern part of Ladakh. Jake glanced at his watch to note that it was close to six in the evening.

On these high passes, the sun rarely set before eight in the evening, that Jake believed was an upper hand which would give them ample time to reach their destination before dark.

As the cruiser raced forward, the cold winds blowing down the snow-capped mountain ranges whistled past gently. The chauffeur had raised the windows, barricading against the strong, cold evening winds.

Jake's growing concern for Taneez's health kept him shifting in his seat. He took note of her condition every fifteen minutes as the climate got nastier with the increase in altitude.

Taneez, however, had reclined in the backseat. Recovering from a combination of nausea and breathlessness, she had fallen sleep.

In the rear-view mirror Jake watched her sleep. She seemed graceful. Her eyelashes, her full lips and thin curl of hair falling over her cheek made her appear like a sleeping beauty.

Sudden jolts pulled back Jake from his distraction. When he looked at the source, he found their Land Cruiser had turned right from the tarmac road, riding over small rocks and boulders before hitting a jeep track.

Moments later, Jake's eyes were drawn off to one side, out the window, at the lofty bare mountains that trailed one after the other as if each one was trying to outdo the other in terms of sheer magnitude and height. He was struck by the vastness of the mountainous trail that had amazing ascents and grand summits, some crowned by snow that peaked against the clear blue sky while others just bare and brownish, spearing high up in all its glory.

Moving another ten miles along the dusty jeep track, the Land Cruiser headed around the west side of the Tso Kar Lake.

Jake, having acclimatized to the weather, relished the spectacular view of high arid plains, its reflection shimmering in the ever-changing blues and greens of the shallow, salty water of Tso Kar Lake.

Continuing eight miles ahead and keeping to a barren landscape, the chauffeur provided Jake his first glimpse of a nomadic settlement, consisting of houses that were usually constructed on elevated grounds, many facing south and made up of a blend of rock, wood and earth that spoke of an ephemeral lifestyle. On the other side of the jeep track, Jake was pleased to see immense stretches of grasslands, where a group of adorable children with cherubic European looks, strayed around, while Pashmina goats, sheep and yak grazed in the background. With his eyes full of this overwhelming scenic beauty, he slid back in his seat.

CHAPTER 84

Taneez woke up to the meek hum of the Land Cruiser.

She felt lightheaded and took a deep breath, realizing that she was feeling better, possibly acclimatized to travelling in the high altitude. She then glanced out the window and saw the sun sinking on the horizon.

The wind outside had grown violent and was battering against the windshields, making the glass windows shudder. At that moment, she spotted something incredible out of the window, something huge, furry, marching in tandem along their road. Taneez plastered her face to the glass window while reaching out to shake Jake's shoulder with her hand. "Jake, you should see this..."

Jake, asleep in the front passenger seat, groggily pulled himself up and looked out the window. He twisted in his seat in surprise, adjusting to get a better view of something outside the Land Cruiser on the side of the road.

Moving in a grand procession along the jeep track was something exclusive to the region of Ladakh: a herd of huge double- humped Bactrian camels.

This species of double-humped camel, Camelus Bactrianus, is rare to find but exclusive to the cold deserts of central Asia. Weighing somewhere between three hundred to one tonne, its reaches a maximum height of eight feet, with thick long woolly fur and varying in shade from dark brown to sandy beige.

"The ship of the famous Silk Route," the chauffeur said, smiling at his passengers' delightful reactions, given he had spent half his life watching this species of camel wandering this cold desert. "This area is in close proximity to the legendary Silk Route," the chauffeur reminded them.

The Silk Route, Jake recalled from his history lesson, was an ancient trade route stretching over a stupendous four thousand miles, had conducted traders, craftsmen, artisans, monks and nomads back and forth from China to the Mediterranean, linking the various regions of the ancient world of commerce. Its name was derived from Chinese silk, a trade in which had resulted in the creation of this extensive transcontinental network, stretching from China making through India, Asia Minor, up through Mesopotamia, to Egypt, the African continent, Greece, Rome and to Britain.

After Jake had delivered this short history talk of the Silk Route to Taneez, they both watched the herd of Bactrian camel pass by with great appreciation. And for all the assistance this animal might have served, playing a major role in developing international trade relations, providing the principal means of locomotion for traders back and forth from their countries across various regions.

As their vehicle left the herd of Bactrian camels behind, Jake felt a great admiration for the Silk Route. The air here still seemed to resonate with the voices of traders from the distant past and reek with stench of fur of bactrian camel, also, the songs of their majestic antiquity and grandeur, still very much present, all narrating an unbelievable true story of human endeavor for trade that developed two thousand years ago, stretching across a massive four thousand miles.

ӁӁӁӁӁ

Twenty-five kilometers off the main Leh-Manali Highway, the Land Cruiser headed down the valley of Tso Kar, towards what the chauffeur cited to them was a small village called Nuruchang.

Soon, Jake perked up in his seat reading a signboard on the roadside that alerted : **Kongka La Pass ---> 3.5 Km**

His friend had explained to Jake over the telephone hours ago that Kongka La was a secluded piece of land in the highest altitude of the Indian sub-continent, which was also infamously a low-ridge pass located in the Himalayan range where the disputed India-China border overlapped.

In the year 1952, it was in this region of Kongka La that the Indian side had discovered Chinese incursion into India. The Chinese had constructed a strategic road through the traditional caravan route passing from Xinjiang (Sinkiang) to Tibet through the Aksai Chin to move their troops. In the years that followed, this affair triggered frequent skirmishes between these two countries over the border dispute that finally culminated in a major war in 1962, where the Indian armed forces suffered severe casualties and the worst defeat recorded in Indian history.

Various Indian prime ministers have ever since tried sorting out this issue, besides pulling in different other channels like Special Representatives talks to resolve the dispute. Yet, little has been accomplished in this sphere when it comes to clarity on the demarcation of the Line of Actual Control (LAC) on the ground or on military maps.

Jake, however, suspected that this issue had no relevance or connection in whatever way to the secret location cited in the cryptic snake puzzle itself. Before he could give this more thought, a sudden strange sound jolted him upright in his seat. He instantly turned to the chauffeur, wondering if he had heard it, too.

Taneez too sat straight in the backseat, alarmed. Then the sound grew to an ear-shattering thump! thump!

They all recognized the sound: a helicopter.

Taneez peered out of the window, raising her gaze skywards, as a military green European-made Eurocopter Fennec Reconnaissance and Surveillance helicopter swooped into her view with a deafening sound in the sky.

"Indian Army," the chauffeur said, releasing his clutch from the throttle, slowing the speed of the Land Cruiser. "We're only thirty minutes from the Red Zone, a restricted area for civilians."

Jake was puzzled, never having heard of such a location. The chauffeur's gaze followed the helicopter as it roared through the sky, flying past them. Through the front windshield, the chauffeur gazed at the copter as it swung inward, taking a wide circle and then heading back to them.

Beside him, Jake turned anxious. His stomach was in knots, his muscles twitched in fear, suspicious that the Intelligence men were back to get him and his game was up.

The Eurocopter zipped past their Land Cruiser, taking a sharp inward turn and flew in from the other side.

"This is a patrolling unit," the chauffeur informed them. "They keep constant watch over this restricted area."

The Eurocopter flying past their Land Cruiser, started circling them in the sky, like a predatory spider around the prey caught in its web.

The thud-thud of the rotors reverberated with an ear-splitting roar.

The chauffeur slowed down the Land Cruiser and brought it to a halt in the middle of the road, killing the engine. Lowering the windshields, he peered out at the sky just as the helicopter came in from the opposite side and hovered overhead.

The co-pilot in Indian army uniform waved a warning at the chauffeur, a hand gesture that they were approaching too close to the restricted area, followed by another hand gesture to retreat. Understanding the warning, the chauffeur used a combination of hand gestures to indicate that they were heading to the nearby village: **Nuruchang.**

The co-pilot nodded and indicated that they could proceed by giving them a thumbs-up signal. The chauffeur nodded, imitating the gesture. The rotors thumped as the helicopter rose in the sky and shot past them, disappearing behind.

In the backseat, Taneez let out a sigh of relief.

Jake looked at the chauffeur, eager for an explanation. "Red Zone," Jake repeated. "The Kongka La lies in a Red Zone?"

"It is a zone where patrolling units from India and China on either side maintain security," the chauffeur explained as he started the engine and took off. "This is where activities of unknown origin, those that are beyond one's understanding, are known to have occurred."

Jake was intrigued.

Taneez leaned forward, eager to hear every word pouring out of the driver's lips.

"This fact is no stranger than fiction," the chauffeur said as he gunned the Land Cruiser down the tarmac road. "This region is experiencing some kind of anomalies…a reason I strongly believe is why it has been intensely guarded by the Indian Army. I suppose they are trying to cover up whatever is out there that they don't want others to discover."

"You really believe there's something out there?" Jake asked. "Do you know something about it?"

"I wish I did," the chauffeur said, smiling. "But whatever is out there…it's definitely very disturbing. There is something very serious happening in this area. Some call it paranormal." he paused before adding, "Needless to say, the Indian Army is going to great lengths to protect it." Staring at Jake, he concluded gravely, "They are hiding something out there…something very deadly…"

CHAPTER 85

Nothing in the world is as amazing as letting oneself into the arms of the cool winds that sweeps onto the highest peaks of Kongka La, which winds in an endless stretch higher up the steep ascents of the pastured lands and continues behind the stupendous snow-crowned mountains.

"This is incredible!" Taneez admitted she had never seen anything like this stunning scenery. She was mesmerized by the breathtaking beauty of the place.

Truly, nature has so marvelously crafted the highest peaks of Ladakh, where one can feel closer to nature than ever before. To Jake, this experience seemed much more than an a quest, an expedition of having been transported away from his superficial worries and worldly bonds and concerns into a different world, into a new domain where he, for a moment, felt like to resign himself to his place for an eternity.

Standing on a high pass, just before the Kongka La itself, Taneez turned to catch a last glance of the Land Cruiser as it disappeared behind the Tso Kar Valley.

Minutes ago, the Land Cruiser had dropped them at the mouth of a small river in Nuruchang and headed off. Jake had led the way as they walked to Kongka La with the sun falling below the mountain range.

Standing side by side, Jake lowered his gaze to the GPS app on the mobile and checked the coordinates, confirming that the exact location was further ahead of the pass, behind another ascent that was visible at a distance, probably a mile or so from where they stood.

Since everything there appeared to be marvelous, Jake suspected that there was a darker side to it. A dimension as gloomy as the very meaning of the word 'paranormal.'

With dusk setting in, the cold winds blowing past the mountain trail were strong enough to cause frostbite if care was not taken to be insulated. Worried, Jake reached for the backpack his friend had sent and found two windcheaters, gloves, mufflers, woolen caps, boots, sunscreens, sunglasses and a water bottle.

Although all of this was not required, Jake and Taneez quickly pulled on some of the protective gear. Jake postponed setting off towards Kongka La Pass by an hour, considering the security force would be alert and heavily guarding the region at this time of day. Further informing to her that under the cover of darkness, they would resume their climb, concealing their moves, and if they were fortunate enough, as they had been so far on this quest, they might even bump into the place the co-ordinates were pointing to, where the secret was known to be hidden.

A bone-juddering chill knocked Jake from his reverie. Beside him, Taneez felt her jaws tighten, although she was well insulated in the windcheater and gloves.

At close to eight, daylight had disappeared, leaving their world on the mountain peak to be lit by twinkling stars and a waning moon. With due caution, Jake and Taneez set out for the final ascent of Kongka La, whose silhouette was feebly visible in the distance.

Walking under a starry night sky, with the moon overhead and a beautiful girl next to him, was a delightful experience, a surreal dream that he knew was ephemeral that he would cherish for the rest of his life.

"This is the most amazing place I've ever been to," Jake confessed, raising his head to the star-lit sky.

"Truly," Taneez affirmed, lifting her eyes above as they moved towards the ascent.

She observed that the sky was studded with stars and wondered if she were adventuring in some fantasy world, as though walking in the deep caverns of diamond mines. Then again, it was just an illusion that she knew would soon disappear once the sun was out the next day.

This feeling of euphoria was, however, stymied by the shadow of fear that stemmed from the thought of Kongka La and its sequestered atmosphere guarded by the Indian Army and spooky rumour attached to it.

In little over five minutes, they appeared near the top of the pass. Jake noted that the coordinates on the GPS were approaching the exact figures of the cryptic snake puzzle. A positive indication that they were closing in on the final secret location and also, a caution against danger of unknown origin up ahead, a deadly warning of risking their lives, while they were all on their own.

That was when they caught sight of a wispy beam of light with a white lustrous sheen silhouetting the pass above. "There is something on the other side of the ascent," Jake told her.

Quickly, they climbed the ascent. Upon nearing the summit, the beam of light intensified. They pressed forward, arriving at the top of the ascent, when the sight on the other side of the pass caught them off guard.

They cast an astonished glance at one another and back at the place down below.

This time, to their sheer surprise, the location Jake's father had concealed in the cryptic snake puzzle was not a temple, or a cave or some sacred river. It was a large military airbase surrounded on all sides by huge mountains.

"You are sure this is the exact location?" Taneez spoke over the gust of chilly winds.

"Yes," Jake assured her.

Completely silent, they looked down at the vast military airbase, which was populated by a few advanced aircraft stationed on the tarmac, some military aircraft and scores of olive-colored trucks. The fenced compound had elevated lookout posts and a large communication tower with complete area heavily guarded, with armed personnel manning the entrance and the lookout posts.

"Look there," Taneez pointed to their extreme right, where military trucks were entering and leaving the airbase through an iron gate. "I think that's the only entry point."

"But it's not easy to enter. It's approximately at five hundred meters from here," Jake said, roughly estimating the distance.

Taneez nodded in agreement.

Making a quick descent down the steep incline of the pass, they ducked behind one of the boulders that was wide enough to hide them from the guards.

Reaching here, Jake reassessed their position and thought to make for another larger boulder to his right, closer to the entrance. But when he turned to inform Taneez, of this, he drew a startled breath finding she had left the cover of the boulder and now standing out in open, seemingly dumbstruck, with her head raised towards the sky.

Alarmed, Jake sprinted up to her instantly. "Have you gone nuts?"

But she didn't seem to have heard him. She had gone stone cold like a statue, a speechless alarmed sculpture, with her head raised skyward.

When he followed her line of sight skyward himself, he recoiled, sharing her surprise "Jesus! What the heck is this?"

With their eyes wide and slack-jaws they looked at a cluster of strange flickering red, blue and green lights that came tearing down from the sky, emerging from the misty clouds and hovering right over the military base.

"Is this..." Taneez whispered in disbelief, words drying up in her mouth.

"It is," Jake replied in a stunned whisper, realizing that what they were now looking at was unmistakably a disc-shaped aircraft.

Huge and sparkling, it hung mid-air for a good few moments. Its two counter-rotating discs spun around the perimeter of the craft, before the ground beneath it seemed to gape open and the flying disc poured down into a large cavity inside the earth, disappearing as swiftly as it came down churning through the sky.

It happened too swift, as quick as the blink of an eye, rendering them ice-cold and too dazed to react to the sight of an advanced military aircraft that closely resembled a mysterious flying object that Jake thought was fictional or limited to ancient scriptures.

Until now.

CHAPTER 86

Kongka La lies in the region where the Eurasian and Indian crustal plate boundaries have dived under one another to create convergent plate boundaries.

Crustal plate is that rigid layer of the earth's crust which is believed to drift slowly. Consequently, this region is among the rarest in the world where the depth of the earth's crust is twice that of any other place found on this planet. Its this feature that makes this location an ideal region for the creation of underground bases that can sometimes run very deep into the tectonic plates of earth.

Further, Kongka La is amazingly immaculate and pristine, concocted of beautiful rocks and fine and picturesque granite. Owing to anomalies it harbors, neither the Chinese nor the Indian authorities have show any interest in excavating, digging or mining in this area. Nor is any civilian allowed to enter this forbidden territory, lest they find out what lies hidden beneath... Jake and Taneez had just been given a mysterious preview of it.

The sight of a flying machine disappearing underground was unfathomable and its implications incomprehensible.

Jake had quickly hauled Taneez behind the boulder, as powerful searchlights from the lookout post pierced the thick darkness, scanning the fenced area for any signs of intrusion.

With their backs pressed against the boulder, they remained silent for a complete minute. Then, Taneez hesitantly spoke, her gaze distant, "Jake, what...what do you think it was?"

He said nothing. He was next to her, sharing her stupefaction, lost in deep thought, wondering if the flying machine was the secret guarded by the fourth and the final element, earth, as it went pouring down into the depths of it.

Taneez peeped around the edge of the boulder and glimpsed at something. "Jake, there's an opening."

Jake looked over her shoulder at a tunnel opening carved at the base of the mountain, roughly at two hundred meters away from their hiding.

Supported by a concrete abutment, opening seemed as a mouth of a monstrous fish from the tales, through which military trucks were moving in and out.

Using the boulders as cover, they made for the opening, keeping close to the rocks, dodging the revolving rays of the searchlights occasionally as it swerved in vigilantly. They hurried on their foot until they arrived at rear of a series of olive-colored tarpaulin covered military trucks, lined up for security check at the entrance of the base.

Staying low, their sight crossed over to two Indian army soldiers in light green uniform. Jake instantly recognized that these soldiers at work here, were officials from Military Intelligence, now, surveying the back of the truck, in the loading area, before letting the trucks inside the cavern.

Jake's gaze shifted to the truck that was the last in the line.

"Ok, we're going into the loading area of that one."

"Hold on, Jake," she stopped him placing her hand on his shoulder, "those soldiers are checking the loading area. Even if we're through, I'm sure we'll be drilled at the next level of security check."

"Don't worry," Jake assured her, furtively making for the truck.

Taneez followed close behind, tagging him, taking long strides, covering the distance in less than a minute.

ӜӜӜӜӜ

In the truck's cabin, the solider in the passenger seat glanced at the soldier behind the wheel suspiciously, noticing furtive moments at the back of the truck from the rear-view mirror.

"Did you see that?" he asked. "See what?"

Realizing that his companion hadn't seen anything suspicious, the soldier immediately climbed down from the truck and walked straight to the loading area. There, he examined the large wooden crates. All were intact, except one that was angled away from the rest.

Odd.

He took a step forward it to examine, when his receiver beeped in his pocket. He reached for the receiver and held it up to his ear. The voice on the other end seemed to have engaged him completely, diverting his attention from the crate.

"Sure, sir." Ending the conversation, he pocketed the receiver. Giving a dubious stare at the odd crate for a long moment, he returned to the truck cabin.

ЖЖЖЖЖ

Inside the truck, Jake heaved a sigh and looked at Taneez, both hiding behind a wooden crate.

"What about the next level?" Taneez worried. Jake signaled to the heavy wooden crates. "You mean…" she hesitated.

Jake winked at her playfully.

ЖЖЖЖЖ

A while later, the echoes of the engine's growl bounced off the concrete walls, as the truck traveled through a long tunnel. It hadn't taken long before the truck came to a halt.

From inside one of the crates, Jake overheard the cabin door to the truck open and close, the soldiers climbing down from the truck and joining a group of men, who seemed to be clustered somewhere close. Their echoing voices suggested that the truck was stationed in some large solid enclosure. Their resounding footfalls got louder, implying that the soldiers were approaching the back of the truck to unload the goods, which was a bad sign.

Jake began to sweat, worried that they would be discovered any moment now.

"Taneez, you ok?" he whispered.

"So far, so good," Taneez replied, tightly huddled in a crate in the enclosed area. "It's suffocating here, though."

"I know. Hold on for a few more minutes," Jake comforted her. "They are about to unload now. Keep cool and stay down. Don't panic."

His words of assurance did little to console her. The danger of them being caught, and God knows what after that was weighing down on her heavily. *They're coming.*

She tried to calm her herself by taking deep breaths. Her breaths however, grew shorter, as they heard the muffled voices grow even louder. Then suddenly, the voices trailed off, suggestive of the soldiers having strode past the truck.

Jake remained quiet and unmoving for some time, until there was complete silence. Then he popped out of the crate and helped Taneez out.

"Where are they?" Taneez pressed anxiously, emerging from the crate.

"Looks like they forgot to unload us," Jake answered, finding his humor now that they seemed to be safe.

Quickly climbing down from the truck, they found themselves in a large enclosed space that appeared to be some kind of a warehouse carved deep into the dangerous mountains.

CHAPTER 87

The warehouse was hollowed out deep into the belly of the icy mountain.

It seemed devoid of human activity. Under the bright florescent lights, their eyes encountered heaps of boxes dumped on the far side of the warehouse along with self-propelled vehicles, fork-lifters and trucks stationed all around.

They looked around for some opening and found a door at the farthest end to their right. Muffling their footsteps, they hastened across to the corner.

Jake cautiously slid the door slightly open and ensured the space on the other side was empty, prior to pushing through it. Taneez tagging close on his heels, stepped after him into a long, empty corridor.

The corridor looked no different than one found in a hospital—hollow, stale-smelling and brightened by neon ceiling fixtures. But their attention was instantly drawn to a sliding door on the rear wall of the corridor, which had a small observation porthole.

Guardedly, they crept to it and Jake looked through it to discover a staircase that overlooked another large enclosed area, several floors below ground level, and something more in addition. "There's a platoon of soldiers down there," Jake informed her.

He stepped aside and allowed her to have a look. Through the porthole, Taneez noticed a squad of soldiers in a space that apparently was the dining area, with the soldiers looking relaxed, eating or drinking or casually strolling around and chatting.

"We should find another door that takes us to..." Jake broke off when something caught his attention: an elevator right next to the wall.

"This will take us down into the lower levels," Jake said and crossed over to it.

Taneez followed him.

With the push of a button, Jake got the elevator's door open and rushed in with Taneez. The space inside was lavish, brightly illuminated and with an access-control panel mounted to one side. What startled them was the number of floors it displayed.

"Good heavens! Thirty-five floors down?" Taneez looked over at him, gauging its implication. "Can you imagine? That's more than one- fourth of the Petronas Towers of Malaysia down there."

Jake knew what that meant. There was no need to build a military facility so deep in the earth's crust unless the Indian Army was trying to hide something really disturbing. Something that they hadn't wanted anyone to discover.

He also grew nervous, unsure about which level to choose, wondering at the amount of security that might be present at each level. Choosing carefully, he pressed the button for floor fifteen. The elevator jerked as it descended into the bowels of the earth. On the floor indicator panel over the door, the floor level skipped faster than their eyes could blink.

"Be alert," he cautioned Taneez. "We have no idea about the security down there."

Jake fixed his gaze at the floor levels jumping on the digital panel. Their pulse raced as the levels slipped down. Seven…eight…twelve. As it hit fifteen, they both moved to opposite sides and plastered themselves to the elevator wall, trying their best to keep out of direct view when the elevator doors opened.

The door hissed opened, revealing a long deserted corridor. Once confirmed the corridor was deserted, they scampered out from the elevator and walked guardedly, their backs hugging the bare walls of the corridor. As they pressed forward furtively, they covered their noses. The corridor, illuminated with crisp neon lights, had a nauseating clinical stench, of the kind usually prevalent in hospitals.

Jake was suspicious when he found no surveillance cameras installed anywhere.

"This place is terrifying," Taneez whispered. "Like a corridor to some Frankenstein's lab where a monster been cooked…"

Jake ignored her, glancing overhead, feeling the weight of the lofty mountains above them. They walked past several doors along the length of the corridor, casting a cursory glance through the eyeholes. Behind one door, they spotted something of interest.

A solid steel double door embedded into the rear wall of the chamber, secured by a digital door access-control system mounted on the door-frame.

Cautiously, they entered the room and closed the door behind them. Taneez walked up to the steel door and surveyed the door access- control system. Jake stepped up next to her, at which moment, they heard footsteps in the corridor outside.

Taneez anxiously faced Jake.

Strangely, she saw him smiling at her. A split second later, she had gauged his intentions.

"No, Jake. That will be the height of insanity."

ЖЖЖЖЖ

The army officer now lying unconscious on the floor was a senior officer in charge of the base. After knocking him unconscious, Jake had checked his identity card clipped on his uniform.

He looked up at Taneez. She gulped down a lump in her throat. Her anxious face was a sign that she wasn't happy with his move.

"If we wanted to explore what's on the other side of the door, we had to do this. We needed his access key card."

Taneez squatted beside the unconscious officer. She checked his pulse and sighed heavily. *He's alive.*

Jake then rummaged through his pocket and found the key card. He reached for the door and slid the key card through the reader. The lock disengaged and the steel door hissed open.

"What about him?" asked Taneez.

Jake looked around and found a small room to the left. Dragging the officer by his legs, he wrangled him inside.

Taneez was already stepping in through the steel door. After giving the room a cursory glance, Jake ran in after her, crossing the threshold.

The steel door closed behind them with a hiss.

On the other side, they continued onward, through a dim corridor with a low roof and a narrow passageway. A few furlongs in, they found themselves standing on a small barricaded platform, some few square meters across, that overlooked a huge cavernous chasm that was completely dark.

Squeezing Jake's hand, Taneez drew his attention to a flight of stairs to their immediate right, which seemed to disappear into the darkness halfway across. Guardedly, gripping the railings, Taneez began to tread down the stairs with Jake on her side.

The space seemed cold and eerie, with low thrum, giving them the same feeling they had experienced in the secret tunnel below Srisailam.

It didn't take long for them to reach the floor and once afoot on flat ground, on a side wall, Jake managed to find an electric switch board which had a lever. Holding his breath, when he pushed the lever, a series of overhead floodlights burst into life in succession, illuminating a large warehouse.

What held them captivated wasn't the vastness of the warehouse; rather it was what filled up the space that astounded them.

Jake watched with his mouth open in sheer surprise. Beside him, beholding the stunning sight, Taneez took a step forward, whispering, "What in the world are these things like?"

CHAPTER 88

Beheld by an awe inspiring sight, senses slowly returned with clarity that the place was in actuality, an aircraft hangar.

Scores of tall gigantic aircraft ran along the length of the hangar, towering over them, reaching nearly half the height of the hangar. But what had caught them off guard was the structure and design of these aircraft, which seemed to be far more technically advanced than any modern-day ones. Ranging in different shapes and sizes, from cylindrical to saucer-shaped, with two counter rotating discs that spun around the perimeter of the craft. They did not even appear close to warplanes. They seemed as if they had been flown in straight from an alien planet.

As if stung by its vast captivating presence, Taneez had gone completely silent. She swore having never seen anything on this scale, a sophistication in technology having reached so far ahead of what science was yet to grasp.

She reached closer to one of the aircraft and soaked her gaze with its immense hulk. Although she had seen aircraft like this one pouring down into the earth only a while ago but not from up close. She felt like she was strolling through the Star Wars studio, watching dummy models of sci-fi flying machines.

Jake, on the other hand, was contemplating on propulsion techniques since none of these airships appeared to be equipped with technology that would lift and propel the machine with thrust or wings. And that meant only one thing to him.

He turned abruptly to Taneez and said, "These are anti-gravity vehicle", dumbstruck by his own assessment. *How had the Indian military secretly developed this technology?* "And this is a secret military installation where these flying saucers are developed and tested."

Taneez turned full circle, taking in the imposing machines from all directions. They were spread all around her, heavy, lofty and growing gigantic.

Jake continued, "This is the same location the third verse of the second riddle mentions." He reminded her. *"Hidden deep within the mountain far apart..."*

Taneez recalled the riddle.

Rock Temple of Ellora holds a marvel of past,
From heaven it beholds an assembly on earth aghast,
Hidden deep within the mountain far apart,
Unleash the key, guards two voluptuous Ajantan art.

"Now it all makes sense." Jake recounted, his eyes distant. "My father had discovered ancient texts that mentioned the construction of anti-gravity vehicles. And the DIA confiscated it, compelling him and the other three to translate those texts. But I'm not getting this...," he trailed off. "If my father assisted them in replicating this ancient technology then why did they have him killed?"

"It's quite evident," Taneez replied. "Anti-gravity and its allied zero-point energy is a quantum leap in the field of clean energy production. It is the most potent inexhaustible source of energy. It can not only provide our future aircraft supersonic speed but also address much of our energy, travel and transportation, pollution and global warming problems." She paused. "Your father wanted this discovery to benefit mankind. But there are those who wanted to suppress it, because they feared it would pose a huge economic threat. Like those from the Oil and Gas company. They killed him when he wished to make the discovery public."

Jake thought about her deduction. His father being killed for wanting to make the discovery public by filming these flying machines just didn't seem credible. Their deaths served as testament to the lengths the military would go to guard its secrets. But was this secret of anti-gravity technology worth killing? His instincts said otherwise.

"I suspect there's more to the story," Jake said thoughtfully. "A cause that might've been more terrible than meets the eye."

"Well said," a new voice said from somewhere behind.

Thrilled, Jake and Taneez swiveled to see a tall man walking up to them with a bastion of soldiers in tandem, all in army uniforms.

"As you said, there's another part to the story," the man said, coming closer. "The story which is worth your effort to reach so far in here. Thrilling and suspense filled."

The man enjoyed their faces going pale, looking at someone who stood to his left. He was the same officer Jake had knocked unconscious to gain access into this secret installation.

Taneez stepped behind Jake, now looking over his shoulder, her fingers wrapped around his.

"You know something," the man said, "Not even a bird dare flutter its wings around the base without my approval. That being the case did you think we wouldn't be able to see you sneaking into the back of the truck?" He smirked. "Our men would have nailed you then and there, but they obeyed my orders and allowed you in."

Jake was a little surprised to realize that they had probed so deep into this base only because they had been allowed to. The officer whom he had knocked unconscious was proof of this. And, Jake remembered, the soldier who was about to inspect the truck had received a call on the spur of the moment and stalked off without bothering to check the back of the truck.

It was all a setup. A cunning plan deceiving them into the base. The series of events that he had thought of as fortunate, leading him and Taneez into the base safely, was, in fact, a line of bread crumbs that had led them into a trap that now seemed inescapable.

The man stepped forward, introducing himself. "I'm Balbeer Singh, the Director General, DIA."

Not surprising, Jake thought, noting the man's sturdy physique and authoritative manner suggestive of a high-ranking officer.

Casting a long and furious gaze at his detainees, Balbeer Singh signaled for the soldiers and they to fanned out, surrounding Jake and Taneez. With one last glare, Balbeer Singh turned on his heels and stormed away. The soldiers ushered Jake and Taneez after him, holding their gun muzzles at their back.

CHAPTER 89

The soldiers forced Jake and Taneez through a maze of hollow corridors in the base, before they were brought in front of a broad elevator. With a glance, Balbeer Singh waved off the soldiers.

The soldiers left immediately. He then pressed a button and opened the elevator door and motioned for Taneez and Jake to step in, following himself after them. Once inside, he stabbed keys on the control panel and the elevator began to descend.

Taneez felt claustrophobic in the dimly lit cabinet, in a space that could fit only four people at one time. Jake, on the other hand, felt his pulse racing, uncomfortable with the thought of wherever they were now being taken to.

"I think you might enjoy this," Balbeer Singh said curtly, motioning them to turn over.

When they turned to look over their shoulders, they realized they were in a glass elevator, one side of which overlooked an enormous valley. They remained awestruck, trying to make sense of the fact that they now seemed to be descending into a tremendous chasm dug into the earth's crust.

As the elevator slid down swiftly, a brightly illuminated structure emerged at the base, like a jewel from the abyss of an ocean. The structure was a high-tech facility, almost six times the size of a football stadium.

Balbeer Singh appeared on Jake's side and peered through the glass enclosure at the vast expanse of the titanic glass structure. "This is too valuable."

Jake had not reacted. Neither had Taneez. They were soaking in the magnificent view of the huge complex that had slowly materialized as the elevator sliding down.

Dazzling like a diamond, the structure appeared like a metropolitan city with well-laid streets and sidewalks. Its magnitude was unimaginable. The ground beneath their legs shook as the elevator hit the ground. The side of the glass enclosure overlooking the view, slid apart.

Balbeer stepped out with Jake and Taneez, guiding them out and over to a walkway, where a chauffeur-driven electric car was awaiting their arrival.

The car door opened and Balbeer motioned them into the backseat, opting the front passenger seat for himself, before the car took off.

In transit, Balbeer behaved like a polite guide, pointing out living quarters, private apartments, dormitories, cafeterias and hospitals, while explaining to them that close to ten thousand staff were employed in the facility for different purposes.

"Only a handful of people, say a privileged few, have toured this high-tech military research center where sophisticated machinery is developed and operated secretly," he informed them.

Shortly, the electric car dropped them off at the bottom of a flight of steel stairs leading up to a glass complex. Halfway up the stairs, the glass complex seemed to shift and an officer in military uniform welcomed them into the complex.

They followed the officer leading them through a corridor, passing hundreds of cubicles and compartments, replete with the hustle and bustle of men, like ants in their colonies, clustered around workstations, who looked up for a quick glance at these intruders.

"These men you see," Balbeer informed them as they advanced, "are adroit computer programmers and ethical hackers who constantly keep vigil on the database system, tasked with staving off hackers who try snooping into our systems."

Further on, they were led to a different section, which their officer-cum-guide explained was an advanced research laboratory. When Jake and Taneez looked through the glass wall, they saw that it was filled with a crew of men garbed in scrubs, working on never-seen-before equipment and weaponry. In the background, arms, ammunition and various military equipment were cached in glass panels.

"These sophisticated weapons that you see in here have all been invented under the guidance and supervision of some special guests who are exceptionally intelligent," Balbeer Singh said. "You're going to meet them shortly."

Jake stared at Balbeer Singh.

Then, military officer led them to another segment of the facility, deep inside the heavily secured zone.

ЖЖЖЖЖ

One thousand miles away, in a grand mansion at Dollars Colony, one of Delhi's posh localities, opposition leader Ajeet Awasthi raised a toast to Major Rabindranath, celebrating over the successful accomplishment of the operation-The Lost Arcanum.

Athar Khan, having abandoned consumption of alcohol following religious obligation, raised his glass of soft drink, sitting comfortably across from Ajeet on a sofa.

"Finally," Ajeet Awasthi said, holding the disc in his hand, "the most prized treasure is in our possession. And I must appreciate your efforts. It was worth the money I've spent."

Rabindranath acknowledged his compliments with a smile, sipping his drink and enjoying the intense excitement of the politician who had acquired what he had desired for long.

"Let's make this occasion more special," Ajeet Awasthi said as he got up from his seat and walked across to the display panel.

Athar Khan was intrigued. Ajeet Awasthi inserted the disc and returned to his seat with a remote control. The Major too, adjusted his position for a better view. He was basking in the glory of a prize he had recovered as remuneration for the harm the DIA had caused him, which still wouldn't make up entirely for the death of his innocent daughter and wife.

He concentrated as the display screen erupted with crackling static.

Athar Khan leaned forward, trying to make sense of what now transpired on the screen. Ajeet Awasthi sat upright in his seat. Although he had never seen the footage himself, he had been told that its content was quite disturbing. Whoever possessed the disc held the key to an immensely powerful secret that could alter the fate of the government and the world religion itself.

And power is all I need, he whispered to himself.

He watched the footage curiously as the camera panned, showing a gathering of men, all garbed in ritualistic dark robes, having assembled for some kind of religious ceremony taking place within a dimly lit chamber. At the center of the congregation, four men clothed in crimson hooded robes, knelt with their heads bowed in submission at the foot of a priest seated on a high throne.

Major Rabindranath instantly recognized one of the four men. Long ago, Major had assisted this man in the IAF: Balbeer Singh, the Director General of the DIA.

Athar Khan, Major and Ajeet Awasthi watched the video in rapt interest, dead silent. Soon after the priest held his hand over the men as a symbol of anointment and then rose to his feet from the throne, the sight of it thrilled everyone.

"Allah!" Athar Khan recoiled in his seat letting out his surprise in deep shock. "What on earth am I looking at?" he said in Hindi.

"This is the eighth wonder of the world," Ajeet Awasthi said, astounded by the sight himself. He realized that this footage would definitely boost his political career to new highs, to a position no one had ever imagined. "This video is going to make history," he declared with a sense of pride.

ЖЖЖЖЖ

General Balbeer Singh observed his detainee.

Both, Taneez and Jake, looked apprehensively at him, standing before a windowless wall, wondering what was coming. Right then the wall started to move sideways, gradually exposing another transparent glass wall behind it.

Jake took a step closer, peering through the glass wall. On the other side of the glass wall, there was an enormous research laboratory, replete with a crew of men and women in scrubs, standing around computers, sophisticated machinery and something else too…something bizarre…

"What the heck is…?" Jake went mute, in deep trauma, leaning close to the glass panel.

"Where?" Taneez asked curiously, looking around.

Without saying a word, Jake twisted her head in the direction of the thing that shared space with the humans behind the glass wall. As she saw it, her skin goose fleshed.. "Oh My God!"

Balbeer Singh chortled at their expressions and turned to face the eight feet tall, blonde-haired creatures interacting with the humans on the other side of the glass wall. The beings, who were from another planet, commonly recognized as humanoid extraterrestrials.

CHAPTER 90

"*These are magical,* benevolent and spiritually evolved entities that believe in spiritual growth," Balbeer Singh explained, standing next to Jake. "Not the hostile type creatures that the conspiracy theorists otherwise suggests. These are at peace with humans. And they are here to share their knowledge and wisdom that was once disseminated on this planet, now forgotten."

But Jake, paralyzed by the scene before him, was barely listening. He adjusted for a better view of the humanoids. Taneez was too dazed to respond. Her eyes were wide open, staring at the extraterrestrials inside the glass panel. They were garbed in white robes. Their features gave off a distinct golden glow and their long blonde hair framed cherubic faces highlighted by the luminescent blue almond shaped eyes. In every other aspect of morphology, they closely resembled humans.

"They look like us," Taneez said, noting their physical appearance.

"Wrong, " Balbeer Singh denied tersely. "we very much look like them."

Taneez glanced at him, her expression clouded by his statement.

"We look like them," Balbeer stressed without taking his eyes off the humanoids. Although his statement was clear and short, his voice was distant and grim. Taneez felt a shiver hearing him speak so. In his choice of words, she detected a secret that was dark and far more mysterious than the truth of the existence of extraterrestrials itself.

Jake watched the humanoids in stunned silence, at last confirming that his father and the three scientists knew about the presence of these humanoids. The men had been killed for filming these beings. He felt a sense of deception that the truth about the presence of these extraterrestrials was one of the best kept secrets in the world.

He was shaken out of his stupor when Balbeer Singh spoke.

"Let's move ahead," Balbeer guided them to the next section, a little farther. It was a glistening sealed laboratory At its center, a saucer-shaped aircraft was in the final stage of production, docked on a raised platform, several meters above the floor. Beneath it, humanoids were instructing scientists over different sections of the machine.

Positioning them before a large glass panel, Balbeer told Jake and Taneez, "This is another hi-tech section where the humanoids assist our scientists in understanding and adopting their exotic technology so we can recreate it in our facility."

Jake did not seem to react to this information. Taneez was listening, but her attention was drawn to one of those humanoids, which was close to the glass wall.

"This is a process of 'Reverse Engineering'," Balbeer added. "is to reproduce devices such as the ones we know today—computer chips, fiber optics, lasers, night-vision equipment, stealth technology, super tenacity fibers, particle beam weapons, anti-gravity aircraft and much more. All of these inventions, mind you, were loosely inspired by extraterrestrial technology or say, directly adopted. Popular multinational companies easily stole these technologies and got the inventions patented as their own."

Just then, one of the humanoids leaned closer to the glass panel, staring at Balbeer Singh with its two dark blue penetrating eyes, darting an alarming glance at Jake and then at Taneez.

With a slight nod, Balbeer Singh communicated with the humanoid, as if assuring it that they were his guests and could be trusted to keep their presence on earth a secret.

Those dark probing eyes swirled in Jake's direction, before they came to rest on Taneez's. The humanoid blinked crisply, studying the lithe form of Taneez with its almond blue eyes lingering little longer, before it moved away.

Taneez seemed to be in a trance. But Jake despised these humanoids, for claiming his father's life and the lives of his fellow scientists. Who knew how many others had been silenced to keep the secret of their existence on earth?

"This brings us to the end of the journey," Balbeer furnished gravely. "I hope you have enjoyed the tour. Now it's time to do some business."

CHAPTER 91

The extraterrestrial humanoid they had initially thought was a priest seated on a high throne, stood more than seven and a half feet taller. In a white robe, it looked no different from a man, except that it had an aura surrounding it as bright as that reported found on an angel.

The video continued, with the scene shifting from a dark chamber to a brightly lit high-tech laboratory, where humanoids were involved in assisting humans.

Athar Khan's mind had gone distant, rendering him speechless. He felt crushed by the weight of a truth that shook the foundations of his faith; this was something his religion had not cited. The sight of extraterrestrials working with humans rattled his composure, leaving his faith in Islam shaken.

If this was the consequence on Khan alone, then what would the outcome be when the whole world would see this footage, Ajeet thought. All religious heads across the globe would head for the hills for withholding from the faithful the existence of beings more intelligent than humans themselves, existing from the time before man inhabited earth. It would strip religion of its faith and devotees of their trust, leaving them forsaken. The world would be gripped by chaos and people would rampage on the streets, protesting with anti-religion and anti-government banners. And the government would stumble.

And that is all I want. Ajeet smiled widely. *To make way into civilians' hearts and grab the throne to power by revealing the secret that was buried since the beginning of time*

The major reached out to Khan with a consoling hand, settling next to him on the sofa.

"These things have existed since primordial times."

Khan spoke dejectedly in Hindi, "Like everyone else, I believed in the divine truth. A truth that God loved this world so much that he created us in his own image, superior to all life forms, bestowing us with intelligence to differentiate good from bad." He let out a troubled moan.

"And now, the existence of these beings right among us has crushed my belief. The fact that there's someone more intelligent and far more advanced than us has shocked me." Khan looked at the major. "I think we should not let this footage be aired."

Ajeet Awasthi looked at the major anxiously, confused. "I won't let any of you have this disc," Khan said.

Ajeet Awasthi was infuriated. The major motioned for him to calm down. Then he turned to Khan. "You know something? I believe in God and reacted in much the same way as you do now. But I saw those things with my naked eyes." He continued, narrating an old incident that had changed his life forever. "They were right in front of my eyes, like dead children, closed in a crate that one of my corporals accidentally stumbled upon, long ago when I was a major in the IAF, tasked with closely monitoring the shipment of highly confidential consignments.

"I was blown away. Those strange beings gave me many sleepless nights. My curiosity knew no bounds, leading me to pilfer libraries, search the internet and all media for information on the origins of the creatures." The major reached into his pocket, pulled out a cigarette and lit it. Taking a deep drag from it, he went on, "I found no mentions of it anywhere, but in the Bible, the *Vedas* and…"

Khan waited eagerly.

The major took another drag on his cigarette before he revealed. "… and in the Holy Koran."

ЖЖЖЖЖ

"So, what have you decided?" General Balbeer Singh pressed Jake from across the table, stealing a glance at Taneez. Fluorescent lights lit up Balbeer Singh's grave countenance.

A while ago, Taneez and Jake had been led out from the facility and detained in a windowless chamber that had a long wooden table with three chairs around it. "You have seen what your father wanted you too. Those beings which he captured in video disc is now I assume is no longer of any use to you. Hand it over to me," Balbeer Singh spread his hand. "What disc are you talking about?" asked Jake, maintaining his cool.

The general drew a long breath, as if trying to remain calm. "I have to tell you, you're as obstinate as your father. He dug his own grave when he videotaped those humanoids, bequeathing its whereabouts in a link and letting word of the secret leak to an outsider who ultimately conspired to kill him."

Jake remembered that David had told something similar. Yet, he was reluctant to believe it. The man sitting in front of him was powerful and influential. His authority would allow him to fabricate any scenario to his advantage. All that mattered to him was performing his duty with diligence to acquire what he wanted.

Jake leaned forward, crossing his hands on the table. "And you're a good storyteller."

"Well," disgust turned the corner of the general's lips, "one needs to have guts to speak so candidly to a senior official despite being in his territory." His voice was now grating. "Don't assume that you are at liberty to do things as you please—hinder our investigations or violate and invade places like you did crossing our restricted area here. You have no clue what we can do to you and those with you." He paused fixing Jake with a fierce stare. "We can rip your flesh and feed the nocturnal animals that lurk in the mountains. And no one would even know that you are dead."

Jake smirked. "Like you did to my father?"

His question aroused a deep dislike, but the general masked it. "As I told you before, we didn't kill your father." The general stared at Jake before asking, "Have you ever heard of an organization called CSETI?"

Jake didn't respond. Neither did Taneez. Their expression showed no recognition of an organization by that name.

Balbeer Singh considered it for a long moment before he ventured. "It's called the Center for Study of Extraterrestrial Intelligence. An international non-profit organization dedicated to searching and understanding extraterrestrials and their technology."

Balbeer recounted the history surrounding this organization thoroughly, stating that this organization dated back to 1990, founded in USA. With an objective of searching for witnesses to UFO sightings and extraterrestrial events, including government and military officials encompassing various branches of armed services, like the DIA, NRO, CIA, FBI and NASA. The evidence and testimonies of thousands of civilian and military officials included the existence and authentication of top-secret documents confirming the recovery of crashed extraterrestrial vehicles and their occupants. Numerous photographs and films showing extraterrestrials interacting with humans were recovered.

The organization was on the verge of going public with the accumulated documents when the eyewitnesses backed off. They reported indications of strange surveillance. Some had even been threatened with dire consequences if they dared to disclose what they had seen. As a result, the organization was shelved, only to re-emerge after a long gap of two years as an independent non-profit organization, to target other countries.

In the past two decades, there have been too many reports of UFO sightings in India. That spurred the interest of the CESTI which turned its attention towards our country. Collaborating with the influential opposition party leader Ajeet Awasthi and Rabindranath, a former IAF major. One thirsty for power, while the other is insanely obsessed with avenging the harm he thinks DIA caused.

The general paused. "An absolute baseless accusation against our organization. Like the one you are making now, holding us responsible for the death of your father and his team of scientists."

Jake smiled as he asked impassively, "Was this a prequel to the story?"

The general fumed. His palms formed tight fists on the table. "Great!" Jake said dismissively, putting an end to whatever he heard so far. "I can see the efforts you've made to keep those humanoids from the eyes of our nation and the world."

The general didn't speak although an intense rage was taking root in him.

"What gives you the right to keep this secret to yourself, General?"

"I do have rights, Mr. Jake," the general replied curtly. "You know why? The secret you're talking about is dangerous. If it gets out, God forbid, it will have consequences of almost inconceivable magnitude."

Jake's response was a disgusted grunt.

"Those humanoids are spiritual entities. They aren't hostile like you assume," Balbeer Singh said. "They are here to remind us of the very purpose of our existence. To show us what we are destined for and where we are heading, with our negligent lifestyles, pushing our planet to the brink of environmental disaster."

Jake looked away disinterestedly.

"They are assisting us in steering the earth back from the path of devastation and restoring its natural balance. To share knowledge that was once lost and potent enough to empower humans with qualities that will elevate them spiritually to the level of God."

"How about I add one more point to your tale?" Jake interrupted. "NASA, ISRO and other space research organizations were nothing but deception programs."

Balbeer Singh suppressed his anger.

"One lie to cover up another." Jake said plainly. "They were used to deceive people into believing that man's greatest quest—the search for extraterrestrial life in the universe was still in progress. While in reality, the extraterrestrials were right among us, visiting our planet for God knows how many decades or even centuries or countless eons." He broke off and asked accusingly, "Is that what you mean by consequence, General? The truth is that the government would have to explain why they continued to fund these space organizations that in the end would be a waste of taxpayers' money."

"The presence of extraterrestrials is not a bedtime story, Mr. Jake," Balbeer interjected, "that people will forget it the next morning. When the world knows the truth, they'll lose faith in the government and in religion. They will discover..." Balbeer Singh trailed off, holding back from divulging another terrible secret on the spur of the moment, one that was deep and acutely darker than the secret of humanoids itself.

A secret far mightier than the presence of extraterrestrials itself that his brotherhood had been closely guarding since its inception.

CHAPTER 92

To dispel the aura of deep affliction caused by Khan's diminishing faith in God, Major Rabindranath, blowing ceaseless puffs of smoke into the air, went about explaining his research on extraterrestrials. "In the Bible, in the book of Ezekiel, chapter 1, verse 24 describes the prophet's encounter with a flying vessel inside which were living creatures that had the likeness of humans. Then there is Kings 2:11, which says there came a spinning chariot that carried Prophet Elijah into heaven. Jeremiah 4:13 speaks of the chariot of gods that spin and fly swiftly. Zachariah 6:1 speaks of four spaceships emerging from between two bronze-colored mountains."

Relishing his drink, Ajeet Awasthi admired the major's informative walk through the holy scriptures.

"But those verses are with reference to angels," Khan said, "and angels are immortal. They are God's messengers. The ones in the footage are ghostly."

"In that case," the Major said, smiling, "you should understand first that humanoids were mistakenly thought to be angels. To ancient scribes, who penned our religious scriptures, these humanoids with the power to manifest in physical form at will, appeared magical. They looked at their powers rather than their appearance." Major paused before adding, "Beauty lies in the eyes of beholder."

That silenced Khan.

Taking it as a sign that he was convinced, the Major took a sip of his drink before he proceeded. "In the Hindu scriptures, there are numerous references to flying machines of vivid features, brilliant as the sun, with the sound of thunderstorms, rising to great heights in the sky, maneuvered by some highly intelligent entities which were these extraterrestrials."

"Perhaps," Khan interjected, "but I'm sure the Koran does not speak of it. I have read it numerous times. There's absolutely no reference to those beings in the Koran."

The Major smiled. "If only you knew to read between the lines…"

"What the hell do you mean?" Khan said, feeling insulted.

"There are so many things apparent to the eyes, but not to the mind." He took in Khan's apprehensive look. "There are millions who accept these religious doctrines blindly. They feel proud that way, exaggerating a false veneration towards the divine. It's because their self-pride makes them feel self-worth that is actually nothing but what I call hypocrisy."

He looked straight into Khan's eyes. "They know not what they do. They fail to probe deeper into its essence, look under the layers, never understanding its true meaning." Major breathed out. "I'm sorry to tell you that people like you have failed to conceive Allah in full essence."

His words speared through Khan's pride like a lance dipped in poison.

"To understand the Koran completely, take it to mind first and then to heart. That way, your heart is prepared to accept what the mind wants to convey."

Major noticed that Khan was close to losing his temper. He quickly revealed, "The Koran, Sura 27:65 commands, 'None in the heavens or on earth, except God, knows what is hidden. Nor can they perceive when they shall be raised up (For Judgment).'

"It states that like humans, there are other creatures in the universe that will also be raised from the dead on the Day of Judgment. In 19:93-96, we are told that 'Not one of the beings in the heavens and the earth but must come to (God) Most Gracious as a servant. He does take an account of them (all), and hath numbered them (all) exactly. And every one of them will come to Him singly on the Day of Judgment. On those who believe and work deeds of righteousness, will (God) Most Gracious bestow love.'

"These verses accentuate that there are life forms like us who will be rewarded for their deeds during their lifetime. The life form does not mean micro-organisms. Rather, it refers to intelligent life forms, morally accountable beings like humans." He paused and looked at Khan.

Khan was embarrassed hearing Major speak so comprehensively about Koran, who was not from his community but still seemed to have grasped the true essence of those verses from the Koran, reading between the lines in a manner his own eyes had failed to do.

"Further," the major continued, "Sura 65:12 tells us that, 'as God has created seven heavens, He has created, of the earth a similar number... 'As there are millions of galaxies God has also created millions of earths scattered throughout the universe. It should be noted from Sura 65:12 that God particularly uses the word 'earth' than the word 'world', referring to a planet like earth that accommodates life."

Not wanting to hear anymore of the Major's informative walk through religious scriptures, Khan got up from his seat and walked across to the display. Major and Ajeet Awasthi were puzzled by his actions. But as he went on to eject the disc from the player and take it in his hand, they immediately deduced his intentions.

"Have you gone mad?" Ajeet Awasthi said, setting down his drink on the table and standing up, alarmed.

Major, too, stood up. "Khan, give that disc to me."

Holding the disc in hand, Khan averred, "This footage will destroy everything. It will make us question the very basis of our religion." He looked at Major. "*Vedas,* the Bible and Koran, all will lose their significance. They will be worth nothing anymore. We both know the consequences if this footage goes public. Mankind will lose faith in God and start suspecting the very existence of one who created them."

"Give me that disc, Khan." Major took a step forward.

"Major, we can't betray our religion." Khan was gasping now.

"You're overreacting, Khan." Major took another step forward with his hand outstretched for the disc. "The truth has been suppressed for too long. It can't wait anymore. It's time for the show."

"Major, it's in our hand to avert this doom from striking the earth. Let's back off from this deal and destroy this disc. Let this secret be a secret. We will bury this secret forever for the welfare of humankind." Khan began gasping loudly, holding his chest, as if he couldn't breathe. In the next moment, Khan had collapsed to the floor, convulsing. His mouth frothed with traces of blood and he jerked several times as if seizure, before his hefty frame went still for eternity.

Major was too dazed by what happened suddenly. He tried to size up of what had come to pass before his eyes.

Ajeet Awasthi crossed to the spot and squatted beside Khan. He checked his pulse and glanced up at the major. "He embraced death." A wave of shock engulfed the major. "He's dead?"

Ajeet nodded, as he reached for Khan's hand and confiscated the disc. "You killed him?" Major saw him with an eye of suspicion "I poisoned his drink," Ajeet agreed coolly.

"What?" Major felt as if the ground beneath his feet had given away. Ajeet nodded gravely.

Major opened his mouth to rebuke him, but the words were choked by a stinging pain in his chest. When he lowered his gaze towards the source of pain, he found a crimson blot on his chest, blooming swiftly. In that agonizing moment, he realized he had been shot by someone behind him. He turned to discover a middle-aged man walking across the hall with a silencer gun and taking a seat in front of him.

"There's the Master," Ajeet scoffed, joining the man on the sofa.

Major couldn't believe that the throaty voice on the phone three months ago, the one that promised to fulfill his dreams, belonged to this man who had now shot him after recovering the disc.

"We sent your family on a never-ending journey a few years ago," Ajeet Awasthi revealed.

"And now it's time for you to join them," the Master smiled derisively. "Convey our love to your loving daughter and wife."

As the bitter truth abseiled down Major's mind that it was not DIA, but indeed, it was Ajeet Awasthi and Master who had conspired the killing of his wife and daughter, his head was reeling. And then the Master squeezed the trigger thrice.

Major's heavy frame collapsed to the floor, sprawling headlong.

There was not even a whimper or a cry.

Only silence...

CHAPTER 93

The Center for Study of Extraterrestrial Intelligence (CSETI) is an independent non-profit scientific research and education organization, established with the main objective of studying information of extraterrestrial origins.

The Disclosure Project was the first of its kind, introduced under CSETI, to identify firsthand military, intelligence and government officials and other witnesses of classified projects dealing with UFOs and extraterrestrial events. It was part of a comprehensive strategy to accumulate enough evidence for a global disclosure on extraterrestrial presence on earth, all in an effort to mentally prepare civilians to accept the most debated and controversial subject—that they weren't alone in the universe.

Their relentless efforts to make the testimonies public had been thwarted by national security oaths and restrictions imposed on the witnesses, some of whom were also threatened against speaking candidly. For this very reason, the organization had tried to encourage highly influential persons from within government circles to withdraw these restrictions, but so far, their efforts had been in vain.

All operations pertaining to UFOs functioned outside normal channels of government, and most senior personnel were kept out of the loop in this matter. Only a select few had access to these controlled and compartmentalized projects. And the need to maintain high secrecy over the presence of extraterrestrials is believed to be multi- dimensional, General Balbeer Singh had explained.

"They had planned the day of revelation even before they contacted us. They had already decided when they would make themselves public. And it's better that way. They need time. We need time. People need time."

"Time for what?" Jake rebuked in anger, "For your organization which is using one lie to cover up another? The truth is that if the secret about extraterrestrials is out, then alien abduction, cattle mutilation and crop circles will begin to make sense. The government has no explanation for misleading the world for decades, because they simply have no answer for these bizarre phenomenon."

"That's bullshit," Balbeer Singh cried out in protest. "Alien abduction and cattle mutilation is a ploy of some shadowy organizations to defame the humanoids and carry out macabre experiments. And I repeat, these humanoids are here to make truce with us. They are spiritual and peaceful entities and believe in spiritual evolution of mankind. And besides, there are other matters. If people get to know about their existence, they would see them as a threat and would attack them."

He paused narrowing his gaze on Jake. "From the dawn of time, they have overseen our evolution from cave men to an intelligent species. If today, we have been able to come out of the Stone Age into an age of technology and intelligence, if today we are able to build sophisticated space shuttles, track the movements of planets and gaze deep into space at the distant galaxies of the cosmos, it's all because of them." General Balbeer Singh ventured. "We humans are creatures of greed, ungrateful and self-centered. It's simply in our genetics. Although we have adopted their technology, when it comes to acknowledging them, we turn away. And the extraterrestrials will not stand for this. They will abandon us all over again. The way they did thousand years ago. Never to return. Besides, the impact of revealing this secret will be catastrophic and multi-dimensional—religious fallout, apprehension of invasion, global meltdown…"

"Good try, General," Jake cut him off disinterestedly. "Better luck next time."

"Damn you!" the general said abruptly, freeing his pistol from the holster and pointing it at him point blank. "You have two choices to make: one, you give me that disc and I'll let you both go alive or," he nudged the gun's muzzle to Jake's temple, "let's forget the disc and I'll handle you my way."

After a moment of silence, Jake haggled. "How about I add a third option?"

The general did not lower his gun nor his steady gaze.

"Set me free and see if I can change my mind." Jake added. "I might retrieve that disc for you."

Casting furious glances at his detainees, the general stormed out of the chamber, shutting close the door behind him.

CHAPTER 94

Monday, August 14, 2017,
3.15 AM.
Indira Gandhi International Airport,
New Delhi.

In a sparsely populated waiting lounge, Taneez glanced at Jake who seemed to be lost in deep contemplation.

About half an hour earlier, at General Balbeer Singh's behest, they had been airlifted in a helicopter from Leh to the international airport in the nation's capital, New Delhi. Unbelievably, despite trespassing upon a top secret location and witnessing something they were not meant to have seen, they had been allowed to leave.

Taneez finally broke the smothering silence, stating, "I think you should do what the general wants of you."

Jake glanced at her, surprised. "Oh! So, you were influenced by the general's version?"

She shrugged. "You're not getting the point, Jake. You and I were completely taken aback at the sight of those humanoids. It left us terrified. Imagine how people would react if that footage goes viral on the internet."

"It doesn't surprise me at all," Jake confessed, smiling. "These intelligence agencies are the most treacherous organizations in the world. They are really deft at manipulating the vulnerable. They managed to employ AD and Riya against me," he said. "You know what the general's real concern is?" Taneez shook her head.

"The biggest cover-up in the history of mankind is about to be revealed before billions of people and he's the man behind this cover-up. And this footage will not only cause irrevocable damage to the defense wing, but also to his reputation that may even cost his job. He and his organization now see themselves kneeling down before their enemies. At such a helpless juncture, they think I'm the only one who can save them from the doom that is about to strike." Jake exhaled angrily. "And that is something I'm not going to do at any cost."

Taneez tried to calm him down. "What do you have to say about your father? Don't you think your father had something more to tell you through this quest? Through fire, air, water and earth that forms a Star of David, a hexagram, the most mysterious and enigmatic symbol in the world. People believe that it holds a closely guarded secret the world doesn't know."

Jake was silent. He himself had wondered what his father had been trying to tell him. Before he could speculate any further, a passenger announcement alerted Taneez to the immediate departure of her flight to Boston, scheduled for take-off in about half hour.

"Huh!" Taneez reacted to the call. "I have to go."

"You must be longing to go back home." Jake said. He studied her face for any sign of reluctance.

She seemed unsure about how to answer. She sighed. "It's been two week since I've been away from home, Jake. My stay in India was for just a week. But it was worth a lifetime."

"Then why don't you stay for a day or two more?" Jake pressed her. "I want you to see my place and meet my friends…"

"Sounds great, but some other time?" Taneez smiled questioningly. She fished out a paper from her bag, scribbled something on it and offered it to him. "You can reach me on this number."

Jake looked down at the numbers. He wanted to say something, but he resisted the urge. Another announcement, the last call for boarding for the Boston flight, was made.

Taneez picked up her bag and glanced up at him. "Bye, Jake. Take care."

She turned and walked toward the boarding gate. As she drew further away, a strange feeling of unease gripped him. It was the same poignancy he felt whenever someone very dear was departing. He raised his hand to stop her, but then held back. He stood silent, watching her walking away from him. When Taneez reached the end of the terminal, Jake raised his hand to wave at her.

But she never turned. She just kept walking without looking back at him, as if she had not known him, leaving him with loads of beautiful memories and the alluring fantasies he'd been nursing about her of lately.

CHAPTER 95

10.30 AM.
Green View Restaurant.

"Is something bothering you?" the attorney Ravi Raj asked Jake, finding him seemingly lost, staring out into nothingness. Since he had walked into the restaurant, Ravi Raj had seen Jake stabbing at numbers on his cellphone, had been repeatedly trying to place a call to someone. He was sure that some concern was weighing on Jake's mind which now seemed to be disturbing him so much that he had forgotten that he had company and that a set of papers was spread across the table, waiting for his signature.

"Jake," the attorney said in a louder voice, snapping him from his distraction.

"Oh, I'm sorry," Jake came back, glancing up from his cell phone.

Earlier this morning, Jake had placed a call to his attorney, stating that he was ready to fulfill the pending legal formalities for his father's will. The will, dealing with an estate worth more than two million dollars, was spread out on the table before him, but Jake felt drawn to something far more priceless.

He reached for his cell phone again and looked at the name, the cause of his restlessness, in the call log list: Taneez.

He dialed her number for the eighty-ninth time. But like all the calls before, a computerized voice repeated, *'This telephone number does not exist.'*

He felt intense despair seep through his heart. Had Taneez deliberately given him a number that didn't exist? Was it to avoid him, not wanting to stay in contact with him after all that she had suffered because of him? Or had she written a wrong number by mistake?

Setting aside these annoying queries for a while, he concentrated on the will that was laid before him on the table.

Ravi Raj guided him through the formalities and completed the paperwork and handed him the will. As they finished, Jake watched

Rajat Singh and Riya entering the restaurant. He ignored them, but the attorney got up to acknowledge them, ushering them into the opposite seats.

"How is Shikha?" the attorney asked Riya.

"She is fine," Riya replied with a smile, glancing at Jake, who turned away as if she was stranger to him.

Eyeing which, she further spoke to Ravi Raj. They discussed about each others well being as she had known the attorney for a long time. It was Ravi Raj, who had helped settle her marriage dissolution without too many hassles and ensured that she was given a big chunk of her husband's assets as alimony.

Rajat Singh felt alienated in this small group when Jake refused to acknowledged his presence. Soon after, the attorney had walked away, leaving them to contend with whatever was brewing between them. The efforts of AD and Riya to convince Jake that their involvement was meant to be a rescue plan went unheard.

"Someone has rightly said," Jake said dourly, "there can't by any father and sister out of blood ties."

"If you are done, can I say something?" AD asked him sternly.

Jake looked away.

"I'm a senior official," AD continued. 'In my forty-five years of experience, fate has drawn me into situations where I had to sacrifice my own principles for the sake of the oath I had taken to stand by my country during peril. One such decision was taken in your case."

"You mean what I was after was a threat to national security?" Jake asked. "Do you even have any idea what was in that footage?"

"I don't intend to know either," AD replied tersely. "All I know is that you had to be stopped." AD told him about Master, the man behind all the murders, and acquainted Jake with the Major's story before he went on to clarify, "I had the lives of two people at stake. One was my dear friend, the Major, hungry for revenge. And the other was you, Jake, obsessed with finding the actual reason behind your father's murder.

"Both of you were victims of cleverly plotted scheme, commissioned by the duo--Master and opposition party leader Ajeet Awasthi. They entangled you both in a complex life-threatening situation. There was no way out. Believe it or not, it was Riya and I, who carefully assessed the crisis and steered the quest in your favor. But I couldn't help my friend." He was silent for a few seconds. "Major was killed yesterday."

"But we're happy that you're safe and back home," Riya added.

"Safe?" Jake reacted in disbelief. "Do you even know how close to death I was? David would have killed me if Taneez hadn't arrived on time."

AD and Riya were silent.

"Any more clarifications?" Jake asked.

AD and Riya realized that Jake was unlikely to understand their perspective.

"No clarifications. But you should hear this," AD said. "Major was murdered yesterday. And we suspect Master and Ajeeth Awasthi are behind this. They even holds that disc and planning for a global disclosure of that secret very soon."

"So?" Jake raised his brows, spreading his hands questioningly.

"The video disc," AD pressed. "Before it's too late, we need to find and confiscate….."

Jake rose from his seat with a wry smile. "That would be the last thing on my to-do list before I die."

After giving them a contemptuous glare, Jake turned on his heels and wove his way out of the restaurant.

ӜӜӜӜӜ

"What brings you here?" General Balbeer Singh asked quite brusquely, the moment the Additional Director of CBI, Rajat Singh, and assistant officer Riya walked into his chamber and slipped into the chairs opposite his desk.

The previous day, he had gathered information that had revealed that these two CBI officers while pretending to be his allies had secretly aided Jake in his pursuit. Their treachery had cost him the life of one of his able officers, David Craig.

Balbeer was quite surprised that that they were brave enough to enter his chamber so casually in spite of betraying his organization.

"Major was killed last evening," Rajat Singh informed him with heavy heart. "His death was staged to appear as if he had been run over by a truck…and the blame on DIA."

"That was inevitable," the general cut him off. "One who colludes with evil will eventually be destroyed at its hands."

AD and Riya glanced at each other, wondering if Balbeer had known about their involvement.

"Anyway," the general Balbeer continued. "What is bothering you now?"

"The disc," Rajat Singh said, choosing his words carefully. "It's in the wrong hands."

The general straightened in his chair but remained silent.

"We're here to let you know that you have our support," AD added.

"Support?" the general mocked, rising from his chair. "That's a good joke." Balbeer collected his words, and spewed them in anger, "If that disc is out there in the hands of someone with wicked intentions, it's your entire fault." Circling the desk, he let his accusing gazed settle over them. "Your double-crossing has already cost me a prime JIC asset."

AD and Riya understood that he was talking about David Craig.

"Ok," AD said. "We have a piece of information that I think you need to know."

"What is it?"

"The footage is to be released soon."

The general listened to him without offering a response.

"On August 15th," AD said, "on Independence Day."

"That's tomorrow!" General Balbeer burst with great concern.

"Yes," AD replied, "But we are not sure when, where and how."

All three of them were silent, burdened by the crisis that loomed on the threshold like a apocalyptic prophecy about to come true.

ӜӜӜӜӜ

We have a state of national emergency…

Enclosed within the four walls of his chamber, Balbeer Singh couldn't help but go over this thought again and again, since the CBI officers' revelation a few hours ago. Neither could he fathom that the secret about extraterrestrials that his clandestine cabal had been guarding closely, had finally leaked.

And all because of me. A sharp sense of guilt tightened his chest. Circumstances had caused him to be the one who was inflicting this mental anguish on those who had trusted him and invited him into their clandestine brotherhood, making him privy to their inner most secret. If necessary measures had been enacted at the right time, if rigorous actions had been taken as soon as he had discovered the involvement of a shadowy organization, things might have been rather different. He could have been successful in nailing the culprits and recovered the link to the secret by now. Maybe he should have put the word out to the cabal and allowed them to intervene and handle the issue the best way they could to ensure a positive outcome.

But now things had veered out of control. The disc was in the possession of a powerful group of people, each with their own motives, all prepared to unleash the secret that would bring about devastation of a kind the world had ever known.

Setting in motion a chain of events that would have dire ramifications globally. There would be nothing but chaos. Civilians would rise against their governments. Ardent devotees would accuse their religious institutions of keeping a crucial truth from them. The government would be stripped naked in the streets and brought to its knees. The outcomes seemed endless. And worst of all, with this secret, the most shocking revelation would be exposed, the one that tied back to the origin of mankind. The thought of it sent a tremor down his body as this was the last thing he wanted.

Considering the dangers ahead, he decided to have his cabal intervene to deal with the matter, which he should have done earlier when the threat was in its nascent stage. He knew there would be several hands pointing to him as a traitor, accusing him of sheer negligence in keeping the highly guarded secret from leaking.

But he was also confident that among those cluster of hands, there would be one that was protective and caring, one that would allow him a chance to prove his innocence and loyalty to the vow. And that hand, he remembered, belonged to the Lukas Covitz, the Grand Master of the brotherhood.

With immense hope, Balbeer Singh picked up his cell phone and placed a call to him.

CHAPTER 96

Secretariat Building,
New Delhi.

In the stark silence of the state-of-the-art video conference room, General Balbeer Singh sat alone, crossing his hands on the table ruminatively, facing a wall of high-resolution video screens.

In his decades of military service, he had never felt so dejected and doubtful of his own abilities. That his allegiance to his country and more importantly, to the secret cabal, were now being called into question. A sickly pang of guilt that got worse with each passing minute.

An hour ago, he had alerted Lukas Covitz to the matter of the classified footage on the extraterrestrials being stolen. Although displeased at the news, considering the sensitivity of the crisis, he had brought the matter to the immediate attention of the rest of the members of the cabal. As expected, the matter had triggered an emergency-like situation, creating humungous tension and bringing immense loathing and wrath of the members down on him. Given the sensitivity of the issue, Lukas had immediately asked for the Director General of Defense, USA, Mr. Donald Reagan, to intervene by summoning a team of top-notch computer programmers from NSA to gain control of major internet networks across India. This special force was assigned to monitor, track and quarantine any suspicious data being uploaded from anywhere across the Indian sub-continent.

Though the task required a massive amount of technical resources and human effort at disposal, as executing the operation in the virtual ocean of cyberspace was a daunting task with bleak prospects. But Lukas Covitz and other members of the cabal were prepared and had left no stone unturned to ensure that every file in a video format would be blocked from transmission and isolated.

Now, in the wake of the crisis, Lukas had called for an urgent video conference call, due in sometime. Amid the turbulence, Balbeer Singh found solace in the warm support of Lukas, who was sure the matter would be brought under control.

The display screens turned on with three familiar personalities, Lukas Covitz, along with Mr. Donald Reagan from USA, Zhuge Liang from China, and Vladimir from Russia, staring back at him.

Anger burned in their faces. But it was Lukas, his gaze softer than that of the other three, who spoke first.

"What has been the situation, Mr. Singh?"

"A rigorous search is in progress," Balbeer Singh replied, assuring, "I'm sure we'll nab the miscreants and confiscate the footage soon."

Lukas drew a troubled sigh, seeming unconvinced. A hint of uncertainty was evident in his eyes. "That's good. But I still seriously doubt if you can contain the crisis. The enemies we're facing are powerful. They have more resources at their disposal. They can corroborate the events from the footage, which will only make this disclosure more catastrophic."

"I'm sure he will fail at this, too," Donald Reagan interjected.

Balbeer Singh looked in his direction, picking up on the anger in his tone. "That's because he has no clue what danger he has brought upon us. Nor does he understand that if the secret of humanoids is revealed, then so will the secret on the origin of mankind. We just cannot afford it."

"If you have forgotten, then let me remind you," Balbeer Singh countered gravely, "that the secret you're so concerned about is of as much importance to me as it is to you. If you talk about your ancestors having guarded the secret of humanoids since time immemorial, then you should also know that our ancestors protected it, ensuring that the presence of humanoids remained a secret and their advanced technology survived in the scriptures that could eventually be passed down into the hands of those who were worthy."

"Officers," Lukas interrupted, sounding irked. "We're here to address the crisis. I expect your cooperation and inputs on the way out of this situation, not discord." Lukas paused and looked at Balbeer Singh. "Mr. Singh, could you please brief us on the measures you have taken?"

"Sorry to interrupt you, Master Lukas," Zhuge Liang intervened with an expression of surprise. "You still want Mr. Singh to deal with the crisis using his resources that are obviously terribly ineffective and flawed?"

It was as if the Directors were making every effort to censure him and blame him for the dire situation that was looming over the harmony of their nations.

"You have shown enough negligence since the footage was stolen from under your nose. But what you don't understand is that if the footage goes viral, we'll have ramifications on a global scale. It's going to be devastation of a kind the world has never known," Zhuge Liang said.

"My resources are not flawed," Balbeer Singh defended. "It's the enemy we're facing that is more powerful. One of them is a politician, an opposition leader, who exercises powers similar to that of a Prime minister. Under such circumstances, we have limitations."

"Then assassinate him," Donald Reagan barked. "It's time to keep the vow you've taken to protect the secret."

There was a sudden silence following that statement. Lukas and Zhuge Liang from China reflected on the fact that doing away with the threat was a remedy in times of crisis. To take lives for a noble cause. History was proof that whenever anybody attempted to compromise the secret about extraterrestrials, they were suppressed, threatened and killed. And they looked upon this inhumane act as an obligation rather than a heinous crime. The assassination of the former American president, Mr. John Fitzgerald Kennedy, was a case in point. Little did the world know that the classified investigation report on his murder mentions the hand of a shadowy organization behind his assassination, which had been orchestrated to stop him from his planned global disclosure on the presence of extraterrestrials. He was one among thousands who were silenced forever.

"His assassination will be in vain, Mr. Reagan," Lukas averred. "The damage has already been done. They might upload the footage on the World Wide Web anytime. In that case, his assassination would only fuel the crisis, not curb it."

In spite of having high-tech surveillance systems in place, complex computer algorithms written to scour every node of network across the country to track and isolate the suspicious file from transmission, they still feared that their efforts were like waiting for a glimpse of the enemy in the dark.

Taking these points into consideration and the small window of time available, Lukas had devised a few more precautionary measures, one of which he now put across.

"Mr. Zhuge Liang, I need you to dispatch a team of hackers to India." Lukas then turned to Balbeer Singh. "Mr. Singh, you need to include them in your security team. Just as an extra precaution."

ЖЖЖЖЖ

The Master, the genius behind the conspiracy, had always maintained secrecy over his identity. He had remained discreet and out of sight when it came to execution of the operation, *The Lost Arcanum*.

Now exploring him from a fresh angle, one that showcased Master's penchant for antique collections, Ajeet Awasthi was taken by surprise.

Sitting back in the luxurious lounge, Ajeet Awasthi allowed his eyes to imbibe the remarkable interiors of the bungalow. The lobby, more like an art gallery, was embellished with canvases of varied themes, from battles of war to those of the modern arts, along the walls, illuminated with sparkling golden light from a beautiful, intricately designed chandelier. The stained glass windows and marble spiral staircase with oak railings, added to the grace of the interiors.

Master returned with glasses of Scotch Whiskey and slipped beside Ajeet Awasthi in the sofa.

"So they're building impenetrable fortress of surveillance in cyberspace...?" The Master mocked, handing a glass to Ajeet. "Those morons will never understand our weapon of destruction, until the damage is done to them."

Ajeet Awasthi smirked, recalling to mind the weapon, which was not in actuality a weapon at all. It was rather a foolproof tool, crafted with such great skill that it would dodge all surveillance systems and relay the footage to the public, unrestrained. And this cunning trick had been organized by Major Rabindranath before his death, who had designed the entire plan of action, flimflamming the DIA, which despite having an avant-garde technological resources at its disposal, had put in place a fragile strategy for tackling the sensitive situation on Independence Day.

Ajeet's attention shifted to the screen which flickered to life as the Master pressed a button on a remote. Their eyes now imbibed the face of Major, giving his testimony about the extraterrestrials. The thirst for vendetta was very much evident in his deep-set eyes.

Ajeet Awasthi could still sense it, as he had when the major was recording his testimony before appending it to the original footage.

"He was a truly hard-nosed bloke, though crippled," Ajeet admitted and faced the Master.

"He was crippled indeed, but from here," the Master said, pointing to his own chest. "He was deprived of love, the love of his wife and his daughter." Sipping his drink, he said thoughtfully, as if speaking from experience. "Love is fatal. It gives people a reason to live…and to kill."

Ajeet Awasthi did not seem to be listening to him, clearly preoccupied with something else.

"What is it?" Master asked, sensing his distraction.

"I was imagining how people would react when they discover the involvement of their own government in the biggest cover-up in history."

Master grunted. "All those who are in that footage with those humanoids will be dragged into the streets. stoned to death for keeping this secret from the world."

They continued to ponder on the endless outcomes from the disclosure, relishing their drinks with a blissful sense of euphoria.

CHAPTER 97

Tuesday, August 15, 2017,
6 AM.
New Delhi.

Structures of national importance was bedecked with exceptionally vivid lights on the eve of Independence Day, as the first ray of sunlight touched the vast roads of the nation's capital, New Delhi, on the day the country would celebrate its Independence Day.

On the wonderful occasion of this national event, special traffic diversions are made for the smooth flow of traffic. Every crossroad, street and arcade in the city was heavily secured, and patrolling wagons continued to watch over the sensitive points. One location, however, was secured to the fullest.

Receiving word on which, Balbeer Singh, seated in the backseat of a speeding limo, finished a call with a security official.

As planned, computer programmers from China and Russia were allowed access to major internet networks across the world, with Indian network placed under intense scrutiny. As an extra precautionary measure, tabs was placed on television broadcast centers, in every studio of every news channel across the country that seemed susceptible to attack, including the national channel 'Doordarshan (DD1)', which held exclusive rights to live telecast of the prime minister's Independence Day address, due in less than an hour.

As the limo crept ahead, General Balbeer looked out of the window, gazing at the city streets that was ornamented like a beautiful bride. The roads, Balbeer realzied, that now wore a deserted look would soon turn into a jam-packed carnival, with thousands of patriots thronging to witness a great event.

This day, unlike any other, was very special day for every citizen in the country. Celebrated with great fervor and enthusiasm, since it marked the most important and historic moment in Indian chronicles.

This day identified the birth of a country as a sovereign nation after three long centuries of British rule. It was the day when the whole of India awakened to a life of freedom in a jubilant mood, with an intense zeal to commemorate the sacrifices and struggles of the great leaders and freedom fighters, who after centuries of struggle, bloodshed, battles and sacrifices, had ended the rule of British and other colonial authorities in the country.

Now, however, seven decades later, Balbeer realized, this day was bound to be unlike those in the past. The high-spirited, cheerful and ecstatic atmosphere of patriotism that usually marked this day, was now on the threshold of being overshadowed by a sinister plot concocted by some dark forces, exceedingly wise and prepared.

And the notion of it was persistently harassing his peace, calling into question thirty years of his diligent service to the nation.

The sharp ringtone of his cellphone pulled him back from his thoughts. Following an exchange of words, he disconnected the call in disgust. The information that had come on his cell phone was disturbing.

Previous night, with an arrest warrant sanctioned from the CBI Director, his team had raided opposition leader Ajeet Awasthi's mansion, but only to have him absconded. Besides, there were still not enough clues about the identity of the Master, the brain behind the conspiracy. As a result, the containment of the crisis only seemed to become more laborious with each passing moment.

Passing by the bustling market of Chandni-Chowk, the limo coursed through an imperial archway and entered the vast courtyard of a Moghul-era monument, before it came to a stop by a magnificent colossal structure.

General Balbeer Singh alighted from his car, lifting his head in admiration of a red, historical monument of timeless beauty that towered majestically into the serene blue morning sky.

It was a structure symbolizing martyrdom and grandeur, where the celebrations of Independence Day would echo as people gathered to honor the struggle and sacrifices of all those great leaders. It was a place of great significance in Indian history: **the Red Fort**.

ЖЖЖЖЖ

Under the steaming hot shower, Jake tried to calm his frayed nerves.

Earlier this morning, the voice of AD, his commanding officer, had escaped into his answering machine when he had refused to answer his calls. He felt no obligation towards AD who was calling in once again to check if Jake was willing to join hands with his team in tackling the crisis. But he sensed a restlessness clawing his gut, as if there was something urging him to reconsider his senior officer's plea.

Concurrently, a desperate longing to hear Taneez's voice was nearly killing him, especially when she had given him a number that didn't exist. As he rewound to his last few minutes with Taneez at the airport, another troubling query added to his worries.

Don't you think your father had something more to tell you through this quest? Her voice thrummed in his mind with deafening clarity. *Through fire, air, water and earth that forms a Star of David, a hexagram, the most mysterious and enigmatic symbol in the world? People believe that it holds a closely guarded secret the world doesn't know.*

Am I missing something? This question had occurred to him several times last night with no substantial answer emerging so far. Pushing the matter from his mind, Jake turned off the faucet, picked up the bathrobe and wrapped it around his dripping frame.

As he crossed over to the dressing table, a valuable artifact set on the table next to his bed caught his eye.

The magnetic box.

Last night, cradling it in his palms, he had stared at it for hours, recalling its wonderful role in the quest, right from the time it was discovered hidden in the safe-deposit box.

Jake walked to the bedside table and lifted the magnetic box. The silver-colored box, four by three inches and one and a half centimeters thick, still glistened magically. And at its center, the carved arcane symbol of the Star of David, two superimposed inverted triangles, reflecting its geometry in the two-line verse, 'As above…So below…', inscribed in its belly. Mysterious as ever, the words still appeared to conceal a secret that seemed to have dodged history for countless eons, holding a deep layer of meaning.

Gently caressing the surface of the box with his fingers, Jake read the two-line script, revisiting the moment it was first discovered inside the aluminum safe-deposit box, stuck to its roof. Then, all of a sudden, Jake felt a shiver run down his spine sensing that something was not adding up.

He looked down at the magnetic box and thought of the aluminum safe-deposit box, stressing on the combination of magnet and aluminum. As far as he knew, magnets would never attract aluminum—a fundamental concept he had learnt in his school days. *Then how could it have been stuck to the safe-deposit box? How could such a heavy magnetic box stick to the aluminum roof,* Jake pondered…*unless…*

"Jesus Christ!" Jake whispered in utter disbelief when the revelation struck him like a thunderbolt. His head pounded as haze begin to wane away. 'As above…So below…,' the Hermetic adage as in the geometry of the two superimposed inverted triangles, hummed in his mind with a deafening sound. He quickly rushed downstairs for his laptop and powered it on. As he waited for the system to boot, he recalled the two-line script once again.

'As above…So below…'

This two-line Hermetic adage, Jake suspected, held more secrets than he had imagined. If his estimates on magnet-aluminum attraction were true and in sync with the two-line Hermetic adage and the geometry of the two superimposed inverted triangles, Jake was sure that the hunt for The Lost Arcanum was still not over.

He launched the web browser and choosing the appropriate string of terms he hit the search button and curiously waited for the results. As hundreds of results poured in, Jake selected the link that read 'Forms of magnetic behavior in materials.'

When the page loaded on the screen and Jake glanced through the contents, he felt his pulse skip in excitement. *This is impossible!* Jake realized, mystified. *How could I miss this in the first instance? If my guess is true… then I need a key to unlock the secret without which the supposed discovery is useless.*

All at once, like a thin ray of sun light piercing through a stretch of dark clouds, the answer to his question emerged clear. Enlightened by the moment of victory, Jake knew where he had to look for the answers.

Picking up his cell phone, Jake placed two important calls. One to Mr. Melkundi, the bank manager, State Bank of India. And the other to his office secretary, Miss Ishita, at the CBI.

CHAPTER 98

Red Fort is an important landmark in the nation's capital that forms a glorious crown for Mughal Emperor Shah Jahan's medieval walled city Shah Jahanabad (Old Delhi).

This humongous and beautiful citadel, also known as *Lal Qilah,* gets its name from the red sandstone used in its construction. Situated on the western banks of the Yamuna River and enclosed by huge walls, this fort has been fortified by two important gateways, Lahori Gate and Delhi Gate. The first is the main gateway, a prime and imposing portal flanked by semi-octagonal towers facing Lahore (now in Pakistan), which explains its name.

Balbeer raised his eyes to the monument with great admiration and with an immense regard. It was this massive structure, a symbol of Indian independence, testimony to the rise and fall of great kingdoms, a splendid reminder of the glorious Mughal era and solemn evidence to the great Indian victory against the British. From this magnificent fort, in the grassy area above the massive Lahori Gate and below the tall ramparts of the fort, Pandit Jawaharlal Nehru, India's first prime minister, had unfurled the Indian tricolor on August 15, 1947, marking the end of British colonial rule.

And now to celebrate the same occasion seventy one years after Independence, the entire area on the rampart was being geared up for a grand show. The stage was all set for the head of the state, the prime minister, who would shortly unfurl the flag and then preside over the gathering and lead the celebrations. To enhance the experience to true to life, huge display screens were installed at many points in the ground to make prime minster's addressing seen from anywhere across the arena.

Before his mind could take it all in, Balbeer Singh was joined by AD and Riya from the CBI, who led him into the fort, across to the central control room where a network of surveillance systems and other electrical and electronic equipment were installed in a chamber right beneath the rampart to ensure infallible security during the celebration.

ӁӁӁӁӁ

At that moment in the other part of the city, Jake had learnt—after scouring loads of data on the 'forms of magnetic behavior in materials classified as ferromagnetic, paramagnetic and diamagnetic'—that aluminum, a grey, ductile metallic element belonged to the class called paramagnetic, the magnetic attraction of which was a thousand times weaker than that of ferromagnetic materials.

This was enough to confirm his suspicion that the magnetic box could not have stuck to the roof of the safe-deposit box, unless…

Jake felt his pulse race, imagining its implication, as he drove his car swiftly towards State Bank of India. In hurry to uncover the secret, he had managed to dress himself in denim trousers, a red collared T-shirt and a pair of sneakers.

He slowed the car and stopped it by the pavement. As he lowered the glass, a plump female appeared outside the driver's side window.

Jake peered out at his office secretary, Ishita, holding a brown envelope in her hand. A little while ago, he had contacted her and asked for some details to be delivered at a private location. Now following his directions, Ishita had arrived with what he had asked of her.

Jake smiled at her. "Sorry to bother you on a holiday."

"Not a problem, sir," Ishita returned his smile and extended the brown envelope to him.

Accepting it, he told her, "Keep this between us." "I always do, sir." She smiled.

"Thanks," Jake said, appreciating her assistance. He hit the gas and charged the car ahead.

With one hand fixed on the steering, Jake allowed his other hand to slide into the brown envelope and extract its contents, which were forensic photographs clicked at the crime scenes. Among the bunch, Jake singled out three photographs, each displaying the victims, Anurag Chopra, Ramanujan and Jaswanth Sinha. With half his attention on the road, he scrutinized one particular pattern that had been repeated in these photographs.

The pattern made by the victims' right hand fingers.

Although this arrangement of fingers had caught his attention almost instantly at the time murders had occurred, it had taken him a long time to realize that the gestures might been guarding another secret that was hidden until now.

Travelling swiftly through the congested lanes of the capital, Jake maneuvered his car into the premises of the State Bank of India and parked it. He climbed down from the car in haste, take a brisk sprint to the first floor of the building. As he stepped through the main entrance and crossed the large hall of the bank, he exhaled a breath of relief on finding it empty on account of national holiday.

He briskly walked to the end of the hall and opened the door to the bank manager's cabin.

Mr. Melkundi glanced up at him with a serious countenance.

Jake was fortunate in that even Mr. Melkundi had agreed to comply with his request when he had contacted the bank manager some time ago asking for immediate access to his father's safe-deposit box.

"This was quite unexpected," Melkundi said in a serious tone, rising from his seat and walking towards him. "Your desire to access a safe-deposit box on a national holiday is quite bizarre and puts me in great confusion."

Jake took a moment trying to catch his breath after having raced up the stairs. Thinking of the bizarre pattern in the photographs, he replied, "Sometimes, things that appear bizarre are made to appear bizarre... rather, they are made to appear so, to serve some purpose."

Melkundi pulled off his glasses. "You remind me of your father when you speak so mysteriously..." He paused. "Allowing you to access the safe-deposit box on a national holiday is against the law of the bank. But considering your father was a great client, I will allow you that privilege."

Picking up a ring of heavy keys from the table, Melkundi motioned for Jake to follow him. Soon, Jake found himself beside Melkundi, who used a key on the ring to unlock the bank vault.

"Make it quick," Melkundi said, handing him a key for the safe-deposit box and motioning him inside. "I'll be waiting for you in my cabin."

To Jake's relief, Melkundi walked away, allowing him the privacy he needed, to explore the safe-deposit box all by himself.

Quickly stepping into the bank vault, Jake glanced around. The lustrous grey aluminum vault shone elegantly in the light cast by the overhead bulbs. Staring at the massive iron frame holding hundreds of aluminum safe-deposit boxes, he felt the same sense of hollowness and the musty stench of aluminum as he had when he visited the last time.

I'm back to square one, Jake thought as he stepped across to his father's safe.

The quest for *The Lost Arcanum,* which had begun from the safe-deposit box, had come back to where it all had started, after going full circle.

Jake's attention was drawn to the key slot and digital display and digital keypad beneath it. Quickly inserting the key into the key slot, Jake turned it right. The digital display powered on with a click, prompting…

Enter your four-digit PIN

Upon entering the PIN, the safe-deposit lock clicked and the door opened outward, slightly ajar. Jake slid his fingers in his trousers pocket and pulled out the magnetic box, holding it to the light.

A week ago, he had found it stuck to the roof inside the safe box. Now to confirm his suspicion on the property of affinity of aluminum metal, Jake moved the magnetic box inside the safe, guiding it closer to the side walls. The magnetic box clung to the side wall, but when Jake withdrew his hand, owing to its weak affinity between the magnet and the aluminum, the box collapsed under its own weight with a clunk.

A sudden rush of adrenaline washed through his veins. Collecting the magnetic box, Jake gradually guided it upwards, towards the roof of the safe. In a flash, it flew from his palms, levitating upwards, sticking to the roof strongly.

I was right. Jake felt his skin goose-fleshed. *The magnetic box would not have stuck to the roof unless…*

CHAPTER 99

7.15 AM.
Red Fort.

The gargantuan citadel, the Red Fort, rose expansively, jutting out astonishingly toward the bright morning sun.

With two major streets of the city laid out from its two main entrances, the one stretching in front of the Lahori Gate--the original main entrance to the fort, overlooking the main street of Chandni Chowk, beyond a vast open space appeared as prominent as ever. And the other, Faiz Bazar, led from the Delhi Gate of the fort to the Delhi Gate of the city.

There is another prominent monument located nearby on a natural rise in the ground, which is a congregational mosque known as Jama Masjid.

LahoriGate is flanked on either side by half octagonal turrets topped by pavilions. The central section of the gateway consists of a series of small protrusions, each embellished with a white marble dome, evenly spaced between two imposing minarets.

This morning, however, directly across this historical monument, the celebration of Independence Day had just begun to unwind extravagantly. For miles around the arena, flags of varied sizes fluttered in the sky, huge gas balloons were suspended in the sky, swaying vividly, all bathed in the colors of saffron, green and white.

Arrangements were made to provide seating for an astonoshing ten thousand people to the right of the Red Fort in the public enclosure, next to where nearly the same number of school children, clothed in the colors of the national flag, faced the ramparts of Lahori Gate.

The section for VIPs, foreign delegates and dignitaries was laid out on the right side of the rampart, from where the prime-ministerial speech was due in minutes.

The security around the Red Fort was tight, with a multi-layered security cover consisting of thousands of armed personnel from paramilitary forces keeping a hawk-eyed vigil to pre-empt any possible terror strikes. National Security Guard sharpshooters were deployed on high-rises near the fort. As an additional measure, helicopters patrolled the skies.

At all entry points, visitors were checked and their bags examined. The security personnel moved around the arena, ensuring harmony was maintained, coordinating with the special forces. On the other hand, the computer programmers from China and Russia were given high- level access to the production control rooms of national and private broadcasting networks. Tasked to work closely with Indian experts to ensure the relay of only select programs, the experts were now geared up to curb the footage across all internet and television channels.

The stage for the grand occasion was set. Local and digital television channels began to zoom in on their high definition cameras, set over the ramparts of the complex, as soon as the Indian prime minister finished unfurling the flag from the ramparts and proceeded towards the podium to lead the nation in the celebrations.

In the VIP section to the right of the podium, on the rampart, Balbeer Singh took a seat with the Secretary of Defense. Behind them, the main Lahori Gate rose majestically, overlooking the massive crowd that had spread across the arena in great enthusiasm

Riya and AD exchanged suspicious looks when the opposition party members entered the VIP section and settled. As expected, there was no sign of opposition leader Ajeet Awasthi.

+Even General Balbeer Singh had taken note of it.

ЖЖЖЖЖ

The prime minister stepped in front of the podium and commenced his address. Behind him, the eight octagonal columns topped with white turrets loomed marvelously.

The prime minister's voice resonated to the distant parts of the ground, clearly audible to the jam-packed audience. His life-size image was visible on the huge display screen installed along the ramparts.

"My dear countrymen, brothers, sisters and dear children," the prime minister said. "Today, we celebrate, with pride, the 71st anniversary of our Independence. My heartfelt greeting to one and all on this day of national celebration. And I take special pride in saluting the symbol of our freedom and peace, the tricolor."

"Let us all recall and recount the great sacrifice of our freedom fighters, whose undying love for the country and unceasing passion and struggle for the dream of a beautiful India has secured us our freedom and peace that we longed for centuries."

The leader's zeal and words of honor resounded in every region of the Red Fort complex, instilling a great fervor of patriotism and undying passion amongst every civilian who had arrived to witness the event.

ӜӜӜӜӜ

Jake's doubts over the strong affinity of the magnetic box to the roof of the safe-deposit box had vaporized.

Now, standing in the bank's vault, under the bright overhead lights and facing the safe-deposit box belonging to his father, Jake plucked the magnetic box from the roof and admired the two-line verse inscribed within the Star of David.

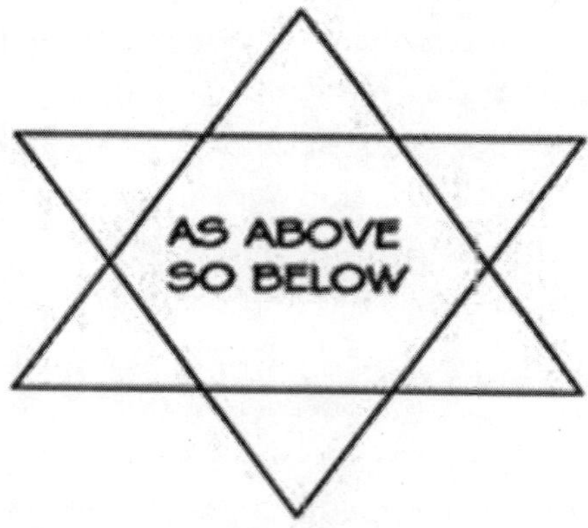

This two-line Hermetic adage and its reflection in the two superimposed inverted triangles forming a single mysterious star known as the Star of David, had been like a sign post throughout the quest, playing a major role in pointing Jake to the path to uncover so many secrets.

From revealing the riddle hidden on the underside of the box, to persuading him to follow the *sadhu* at Srisailam, this millennia- old esoteric combination of geometry and verse, had proven to be mysterious and cryptic.

Now, once again, it was pointing the way for something more that Jake suspected had gone unnoticed.

After reading the two-line verse, 'As above…So below…' again, Jake raised his glance to the safe-deposit box that sat immediately over the one that belonged to his father. It was this safe-deposit box, the verse seemed to be pointing at.

Using the key the bank manager had handed him, Jake activated the digital display of the upper safe-deposit box. It beeped to life, blinking in red, prompting…

Enter your four-digit PIN

Setting the magnetic box aside, he reached into his pocket and pulled out the photographs his office secretary, Ishita, had delivered to him.

What had appeared to be a puzzling piece of evidence at the murder site then, had now unscrambled itself in a way that Jake had never imagined.

In the photographs of the victims—Anurag Chopra, Ramanujan and Jaswanth Sinha—one particular part of their body was highlighted in a bizarre fashion, as though it held a secret in its arrangement: their fingers.

Throughout history, this ancient hand gesture was known as 'hand of mysteries', emblematic of an invitation extended by a divine master to his initiate to discover mankind's greatest hidden secrets. The *sadhu* from Srisailam had used the same gesture, pointing the index finger skywards and then downwards, solemnly declaring, 'As above…So below…'before ushering them to witness the grand art of alchemy.

The triangles inside the rim of the cryptic snake puzzle were also arranged in a specific order, one that this popular axiom eventually helped transform the puzzle into an actual map pointing to location of Kongka La.

Once again, several centuries later, the ancient 'hand of mysteries' had resurfaced, pointing the way toward one more secret.

Discerning its implication, Jake had subjected the gesture to meticulous investigation. The hands of the victims didn't bear the five symbols—sun, lantern, crown, key and a star—that otherwise would be stained on the tip of the fingers of the 'hand of the mysteries.' However, their index fingers and thumbs stretched outward and the rest of their fingers were coiled in a similar fashion. Jake's attention had been fixed on the other hand of the victims, as he found dissimilarities in the pattern there…dissimilarities that expressed numbers.

The four-digit number, the PIN, required to open the safe.

In the first photograph, Jake focused on the right hand fingers of Anurag Chopra. Except the thumb and the index finger that were outstretched, the middle, the ring and the little finger were coiled; all the fingers on his left hand were outstretched. To Jake, the right hand implied the number 'two' and the left hand, the number 'five.' He skipped to the next picture, the one of Ramanujan. Here, the right hand pattern was repeated, while that on the left hand four fingers were outstretched and the thumb was coiled. *Number two and number four*, Jake noted. He looked at the third picture. The right hand pattern recurred, but one on the left, the index finger and thumb were coiled while the rest were outstretched. *Number two and three…*

After unscrambling the sequence of numbers from the pattern, Jake realized that the number 'two' had recurred while the rest of those displayed by the left hand, differed by one: *two and five two and four two and three.*

Committing those numbers to his memory, Jake raised his fingers to the digital panel and punched in the four-digit number, using the sequence: 2345. As soon as he hit the 'Enter' button, there was a long beep: 'Wrong Pin.'

Jake punched in again, using the combination of 2453 this time. 'Wrong Pin', again.

At the fourth attempt, Jake got the sequence right: 2543. The safe-deposit box instantly opened with a click.

Having arrived at the moment of what had been waiting for its time, an unknown energy surged through Jake. With a trembling hand, Jake opened the door of the safe.

His eyes went wide in disbelief.

Lying inside the safe-deposit box was something big and ancient looking.

CHAPTER 100

"*On this joyous occasion,*"the prime minster said, "I ask you all to join me in saluting the endeavors of all our citizens, who, over a span of seven decades, have contributed towards building a new India."

His picture loomed on the huge screen below the rampart and on the small screens that were installed across the arena to the left and right, inside the railings protecting the lush green lawn.

"Let us all bow our head in memory of those brave *jawans*, who have sacrificed their lives for our unity, integrity and progress."

The words echoing across the arena failed to register with Rajat Singh who, along with Riya, had been tasked to work closely with the security team. He was as alert as a predator, listening closely to every notification crackling from his microphone on the status of the operation, while his vision, like that of a hawk, skimmed the heavily guarded entry points in the hope of nailing any suspicious activity.

A worry loomed large over him: thus far, there was no news on the whereabouts of the Master, the criminal mind behind the conspiracy, whose identity challenged even the skilled minds of the CBI.

"Seventy one years ago," the voice of the prime minister sounded crisp and clear, "the great people of India steered the nation on the path of freedom, marking the beginning of a new journey as a free nation, inspired by the message and moved by the vision of Mahatma Gandhi." He paused. "Mahatma Gandhi's dreams of a free India will only be fully realized when we banish poverty from our midst.

"As I raise my head to see the tricolor flutter high in pride, my thoughts roll back to the years when I had envisioned a new flourishing India. A country that is united regardless of being fragmented into diverse pieces, a country whose feathers of harmony are not ruffled by the disgrace of differences in caste, creed and gender, a country that lives in peace with all neighboring nations, a country where…"

The prime minister's voice was interrupted by a screech of static that died out all at once. There was complete silence. The crowd stared back at the ramparts, clueless. The prime minister tapped the mike. It didn't work. He looked back and stepped aside as the technical support team arrived at his podium to fix the technical snag. At that moment, the speakers seemed to come to life, but with the sound coming from an entirely different source…

The technical support team stood perplexed. The prime minister looked on puzzled.

AD, Riya and the top security personnel down in the arena were dumbstruck and General Balbeer Singh sprang up from his seat, as all of them got their first glimpse of the terror that had just materialized on the other side of the rampart.

In complete silence, the entire crowd heard a new voice crackling out of the speakers, a man's ghostly image looming on the huge screen across the arena.

The man who was familiar to all as the opposition leader Ajeet Awasthi.

ӁӁӁӁӁ

This in incredible….

The safe-deposit box now lay wide open. Inside, Jake had discovered quite a large and heavy metal chest roughly one square foot in length and breadth. With a little effort, he lifted the heavy chest out of the safe and cradled it in his hands, touching its surface. The corners of the chest were elegantly fashioned with an intricate lacework of mysterious symbols, while one familiar symbol was carved into the center.

Just beneath the symbol, there was a keyhole, its size perfect for the key that Eileen had handed him. Jake reached for the key that hung from his locket. This indeed was the final key to the secret…*The Lost Arcanum.*

Before he could explore the contents of the chest, something drew his attention to the inside of the safe-deposit box: a white envelope that lay on the floor of the box. He placed the chest back in the safe and pulled out the envelope. Inside, he found a handwritten letter, addressed to him by his father.

Jake,

Today, as you read this letter, I'm the happiest father in the world as you've returned to me after all these agonizing years. I feel relieved as the burden of responsibility, of protecting this chest, that I've been carrying for decades has finally been lifted. I'm not sure if I'll ever be able to embrace you in my arms at this wonderful juncture, but I wish I could.

It's been so long since I embraced you. And it seems like yesterday that I cradled you in my arms and I try to cuddle you every day. But the distance between us is vast and humiliating. People always told me that you're my clone, a facsimile, a mini-me. If only they knew how proud it made me hear that..

There is something very important that you need to know. That I was so conspired against that I was separated from Katherine and you, severing the very thread that weaved our loving family together.

Contrary to your understanding and that of Katherine, I shared a sororal relationship with Eileen, a platonic bond that was exaggerated and projected as illicit. Katherine fell prey to an illusion and misinterpreted the actual nature of our bond without trying to learn the truth. And she imposed on me a penalty for a sin that I was never guilty of. The most terrible punishment a wife has ever brought down upon her husband, of estrangement from her life and from his beloved son. I always desired to tell you that it was the will of Katherine that I stay away from you. You can't imagine the intensity of suffering I endured over the years, being away from you and Katherine. It was a life of hardship. I have no words to describe my love for you both. Alas, I couldn't prove the same. This love is an unceasing feeling that I have realized will go along with me to my grave.

My dear son, it was too late by the time I discovered that I had been framed. A gruesome scheme that was orchestrated to confiscate the secret the three scientists and I possessed. An ancient secret that we named The Lost Arcanum. As old as time, the secret is deadly and shocking and if revealed will rock the civilized world. In the wrong hands, it will bring the world to its knees.

I am certain to face a terrible and painful death. It does not matter. I will die for what I possess. There has been blood...and there will be more...and all for a noble cause, which I'm going to disclose to you now...

With his heart seething with pain, Jake continued to follow his father's words, which narrated the events, starting from the discovery of the monastery in the baking sand of Thar Desert, the discovery of the secret chest and Balbeer Singh setting up a secret committee with three science experts.

One significant clue was left behind, that of the ancient hand of mysteries, which I had overlooked in the wake of the DIA summoning me for immediate research on those recovered scrolls. I later returned to the excavated monastery with the conviction that I would unearth a treasure of incalculable worth. And as I had suspected, this hand of mysteries, which has from ancient times guided the privileged to valuable knowledge with held from the unworthy, gifted me with something momentous—a metal chest containing an incredible treasure of priceless, arcane and mysterious scrolls that was once guarded by a clandestine society known as the Brotherhood of the Serpent.

The origin and history of this brotherhood is steeped in mystery, which you'll learn as you read further. But it would be a great injustice if I did not mention that the men who made up the brotherhood were courageous and audacious, driven to protect and safeguard what they believed was the sacred knowledge inscribed within the scrolls passed down through generations by their forebearers and which contained a shocking revelation about the origins of mankind.

The scrolls contain a very dark knowledge that was not spoken of on this planet for more than seven thousand years. One that is enigmatic and arcane and has been concealed from mankind from the very beginning. Before I dwell deeper into the historical fabric of this brotherhood and reveal the secret they had safeguarded for seven thousand years, it's extremely important for you to understand that the evolution of intelligent life on earth has always challenged the ingenuity of mainstream science. Where ancient and medieval scholars expounded the hand of God in the creation of intelligent life-form, modern experts concurred with Darwin's theory of evolution and natural selection. If they only knew... Darwin's theory of the evolution of human species from apes was heavily flawed. It has severe discrepancies and has no absolute credence to what has been said about human evolution from a scientific point of view. How did the human species evolve from apes, suddenly turning into an intelligent race that went on to build the most technically advanced civilization on earth?

In addition, there is no fossil record available either. No fossil of a half-ape half-human has been found to support the theory of evolution. This scientific effort can be looked upon as nothing more than a desperate attempt to believe and prove something that actually wasn't true about the evolution of the human species at all.

However, in the race to unravel the greatest conundrum on the origin of humanity, a much darker secret has eluded history. A significant missing fragment of timeline that was expelled from common knowledge, which if revealed would perfectly fit the gap left in Darwin's theory of evolution—the great leap from Homo-erectus (ape-like ancestors) to Homo-Sapiens (modern man). Intelligent man appearing out of nowhere from his anthropoidal cousin is simply too bold a theory to be accepted as a mere coincidence.

My son, it's really disheartening to learn that what we all thought we knew about our origin was the biggest lie the world has ever been fed. A great hoax in the history of mankind devised to conceal an explosive secret. Held by the ancient scribes as the most sacred epoch in the history, the missing link was a secret and remarkable event that filled this vast void of time—the existence of a highly intelligent and technologically advanced race called Elohim, those who from heaven to earth came.

CHAPTER 101

"My deep apologies for the inconvenience," politician Ajeet Awasthi's phony voice resounded crisply, leaving the entire crowd in the arena puzzled by his sudden and unexpected appearance.

"But this was important. There might've been no better moment than this one, on Independence Day. I can sense your perplexity at my sudden and unusual arrival. In the next few minutes, your confusion about my intervention will vaporize. My presence will begin to make sense. Before that, I need your cooperation. I require your support in the form of silent observation. I want your attention on what I'm going to reveal which is surely going to leave you all astounded."

The security officials with their submachine guns near the podium were about to fan out to curb the opposition leader had not the prime minister signaled to them to back off. He also intervened and stopped Balbeer Singh, clearly gesturing him to wait, as he attempted to bring the situation under control.

The prime minister clearly wanted to know what the opposition leader was up to.

Appearing to the left of the podium on the ramparts, the politician Ajeet Awasthi looked down at the crowd beneath him. Despite the heavy security arrangements, the intrusion of the opposition leader had greatly astonished the security officials, leaving them doubting their own abilities in catering to the acute security on this national event.

"My dear friends, before I proceed, let me make one thing clear to you. I'm not here to accuse anyone or pinpoint the inadequacies of our ruling government for political gain. If I'm here today, standing before you all, I must have a valid reason, a rationale that must serve a purpose. One that is high above all our material desires."

The populace gazed palely into each others faces, confused, expecting some absurd drama that usually followed whenever any Indian politician showed up in front of victims of calamities with food and water to gain their favor by accusing the ruling government of ineptitude.

AD came sprinting up with Riya and stopped at the foot of the rampart, scanning the scene from the ground. He glanced at the cameras installed on the rampart that zoomed in onto the politician.

"How in the world did he get up there?" AD said in awe.

Riya, sharing his surprise, touched her throat mike and spoke to security personnel.

"Officer, what is going on?"

AD stood beside her, minutely studying the figure of Ajeet Awasthi on the rampart, finding something fishy. A few seconds of meticulous observation later, his jaws dropped in surprise. "Oh God! This can't be happening."

Riya turned her attention to him anxiously.

"No wonder he escaped the security," AD said, now having understood, gazing at the figure of the politician.

"What?" she sounded confused.

AD turned to her in amazement. "He has tricked us..."

ӜӜӜӜӜ

Jake felt a pang of surprise and horror on learning that the infamous missing link that discredited the Darwinian theory was an alien race called Elohim.

Elohim were spiritually evolved beings from a distant planet that had come to earth. They had the power to transform energy and light into matter and create and recreate anything at will. They arrived at that point of time when earth had taken the brunt of a collision of catastrophic asteroids. Celestial debris disfigured its geological morphology, breaking Pangaea into Laurasia and Gondwanaland. The intensity of the impact was so great that it wiped out any traces of gigantic animals and all signs of life that once populated the planet. All that remained of the catastrophe was the race of Homo-erectus that sought refuge in deep caves during the cataclysm. When they emerged, they found themselves amidst the chaos. Thick smoke emerging from the charred ruins clouded the skies and engulfed the land mass, spreading darkness across the planet. Wilderness stretched across continents, stillness hovered over the vast expanse of oceans.

Disheartened by the sight of Homo-erectus living in a state of ruin, the Supreme Being of the race patiently spent six days and six nights, equivalent to sixty hundred days of light and darkness, to restore the earth's natural equilibrium. He cleared the skies and allowed the light to sweep the earth. He then touched the waters and they teemed with life and made the plants and trees fill the lands and animals to populate the forests. Even so, he felt something was amiss in his creation. At which point, of all the life forms that had survived, Homo-erectus caught his fascination with its slight signs of intelligence.

To perfect his creation, to hone the product he had imagined, the Supreme Being mixed the blood of the Homo-erectus with that of his own race and by genetic manipulation, he created the first man and woman on earth by giving them a bodily form similar to his own.

Deep inside, however, something made the Supreme Being uncomfortable. Since man and woman were hybrids, born out of the mixed blood of his own race and that of the earthly primates, he wondered if his purpose in creating them would be served as they would indulge in disgraceful acts that would impede their spiritual growth. He feared his offspring had strong propensity of animal instincts, which would bind them strongly to physical needs rather than reflecting on their spiritual requirements that they were otherwise created for. He wished his creation to contemplate their divine consciousness, like his own race, more concerned with honing the inner soul and its evolvement into the quintessential, rather than catering to the temporary needs of the outer physical shell.

Concerned, he brought the man and woman into his solemn presence, blessed them to be fruitful and have dominion over everything that rested below the skies and placed them on earth. He gave them the fruit of the tree of life: the knowledge that instructed the man and the woman to live their life within the confines of certain moral principles governed by nature, which was required for spiritual growth by self-awareness. But he strictly warned them against having the fruit from the tree of knowledge, which would give them a taste of evil instincts, which would hinder their spiritual growth and bring upon them death, certainly.

But it wasn't long before his warning was disregarded. His order to abstain from having the tree of knowledge was unheeded. Ignoring what they had been strictly warned against, the man and the woman indulged themselves by eating from the tree of knowledge and committed sin by disobeying the Supreme Being.

Enraged by their act of disobedience, the Supreme Being brought down upon them the irrevocable curse of mortality and a wrath that would stretch for eternity, condemning them to a life of toil ever after. Through sorrow, the woman would bring forth her children and the man would rule over her. For harkening unto the voice of the wife, the man was so cursed that he would toil and work the soil and from between the thorns and thistles, he would reap his food.

Their sin led to the fall of humanity from heavenly bliss and the spark of universal spirit in them was trapped in flesh and bones.

From immortal beings, they turned into mere mortals.

CHAPTER 102

A *gloomy silence* gripped the entire crowd at the Red Fort. The lively, vibrant and enthusiastic atmosphere that had existed only a while ago had turned suspicious at the unexpected scene of opposition party leader Ajeet Awasthi presiding on the occasion of Independence Day, instead of the prime minister of India. The scene was just too much to take in. The crowd could not help but wonder at the drama that was now unfolding on the rampart.

Still confused by the way the event had shaped up, the Indian prime minister turned to Balbeer. "It's such a disgrace that your security team is flawed. It should be me speaking at this event."

Balbeer Singh faltered. "I just need one minute, sir. If you let me, I'll have the situation..."

"It's too late, General." The prime minister cut him off. "The damage is done. When you had to, you failed. All we can do now is sit and watch. There are a bunch of cameras capturing this event, telecasting this live on television screens across the nation."

Balbeer ascertained that he was right, by looking around at the cameras installed along the ramparts.

"These opposition parties are like vultures," the prime minister said calmly, "always on the lookout to feed upon our mistakes and make it an unnecessary national issue. And that is something I'm not going to allow at any cost. Not on this national day."

"I understand, but..."

"You're finished here," the prime minister angrily cut him off again. "Just stay quiet and do nothing."

Balbeer Singh nodded. His face was ashen. His conscience was gnawing at him for his inability to devise a foolproof plan to avert this crisis, in spite of having top-class security personnel at his disposal.

The prime minister cast a curious glance at the public who seemed prisoners to the politician's proceedings. He looked at the cameras on the rampart that captured the entire event, making his picture available on the large screens set across the arena and also on national channels across the nation.

"I strongly disagree when our honorable Prime Minister asserts that India is a free nation," Ajeet Awasthi continued gravely. "And it sounds very unrealistic when he talks of our nation being touched by the hand of peace, progress and development."

The people grumbled among themselves, marveling at his bold statement.

Balbeer moved away from the prime minister and peered down the rampart at the security team. They had converged below in precise position, their hands on their weapons, ready to take down the opposition leader on his order.

Sometime back, Balbeer Singh had received an input from the chief security personnel that the team of techies flown in from Russia had secured all the points of satellite and broadcast networks, including the domains that were more susceptible to attack. But the enemies seemed to have waged the war right into their face. Nonetheless, this was not the time to lag behind and watch the enemy takeover. Balbeer touched his throat mike, radioing the command to the security personnel.

"I don't know how, but I want that bastard out of the rampart. Right now!"

"My dear people, in my opinion, there's nothing we should be proud of." Ajeet Awasthi continued, "I agree our country has made its presence felt globally, but it has done little to address the needs of the common man. The rich are prospering, while the poor are rendered more impoverished."

The general's radio beeped. He instantly pressed the button and heard AD speaking. He was somewhere below the rampart, coordinating with the security team.

"What?" Balbeer barked on hearing AD's response. He turned abruptly, looking over at Ajeet Awasthi in a new light. "That can't be true..."

"The truth is all you see right now, General," Rajat Singh retold and hung up.

Feeling desperate, Balbeer slipped his hand into his holster and freed a silenced gun.

The tantalizing voice of the opposition leader was resonating deeply, biting into the jam-packed arena of the Red Fort.

"Corruption has affected our economy and crippled efforts at banishing poverty and unemployment from our midst." Ajeet Awasthi paused. "As per the latest source, our economy is now growing at historically unprecedented rates, which enables us to generate the resources required for eradication of poverty, for education and health care for all." He swept his vision across the crowd. "In that case, where is the money going? Why do we still suffer from poverty, unemployment, poor health care and education facilities even after seventy years of independence?"

Balbeer Singh raised his silencer-equipped gun, gripping it tightly, aiming at the opposition leader. Calming his nerves, he placed his fingers on the trigger.

The input from AD was really very disturbing, which suggested horrific outcomes. Every word that he had heard whirred in his ears. Sucking in a deep breath, he pulled the trigger.

ӜӜӜӜӜ

By now, Jake had recognized the Supreme Being from the race as *'Jehovah'* from the book of Genesis, the first book from the Old Testament of the Bible. And the information that followed was enough to confirm his suspicion and something more he had not been aware of.

The Supreme Being from the extraterrestrial race of Elohim and his arrival on earth... isn't it synonymous to what has been narrated in the Biblical texts? Well, the Bible is not the only book that speaks of celestial beings that descended to earth in the remote past and influenced human civilizations. These events were also reported by many ancient settlements such as the Greeks, Egyptians and Romans, but with slight modifications to the story. Further, closer comparison between the Hebrew Bible and the ancient Sumerian texts dating back to 3500 BCE reveals many similarities. Not just their stories, but even their languages share commonalities. Adam is the man in Hebrew texts, while Adamu is what the Sumerians called the first man. In addition, there is massive information buried in the ancient Hindu texts which describe these extraterrestrial humanoids intervening during the time that was known as Rama Empire, which shows very strong similarities to

Sumerian texts. Their gods and goddesses were the same, their personalities, their behavior, their war technology and their architecture were all similar. They all give the same explanation of how these beings were space travelers who visited earth in starships, decked in strange clothing, possessing some extraordinary magical powers.

And with these magical powers, they would manifest anything at will. They embodied power and authority, forming the theological background for many civilizations, like Canaanite and Israelite traditions. The Supreme Being of the Elohim became the Supreme God, who later became the object of the devotion of Abraham, Isaac and Jacob in the Hebrew Bible. For mankind's disobedience, he kept them from the knowledge he deemed forbidden. The knowledge which would give mankind the power to create anything, any matter at will. He decided not to share the mysteries of the universe with humans as he believed they were fashioned from mixed blood in which bestial instincts were more powerful and pronounced, keeping them bound to superficial pleasures and thus hindering their spiritual growth. To realize the full potential of this knowledge, they were first required to hone their *spiritual evolution.* His reason behind keeping the technology and the mysterious knowledge can be looked upon as the same reason America was against Africa and the Middle-East having nuclear technology. In the wrong hands, the secrets were devastating.

However, that didn't mean he wished to conceal the knowledge entirely from humans. In the period that followed, he devised a scheme to allow humans to benefit from the knowledge without actually giving them direct access to it. To carry on this humongous task, he chose honest, noteworthy individuals and entrusted them with the forbidden knowledge. Lest the knowledge be lost or be misused, he insisted they protect and share it among those who were worthy, to keep it alive and to maintain and spread the divine consciousness as the only true God. And his followers formed a society in secret that came to be known as The Brotherhood of the Serpent. They shared all the knowledge carefully within their circle and kept it alive.

The metal chest, which now you possess, contains scrolls of texts containing the knowledge that Elohim had deemed forbidden. Some of this I have made a part of your quest.

The alchemy: there is a detailed explanation dedicated to the mysterious potion known as 'nectar of immortality', the supposed drink of gods, which rendered immortal anyone who consumed it. In the same manner, the Philosopher's Stone, brought down to earth by the Elohim, had the potential to convert base metals into gold. Now, imagine if the recipe for the nectar of immortality or the secret of making the Philosopher's Stone slipped into the hands of someone evil? Would there be an end to the monstrosity?

So is hidden for the same reason, the secrets of anti-gravity and the techniques to manipulate human thoughts such that it can manifest anything and everything at will are also hidden. Likewise, the presence of Elohim in the deep valleys of Kongka La, below the earth's crust, should be guarded. That is their old home. The one they had abandoned long ago.

In any case, the world will crumble under the weight of the truth that God, whom the sacred doctrines cited as hovering in the skies and whom mankind has revered for an immeasurable period, actually belonged to an advanced extraterrestrial race that came to earth from heaven.

Humans will simply not accept that they were genetically engineered hybrids, forged into flesh and bones by the Elohim, who created them in their own image.

CHAPTER 103

It was a mind-numbing sight: the bullet charged from the silencer-equipped gun, pierced Ajeet Awasthi's chest and left him uninjured.

General Balbeer Singh turned to ice.

There was no blood and the opposition leader showed no panic. He remained unscathed, his voice as unwavering and confident as ever, touching every person in the crowd with his mind-transforming speech.

AD was right, the general thought, lowering his gun. The opposition leader was missing physically. His figure on the ramparts of Red Fort was a virtual image, one that was artificial creation projected from some source to produce just a beam of focused light on the rampart.

In complete dismay, the general realized that the opposition leader had deceived the crowd, the dignitaries and the Indian prime minister, who still assumed he was physically present among them and continued to listen to him.

But AD had revealed that his fraudulent appearance was nothing but holographic 3D projection technology, which was now projecting a video clipping of the politician from some unknown location through a network of satellites.

With terror gripping his flesh, the general sensed that they were now facing an enemy who waged a terrible war from behind an impenetrable virtual fortress.

ЖЖЖЖЖ

Holographic three-dimensional video projection is an imaging technique whereby a 3D image is first recorded using an array of cameras, capturing the object from different angles and positions before it is digitally encoded in a fast-pulsed laser beam on emulsion of light-sensitive film. The developed film, when re-exposed to laser light or normal incandescent light, recreates in space all the points of the light that originally came from the object such that the resulting image has all the dimensions of the original object, like depth, size, shape and texture, seeming real and life-like. However, if touched it would reveal nothing but a focused beam of light there.

Five years ago, General Balbeer Singh had overseen a secret project in DIA on 3D holographic technology when the concept was in the nascent stage of development. Developed as a covert technology, the 3D holographic projection technique was secretly implemented by many countries as a component of Psychological Operations, which had the capability of projecting persuasive images and 3D images of cloud, smoke, rain, buildings and terrain models across a large area of the battlefield through satellite. This was effective in strategic optical deception and cloaking, for providing momentary distraction while engaging enemies in war.

This 3D image, termed holographic telepresence, is recorded in one location and displayed in another in real-time. It can be done anywhere in the world and is supposed to be the world's first practical 3D transmission system that works without the viewers having to wear special glasses or other optical devices. Surprisingly, years after this technology was pushed into oblivion by the military, holographic telepresence was back, projecting the pre-recorded video of the opposition leader on the ramparts of the Red Fort through satellite, looming ominously over the joyous occasion of Independence Day, misleading the crowd that had mistaken the virtual image to be a genuine presence.

The general hurried down the stairs behind the rampart, as he spoke to AD on the mike,

"Like you said, he is physically missing."

"General, their moves are unpredictable." AD replied. "They are far more prepared than we think they are."

"That's quite certain from what I see now on the rampart," the general agreed, breathing fast. "From what I know on how they have used this technology, they have manipulated a domestic dish antenna from some nearby location. We need to trace it and block the signals."

"Sure, General. I'm in the control room. I'm sure the security team will be able to resolve this soon."

"Update me once you're onto something. I need that video to be stopped as soon as possible."

With those words, Balbeer Singh signed off, hastening towards the arena.

ЖЖЖЖЖ

Some five miles away from the Red Fort, Jake, jolted by a string of revelations, paused for a long moment, standing before the safe-deposit box, letter in hand, pondering his father's opinion on the presence of extraterrestrials on earth.

Surprisingly, contrary to his belief, Jake's father desired the truth about the presence of extraterrestrials to be concealed, to be buried forever. Going by which, Jake had now decided to comply by his father's will. He was not finished with the letter, but against completing it as of a major and very crucial concern was weighing down on his mind.

To stop the footage from going public.

Jake brought his hand to rest on the iron chest lying inside the safe box, sensing the endeavors of his father and his three colleagues to support the cause of the Brotherhood of the Serpent, who wished to keep the forbidden knowledge alive but out of the hands of the unworthy.

With his hands resting on the chest, Jake took a solemn oath, caressing the iron chest: *I will preserve and protect the dangerous knowledge for the well being of mankind.*

With that thought echoing in his mind, Jake checked the time; it was close to nine.

My country is in danger, Jake thought. *It needs me. I must avert the disaster before it strikes.*

With strong conviction, Jake locked the safe-deposit box, stuffed the half-read letter in his pocket and sprinted out of the vault.

CHAPTER 104

Cyber attacks have become a major concern for the Indian government, with its national security agenda prone to intrusions and web defacements.

One such attack had occurred recently after New Delhi's nuclear weapons testing. The intrusions and discreet eavesdropping ever since, on some of the classified data from the nation's repository of defense, had increased, revealing unshielded areas on the inside, exposing Indian government's sheer negligence toward securing world-class IT infrastructure security solutions.

As most computers are connected to each other and share the same operating system, communicating with other computers via a standard set of TCP/IP protocols, curbing the eavesdropping becomes invariably a difficult task. Worms and viruses, obtrude into vulnerable networks to pilfer data tables, degrade communications, disrupt commerce or impair critical infrastructure such that the nation incurs great losses.

This morning, however, India was under one such major attack over again. The malignant force of the conspirators was underway, with their nefarious purposes being channeled through the nation's network of computers and satellites, which were transferring the signals of the holographic image of the opposition leader Ajeet Awasthi from an unidentified location with depth, sharp perception and crystal clear sound.

"Indeed, the Indian government is catering to the excessive needs of defense," Ajeet Awasthi revealed. "They are wasting taxpayers' money on top-secret defense projects, projects that are deemed classified." He looked gravely at the crowd. "These projects are dark and mysterious and very few know about their existence. And the ones who try to reveal it are either oppressed with deadly warnings or silenced forever."

Down in the arena, opposite the rampart, General Balbeer Singh stood helplessly with the security personnel. He felt his chest tighten with anxiety of loss. Soon after learning that the politician could not be stopped owing to his ghostly virtual manifestation, he had ordered a power shutdown in the areas in close proximity to the Red Fort to cripple dish antenna receivers, while managing uninterrupted power supply for the occasion through huge generators.

In spite of this, the holographic projection streamed uninterrupted. Opposition leader Ajeet Awasthi went about unleashing his evil intentions, to strip the government nude and reveal the secrets that Balbeer Singh and others like him had been protecting for decades.

ӜӜӜӜӜ

In an isolated corner of the arena, to the left of the rampart, Riya clicked off her throat mike after talking to the security personnel.

She sprinted quickly across to General Balbeer Singh.

She was coordinating with the security personnel, whom the general had deployed to search the high-rises in the vicinity of the Red Fort, to look for a receiver, likely powered by batteries, discreetly projecting the 3D holographic video of the politician.

She was halfway there when she heard her cell phone ring. The name of the caller surprised her. Flummoxed, she connected the call and spoke.

"Jake?"

"Riya, listen to me." Jake's voice had an unusual urgency. "I will explain everything. But first tell me what the situation at Red Fort is?"

Riya gulped down a knot of ease. "As expected, we have a major crisis, Jake,"

She briefly explained to him the entire situation at the Red Fort.

"Okay, I'm heading towards the Red Fort. I will be there in about five minutes." Jake spoke fast. "We'll have to stop the footage before the world gets to know its contents."

Hopefully, Riya prayed as she hung up the phone.

ӜӜӜӜӜ

In a security chamber immediately below the rampart where the fake 3D image of the opposition leader was being projected, a thin bespectacled information security analyst sat perplexed in his seat in the control room.

He ran his hand through his soft hair, wearing a troubled look on his face. He was staring at the output from his laptop and raised a worried glance at a wall of screens before him, projecting various parameters of data in graphical and tabular forms from a monitoring tool.

For the past five minutes, along with a pack of professional hackers, he had traced, isolated and blocked all wireless signals of various frequencies bouncing in the vicinity. Computer programmers from Russia sitting in different broadcast centers across the city, on the other hand, were controlling the telecast of various broadcasting network channels and had reported no evidence of enemy intrusions. Despite this, the frequency band of the 3D projection had infiltrated their sophisticated monitoring tools, eventually making it nothing more than a wild goose chase.

From meticulously gathered data, the security analyst could infer only one thing. Letting out a troubled moan, he glanced over his shoulder at AD.

"The source is untraceable, officer."

AD masked a worried look.

"As we suspected, the video file is not being relayed through national or private broadcasting networks which are under our constant vigilance." He paused, feeling uneasy about divulging the bad news. "The holographic video file is being relayed through a secure connection that seems to have dodged our monitoring systems."

"Which means?" AD insisted anxiously.

The security analyst tugged at his glasses. "Whoever is behind this seems to have acquired an exclusive broadcasting connection with maximum bandwidth to telecast the video file."

AD felt a searing chill in his gut. "You mean you can't trace it?" "Can't say for sure, but they are working on it." The security analyst pointed in the direction of his team, who were constantly conversing with their Russian counterparts on the phones and working on their laptops. "We need time."

Time is what we don't have now, AD thought, looking away, distraught.

"Sir, you should see this," one of the programmers from the team intervened, demanding the security analyst's attention.

AD and the security analyst joined him and looked at his laptop screen over his shoulder.

"I have singled out a signal that seems to have escaped our monitoring tools."

"Finally," the security analyst said in excitement. With a clap of his hand, he garnered the attention of his team members. "Guys, we have zeroed in on the threat. Now, I want each one of you to chase that specific frequency band and distort the signals beyond the recognition of the receiver." He rushed to his workstation, directing his team members gravely. "This is the only way we can bring the situation under control. So, get cracking."

As he followed the security analyst to his seat, AD pressed, "What's the prospect of this action? Can we stop the relay?"

The security analyst gazed at AD. "Hopefully."

Hopefully? AD ground his teeth in frustration. *Damn hope!* His mind was clearly weighing the terrifying implications if the telecast of the video was not curbed immediately.

At that moment, General Balbeer Singh radioed him. He pressed the throat mike and passed on an update on the progress report that seemed to only anger the general.

AD consoled him, "Nonetheless, we're trying our best to contain the crisis, General."

"That's a dicey task, officer," the general replied sighing deeply. "I'm afraid the outcome will be futile."

After adding it, the general, in a hurried tone, instructed AD on an alternative plan of action to control the crisis. He finished with his instructions. "Call the INSAT Coordination Committee. And tell them it's a state of national emergency."

"Okay, General."

Clicking off the radio, AD took critical note of the graphical information illuminated in colors of red, blue and green, spread out on the wall of screens in front of him.

Then quickly, he drew closer to the security analyst. "I want the frequency band of that signal." Turning to one of the security personnel from the defense wing in the room, he ordered with a sense of urgency. "Pull up the contact number for MCF. I need the service to this frequency shut down, immediately."

CHAPTER 105

Less than two miles from the Red Fort, on the wide stretch of Lodhi Road, Jake threw the gear stick to fourth, reaching a speed of eighty kilometers per hour on his car.

A little while ago, Riya had walked him through the situation at Red Fort, which was reaching its critical point while also recounting how INSAT was acting as a conduit in pushing the nation to the threshold of devastation.

Jake still couldn't fathom how INSAT was involved in all of this.

INSAT or the Indian National Satellite System is a series of multipurpose geostationary satellites that was launched in 1983 by ISRO for television and radio broadcasting, meteorological services and search and rescue operations. Considered the largest domestic communication system in the Asia-Pacific region, around twenty-four satellites have been launched as part of the INSAT program. Of these, the INSAT-4 series satellite serves the Tata Sky and Star Group companies for distributing their DTH services.

Today, however, after rednering thirty-two years of prompt satellite services to Indian nation, for the first time in its history, its services were being manipulated for wrong reasons, projecting a holographic 3D video being relayed on an exclusive frequency band.

Expelling the thoughts from his mind, Jake placed a call to Riya while steering his vehicle with the other hand. When Riya answered, he asked, "What's the update from the control room?"

"The security analyst and his team are trying to distort the signal of the frequency band beyond the recognition of the receiver."

"I don't think that will be possible," Jake said, steering his car left from the traffic signal. "The signals are encrypted such that they can be decrypted only if the receiver has the correct decoding satellite receiver with decryption algorithm and security keys." Jake paused. "That way, the question of distorting the signal arises only if they are able to decode the encryption and make it legible first."

"They might know what to do," Riya said. "They're giving it their best shot. And AD is however working on an alternative plan to get the services to that frequency band shutdown."

ӁӁӁӁӁ

Normally, in an ideal satellite transmission process, international and local turnaround channels have a distribution center that beams their programming channels to a geostationary satellite. Using large satellite dishes, broadcast centers pick those analog and digital signals, convert them into high-quality digital video and run them through an MPEG-2 encoder to obtain a video format of appropriate size and format for the satellite receiver. Once this process is completed, the compressed video is encrypted by the provider to keep people from accessing it for free. The broadcast center then shoots the encrypted compressed signal to one of its satellites which picks up the signal, amplifies it and beams it back to the receivers on earth.

Now, one among those millions receivers installed somewhere around the Red Fort, was projecting the politician with total clarity of sound and video.

"But, the truth can't be suppressed for long," Ajeet Awasthi went on. "Our right to transparency cannot be ignored anymore."

"Each year, around three hundred billion dollars are allocated to defense in the union budget, which is a massive one-tenth of our country's overall budget." He stilled for a moment. "Have you ever wondered why such a large chunk is set aside, while the needs of the military can be met at half the cost?"

The statement had the crowd on the edge of their seats.

"Damn!" Balbeer Singh was getting frustrated. He and his team of security officials were receiving a fair amount of contemptuous glances from the audience, who seemed to have been influenced by the deceptive speech of the opposition leader Ajeet Awasthi.

The Russian Director General of Defense Mr. Vladimir Gobarchev had shown serious concern when Balbeer Singh had reported on the crisis. His voice was shaky, impregnated with stark fear that the situation was gradually slipping away from their control. Yet, Lukas Covitz had maintained his cool, urging Balbeer Singh to keep the battle moving, boundaries of self defense pushing

While he was still figuring out a way out of this hell, he received an international call on his cell phone. Balbeer Singh knew it would be Mr. Donald Reagan, the Director General of Defense, USA.

He heard him barking as soon as he connected.

"What the hell do you think you're doing? The footage is being played right in front of your eyes. And yet, I see you doing nothing to curtail it?"

"Do hell with you!" Balbeer Singh burst out in fury. "This sensitive issue is as much my concern as it is yours. If I have gone lengths to protect the secret from the world for decades, then I will continue to do whatever I can to ensure that the secret is never to be revealed. Now..."

Before he could complete his sentence, he heard a click indicating the call had been cut. A surge of relief swept through him, finally having vented his long-suppressed anger on Donald Reagan. He lowered the cell phone with an understanding that sometimes one needed to stand their ground, to fight back and protest when needed.

ӜӜӜӜӜ

Rajat Singh studied the contact number of MCF that the security official had written on a piece of paper and handed to him. Dutifully, he stabbed those numbers on the keypad and held his cell phone to his ear.

MCF or the Master Control Facility, is situated in Hassan, Karnataka, from where the geostationary and geosynchronous INSAT satellites are monitored and controlled. Of three hundred staff members belonging to various engineering disciplines, technical branches and administrative areas, around eighteen are on a twenty-four/seven shift headed by an operations manager.

Rajat Singh was lucky to speak to a female employee who, comprehending the situation at Red Fort, had reacted immediately, putting him on hold while she processed his input. It was not long before she came back on the line and spoke with slight unease.

"Sir, from what I can see, the service to that frequency band is already inactive."

"What the hell...?" Rajat Singh burst out, glancing up at the display panels on the wall. He could still see the video being streamed on the rampart. "Cross-check again. I'm sure you're missing something."

"I'm sorry, sir," the female voiced insisted, "As I told you, the services to that frequency band were active only a while ago. Now, though, its in an inactive state."

AD clenched the cell phone tightly in astonishment. "How can that be possible? I still see the video being streamed."

"From my best guess, what you see is the recorded telecast," the female informed him. "You might've detected the signals in an active mode when the recording was in progress."

"Damn it!" AD cursed, hanging up. He lowered his cell phone and stared at the screen helplessly. He felt a deep sense of fear; their efforts were going in vain and the situation was slipping out of control.

CHAPTER 106

Peripheral security around the venue and the buildings surrounding the Red Fort had been tightened by deploying the elite Special Protection Group (SPG). The Intelligence Bureau and security agencies had also deployed trained commandos at various points in the city.

However, in spite of the best security arrangements, the enemies had penetrated the citadel in a manner that was beyond human control: through holographic technology.

For Jake, the current scenario at Red Fort seemed to be a state of virtual pandemonium.

"Jake, we're sinking."

Jake could hear the distress in Riya's voice as she continued to update him on the response from the MCF while he headed towards the venue.

"Now our only hope is the receiver," Jake reminded her. "I'm sure the receiver is hidden somewhere around the venue. Somewhere close by, in plain sight." Jake fell silent, thinking how the answers to the riddle had also been embedded in plain sight.

"Riya," Jake said, "can you send me a live feed of the venue from your mobile?"

"Sure, but what are you intending to do with it?"

"Well, what would an investigator do at a crime scene?"

Riya was silent for a moment, before she ventured, "Investigate?"

"Exactly."

ЖЖЖЖЖ

"My dear people," Ajeet Awasthi voiced in high spirits, "in the next few minutes, you'll discover why our government has been secretly spending three hundred billion US dollars in the deep valleys of Himalayas on something that will baffle your imagination."

As the opposition leader continued to lure the crowd with his deceptive speech, members from his alliance party at the venue whispered among themselves, finding him determined and seemingly unstoppable. From his assured voice and unwavering confidence, they were certain he was leading up to something on this day, an achievement that would ensure their power in the forthcoming general elections.

"I have someone who will guide you through the rest of the story. Someone who has gone to great lengths to uncover the secret," Ajeet Awasthi ventured, "Mr. Rabindranath. A former IAF major, who recorded some classified footage minutes before he was killed in a road accident. His death, unquestionably, was a conspiracy to keep the silence over what he knew. And in the light of his death, we have his testimony in the form of footage that will introduce you all to the darkest side of this government."

Down in the arena, the general was receiving on update from AD on the response from MCF when he heard the opposition leader making another terrifying statement. Reflexively, he turned his head towards the holographic image of Ajeet Awasthi on the rampart, who had raised his hand, pointing at the large screen down at the rampart.

"Dear people, here is the footage that discloses the secret of the truth the Indian government has been hiding from us and from the world for decades."

Damn! The general hastily called the control room, screaming. "Put off the display screens right now."

ЖЖЖЖЖ

Earlier, Riya had been flustered when Jake had contacted her unexpectedly and had asked her about the situation at Red Fort.

After all the misunderstanding between them over the past few days, she had never anticipated that Jake would call her. Despite being at loggerheads over keeping whatever secret from the public, now Jake had agreed to fight to bury the secret. He showed keen interest in joining the battle being waged against evil.

The thought was unsettling though she felt reassured that Jake was back on their side at this crucial point, when the situation was slipping out of their control with each passing moment.

Now, focusing her attention entirely on the task at hand, she obediently followed Jake's instructions, holding her cell phone high and began to pan the camera gradually, capturing the high-rises, trees and other monuments surrounding the Red Fort, moving in a slow circle, sending a live feed to Jake's mobile.

ӁӁӁӁӁ

General Balbeer Singh was thwarted yet again when another video was streamed onto the huge screen installed below the rampart. Although he had ordered power to the screens to be cut off, this effort of his, like others earlier, had bit the dust.

On the huge screen, a familiar face came to life, of former IAF major, Rabindranath.

"Officer," the general screamed into his throat mike, "Why is it taking so long to shut-down that screen?"

"We have a serious problem, General," AD replied, sounding alarmed.

The general's hands trembled, sensing another failure.

Drawing a long breath, AD reported, "General, the screen has already been shutdown. But the video being streamed onto the screen is another projection. It's a 2D video, which, as per my best guess, is being projected by the same receiver which is simultaneously projecting the 3D holographic video on the rampart."

Holy Mother of God! The general helplessly observed the two projections, a 3D holographic video of the politician on the rampart and the 2D video on the screen, which were now being beamed from a single receiver, hidden somewhere in an undisclosed location around the venue.

Disquieted, he started ticking off the minutes before he and his secret cabal would be exposed and the beliefs of civilians trampled under the secret that was now being revealed.

CHAPTER 107

Still unaware of the crafty game that was evolving at the venue, the naïve crowd, shaken by the unprecedented sequence of events, silently watched the video being played on the huge screen below the rampart.

The power supply cut had angered national and private broadcasting channels holding the rights to the transmission of this monumental speech. Security officials did their best to control the miffed cameramen who continued to record the event.

The scene on the screen shifted to Major Rabindranath sitting on a couch, facing the camera. His furrowed eyes were soaked with vendetta and his lips quivered as he went on to unleash his poignant tale. He spoke in a modulated tone, revealing how the Indian government was running sinister, undercover projects disguised as research and development programs in the remote valleys of the Himalayas and how it was responsible for his family's death, which had been orchestrated as a warning to maintain silence over those secrets.

Rajat Singh joined General Balbeer Singh in the arena facing the rampart and the screen. Tears welled up in his eyes as he watched his dear friend Rabindranath, his now dead friend. He felt great sympathy for the man who had dug his own grave by agreeing to work with those who had actually orchestrated his and his family's death.

ЖЖЖЖЖ

Jake managed to glance back and forth from his cell phone screen to the road ahead, as he sped his car towards the Red Fort. He was meticulously scanning the live feed of the area around the venue that was being fed through Riya's cell phone.

"Is the angle of the view okay?" Riya asked, simultaneously panning the camera.

"Angle it up a little, "Jake instructed her. "Focus only on the tall buildings and structures."

"Okay."

The video panned delicately, starting from the point where the Lahori Gate of the Red Fort directly overlooked the large Jain Temple, also commissioned of red stone, looming behind the trees. The camera continued to gradually pan to the right, capturing flagpoles, trees, gas balloons suspended high in the sky and the broad road leading out of the venue before it stopped for a split second at the Lahori Gate itself, capturing the opposition leader looking down at the screen below the rampart.

Then, the focus continued onward, moving past the screens, flagpoles, gas balloons, Jama Masjid, trees, before reaching Jain temple, completing a three hundred sixty degree sweep, making it back at the point it had started.

"Pan it once more," Jake said letting out an unsatisfied breath. "I think I'm missing something here."

"Sure," Riya panned the camera again. But as she did, it was somewhere between the rampart of Lahori Gate and Jamma Masjid Jake noticed something unusual.

"Pause," Jake said abruptly. "Pan the camera back a little."

As she did, something that had drawn Jake's attention earlier appeared clearly.

"That's it!" Jake said aloud, exhilarated. "What's that?" Riya pressed.

"I got it," Jake said aloud. "But what is it, Jake?"

Jake's spoke fast. "I was right. Like I told you, it's indeed hidden in plain sight."

"Jake, we don't have much time left. Tell me and I'll set it right now."

"No, Riya. I'm responsible for this mess. Now, I get to bell the cat myself. Let me handle this. I'll fix it. Please."

After a prolonged silence, Riya agreed. "Okay. But know that we have no much time left. How far have you reached?"

"Two more minutes and I'll be there." He spoke hastily. "But I need a favor from you." He paused and added, "Actually, two."

"And what are those?"

"Steer clear the path along the main street of Chandni Chowk all the way up to the main entrance to the Red Fort." Jake said. "Right, now."

"And the other?" Riya pressed, waiting curiously. Jake divulged what he needed.

After a silent second, Riya, who found his demand a little strange, conceded, "Okay, you'll have it."

ӁӁӁӁӁ

AD found it hard to look at General Balbeer Singh's state, which seemed pathetic. A man who had always seemed undaunted and determined and audacious in the face of threat, was now standing with his hands folded and his once erect shoulders sagging in defeat.

He and his organization had endeavored for a lifetime to keep a secret from the eyes of the world and it was now about to be revealed before a large crowd, in fact, before the whole of the country and the world.

Sixty seconds ago, the crowd had witnessed a gruesome scene on the screen—several pictures of the mangled dead body of Major Rabindranath, seemingly involved in a road accident. Numerous brows in the crowd had rose in frowns and the simmering anger suggested they had believed Awasthi's claim that this was a conspiracy by the Indian government. They had no clue that Major Rabindranath's death was cleverly orchestrated by the CSETI to gain their favor.

"Dear friends," Ajeet Awasthi said, sweeping his glance across the crowd. "The major was one among those brave civilians who dared to go public despite knowing that he would be killed. And there are many crimes that have occurred out of our knowledge. One such incident had taken place in the very heart of our Delhi city. Three renowned Indian scientists were killed in broad day light and surprisingly, these ruthless homicides never came to light. Or say, they were not made to surface because our government is involved in this conspiracy. However, we have recovered those evidences for you all to see, for you all to lay your eyes upon what is being clandestinely orchestrated by our government." Ajeet Awasthi pointed to the screen at the slide show of crime scenes of three scientists.

First one revealed Anurag Chopra with knife stabbed in his gut, followed by that of Ramanujan lying face down in a pool of blood and then of Jaswanth Sinha smothered in blood. Noting down these horrific images, crowd let out a low cry.

Frown and disgust marked their faces.

"It's such a shame." Ajeet Awasthi said. "In the name of peace, the government is committing heinous crimes, inflicting terror on innocents, claiming the lives of those who demand transparency over our right to know what is being hidden out there in the Himalayas." Ajeet Awasthi broke off with an audible heavy sigh. "Yet, the truth can never be suppressed for long. The truth shall find a way to set itself free."

Amid this chaos, an event which has spiraled out of control was reaching its climax, AD's spirits surged on hearing that Jake was arriving at the venue.

Riya had informed him that Jake could probably lead them to the receiver the entire security force was still hunting for. AD kept himself abreast of the security team, preparing to clear a path for Jake from the crossroad of Chandni Chowk up till the venue.

Oblivious to the commotion up at the venue, the opposition leader's holographic image read out the story of Major Rabindranath to the crowd, relating how he was conspired against for recording the footage and leaving it for the world to see. Reflecting on his sacrifice with a few words of praise and condolence, he then proceeded to play the footage.

The footage gradually panned into the secret base, diving into the realms beneath the earth's crust and focusing on a lofty high-tech facility spearing outward from the cavern floor.

"This video was shot at a secret base in the deep valleys of Kongka La. It's one of the least accessed areas in the world and also, the most mysterious place on earth with China patrolling the other side. Any human activity and trespassing is forbidden here," Ajeet Awasthi narrated.

"You know why our government has, for decades, including that of China, has been reluctant to speak about this no man's land? Because there are more nations involved in this cover up." He looked across at the crowd, gravely, saying, "Well, the answer is right before your eyes."

"This hi-tech facility," he commented as the video feed showed the next scene, "huge and cavernous, almost four times the size of a soccer field, is built underground and consists of thousands of living quarters for scientists and employees, including advanced laboratories for carrying out secret research that appears grossly unconventional."

CHAPTER 108

The prime minister seemed appalled by this revelation.

Although, he held the most powerful position in this democratic country, he felt a stab of rage for being kept out of the loop of classified projects that were being operated covertly in the country.

The crowd seemed to feel disgust against the government, as they witnessed the grimmer aspect of the DIA, concealed in a hideout, away from human habitation, conducting research beneath the icy mountainous environs that they revered as holy.

"This visual is from one of the compartmentalized areas in the facility," Ajeet Awasthi continued as the scene shifted to humans in clinical scrubs, who bustled around the facility with outlandish machinery in the background. "This is a place where the classified experiments are conducted. Sophisticated aircraft and weapons are researched, built and tested. Around five thousand employees work in this facility. And their remuneration is five times than that of a top IIM graduate working in an MNC."

In the VIP section, the opposition party members were waiting for the entire video to be aired. Without any doubt, they knew the ruling government would soon stumble off its throne. Although they were drawing a fair amount of suspicious, anger-soaked stares from other party members, they masked their excitement by pretending to browse and talk on their cell phones.

"Dear friends, the government is shelling a whopping ten billion dollars annually for the maintenance and operation of this military installation alone," Ajeet Awasthi continued. "If this amount is put to appropriate use, it could cater to the common man's needs. Poverty can be driven from our midst and other critical issues like unemployment and inflation can be resolved."

ЖЖЖЖЖ

Down in the arena, all was set.

As per Jake's demand, the roads around Chandni Chowk had been emptied. Commandos skimmed the lanes, ensuring that no vehicles were present on the road, making space for Jake's car that would arrive at any moment.

But the last thing Jake had asked for had completely confused Riya.

She dropped her gaze to the weapon resting in the hands of a commando standing beside her: a PF-89 single-shot rocket launcher.

What is he planning to destroy with this powerful weapon? Riya thought, wondering what must have drawn Jake's attention where her own eyes had failed to spot the hidden receiver. Curiously, she flipped her cell open and replayed the feed she had sent to Jake's mobile some time ago. She fast forwarded the video up to the moment when Jake had insisted she roll back the camera. She watched that specific part of the video. From what she discovered, Jake's attention had wandered along the array of gas balloons suspended in the sky by thin strings tethered to the ground along the outer perimeter of the venue, flaring out in a semi-circle from the north to the south end of the Lahori Gate. She was playing the part of the video that panned south-west from the rampart of Red Fort, continuing onward.

Then she saw it too.

Oh My God! Riya felt her skin grow cold—the result of both, of excitement at spotting the anomaly and fear of what would come of it.

She abruptly turned, raising her sight to the array of gas balloons swaying high. Among the scores of balloons, one specifically stood out, completely still, not moving, as if a heavy metal ball was suspended in the air.

Before she could even react at having zeroed in on the location of the receiver which was placed in the gas balloon, she found herself instinctively turning back and looking across the venue at the loud revving sound of a Honda Civic hybrid, emerging out of the Chandni Chowk intersection and pacing swiftly towards the entrance.

A smiled creased her lips, instantly recognizing the car and the person inside it: Jake.

It was time to defend the nation from the enemy, she reminded herself. It was a time, she realized, that rarely comes in history, when the nation that had taken its civilians under its wings protecting them from countless moments of dangers, saving them from the enemy and proffering the security to lead a peaceful life, had now reached out to them to return the favor by saving it from the deep peril that was about to strike.

Squaring her shoulders, she lifted the rocket launcher from the commando's hand and sprinted in the direction of the entrance.

ӜӜӜӜӜ

Retreating into the control room, General Balbeer Singh cupped his face in his palms in dismay, watching the 2D footage unraveling on the screens outside in the venue. A searing pain seemed to envelop him. His hands shook when his relentless efforts seemed to have failed. The screen was showing a gathering of men, all garbed in ritualistic dark robes, having assembled in some kind of religious ceremony taking place within a dimly lit chamber.

He had never wished the eyes of the world upon the extraterrestrial humanoids. Neither had he imagined his oath of allegiance, the vow to secrecy about the presence of extraterrestrials, would be shattered. This secret, Balbeer Singh knew, had been one of the best guarded in the world…until now.

Balbeer Singh was nursing such despairing thoughts when Rajat Singh appeared in front of him, squeezing his shoulder, demanding his attention.

"You should see this, General," Rajat Singh said, drawing his eyes towards a screen in the corner that fed the live feed of the entrance to the venue.

Balbeer Singh leaned forward, watching the feed closely. What transpired on the screen took him by surprise. Riya running towards the entrance of the venue with a rocket launcher cradled in her hand, looking at a man sprinting across to her.

"Zoom in," he informed the security analyst, adjusting for a closer look. His eyes narrowed when he recognized the man.

Balbeer Singh turned to Rajat Singh in anger.

"What the hell are they up to?"

Rajat Singh said without looking at him, "They are up to destroying the hell itself."

ӜӜӜӜӜ

Jake felt a heavy rush of adrenaline discovering Riya sprinting in his direction with the rocket launcher he had asked for.

As he came to a stop by Riya, she extended the rocket launcher to him.

"This way," she said huffing, handing him the rocket launcher and guiding him along the outer perimeter of the venue, towards the right, facing the rampart. "You'll have a perfect vantage point along this path."

Jake smiled at her, accepting the weapon. He understood that she had located the source of crisis. The target: the gas balloon.

Jake gave a strong nod, thanking her for not acting on the target even after locating it, allowing him the privilege.

"Jake, you need to hurry," she reminded him. "Time is slipping."

Jake nodded and bolted along the outer perimeter of the venue of the Red Fort with the rocket launcher, past the commandos and security guards stationed along the outer perimeter.

In about ten seconds, Jake reached a point outside the venue from where he had a perfect view of the target: a gas balloon, suspended approximately two hundred meters above the ground.

He lifted his head to the target and ranged the rocket launcher, bolstering the long cylindrical body on his right shoulder.

A PF-89 single-shot rocket launcher is a class of shoulder-fired missile that has free-flight, is fin-stabilized and carries ammunition—rocket-type cartridge self-contained within a fiberglass-wrapped launch tube. It weighs only eight pounds and is designed such that when fired, the long cylinder tube expels the exhaust gas from the rear end of the launch tube, thus minimizing recoil.

Jake wrapped his left hand over the forward grip for maximum leverage and gripped the trigger with his right hand index finger. Staring through the launcher's scope, he raised it enough to place the crosshair in perfect alignment with the target.

Some two years ago, Jake had acquired sufficient training in handling ammunition of various kinds. It was meant to be training for preparedness in times of crisis. Although he had never handled a rocket launcher before, his training stood him in good stead.

Adjusting for a firm grip, Jake double-checked its range—two hundred meters. A vehement cry from the opposition leader and a low growl from the crowd filtered through his ears. He let it all fade into the background as he concentrated on the target.

Steadying his breath, Jake tightened his index finger over the trigger and squeezed it.

The projectile burst out of the launch tube with a sharp whistling scream and roared into the sky with a fiery tail, following a straight trajectory towards the target.

Due to the low recoil, although Jake staggered backward he was able to gain his balance after the backend of the launch tube spewed exhaust gases. His eyes were fixed on the trail of the projectile as it rammed into the gas balloon, exploding on contact.

There was a sharp explosion that shook the crowd.

The gas balloon erupted into flames, sending a fiery rain of debris down to the earth.

ӜӜӜӜӜ

There was a heavy outcry of joy within the control room as the demonic 3D holographic image of the politician Ajeet Awasthi and the deadly 2D video vaporized instantly.

Balbeer Singh switched his anxious glances between the screens that showed the live feed of the fiery explosion in the sky and the other one showing the rampart. With the explosion of the gas balloon, the 3D holographic image of the politician had vanished.

"Yes! He's done it," Rajat Singh cried aloud in excitement beside Balbeer Singh. "I knew he would do it."

ӜӜӜӜӜ

Though the impact had a small explosion radius in the sky, it was loud enough to have drawn the attention of all the eyes in the crowd. A stunned silence seeped through the crowd. While their eyes were still wide, trying to make sense of the nature of the blast, a screech of a mike had them all looking back at the rampart.

"This is the Red Fort security force," a demanding voice spoke. "The explosion in the sky was an accident, the result of a hydrogen gas balloon coming in contact with fire. There's no need to panic. The situation is under control."

The crowd, nevertheless, were caught off guard not over the explosion but at the sudden disappearance of the politician from the rampart and the blank screen that remained.

CHAPTER 109

Jake stood speechless down the rampart, facing the crowd. He tried to catch his breath after his short sprint from where he had fired the rocket launcher to the point down the rampart, in the arena, from where his six-foot tall frame was clearly visible to the crowd.

Seemingly determined, Jake skimmed his glance along the length of the crowd, as if he wanted to reach out to each one of them personally and convince them about what he was out here for, but he fell short of words.

ЖЖЖЖЖ

"Give him a mike," Balbeer Singh radioed from the control room to the security personnel out at the venue. Then he looked at the sound engineer. "Turn the volume up high," he said, before turning to the security analyst. "Power up the screens and bring his image up on the screens. Focus on him and telecast it on the national channel." He said with a renewed sense of energy. "I want the entire nation to watch him speak."

ЖЖЖЖЖ

Jake hesitated as he spoke into the mike. "The blast in the sky was not an accident. In fact, it was a small effort to save our nation from the doom that had almost struck."

The crowd murmured.

"It wasn't any terrorist attack, but it wasn't lesser than that either," Jake said, his breathing was shallow. "When people from our own country, bred on the very soil where we all belong try to betray our nation." He paused gathering his courage to speak before the humungous crowd. "And our opposition leader, sometime ago, accused our government of deception. He went on to show a confidential footage claiming the involvement of the government in running secret projects."

Jake steadied his breath. "If that was true, then he should've had the courage to stand before you all physically and speak."

The crowd began mumbling, unsure what to make of this.

"But he has tricked us all into believing that he was physically here, while the truth is that he was not. Through a receiver hidden in the gas balloon I blasted, he was telecasting a 3D holographic recorded footage, making us all believe he was actually here."

A low murmur rose among the crowd.

"Before you all begin to wonder at my identity and question my authority to speak here, I want to let you know that I'm son to one of the murdered victims whose images our opposition leader, Mr. Ajeet Awasthi, had shown on the screens." Jake informed the crowd that the murders were, indeed, part of conspiracy orchestrated by the opposition party and tricked them into believing the government was behind it.

"That's how we've been led astray all the time by these politicians." Jake said. "That's what they are good at. And sadly, that's where we Indians are weak. We let ourselves be deceived and tricked by these wolves, lurking in the shadows of this beautiful country. In the name of peace, unity and integrity, they make false promises. They are manipulating our innocence to quench their greed for power and wealth."

Jake paused, sweeping a glance over the venue. He was silently relieved that the crowd was now listening to him attentively. "However, I do not wish to waste your time. Not when there is this exuberant and jubilant mood of Independence Day, not by talking about some corrupt individual who like many others down the decades, has done nothing other than pilfer the country of its grace, pride and dignity, marring the wonderful achievements of our great leaders from the past and laying their endeavors to waste.

"But I want to remind you that the opposition leader Ajeet Awasthi tried to show good things in a bad light. He wanted to compromise our sensitive military data by means of treachery." He paused and took a deep breath. "If that gas balloon containing the receiver had not been destroyed, then our nation's security would have been compromised. He put our country's arsenal, developed over decades of research and development, at huge risk by sacrificing it on the altar of supposed transparency. He was trying to expose us to our enemy. In a way, he was making us vulnerable to threats from neighboring countries, allowing them a chance to have a fair idea of our strengths and weakness."

Jake was silent for a long intense moment before continuing. "If he says that our government is wasting taxpayers' money for funding these classified projects, I don't agree with him." He seemed incredulous. "I'm a taxpayer too. I have never felt that our government is misusing my money. What concerns me most is my security. It is of utmost importance to me and to you all."

Jake pondered how his own opinions on this matter had changed from the last time it was discussed, with Balbeer Singh at the secret base in Kongka La.

"I'm an ordinary man and come from a family like you all. I work nine to five to earn my bread. In other words, you can all look at me as one among you." His voice grew softer. "I love my country because I feel safe and secure on this soil. And that's because I have someone who ensures my safety, guarding the borders of our country so that I live in peace and joy."

The crowd, the 'someones' that Jake referred to, understood that he was talking about them: the Indian soldiers.

Jake still couldn't believe that his view on the classified project had changed so drastically. He found it hard to swallow the thought that he was in a way helping the DIA to keep the secret buried, to close the lid over what he had thought was not right. But his father required him to do so. Not for any individual, but for the country and for the welfare of mankind.

"Don't you love your country the way I do? Don't you all wish your country to be safe and secure?"

The crowd remained quiet, reflecting on his question. "Dear friends, if not now, then never. This is the time to ask ourselves that how much do we all love our country?"

He paused for the crowd to give the question some thought.

"Be thankful to God that your children are not forced to hold weapons instead of toys. Be grateful that your mother, father, sisters, brothers and wives enjoy a life that's far from the rule of militants who wage war in the name of religion. And that's because of our brave Indian *jawans*, our gallant soldiers, who guard us from dangers. They stay awake during freezing nights, patrolling our borders, bearing extreme climatic conditions so that we sleep in peace.

"So, if our government allocates a chunk of its budget for improving the defense system of our country, what wrong do you seen in that? All their efforts, be it a massive budget allocation or running secret projects, are aimed at ensuring the safety of those who are guarding our peace." He was silent for a few seconds. "Our government is protecting those who protect us."

Jake looked at the crowd somberly, making sure his point heard across. "Every country maintains silence over their defense systems. They have protocols in place which ensure that sensitive data on strategic plans and the development and implementation of technologically advanced weapons systems remains privy to their own defense organization. That way, every country is immune to attacks from their enemies." He paused again. "And our government has done what was needed to be done to preserve classified projects, keeping it from the common mans knowledge.

"I believe that you all are wise enough to ignore the manipulations of the opposition leader. You are educated enough to differentiate bad from good and right from wrong." The crowd was silent.

"Our great grandfathers lived the lives of slaves for decades. Let that not happen to us all again. We have freedom of speech. Speak your mind, see things the way they are and act accordingly. Never let these hypocrites ride your mind."

Jake looked across at the crowd. "That is all I had to say. And yes, I love my country. I'm proud of my brave *jawans*. And I look up to my government with deep respect, because the work of the government is the work of God." He went silent for a beat. Then he turned toward the rampart, looking high over at the national flag fluttering beautifully in the breeze. Loudly and in high spirits, he saluted the Indian flag, voicing fervently, "Jai Hind!"

And, clicking off the mike, he stood there silently watching the crowd for a long beat, before weaving his way out through the crowd toward the exit.

CHAPTER 110

All is well that ends well.

The popular proverb was fitting, after the turbulence at the historic arena of Red Fort simmered down to normalcy.

Finally, the prime minister felt some relief. He was back on the ramparts and stood before the same crowd, who over the past thirty minutes had been taken on a roller coaster ride of unprecedented events. From the dais, the head of State resumed his interrupted speech.

"I have nothing much to say. Not after what the young man, Mr. Jake Stevens—a simple man with extraordinary vision and perception— had to say." He pursed his lips thoughtfully. "To be honest, even I, at some point of the opposition leader's speech, was carried away by his assertions. I felt offended that I had been left out of the loop on certain classified projects. Then, Jake Stevens helped me see things through his eyes. I felt again the love for my nation through his heart. I'm glad that on this day, I got to hear a determined and diligent voice that resonates with such passionate enthusiasm for our country. It is a great honor for me to witness such an event during my tenure."

Down in the arena, General Balbeer Singh strode past security officials in pursuit of Jake, who was moving towards the exit. The prime minister had shown a keen interest in meeting Jake and congratulating him for the role he had played. But soon after addressing the crowd, Jake had walked off. He strode towards the main entrance, to where he had parked his car.

Now quite close, Balbeer Singh called out to Jake.

Jake stopped and turned to face him. The look of seriousness was still on his face.

"The prime minister wants to have a word with you in private."

In the background the voice of the prime minister resonated through the speakers.

"My dear brothers and sisters, seventy one years ago, great men gave their lives to secure our freedom. And today, on this day of independence, a gentleman has fought to set us free from our delusions.

This day, in the truest sense, is a day of independence. We have been freed from our false beliefs, from disloyalty, from the domination of immorality and from the bondage of our irrational minds."

Blocking the sound from his ears, Jake concentrated on something that was weighing on his mind heavily.

"My father was not a traitor," Jake said with severity. "He was a man with extraordinary vision. A vision that made me save you from the crisis that otherwise would have struck you and your secret cabal today."

The general was surprised. *He knows about our cabal?*

Jake read his confusion but didn't wish to drag it on. "And it's because of my father that the country that would have been shredded into disharmony by now, remains in tranquility."

Fixing him with a serious stare, Jake turned and walked out of the arena.

General Balbeer Singh went stone cold. Had Jake's father George Stevens recovered something more from the ruins of the monastery? Apart from providing a clue on the secret of extraterrestrials, did this also mention their cabal—the ancient and oldest brotherhood in the world: The Brotherhood of the Serpent?

CHAPTER 111

Wednesday, August 16, 2017,
1.30 PM.

Jake sipped his fourth mug of coffee, settled in a restaurant, hoping the excess intake of caffeine would give extra boost to his central nervous system, making it more alert to the unanswered questions that continued to torment him.

The previous day, after exiting the Red Fort arena, Jake had enjoyed a day of solitude. Switching off from the world, worries and tasks, he had severed all means of communication with the CBI temporarily, retiring into his apartment.

That's how it had always been, taking time for himself. In solitude, he would reflect upon all that agitated him. He would shake the sting of it, mend shattered nerves and then recuperate.

But last night, it had been a tad difficult. When the entire nation retreated to bed in peace, he lay on his back on his bed, staring at the ceiling. The whole day's events cascaded over him, flashing past in quick succession before his eyes, one frame after the other—scenes that had moved him deeply, disturbing him.

He tossed and turned on the bed. Yet, he couldn't dodge the worries that came spinning back at him like a returning boomerang. One thought that dominated over all the other was of a priceless artifact that he had left locked in the safe in the wake nation calling him: the metal chest.

He could still smell the ancientness of the metal chest and feel it the mysterious insignia of the brotherhood carved deeply into the metal chest, under his fingers. A symbol within a symbol: a hexagram star inscribed with a snake feeding on its own tail.

As he pondered, its mysteriousness was quickly replaced by another mystery: Taneez.

Had she safely reached Boston? Why did she leave me with a contact number that doesn't exist? The questions continued.

This morning, when he got back in touch with the world the first thing he heard on his answering machine was a recorded message from Riya. The message said that opposition leader Ajeet Awasthi had been nabbed by the CBI in close vicinity of the Red Fort when he tried sneaking out in the dark of night. He seemed to have been holed up in an underground bunker from where he was controlling the relay of the footage. Further interrogation served no purpose as he accepted that the disc was now under the control of CSETI.

The message had caused Jake deep unease. The brain behind the conspiracy, the supposed Master behind the murders and the one who had called his mother Katherine on that fateful night was still missing. There was no clue on this man in the Intelligence.

As he sipped from his mug, a message popped into his cell phone with a beep.

He checked and found a message from the bank manager of State Bank of India, Mr. Melkundi, requesting him for an urgent call back.

Jake feared that if Melkundi had discovered the metal chest. He stabbed the buttons on his phone and called the manager. After several rings, Melkundi answered.

"Jake? Where are you? I tried to get in touch with you yesterday."

Sensing the apprehension in his voice, Jake pressed immediately,

"What's the matter?"

"I have something important that might interest you."

Jake felt his head throb, wondering if he had left the locker with the metal chest inside it unlocked when he'd hastened out of the vault yesterday, which the bank manager might have later discovered. With his pulse racing, he tried to maintain his composure as he spoke, "What is it?"

"You remember our first meeting? I told you there was a stranger who sought access to your father's safe soon after his death?"

"Yes," Jake replied, recalling the man he suspected might be behind the mysterious phone call to his mother. "What about him?"

"I saw him yesterday."

"What?" Jake blurted out, unable to control his surprise. "Where is he? What does he look like?"

There was a long silence and then the manager said, "Why don't you see for yourself?"

Jake waited for him to elaborate.

"I took a picture of him on my phone. He was out with two men. I'm sending his picture to you right now."

A minute after Melkundi hung up, Jake was looking at an image on his cell phone's screen. The image revealed three men, one of whom Melkundi had circled, obviously the stranger who had paid him a visit insisting on access to Jake's father's safe.

But Jake's attention immediately drifted to another individual in the image, a figure in the background to the extreme right, someone well known to Jake.

What the hell is he doing with them? Jake was unable to suppress his shock. *Which means*.....Things became clear and he saw it in new light. *Son of a bitch!*

ӜӜӜӜӜ

"Who is this man?" Riya asked, raising her brows suspiciously.

Soon after seeing the image, Jake made sense of everything; the face of deception that had been in the shadows for over two decades was finally out in front of him with striking clarity. He felt paralyzed by the gravity of the revelation. The face he had always admired had a dark side to it. Realizing this, he had reacted on impulse and had immediately contacted Riya, asking her to join him on the way. Also placing a call to the CBI to dispatch an armed force to clean up one last mess that had been pending for a very long time—the Master, the missing piece of the puzzle behind the operation, *The Lost Arcanum.*

"He's Athar Khan," Jake answered, adding, "one of the men from that shadowy organization. He was found murdered the same day Major Rabindranath was killed in a road accident. Though his body was found drowned in a drain."

Riya analyzed the image and asked, "If he's dead then what is still bothering you, Jake?" She took in his furious expression. "What is it Jake? Where are we headed to?"

"Look to his left," Jake said, clarifying, "to the extreme right corner."

When Riya did, her eyes gaped wide. "This is unbelievable." Shell-shocked, Riya was now staring at Jake's cell phone screen, at Master, the mastermind behind the conspiracy. "I can't believe it's him," she said in awe, turning to Jake. "I can't imagine him in this disguise."

Now with the trap in place and the CBI backup team keeping close behind them, he cautiously maneuvered his car and brought it to a slow stop, killing the engine before a magnificent mansion situated in another upper-class locality in the suburbs of New Delhi: Hauz Khas.

CHAPTER 112

A *torturous pang* of disgust constricted Jake from within, as he struggled to swallow the truth that the man he had trusted so blindly had stabbed him in his back.

Riya, was disturbed as well. She couldn't imagine that this man's elementary appearance of moral excellence concealed a dark and terrible disloyalty and betrayal.

They alighted from the car, ensuring minimal noise and headed straight to the main door, passing through the unmanned entrance gate. At the doorstep, Jake pushed the door bell and waited.

He frowned at Riya as she held in position a 0.75 caliber gun. "It's too early for that," he said, motioning for her to lower it. "We've got to give him a chance to make his last wish."

She holstered her gun in her waist belt.

The door opened. An old man with sagging skin inquired into the identity of the guests on the doorstep. Then an uncertain flickering of lashes was followed and recognition flared in his old eyes. He cast a welcoming smile and ushered them in.

Many times in the past, Jake and Riya had visited this mansion and had been served by the same servant. Now, they inquired into his well-being as he served them with water and disappeared upstairs to inform the owner of their visit.

Sitting back in the luxurious lounge, they took in the remarkable interiors of the bungalow. The lobby, more like an art gallery, was embellished with canvases along the walls, illuminated with sparkling golden light from a beautiful, intricately designed chandelier. The stained glass windows and marble spiral staircase with oak railings, added to the grace of the interiors.

"A gift from CSETI," Jake announced to Riya, hinting at the assets.

Footfalls on the stairs drew their attention. When they turned, the man, decked in his usual professional attire, walked down the stairs, wearing a pleasant smile, "This is a surprise."

Jake picked up a hint of apprehension and anxiety in his faltering voice.

The man walked over and took a seat in front of them.

"What you would like to have?" he asked, smiling, trying his best to conceal his concern over their sudden appearance at his place. But Jake still saw that raw fear in his eyes.

"Nothing, thanks!" they refused in unison and smiled, as if they were here on some official business rather than one of the many casual visits they had paid earlier.

Seemingly relieved by their responses, the man pressed. "So what brings you here? I mean…" he faltered and re-phrased, "You could have visited my office if the matter wasn't urgent instead of travelling all the way here."

Jake understood the man's eagerness to learn the reason of their visit. He took a deep breath and meeting his gaze head on, said tersely, "Your cover is blown."

The man said nothing, still weighing what he had heard. "You have been exposed," Jake repeated.

"I beg your pardon," the man tried to feign ignorance. "What are you talking about?"

Jake breathed noisily. "What would you liked to be called? Master? The one responsible for orchestrating the operation, The Lost Arcanum? Or would you still wish to be known by your old identity, Mr. Ravi Raj?"

ӁӁӁӁӁ

With his fake identity torn apart and his cover blown, there was nothing the attorney Ravi Raj could do. Sweat beaded on his forehead and fear of exposure was imminent in his eyes.

"You claimed to be the dearest friend of my father," Jake said staring at him contemptuously, "But you stabbed him right in his back?"

Ravi Raj grew anxious. He stumbled as he rose from the sofa.

Jake and Riya were alert at once, but held back when they saw Ravi Raj trying to steady himself and advance towards the mini bar, where he poured out a drink.

Strangely, when he turned, he was smiling cunningly.

He let out a soft chuckle, sipped his drink and asked, "Am I not a good actor?"

He casually walked to the sofa and dropped into it. "No matter how cautiously I guarded my objectives and covered my tracks, you wolves somehow sniffed it out. But this time, I will not repeat…"

"You called my mother that night," Jake cut him off. "Why did you wish their separation?"

The attorney was silent.

"He trusted you more than anyone else." Jake was gritting his teeth. "Why did you do this to my father? Damned!"

The attorney placed the glass on the table and threw a glance at Riya before fixing it on Jake. "It all started fifteen years ago, when your father introduced me to your mother, Katherine. She was beautiful. I fell in love with her."

Jake was stunned.

"I desired her intensely but she was faithful to your father. And I disliked that."

Jake tightened his fist. Sensing his fury, Riya placed her hand on his shoulder, urging him to keep calm.

"Everything changed when your father invited me for a drink to his home. In a drunken stupor, your father confessed to having recovered some scrolls that contained a devastating truth. He cited something about The Lost Arcanum, the footage that was evidence to the presence of extraterrestrials in India. I tried to squeeze more information out of him, but he never brought up that matter again.

"I hadn't taken it seriously until three years ago,, when I came into contact with CSETI. When I understood what the organization was about, I met the panel members in Washington DC for further discussions. We needed heavy funding to blow the cover off the secret and that's where Ajeet Awasthi, the opposition leader, stepped in. And this is how the operation, The Lost Arcanum, began."

Jake knew that *The Lost Arcanum* was not just about extraterrestrials as the attorney had assumed. It was, indeed, something more, about a link to the arcane repository of forbidden knowledge that was hidden from the world and that except him, no one knew.

"I saw that operation as an opportunity and called your mother Katherine that night, instilling a seed of suspicion about his extra-marital affair with Eileen, although he never had one. I thought that in doing so, I could accomplish two goals. By isolating your father from his family, I would give him my shoulder to lean on in his solitude and get him to speak about the secret again. But he never did. He gave up his life, but did not reveal the secret that he guarded.

"After George had deserted you both, I thought Katherine would be mine. But she remained faithful to your father even through her death.

"I didn't achieve my goals, but I discovered that apart from your father, Ramanujan, Anurag Chopra and Jaswanth Sinha had also known about the secret. I got them killed one by one. Strangely, all of them gave up their lives but did not reveal a word about The Lost Arcanum."

Jake and Riya listened, as he continued.

"The only way left for me was to check your father's lockers with the State Bank of India—another possible location where I thought I could find some clue to the secret. But the person I had sent was denied access. I came to you with the will. I was sure you would at least look into it once, which you later did. But by then, the operation had begun. The rest is history." The attorney shook his head. "As for now, you both will see what will happen."

Sensing that he was up to something fishy, Jake and Riya instantly drew their guns from their holsters and brandished them in his direction, only to realize they were too late. They already had gun muzzles nudging their skulls from behind.

Behind them, two armed thugs had emerged stealthily and caught them on point blank.

A scornful, devilish laugh escaped the attorney's lips. "Any last wish?"

The answer came from somewhere far behind. "Yes."

The response drew everyone's eyes to the main door that burst open with armed men from the CBI pouring into the hall swiftly. Using the distraction, Jake and Riya snapped the guns from the thugs, gripping them by their arms and yanking them by force, making them fly over the sofa in a semi-circle and crash to the floor.

The attorney reached for his own gun, but Rajat Singh stepped into view from the shadows and dispatched it to the floor with a single shot from his pistol.

The CBI team pinned the thugs face down on the floor, fastening their arms behind their backs.

"If you think the game is over," AD warned the attorney gravely, "then you're wrong."

Ravi Raj took a step back, his eyes filled with fear.

"Not until...now," AD said leveling his gun at the attorney and emptying three bullets into his chest until the man's hefty frame slipped to the floor and lay still.

Jake and Riya walked around to AD and watched the attorney lying face down on the floor, blood seeping out from his chest.

With three bullets buried in his chest, his years of corrupt, immoral practices came to an abrupt end that would stretch for eternity.

CHAPTER 113

7.20 PM.

Jake gave his formal attire a last once-over in the rear-view mirror, as he steered his limo into the forecourt of Rashtrapathi Bhavan.

Ahead of him, a sprawling tarmac beckoned, with a Jaipur column at its center, royally piercing the magnificent skyline of the nation's capital. Beyond it, the dome of the main structure of Rashtrapathi Bhavan, once home to the viceroy of India, dazzled, appearing colossal, almost like the Capitol Building of Washington DC.

Both the structures symbolized power and freedom.

He pulled his car into the parking space and killed the engine. Ensuring he was carrying his off-white cashmere blazer on a silky black shirt and trousers quite elegantly, he slipped out of his car and walked to the main entrance of the building.

The facade of the Rashtrapathi Bhavan is supported by massive colonnades under which a flight of long and broad alabaster stairs overlooks the forecourt. Threading his way through the portico, he arrived at the reception, where he was photographed and given an entry pass. As he moved onward, he passed by the Marble Hall and then the Durbar Hall which was situated directly under the dome. Many head honchos from the corporate and industrial world matched his pace, presumably to the same venue.

Another minute of walking brought him to the threshold, where a security guard held the door open, ushering him into the Ashoka Hall.

During colonial rule, this hall had served as the ballroom for the viceroys. It was a beautiful hall with a wooden floor, vaulted lobbies of grayish marble and a gallery on the east. The large paneled mirrors and chandeliers bathed the hall with a vibrant golden glow. The overall effect charmed Jake as he stepped in and strode the length of the hall.

Jake was told big names from different walks of life peppered the hall along with foreign delegates and dignitaries for whom the Indian government had arranged a small get-together post the Independence Day celebrations.

Jake couldn't dodge cursory glances from guests as he wove through them, making his way deeper into the hall. Some recognized him from his heroic act yesterday at the Red Fort, while others simply stole a momentary glimpse of him, before returning to their drinks and conversations.

Off to a side, he found a gathering of men and women. Even from this distance, Jake could recognize the person who stood with his back to him: Rajat Singh, in a neatly pressed navy blue suit.

Jake breathed a sigh and a thin smile of relief creased his lips on finding AD. He was worried he would be lost diving into this vast sea of big-shots.

Surprisingly, in the very next moment, his smile evaporated and his footsteps slowed down, coming to a stop as AD turned to him, smiled and then gingerly stepped aside, allowing him to see a couple of foreign delegates.

A look of disbelief masked Jake's expression as he noted the duo. A sturdy framed English man clad in a tuxedo was flanked by a familiar woman. In a delicate sequin-embellished one-shoulder black gown hemmed to a fish tail, she looked stunning. Her hair was swept to one side, showing off the asymmetric style of her dress.

He looked between them and then at AD who did not seem to have realized that Jake already knew one of the duo. AD cleared his throat and introduced, "Meet Mr. Raynard Wulff."

Mr. Raynard Wulff was of German descent, six feet tall with blonde hair, yet his high cheekbones made him look more like a Native American.

But Jake's attention was fixed on his companion, the lady in the black gown.

Noting which, AD said, "And this is Zeenat. They have come from Boston on research work. They are guests of General Balbeer Singh."

Jake didn't smile. He remained serious, his eyes showed no signs of geniality.

AD was surprised but didn't give it much thought. He excused himself and walked Mr. Raynard Wulff to a small group to one side to introduce him to other guests.

Zeenat stood there, trying her best to avoid Jake's fierce gaze. The awkwardness of silence was weighing on her shoulders, that she attempted to break. "Nice to see you again, Jake."

Jake took a deep breath and said, "Excuse me."

He then turned and strode away, leaving her alone amid the chaotic murmur of the guests.

She didn't make an attempt to stop him as she had expected this reaction.

Exiting the Ashoka Hall, he emerged into the loggia, which overlooked the amazing Mughal Gardens. This place, which is often used to serve tea for guests after functions in the Ashoka Hall, now wore a deserted look, providing him the moment of privacy he needed given that he had been shaken to the core having learnt something he never expected.

Basking in the silence of the lobby, he watched some unique pieces of furniture on display, before he turned to face the Mughal Gardens to his right. Home to some of the largest varieties of flowers, Mughal Gardens modeled after Persian style architecture garden forms an enormous stretch of beautiful tulips, large dahlias, roses of numerous colors, lilies and the rare, bright Iris. Unfortunately, the cocktail of beauty and color was now dulled by the night sky.

A light rustle drew his attention.

Zeenat arrived beside him and watched the splendor of the Mughal Garden at rest.

"This place is peaceful."

"It is," Jake said plainly.

"Listen, I'm sorry," Zeenat began, "I know I shouldn't have lied to you, but I have reasons of my own."

"But that doesn't explain why you had to fake your name to me," Jake interrupted her. "Just read your name backward and there we have Taneez, whom I met. The one who I thought was honest with me."

She stole her gaze away, feeling low. "I'm sorry."

She took a step to leave, but Jake held her hand. "What made you lie to me?"

She faced him with her eyes lowered, accepting her mistake.

"You know something," Jake said, clasping her hand between his palms tightly. "I missed you a lot. I just can't explain what I went through when you left me with a wrong number."

She remained quiet. Her eyes were still trained on the ground.

Slipping his other hand around her waist, he gently pulled her closer, until she was close enough to feel his whisper on her skin. She twisted in his arms, trying to wriggle free herself. Then, she gave up in submission, as if she found the solace there she had longed for ages. She relinquished herself to the warmth of his embrace.

"I always wanted to tell you this," Jake leaned closer, his lips closing in on hers. "I need you."

She closed her eyes, feeling his warm breath bristle her skin. "Taneez," Jake said leaning even closer, his lips almost touching hers, "I..."

Zeenat forced him away, twisting from his grips, turning her back to him. Jake was not surprised by her behavior as he had expected this.

She was now breathing fast, her heart pounding. "This can't happen between us."

"Why?" Jake insisted. "Why can't this happen between us?"

She took a troubled breath and replied, "You and I can't be together, Jake. We're not destined for each other. We're from different worlds and cultures. And the distance between us is far greater than you can imagine."

Jake let out a faint smile of pity, as if he was not expecting this reaction from her. "It's sad to see you restrict me by physical boundaries."

Zeenat did not reply.

"No matter how distant our worlds are," Jake insisted, "But I would still want to..."

"Heaven and earth," Zeenat said, almost a loud, "that's the distance between us. You cannot fill that gap."

Jake smirked in disbelief. He had never expected that Zeenat held such opinions that created a rift between two people in the name of religion and the superficiality of materialistic aspects. Her actions suggested that she didn't wish to stretch the matter anymore. Neither had she liked what he wanted. Maybe she did not nurture the same feelings for him that he had for her.

As they both stood there in the deserted lobby, trying to undo the unease from the last minute, a distant and hollow silence stretched between them.

Zeenat gazed at the Mughal Garden, her thoughts far away. Deep inside, she struggled against this fragile situation. She knew she was losing herself entirely to Jake. She never wanted to let this happen to her. Yet, some feelings had accumulated like water in a reservoir. A single crack through the wall was enough to send the barrier collapsing and the water flooding the landscape. Something similar was now happening to her. Despite her best efforts to curb her feelings, her emotional barrier had finally burst open, flooding her feelings.

"If you think I'm being immodest, superficial and narrow minded, then you're wrong." She gasped shaking her head. "It only shows you didn't understand me. From the day I met you, I was attracted to you. There was something in you, a spark that kept me close to you. And I realized this when you left me in the middle of the journey and went on your own to complete what you'd started."

She paused as she stared into the vibrant skyline of Delhi. "And there was a reason I gave you a non-existent contact number. I never wanted to get in touch with you again. I know it sounds strange, but I didn't want to be in a relationship that has no future. Moreover, you don't know who I am and where I come from." Zeenat broke off briefly, wondering if Jake understood her. "I feared that I would lose myself to you, melt in your arms. And I didn't want this to happen to me."

Zeenat felt his warm hand touching her shoulder, giving a soft squeeze that held the promise of a lifetime and the assurance that they were made for each other. He leaned over and kissed the nape of her neck. She felt a sensual shiver down her spine. She fought the urge to retreat back into his arms, which assured her solace for eternity.

"Please, go away." It was a passionate whisper. "I don't want to break in your arms. I'm too fragile. Please leave me alone."

She found his arms curling over her waist Unable to suppress her long hidden feelings anymore, she twisted on impulse and leaned her head against his chest, "I need you too," she whispered and then hugged him tight, breaking into tears. "I love you and I want you."

"I was expecting this, honey."

The response rocked her as she rested in his arms, her teary eyes now wide. It was not the reply that shook her, but the familiarity of the voice.

Stunned, she forced herself out of his embrace and found staring directly into the familiar features of Mr. Raynard Wulff.

He smiled. "I was waiting for this moment."

Zeenat couldn't believe that this was happening to her. She looked over his shoulder, searching for Jake, but found that he was gone, suggesting that he might've left even before he'd learnt about her feelings.

Raynard Wulff drew her back into his arms, averring, "Once we're back in Boston, we'll exchange rings."

Sad that her feelings had gone unheard, she remained in his arms against her will. She knew she didn't belong there. Neither did she have any feelings for this man, nor would she ever.

Resting in his embrace, her heart yearned for nothing but the one man she truly loved: Jake.

CHAPTER 114

Jake wiped away a small drop of tear that trickled down his eyes. If the pain from his feelings was so excruciating and bitter, he wished he had never had them for someone who built walls on the basis of races.

Lying on the bed staring at the roof, he could not help but revisit all the moments he had lived with Taneez on their journey from Srisailam till they parted ways at Delhi airport.

Surprisingly, he couldn't recall even a single moment on their journey when he had felt that she was holding such opinions, of those that brought rift between the loved ones on the basis of old held beliefs of racial supremacy.

Those were the opinions born of him misconstruing Taneez. If only he knew that Taneez also shared his feelings and never built any walls on the basis of racial status or religion as he had perceived.

It was neither of their faults.

The fault was in the timing, in the transit of their stars, making their fate too unfortunate to bring them together, bind them with the bond of love. If he had delayed his exit from the lobby by a minute, he would have discovered her feelings. Probably, she would have been in his arms, confessing her emotions for him.

But that was a possibility that didn't come to pass.

ӁӁӁӁӁ

Splashing cold running water into her eyes, Zeenat turned off the faucet, trying to blink away Jake's image that persistently formed under her eyelashes that refused to fade.

One that she now realized kept recurring more out of a deep emotional bond that had shaped up unknowingly between them than just out of each others company.

"Are you okay, honey?" a voice inquired from the living room outside.

"Yes, dad," Zeenat reassured, her voice wavering, choked of emotion.

After leaving Rashtrapathi Bhavan halfway through the gathering, his father had drove her back to hotel room with his fellow man and Raynard Wulff. She had excused herself from the group in the room outside on the pretext to freshen up but her father seemed to have sensed her mental turmoil, wondering at the cause behind her sudden emotional breakdown.

She splashed more water on her face, pulled a towel from the stand and dabbed it all over, ensuring no signs of her mental turmoil reflected in her eyes.

When she walked back to join the group, she found Raynard Wulff handing over glass of drinks, one each to her father and to the other man.

Her father, Lukas Covitz, the Grand Master of the secret brotherhood of the Serpent, sat across from the other man.

Balbeer Singh.

The Director General of Defense Intelligence Agency.

He sat on the plush spread of sofa, legs crossed, his neatly pressed dark brown suit adding a sparkle of dignity to his demeanor.

"I savored Jake's reaction spotting you with great delight." Balbeer said, smiling widely. "As if ground beneath his legs was swept." he paused and said, "Or say, resembling a mouse snatched off a pie of cheese."

Zeenat didn't react. Her stoic expression, clearly indicated she had disliked the statement made against Jake.

"Ah yes," her father interjected, identifying it, saving her from the awkwardness, "why don't you take off some time for yourself. A walk out on the terrace, I suppose, would do the magic."

Zeenat looked at her father, knowing he wanted to salvage her from this moment.

Nodding, casting a long serious stare at Balbeer, she excused herself. "I'd better go get some fresh air."

ӜӜӜӜӜ

With a terrible heartache, he stared into the deep void of loneliness that had formed before his eyes. Losing someone was a great agony. He had lost all those he had loved the most—his father, his mother and now, Taneez. They had all departed from him on a path that held no promise of return. That's how life had always been. Dreams and hopes never came with a promise, but with a price tag of pain that one would endure all their life.

Letting the realization dawn, he tried to close his eyes and sleep, only to find her face forming under his eyelids, replaying the last memory of her pushing away his arms after he had revealed his feelings for her. He already knew her answer when she parted her lips in denial, but in those blue eyes of hers, he had seen a hint of a lie lingering, which unnerved him.

He replayed the entire conversation, going over every word she had said.

You and I can't be together, Jake. We're from different worlds and cultures.

And the distance between us is far greater then you can imagine.

"No matter how distant our worlds are." Jake had insisted, "But I would still want to..."

"Heaven and earth," she had interrupted, "that's the distance between us. You cannot fill that gap," she had said impassively.

Heaven and earth, Jake thought, feeling sad. If she had so desired, he could have even made heaven and earth one. But she didn't need that. And her stoic expression was proof of that.

Heaven and earth, he recalled her words again, realizing how it echoed the Hermetic axiom, *'As above...So below'* also reflecting the Star of David, two independent superimposed triangles which when pulled apart, meant heaven and earth.

Abruptly, he sat upright in bed, shaking his head, trying to understand if that was what she had meant, the Star of David, when she had cited heaven and earth, which was a vast, immeasurable and unbridgeable gap.

Intrigued, he slipped out of bed and walked over to the table where he had kept the letter his father had bequeathed him.

Yesterday, in the rush to save his country from peril, he had abandoned the letter halfway through. Now as he reached for it, her lines resounded in his ears. We're from different worlds and cultures. And the distance between us is far greater than you can imagine.

What had she meant? Was she talking in metaphors or in a literal sense? As the questions nagged at him, he opened the letter and resumed from where he had stopped.

The symbol of Ouroboros—the snake feeding on its own tail—and the geometrical pattern of two, inverted, superimposed triangles were altered through the course of history by many clandestine societies and religions across the world to fit their own belief systems, further corrupting their true meaning. Various faiths referred to the Ouroboros as a 'tail eater', which signified bodily birth followed by bodily death and then rebirth, or simply, renewal, infinity and eternity. But this symbol originally stood for the Biblical serpent and a reminder of mankind's disobedience, which caused the fall of humanity from grace.

The six-pointed hexagram was an archetypal sign of the sacred union of opposite energies. The upward triangle symbolized matter rising into spirit, while the downward triangle meant spirit descending into manifestation. If the intertwining of these triangles signified Yin and Yang in Chinese philosophy, also appearing in the seal of Solomon and on a dollar bill, forming a secret icon of Freemasonry, it also stood for the cosmic dance of Shiva and Shakti. But it was popularly known as the Star of David.

Although it was known by many names across cultures, with variations in its significance and meaning, it was mightier and darker than what we all thought we had known about its origin. It was inconceivable until one knew to gaze at the night sky and spot a precise star.

The star which guided you in your quest, acting as a guidepost through its various interpretations, 'As above... So below', as the upright triangle of Fire and the downward triangle of Water, serving as markers for four cardinal directions, pointing to Kongka La—the hiding place of the Elohims on earth, is the same star that also points to their home in the sky.

In actuality, the Star of David is a map, a star map.

A map? Surprise knocked off Jake's senses. *The star is a map?*

The six-pointed star is a star map. It leads to the actual home of Elohim, out there in space, to a star where they came from.

CHAPTER 115

Pieces were finally falling into place.

Each fragment of the historical symbol, the six-pointed hexagram, emerged out from the shadows into the light, completing the final jigsaw puzzle offering up the factual meaning of a popular event from the Bible that had baffled the world for over two millennia.

The six-pointed hexagram symbol had been a recurring theme across all cultures and civilizations in human history.

Jake began to work on the schematics of the hexagram star, grabbing a blank sheet and pencil from the desk.

In Judaism, this star was known as Magen David—meaning, *The Shield of David*. And in Arabic literature by Kabbalists, it was used in segulot – a talismanic protective amulet known as *Seal of Solomon*. Later in seventeenth century, it became widespread in European countries and came to be associated with Jews who used it to mark their synagogues as a place for Jewish worship.

Today, however, after thousands of years, the same star seemed to have a different connotation, one that was steeped in mystery. Had it slipped from the annals of history, or perhaps was purposely been made to as it carried an encrypted message about our origins?

To prove its validity, Jake completed the first draft of how the star would appear if the two inverted superimposed triangles were pulled apart until it looked something like this:

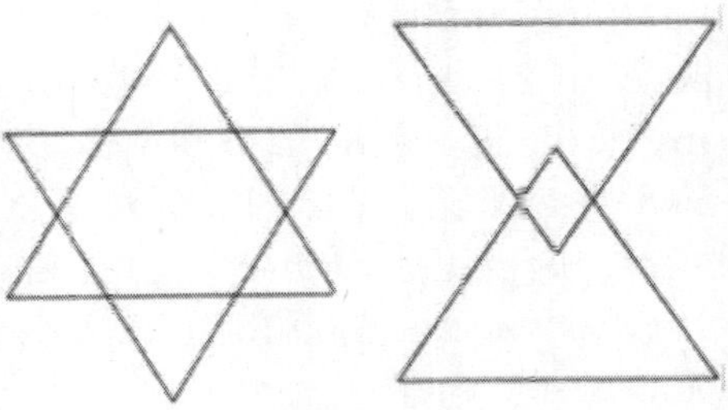

What am I missing here? The thought chafed at him.

Extremely curious, he brought out his laptop and powered it on. He used a search engine to look for hexagram star. Websites with matched words piled up on the screen.

He clicked open one website.

What caught him off guard was the shape of the Orion constellation depicted in the sky, which resembled closely the sketch of the detached superimposed triangles he had drawn.

He placed his sketch alongside a picture of the Orion Belt that appeared like an hourglass.

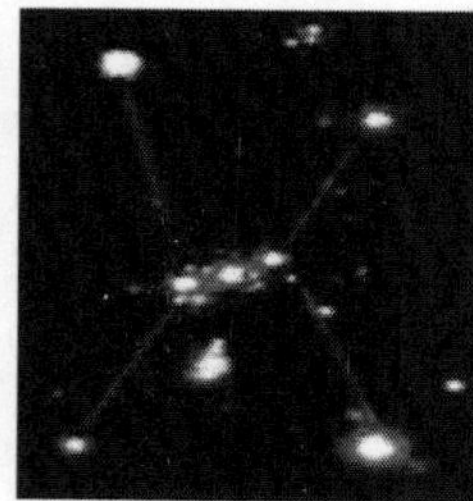

Bright stars marked each corner of the hourglass, but three prominent stars which traversed in the middle, were aligned in a straight line towards the east pointing to a blazing star. Namely: **Alnitak, Alnilam and Mintaka**.

Familiarity of an ancient event struck him. From the Bible. Then things became clear. These three major stars from the Orion Belt seemed like a coded language in the Bible.

The Magi.

ӜӜӜӜӜ

Taneez stepped out of her hotel suit, allowing her father, Balbeer Singh and Raynard Wulff, space for their private talks.

As she spanned the length of the long deserted hotel corridor her opinion about Balbeer Singh grew bitter. He had not known her identity until this night, that she was daughter to Lukas Covitz, the Grand Master to his brotherhood of the serpent.

Her mind churned back to the time when this man, post his inclusion in the brotherhood, had arrived at her mansion with disturbing news about the secret they guarded. Showing the photographs of bizarre murders of victims, he had related the events to be that of an organized crime. A handiwork of some intelligent mind that he supposed could be privy to the secret they thought only they had been to, guarding since the beginning of time the one to do with presence of Elohim on earth.

However, it wasn't the information Balbeer Singh had offered that had caught his father, Lukas Covitz, off guard. It was the photographs that showed a mysterious pattern formed by the hands of the victims before they had died that Balbeer Singh was oblivious to. The ancient and mysterious icon--a sign of thumb and index finger pointing upward while the rest of the fingers coiled to form a mysterious hand gesture. The one that had baffled historians for a millenia.

For this hand gesture was an ancient invitation designed by the enlightened souls to summon one who proved himself worthy enough to learn knowledge, along with many other, the greatest untold secret on the origin of mankind.

These murders were evidence that those victims were in possession of one of the copies of scroll they named as *The Lost Arcanum* that were written in multiple languages and shipped across into different lands.

Assessing the situation, her father had felt an urgent need to intervene and seek where they might have hidden the Lost Arcanum or if the victims had bequeathed to someone? Was that someone worth protecting what had been passed under their custody realizing its repercussion if it fell into the wrong hands or would he himself misuse the knowledge for personal gain? Questions like this had compelled her father to task Zeenat with finding the man who possessed The Lost Arcanum that ultimately bought her down to India for the first time. And by the time she had tabs on the latest news on the investigation of the murders, Jake was on the run. Keeping her identity hidden from Balbeer, squeezing every possible intel on Jake from the circle of Intelligence Agency, she had gained knowledge that he had escaped down to south India, into some hills, finally tracking him at Srisailam.

Zeenta arrived near a flight of stairs at the end of the corridor where a blue signboard announced the way to terrace. As she took the first step, Jake's face flashed before her eyes, and her last words to him hummed in her ears.

You and I can't be together. We are from different worlds and cultures. Yet he had insisted her saying *No matter how different our worlds are I still want to*…at which point she had interrupted.

Heaven and earth...That's the distance between us. You cannot fill the gap.

ЖЖЖЖЖ

Jake was overwhelmed by the sheer gravity of truth that was now weighing upon him.

According to the Gospel of Matthew, the three wise men known as Magi, travelled from the East to find the star that guided them to the birth place of Christ.

This night, however, Jake wondered if three wise men were literal personalities or just figurative terms referring to a trio of star guiding the way to the blazing star. *Could the Magi in the Bible have been symbolic of three stars from the Orion Belt pointing to the blazing star?*

It made sense. The star could not have appeared so low in the sky as to point out any precise location on earth. *Then what would it have meant?* Jake got a slight hint of what must have been implied in the Bible with the Magi.

His breathing became faster as he stared back at the image anxiously.

Things were only getting complicated. With his deep probing, the mystery of the star was growing larger in scope.

Ignoring the eastward direction, Jake followed the alignment of the three stars due west, in a straight line that went past two important clusters of stars. When he read through the names of each cluster, his jaw dropped in awe and his eyes were pinched in terror. As suspected, there was a mention of these clusters of stars in the Bible too.

Is it where…? Intrigued by the discovery, Jake abruptly rushed to his bedroom and searched for his telescope.

His heart pounded with the realization that all he had uncovered about the stars in the last few minutes, their connection with the Bible and other ancient doctrines was just too much to be a coincidence. Allegorically, the sacred doctrines were clearly pointing to these stars in the sky. And all the lines that spoke of heaven were referring to these stars.

The telescope was in one of the drawers. It had belonged to his father and he had often used it to look at the night sky, staring at the stars. Now Jake wondered was his father used it to see something what he was now trying to look at?

He grabbed it and ran up the stairs to the terrace. As he climbed the stairs, a bone-chilling truth about the lines spoken by Taneez struck him like a bolt of thunder from out of the blue.

You and I can't be together Jake. We're from different worlds.

Jake tripped a step but regained his balance, wondering if with those lines Taneez was literally pointing out to him that she came from heaven?

ЖЖЖЖЖ

She tripped a step, when the truth struck her like a bolt of lightening. She regained her balancing holding the railing, going over each and every word that his father had voiced to her.

Heaven and earth, his father had told her. *That's the distance between you and the earthlings.*

That was true. The distance between her and every other man and woman on earth was that of heaven and earth.

A grave truth his father, Lukas Covitz, had told her for the first time soon after she had returned home in Turkey post her completion of her graduation from University of Boston.

Facing his back to her, with a eyes that had gone distant out the window staring at the magnificence of brightly illumined skyline of Turkey, he had made her privy to her family's long kept secret. The one that spoke about their origin. That she, like him and her mother, didn't belong to any earthly heritage. That the history of their descent was steeped in a secret that was as dark and as old as time itself, rooted deep at the point in the epoch when highly intelligent and spiritually evolved race of entities called Elohim had come to planet earth from distant corner of universe. Tracing back his family tree, he had revealed how distinct his ancestors and their descendants were from the rest of the population of the world as they, unlike rest, were procreated by immaculate conception, carrying blood that was pristine and exclusive to Elohim.

But soon after the Elohim departed from this world, their generation lost the ability of immaculate conception and turned to worldly means of propagating their population. Yet, they had managed to preserve the purity of the blood line by intermarrying among families that carried heritage of Elohim.

Following this stunning revelation, Zeenat had corroborated the need for her father to bring up his children in a tight and closed circle of orthodoxy, barring them from developing any kind of contact with the outside world. They were the last of descents of Elohim to be left on earth. However, under strict obligations, her father had let her pursue education abroad along with Raynard Wulf, another of Elohim descendant--a man her father had chosen to marry her.

That which she had kept most sincerely.

And also, this family secret of hers from Jake, save for leaving behind hints she knew Jake would decode in the lines….

Heaven and earth…..That's the distance between us.

ЖЖЖЖЖ

Heaven and earth, Taneez had said. *That's the distance between us.*

Did she imply me to discern that she was a direct descendant of Elohim, those who came from heaven? Jake pondered the brunt of her implications as he took two stairs at a time. *Did she genuinely mean that the blood streaming through her veins was pure and of those extraterrestrial beings, unlike him, who had the mixed blood of Elohim and the ancient Homo-erectus?*

A blend of astonishment and horror washed over him as he tried to fathom the truth. He couldn't believe that the girl he had at his side in the quest, running shoulder to shoulder, dodging bullets, staving off dangers, was indeed from the race of Elohim, who carried the pure blood of those who had left planet earth several millennia ago.

If so, why did she come to earth? What was the purpose behind her meeting him? Was she searching for the same secret his father had concealed? As these questions nagged at him, he decided the answers to these questions had to wait.

Clutching the telescope in one hand, he unlatched the door at the end of the stairs and shoved it open, bursting into the cold breezy night, staring directly overhead. He slowed down and spun on his foot, taking in an amazing vista of a clear night sky spectacularly interspersed with the sparkling, silvery glitter of stars.

Like a diamond in the sky, a line from a nursery rhyme hummed in his ears. *Truly, the stars in the sky has the glitter of diamonds.*

ЖЖЖЖЖ

Like a diamond in the sky...Zeenat concurred too, standing on the hotel terrace, staring directly into the sky that glistened with stars like a diamond in the sky..

The brightly lit opulent high rise structures surrounding the hotel did little to draw her attention as she continued to look in specific direction, as if searching a precious diamond amongst scatter of stars in the sky.

ЖЖЖЖЖ

Jake skimmed his vision along the northern sky, searching for three prominent stars from the Orion Belt and spotted it on the eastern horizon. Lifting the telescope to his eyes, he adjusted the focus on the three prominent stars, fine-tuning it, until its brilliant sheen reflected off the lens.

He had read that the three great pyramids of Giza celebrated these stars as their construction and location on earth precisely mimicked position of these stars in the sky.

He swiveled the focus towards the east and spotted the blazing star. Knowing the path was right, he refocused on the three stars from the Orion belt and extended an imaginary line upward and to the extreme right, following its alignment westward. Then he stopped abruptly, as he identified the first star cluster in the path. Though faint, its 'V' shape was sharply apparent: the constellation of Taurus the Bull.

The bull's eye and face was plainly marked by the fine V-shaped cluster of Hyades. And a bright star in that cluster marked the end of the lower arm of the V, making it appear like the bull's fiery eyes.

It had a name, too: **Aldebaran.**

Aldebaran, also known as 'the follower', appeared to be orange. This star from the cluster of Hyades points westward straight to another cluster in the same constellation of Taurus the Bull: The Pleiades.

When Jake fine-tuned the lens of the telescope, he was mesmerized by the sight of seven stars from the cluster of Pleiades, so arranged that it appeared to form the bull's leg.

All the stars had a sharp and icy blue glitter

As per ancient records, these seven stars were known as 'Seven Sisters' and went by various names across all cultures and civilizations.

Indian sacred doctrines recognized these stars as Krittika or Kartika. In the New Testament's book of Revelation, Jesus Christ taught John and his close disciples about the mystery of seven stars and the seven golden lamp-stands, saying that the seven stars were the angles of seven churches and the seven lamp-stands were the seven churches. He was symbolically referring to the seven stars from Pleiades.

Everything was moving fast, faster than he could grasp.

Jake was meticulously skimming along the seventh star of this cluster, the tiny star which marked the end of the bull's leg, which should be pointing to a specific star as mentioned in the reference star map material.

A little fine-tuning of the scope presented Jake with the star he was looking for. As bright and white as the sun against the black velvety fabric of space, the tiny star glistened against the lens of the telescope.

This is it, Jake thought, flabbergasted. *This is the actual blazing star the Bible speaks of, not the one along the east, but the one aligned westward, that was concealed for a reason, to guard the greatest secret on the location where all the life had taken root.*. From here, the seed of life was brought to earth by the Elohim.

And that is where Taneez came from, Jake finally had the truth uncovered.

ӜӜӜӜӜ

As chill wind swept her hair into tangles, she groomed it in place, at which point, a tender hand found her shoulder and squeezed them.

She didn't turn, knowing it was her father.

Lukas Covitz.

He stood beside her, gazing at the night sky.

Silence that now stretched between them, as they both continued to gaze at the night sky, was same as that was on the night after everything his father had revealed to her family secret. One about their origin. He had continued by walking her through serious of events that had ensued after the exodus of their ancestors from their native land of Ur-an ancient city in Mesopotamia, now a modern day city of Tell el-Muqayyar, south Iraq.

The event of migration, her father had emphasized, was more out of need to protect and safe guard esoteric wisdom in the scrolls than from running for their own lives from the enemies of western world.

The travails of carrying the treasure of wisdom out of harms distance the brotherhood had endured in the past, her father had confessed, was nothing less than carrying the Ark of the Covenant itself during the great exodus. Burdened with the responsibility of safe guarding the scrolls, her father had told, there was no fear as terrible as getting captured with the scrolls as that was the last thing their brotherhood had wanted. Besides, concealing their true heritage of that of Elohim was equally challenging as it was preserving the purity of their bloodline.

That night, Taneez had grasped the gravity of the truth her father wanted to convey through the history of the brotherhood and had committed herself completely for the cause.

Tonight, however, in spite the same gravity tugged at her heart, reminding her obligations and her purpose in supporting the cause, her resolution faltered. Because of Jake.

ЖЖЖЖЖ

Gazing at the blazing star along the west, Jake had to admit that some of the instances in the Bible had been altered. The actual location of the blazing star in the sky was misinterpreted in the Bible by the scribes or possibly concealed purposely from mankind for a reason. Although most civilizations cited the importance of these constellations of Orion, Taurus and Pleiades, they were all taken to be some fantastical story.

Watching the Blazing Star, Jake felt his ego diminish before its brilliant sheen. He felt a stab of guilt, a sickly pang of disgust at mankind's pride, vanity and ignorance that showed no concern towards what had been said in the sacred doctrines. We believed we were at the peak of the intelligence scale and that there were none like us on this planet. We assumed new technological breakthroughs were being pioneered by us. We believed that we were the first to do anything technological or marvelous upon earth. But we were all selfish and have forgotten our true past. If those beings from heaven had not come to our planet, if they had not interfered and guided our evolution from beasts to intelligent creatures, we would have been sticking to gloomy corners of caves, gnawing on raw flesh and grass. Their helping hands ushered us out of caves and set us on the path of progress, freeing us from barbarism and making us a more ethically developed species that went on to build scientifically great and advanced civilizations on earth.

Jake lowered the telescope from his eyes as a bitter and poignant thought occurred to him. That humans waged wars in the name of religion, allowed racial discrimination and nurtured hatred, set boundaries on the basis of caste and creed, yet barely realized that we all were tied back to each other in some way, held to one another by an invisible thread that weaved back into the past, into the prehistoric epoch, connecting us all to a common root. We had the essence of the supreme being from the Elohim whom we all called God in all of us, streaming through our blood, reaching down to every cell in our body, which in itself was the most potent of any truth upon earth. We worshiped the same God, but in different names, in different languages, in different forms, oblivious to the fact that we all shared a common ancestry, which was a truth mightier than any religion upon earth.

Indeed, there was no religion; knowledge of God was in itself a religion.

Jake imagined a cave dweller from the Neolithic Age gazing at the starry night sky, holding the fingers of his young ones and pointing the other hand skyward, far into the horizon, showing him the same clusters of stars.

He watched the star-pattern with wonder-soaked eyes and recalled what his father had told him on the day he had left him and his mother. That he would return on the day when he would be gazing at the stars. From that day onwards, Jake got into the habit of running to his terrace and watching the stars, thinking that his father's return was somehow tied to those stars. If only he had known that it all would make sense now, decades later. His father had spoken cryptically implying that he would return on the day when Jake fully comprehended the secret of the origin of mankind was buried in stars.

ЖЖЖЖЖ

Zeenat leaned her head on her father's shoulders, shifting in his arms, both staring at the night sky, at the precise star from where the seed of life was brought to earth.

"I know what it feels like," Lukas said, sharing his daughter's emotions, tugging his hold over her, gazing at the star. "But we all are here to serve a bigger cause, one that we're destined for."

Zeenat knew what he had meant. That they were the direct descendant of Elohim. Carrying pure blood of Elohim through generations, preserving the real heritage by intermarrying with those from the same bloodline. They needed to preserve it that way. No matter what, they had to maintain the bloodline in all its purity. Which in turn meant they needed to distance out themselves from the earthling.

And Jake was an earthling too.

"I wish I never had met him," Zeenat averred, her voice heavy with grief.

Lukas remained quiet, knowing there was nothing he could do in that matter. Except for encouraging her to accept the separation of her from Jake as a will of destiny to serve a greater cause, there was barely anything he could have done. As he had vowed to protect and preserve, alike many of his ancestors, their ethnicity from contamination and prolong the pure heritage of Elohim on earth.

Now letting her rest on his shoulders, he felt as helpless as ever. A father who reluctantly had turned a deaf ear to his daughters wishes.

Knowing, she would never meet Jake again, nor see him, Zeenat eyed the blazing star....sending a silent prayer for safe keeping a diamond she will cherish all her life.

A diamond that she held as most prized and adored.

Jake.

ЖЖЖЖЖ

Knowing they were not destined to become one, Jake's lips parted sending out a silent prayer to the blazing star for safekeeping a diamond he will treasure for the rest of his life.

A diamond that he held as most precious and dear.

Taneez.

As he stood there with heavy feelings, he felt his father's presence beside him, his fingers curling over his and a hand pointing at the same stars from the star map.

He felt his voice, filled with awe and reverence: *That is where life began in the universe and that is where they came from. From there, our creators carried the seed of life to earth, living the trail of our origin back there. And one day, when our souls shed our mortal shell and detach from karmic cycles, they will be deemed fit to return to their home in heaven.* His father's voice turned into a whisper. Jake turned and found his father smiling. *We shall all then return to that star in heaven where we came from, because that is where we all belong.*

Then he disappeared, leaving Jake behind with nothing but the secret of our origin that had been withheld from the world since the beginning of time: that we all came from the same star to which we all shall return one day…as that is where we came from, as that is where we all belong…

AUTHOR'S NOTE TO READERS

I have tried my best to base my book in the real world while dabbling in the concepts that had intrigued me.

Now I take this moment to separate fact from fiction. So here we go:

HIDDEN TREASURE AT SRISAILAM:

On the hills of Nallamala, historians have located an eleventh century hidden passageway leading to a secret chamber that once was a laboratory used by the alchemists, Gorkhnath—a sorcerer and powerful alchemist. The laboratory was found to be stashed with earthen wares, hearth and some unidentified instruments for the use in experiments. Scholars believe that these hills are riddled with more such concealed passageway, one of which possibly leads to a treasure of inestimable worth the legend speaks of. Very few have the knowledge that the ancient alchemists from this region have left the clue to the location of treasure on the bas-reliefs on the outer walls of Mallikarjuna Temple. Some people have even reported of having spotted the passageway, which is protected by powerful Garuda Mantras. Those who tried crossing its threshold have met with fatal accidents. Some of them have even lost their lives. However, my journey to these hills was indeed for the hunt for treasure—treasure not being gold, but researching on the facts to establish solid proof that ancient Indian alchemists really perfect the arcane art of making gold from worthless metals, which I think I have accomplished. And sadhu was my creation though the concept of vibrational frequency and different dimensions discussed are true. For further reading, I suggest a book 'The Alchemical Body: Siddha Traditions in Medieval India' by David Gordon White. You may also check these sites on concepts like frequency and vibrations.

http://www.one-mind-one-energy.com/Law-of-vibration.html
http://altered-states.net/barry/newsletter463/
http://soundcurrentrider.com/FrequencyMatrix.html

CAVES AT ELLORA:

The concept of careful alignment of these caves with the position of the stars is true. Some face south and some towards west. But the caves that serve as temples are mainly oriented towards east, facing the rising sun, unraveling an advanced understanding of celestial phenomena by the ancient Indians. Modern scholars propose that these caves were difficult to be built unless there were some sophisticated high-tech gears and equipment available to make it perfectly oriented towards the solstices. They propose an alternative theory that these caves could have been some kind of subterranean space used by ancient aliens. There are numerous videos available on youtube concerning this theory. For further details on the enchanting sculptures and stone work at these caves, I recommend these websites.

https://en.wikipedia.org/wiki/Ellora_Caves
http://asi.nic.in/asi_monu_whs_ellora.asp

GANGES AND ITS MIRACULOUS PROPERTIES:

The claims concerning the Ganges' amazing self cleansing properties because of the presence of Bacteriophage and high oxidation level is based on the facts. The crystalline structure of water molecule of Ganges responding to external vibrations arising from the thoughts and chants may sound farfetched, but it is true. Despite vast stretches of damming and pollution along the upper reaches of this river, its properties remain unaltered, especially where devotee interact with her, offering prayers and chant mantras to her. To understand full extent of this concept, go seek out Japanese author, researcher and entrepreneur Dr. Masaru Emoto's book titled 'Messages from Water.' For further information, check these web links:

http://www.tribuneindia.com/news/uttarakhand/community/waters-of-boon-unlock-joys-of-heart/147669.html

http://www.npr.org/templates/story/story.php?storyId=17134270

https://explorecuriocit y.org/ Explore/ArticleId/2530/bacteriophages-and-the-mystery-of-the-ganges-2530.aspx

KONGKA LA:

As discussed in this book, this is one of the least accessed areas in the world, a low-ridge pass anda no man's land in Ladakh. Thesouthwestern part of this pass is held by the Indian side while the northeastern part is held by China and is known as Aksai Chin. Though India and China had come to an agreement that neither side will patrol the area, for some unknown reason, they keep an eye on it from distance, perhaps, due to strange anomalies this region is experiencing. Locals from either sides of pass have reported strange lightings in the night sky, and some have even spotted UFO's hovering in that region. According to rumors, there is UFO underground base through which they have seen UFO's emerging out. This rumor hadn't gained credence until in 2006 when Google Earth's satellite imagery released astounding images of this region that baffled the world. The detailed terrain model of 1500:1 scale of Kongka La pass from the satellite had revealed buildings and tower post which resembled closely to a military base. If India and China are not patrolling this area, then to whom does this military facility belong to? Or it's maintained and operated mutually by both the countries to conceal God knows what and for how long, lest the world would discover what lies beneath? This idea formed the premise for my book. Well, I have taken liberties in stating this location as once home to Elohim. For further details, go for these websites.

http://factslegend.org/20-interesting-kongka-la-pass-ufo-base- facts/

http://thevoiceofnation.com/politics/ladakhs-kongka-la-pass-is-the-mother-of-all-mysteries-does-it-have-a-ufo-hub-or-a-secret-air- force-base/

http:// www.latest-ufo-sightings.net/ 2014/ 08/ possible-underground-ufo-base-in-kongka-la-pass-himalayas.html

http://www.hiddenmysteries.org/mysteries/ufo/hima-ufobase. html

http://hauntedindia.blogspot.in/2014/05/kongka-la-pass-in-aksai-chin.html

THE CENTER FOR STUDY OF EXTRATERRESTRIAL INTELLIGENCE (CSETI) AND DISCLOSURE PROJECT:

Both organizations are real and fully functional, each with their own objectives, though I have taken liberty in my book, blending them into one corporation. I suggest checking these web links for more details on their objectives and functions.

http://www.disclosureproject.org http://www.cseti.org

3D HOLOGRAPHIC TECHNOLOGY:

This technology was developed by many countries and remained classified for decades. As a component of Psychological Operations with the capability of projecting persuasive images in the battlefields through satellite, this technology is effective in strategic optical deception and cloaking, for providing momentary distraction while engaging enemies in war. For more details, read these articles.

https://www.wired.com/2010/12/military-one-step-closer-to-battlefield-holograms/

http://bigthink.com/dr-kakus-universe/advances-in-holographic-technology-could-have-far-reaching-implications

http://www.historycommons.org/timeline.jsp?us_military_general_topic_areas=us_military_weaponizationOfSpace&timeline=us_military_tmln

BROTHERHOOD OF THE SERPENT:

This is the oldest secret society and a cult of snake on earth, a disciplined brotherhood that was formed to disseminate spiritual knowledge and attain spiritual freedom. It is believed that owing to fall of humanity from the heavenly grace in the Garden of Eden, the Elohim—those who from the heaven to earth came, had branded this knowledge as Forbidden and concealed it from mankind, lest it would fall into wrong hands. Modern scholars propose that this is the same cult that established the infamous Illuminati, Rosicrucian and Knights Templar, who in turn control the world's myriad secret societies, fraternities and organizations. Though the nature and the magnitude of the secret that lies buried at the heart of these organizations is still unknown, a fair amount of whispers on whatever is closely guarded has escaped, one to do with the ancient alien race behind the creation of mankind. If you like to read more about this theory, check out author Zecharia Sitchin's books on Annunaki—an ancient alien race behind human creation. Coming to the star map theory, I have reproduced one of the map, drawing ideas from popular website of author Wayne Herschel. I recommend reading his extensively researched book titled 'The Hidden records.' I also suggest the readers to check his website that has plethora of mind blowing star maps from different civilizations and countries around the world on offering. And don't forget to check these other websites I have used in my research.

http://www.bibliotecapleyades.net/vida_alien/godseden/godseden03.htm#Brotherhood

http://www.ancient-origins.net/myths-legends/tracing-origins-serpent-cult-002393

http://www.thehiddenrecords.com/index.htm
http://www.thehiddenrecords.com/key-of-solomon.php

About the Author

Based in Bangalore, Navin Reuben, a graduate in engineering, loves teaching when he is not penning down his novel. His keen interest to probe into the unknown realms of antiquity and uncover the hidden layer of untold mysteries has been the cornerstone for his first novel. In this book, he has endeavored to bring humanity as close to the truth as possible on the roots of its origin. Also, he greatly believes that the line between science and religion is blurring at a pace so fast that the day is not far when science will lean strongly on our ancient sacred scriptures of the world. For it is there, the answers to all the mysteries of the world, unknown forces and unexplained marvelous structures of the past, which have been a conundrum to the genius minds, which lie buried and are accessible only if one knows how to read between the lines.